OXFORD WORLD'S CLASSICS

THE CASTLE

ANTHEA BELL is a freelance translator from French and German, and the winner of many translation awards. She has translated the entire *Asterix* series, with Derek Hockridge, and many adult novels, including W. G. Sebald's *Austerlitz*, a large selection of novellas and stories by Stefan Zweig, and E. T. A. Hoffmann's *The Life and Opinions of the Tomcat Murr*.

RITCHIE ROBERTSON is Fellow and Tutor in German at St John's College, Oxford. He is the author of *Kafka: A Very Short Introduction* (2004) and editor of *The Cambridge Companion to Thomas Mann* (2002). For Oxford World's Classics he has translated Hoffmann's *The Golden Pot and Other Stories* and introduced editions of Freud and Schnitzler.

OXFORD WORLD'S CLASSICS

FRANZ KAFKA

The Castle

Translated by
ANTHEA BELL

With an Introduction and Notes by
RITCHIE ROBERTSON

OXFORD
UNIVERSITY PRESS

OXFORD

UNIVERSITY PRESS

Great Clarendon Street, Oxford OX2 6DP

Oxford University Press is a department of the University of Oxford.
It furthers the University's objective of excellence in research, scholarship,
and education by publishing worldwide in

Oxford New York

Auckland Cape Town Dar es Salaam Hong Kong Karachi
Kuala Lumpur Madrid Melbourne Mexico City Nairobi
New Delhi Shanghai Taipei Toronto

With offices in

Argentina Austria Brazil Chile Czech Republic France Greece
Guatemala Hungary Italy Japan Poland Portugal Singapore
South Korea Switzerland Thailand Turkey Ukraine Vietnam

Oxford is a registered trade mark of Oxford University Press
in the UK and in certain other countries

Published in the United States
by Oxford University Press Inc., New York

Translation © Anthea Bell 2009
Editorial matter © Ritchie Robertson 2009

British Library Cataloguing in Publication Data

Data available

Library of Congress Cataloging-in-Publication Data

Kafka, Franz, 1883–1924.
[Schloss. English]
The Castle / Franz Kafka ; translated by Anthea Bell;
with an introduction and notes by Ritchie Robertson.
p. cm. — (Oxford world's classics)
Includes bibliographical references.
ISBN 978-0-19-923828-6 (pbk. : acid-free paper)
1. Bureaucracy—Fiction. I. Bell, Anthea. II. Title.
PT2621.A26S33 2009
833'.912—dc22
2009005381

Typeset by Cepha Imaging Private Ltd., Bangalore, India
Printed in Great Britain
on acid-free paper by
Clays Ltd., St Ives plc

ISBN 978–0–19–923828–6

CONTENTS

BIOGRAPHICAL PREFACE

FRANZ KAFKA is one of the iconic figures of modern world literature. His biography is still obscured by myth and misinformation, yet the plain facts of his life are very ordinary. He was born on 3 July 1883 in Prague, where his parents, Hermann and Julie Kafka, kept a small shop selling fancy goods, umbrellas, and the like. He was the eldest of six children, including two brothers who died in infancy and three sisters who all outlived him. He studied law at university, and after a year of practice started work, first for his local branch of an insurance firm based in Trieste, then after a year for the state-run Workers' Accident Insurance Institute, where his job was not only to handle claims for injury at work but to forestall such accidents by visiting factories and examining their equipment and their safety precautions. In his spare time he was writing prose sketches and stories, which were published in magazines and as small books, beginning with *Meditation* in 1912.

In August 1912 Kafka met Felice Bauer, four years his junior, who was visiting from Berlin, where she worked in a firm making office equipment. Their relationship, including two engagements, was carried on largely by letter (they met only on seventeen occasions, far the longest being a ten-day stay in a hotel in July 1916), and finally ended when in August 1917 Kafka had a haemorrhage which proved tubercular; he had to convalesce in the country, uncertain how much longer he could expect to live. Thereafter brief returns to work alternated with stays in sanatoria until he took early retirement in 1922. In 1919 he was briefly engaged to Julie Wohryzek, a twenty-eight-year-old clerk, but that relationship dissolved after Kafka met the married Milena Polak (née Jesenská), a spirited journalist, unhappy with her neglectful husband. Milena translated some of Kafka's work into Czech. As she lived in Vienna, their meetings were few, and the relationship ended early in 1921. Two years later Kafka at last left Prague and settled in Berlin with Dora Diamant, a young woman who had broken away from her ultra-orthodox Jewish family in Poland (and who later became a noted actress and communist activist). However, the winter of 1923–4, when hyperinflation was at its height, was a bad time to be in Berlin. Kafka's health declined so sharply that, after moving through several clinics and sanatoria around Vienna, he died on 3 June 1924.

The emotional hinterland of these events finds expression in Kafka's letters and diaries, and also—though less directly than is sometimes thought—in his literary work. His difficult relationship with his domineering father has a bearing especially on his early fiction, as well as on the *Letter to his Father*, which should be seen as a literary document rather than a factual record. He suffered also from his mother's emotional remoteness and from the excessive hopes which his parents invested in their only surviving son. His innumerable letters to the highly intelligent, well-read, and capable Felice Bauer bespeak emotional neediness, and a wish to prove himself by marrying, rather than any strong attraction to her as an individual, and he was acutely aware of the conflict between the demands of marriage and the solitude which he required for writing. He records also much self-doubt, feelings of guilt, morbid fantasies of punishment, and concern about his own health. But it is clear from his friends' testimony that he was a charming and witty companion, a sportsman keen on hiking and rowing, and a thoroughly competent and valued colleague at work. He also had a keen social conscience and advanced social views: during the First World War he worked to help refugees and shell-shocked soldiers, and he advocated progressive educational methods which would save children from the stifling influence of their parents.

Kafka's family were Jews with little more than a conventional attachment to Jewish belief and practice. A turning-point in Kafka's life was his encounter with Yiddish-speaking actors from Galicia, from whom he learned about the traditional Jewish culture of Eastern Europe. Gradually he drew closer to the Zionist movement: not to its politics, however, but to its vision of a new social and cultural life for Jews in Palestine. He learnt Hebrew and acquired practical skills such as gardening and carpentry which might be useful if, as they planned, he and Dora Diamant should emigrate to Palestine.

A concern with religious questions runs through Kafka's life and work, but his thought does not correspond closely to any established faith. He had an extensive knowledge of both Judaism and Christianity, and knew also the philosophies of Nietzsche and Schopenhauer. Late in life, especially after the diagnosis of his illness, he read eclectically and often critically in religious classics: the Old and New Testaments, Kierkegaard, St Augustine, Pascal, the late diaries of the convert Tolstoy, works by Martin Buber, and also extracts from the Talmud.

His religious thought, which finds expression in concise and profound aphorisms, is highly individual, and the religious allusions which haunt his fiction tend to make it more rather than less enigmatic.

During his lifetime Kafka published seven small books, but he left three unfinished novels and a huge mass of notebooks and diaries, which we only possess because his friend Max Brod ignored Kafka's instructions to burn them. They are all written in German, his native language; his Czech was fluent but not flawless. It used to be claimed that Kafka wrote in a version of German called 'Prague German', but in fact, although he uses some expressions characteristic of the South German language area, his style is modelled on that of such classic German writers as Goethe, Kleist, and Stifter.

Though limpid, Kafka's style is also puzzling. He was sharply conscious of the problems of perception, and of the new forms of attention made possible by media such as the photograph and cinema. When he engages in fantasy, his descriptions are often designed to perplex the reader: thus it is difficult to make out what the insect in *The Metamorphosis* actually looks like. He was also fascinated by ambiguity, and often includes in his fiction long arguments in which various interpretations of some puzzling phenomenon are canvassed, or in which the speaker, by faulty logic, contrives to stand an argument on its head. In such passages he favours elaborate sentences, often in indirect speech. Yet Kafka's German, though often complex, is never clumsy. In his fiction, his letters, and his diaries he writes with unfailing grace and economy.

In his lifetime Kafka was not yet a famous author, but neither was he obscure. His books received many complimentary reviews. Prominent writers, such as Robert Musil and Rainer Maria Rilke, admired his work and sought him out. He was also part of a group of Prague writers, including Max Brod, an extremely prolific novelist and essayist, and Franz Werfel, who first attained fame as avant-garde poet and later became an international celebrity through his best-selling novels. During the Third Reich his work was known mainly in the English-speaking world through translations, and, as little was then known about his life or social context, he was seen as the author of universal parables.

Kafka's novels about individuals confronting a powerful but opaque organization—the court or the castle—seemed in the West to be fables of existential uncertainty. In the Eastern bloc, when they became accessible, they seemed to be prescient explorations of the fate of the individual within a bureaucratic tyranny. Neither approach can be set aside. Both were responding to elements in Kafka's fiction. Kafka worries at universal moral problems of guilt, responsibility, and freedom; and he also examines the mechanisms of power by which authorities can subtly coerce and subjugate the individual, as well as the individual's scope for resisting authority.

Placing Kafka in his historical context brings limited returns. The appeal of his work rests on its universal, parable-like character, and also on its presentation of puzzles without solutions. A narrative presence is generally kept to a minimum. We largely experience what Kafka's protagonist does, without a narrator to guide us. When there is a distinct narrative voice, as sometimes in the later stories, the narrator is himself puzzled by the phenomena he recounts. Kafka's fiction is thus characteristic of modernism in demanding an active reading. The reader is not invited to consume the text passively, but to join actively in the task of puzzling it out, in resisting simple interpretations, and in working, not towards a solution, but towards a fuller experience of the text on each reading.

INTRODUCTION

KAFKA'S last novel centres on a simple and compelling cluster of images. A rural castle, the property of an absent nobleman, is run by an administrative staff who dominate the village beneath the castle. The protagonist, K., coming from outside and ignorant of the village and the castle, has painfully to learn their ways and to discover that, despite all his efforts, he cannot gain access to the castle. So far, this may seem to match the associations of gloom and oppression suggested by the term 'Kafkaesque'. Kafka, however, has much more to offer than the 'Kafkaesque', and if one can put aside such presuppositions, *The Castle* provides many surprising discoveries.

The reader of *The Castle* is likely already to know *The Trial*, and may think that Kafka has simply replaced one opaque, hierarchical authority, the court, with another, the castle.[1] In their texture, however, the two novels differ considerably. In contrast to the anonymous city of *The Trial*, *The Castle* has a vividly presented material and social setting. We are in a remote village, in the depth of winter. The snowbound village is repeatedly evoked: 'more and more little houses, their window-panes covered by frost-flowers', 'a narrow alley where the snow lay even deeper. Pulling his feet out of it as they kept sinking in again was hard work' (p. 13). We feel how exhausting it is to have constantly to struggle through the deep snow. Moreover, the village is a community, with friendships and hatreds that go back through the generations. We learn about the village's two inns, the humble Bridge Inn and the more pretentious Castle Inn, and about how the latter's landlord and landlady acquired it; we meet the families of the tanner Lasemann and the cobbler Brunswick, and hear about their standing in the village; and we are told at great length about the family of Barnabas, the castle messenger, and how the family are in bad odour because of their refractory attitude towards the castle. And whenever a new figure is introduced, he or she is neatly characterized, so that even those who appear briefly—the carter Gerstäcker, the village schoolmaster, the schoolmistress Gisa and her languishing suitor Schwarzer—are vivid presences.

[1] For a detailed comparison, see Richard Sheppard, '*The Trial/The Castle*: Towards an Analytical Comparison', in Angel Flores (ed.), *The Kafka Debate* (New York: Gordian Press, 1977), 396–417.

This community is also the setting for a love story. Unlike the callous and self-centred protagonist of *The Trial*, the main character here is at least briefly capable of love, and the rapid development and decline of his love-affair with Frieda has moments of poignancy not found earlier in Kafka's work. These features offset the extensive conversations about the puzzling ways of the castle authorities, which correspond to Kafka's profound concern with ambiguity, but which sometimes make one feel that the novel could have benefited from the work of an editor. Kafka did not complete the novel; like his others, *The Trial* and *The Man Who Disappeared*, it was published after his death by his friend Max Brod.

If we seek access to the novel through Kafka's biography, we shall be disappointed. The snow-covered environment is that of the ski resort of Spindlermühle in the Tatra Mountains, where Kafka stayed in January 1922, while the rural community no doubt reflects his experiences in Zürau, where he stayed on his sister's farm in the winter of 1917–18. The emotional drama goes back, in complex and untraceable ways, to his relationships with the Czech journalist Milena Polak, née Jesenská, and with Julie Wohryzek, his second fiancée. But the isolated setting of the novel, and its quasi-fantastic social system, enable Kafka above all to explore and dramatize some long-standing intellectual preoccupations.

One of these was the idea of a community. Kafka's personal writings constantly express his sense of solitude, his isolation from his family, his need to find a substitute in writing, and his wish to found a community by marrying and starting a family. But, while attracted to the community as an ideal, he was also sharply aware of the frictions arising from living with even one other person. When he and Felice Bauer stayed together in a hotel in the summer of 1916, Kafka recorded in his diary how laborious it was to live together, adding: 'only deep down perhaps a narrow trickle worthy to be called love' (5 July 1916). Integration into a community such as the fictional village would be many degrees harder. Hence K. the outsider is treated with condescension, contempt, and outright dislike by the villagers, and allowed only a marginal place in their community as janitor in the village school. His situation has been compared to that of Jews seeking a place in European society.[2] But to interpret the novel accordingly would be too narrow.

[2] See Hannah Arendt, 'The Jew as Pariah: A Hidden Tradition', in her *Reflections on Literature and Culture*, ed. Susannah Young-ah Gottlieb (Stanford: Stanford University Press, 2007), 69–90.

The novel is also concerned with authority of various kinds. The castle is said to belong to Count Westwest, whom we never see. In his absence the castle is run by a huge staff of bureaucrats, arranged in a hierarchy, who manage the affairs of the village. There is much satire on bureaucratic confusion and inefficiency. But it is also clear that the bureaucrats arrogate to themselves the respect formerly paid to the vanished aristocracy. Kafka was writing just after the collapse of the Austro-Hungarian, German, and Russian empires. His novel asks in part what will take the place of traditional authority.

Alongside political power, the castle and its staff receive religious devotion from the villagers. The many religious overtones in the text have sometimes been interpreted as meaning that the castle has an enigmatic religious significance: thus Max Brod called it the abode of divine grace.[3] Erich Heller memorably challenged this interpretation by pointing to the misbehaviour of the castle bureaucrats: 'The castle in Kafka's novel is, as it were, the heavily fortified garrison of a company of Gnostic demons, successfully holding an advanced position against the manoeuvres of an impatient soul.'[4] But this may be both extravagant and misguided. The castle is enigmatic: we cannot tell what power it contains—if any. The image may have been suggested by a passage in Schopenhauer's great philosophical work *The World as Will and Idea*, where Schopenhauer argues that scrutiny of the world can never tell us about the true, inner nature of things: 'we can never arrive at the real nature of things from without. However much we investigate, we can never reach anything but images and names. We are like a man who goes round a castle seeking in vain for an entrance, and sometimes sketching the façades.'[5]

Perhaps the castle contains no secret. It may be more appropriate to see it not as a real spiritual authority, whether benign or malign, but rather as 'the emblem for the modern, secular, post-religious era',[6] and as the projection of people's desire for a spiritual authority. As in *The Trial*, where we are invited to wonder why Josef K. submits

[3] Max Brod, 'Nachwort', in Franz Kafka, *Das Schloß* (Munich: Wolff, 1926), 492–504 (p. 496).

[4] Erich Heller, 'The World of Franz Kafka', in his *The Disinherited Mind: Essays in Modern German Literature and Thought* (Cambridge: Bowes & Bowes, 1951), 157–81 (p. 175).

[5] Arthur Schopenhauer, *The World as Will and Idea*, tr. R. B. Haldane and J. Kemp, 3 vols. (London: Routledge & Kegan Paul, 1957), i. 128.

[6] Stephen D. Dowden, *Kafka's Castle and the Critical Imagination* (Columbia, SC: Camden House, 1995), 127.

xiv *Introduction*

to the authority of the court, so here Kafka is examining the psychological mechanisms that lead people to believe in a spiritual authority and submit to its demands—demands which are based in their own desires and hopes, and thus ultimately in their own power. Kafka summed up the problem of authority in a little parable written on 2 December 1917:

They were given the choice of being kings or royal messengers. Like children, they all wanted to be messengers. Therefore there are only messengers; they rush through the world, and as there are no kings, they shout their meaningless messages to one another. They would gladly put an end to their wretched condition, but they dare not because of their oath of loyalty.[7]

This closed circle—servitude to an authority that one has oneself created and could in theory destroy—is the condition of the villagers in *The Castle*. K. challenges that authority; he is a land surveyor, whose work consists in rational calculation, and thus a representative of the disenchanted, post-religious modern world. But he is also susceptible to its appeal.

Within Kafka's work, the castle and its hierarchy seem to be an expansion of the legend of the doorkeeper which the chaplain told to Josef K. in *The Trial*. There, a countryman comes to the gate of the Law, as K. comes to the village, and is told by the doorkeeper that he cannot enter yet; the man spends his whole life waiting submissively for permission to enter, only to be told, as he dies, that the entrance was intended specially for him. The doorkeeper resembles the castle official of whom K. sees a portrait soon after his arrival: both have big beards and prominent hooked noses. Both are members of a hierarchy: we hear later in *The Castle* of a warden with several deputy wardens, besides officials and secretaries, while the doorkeeper evokes a series of further doorkeepers and says: 'The sight of just the third is too much even for me.'[8] A similar phrase occurs in *The Castle*, when the landlady of the Bridge Inn asks K., 'how did you bear the sight of Klamm?' (p. 47). The doorkeeper professes to be 'powerful', and the word is used in a similar undefined way by the landlord, who describes officials, but not K., as 'powerful' (p. 10). K. imagines Klamm's door being guarded by a 'doorkeeper' (p. 108).

[7] Kafka, *Nachgelassene Schriften und Fragmente II*, ed. Jost Schillemeit (Frankfurt a.M.: Fischer, 1992), Textband, p. 56.

[8] Kafka, *The Trial*, tr. Mike Mitchell, Oxford World's Classics (Oxford: Oxford University Press, 2009), 154.

The castle is defined by its contrast with a traditional religious building: not with a synagogue, as one might expect given Kafka's increasing consciousness of his Jewish identity, but with a church. As K. looks up at the castle on his first morning in the village, he compares it with the church in his home town:

In his mind, he compared the church tower of his childhood home with the tower up above. The former, tapering into a spire and coming down to a broad, red-tiled roof, was certainly an earthly building—what else can we build on this earth?—but it had been erected for a higher purpose than these huddled, low-built houses and made a clearer statement than the dull, workaday world of this place did. (p. 11)[9]

This passage may be cautiously agnostic, but it concedes that the church spire at least points to some goal beyond ordinary life and has a clarity that stands out from everyday existence. The castle lacks any such clarity. It looks neither like a feudal fortress nor like a modern mansion, but like a collection of two-storey houses. If you had not known it was a castle, you would have taken it for a small town. That implies that prior belief, perhaps the eye of faith, is needed to see it as a castle at all.

In many other ways the castle is ambiguous. When K. first arrives in the village, the castle is invisible, hidden in darkness, without even a glimmer of light showing, and K. gazes up at 'what seemed to be a void' (p. 5). The next day he finds it impossible to get to the castle on foot, because the village street that seems to lead there curves away from it, and the carter Gerstäcker flatly refuses to drive him to the castle. When K. expects the messenger Barnabas to lead him to the castle, Barnabas, having misunderstood K., in fact goes to his own house. Barnabas himself is not sure that the offices in which he is made to hang about are really in the castle, or that the official from whom he receives orders is really his employer Klamm.[10]

Klamm too is bewildering. His name—one of the few names in the story that one can interpret with some confidence—suggests the Czech word *klam*, 'illusion'. K. does in fact see Klamm when Frieda encourages him to look through a peephole into the inn room where Klamm is sitting at a table with his beer. Klamm is facing the peephole, as though posing for a photograph, thus affording K. a 'photographic

---

[9] See the comments on this passage in Dowden, *Kafka's Castle*, 127.

[10] On the shifting and uncertain nature of the physical world in this novel, see Deirdre Vincent, '"I'm the King of the Castle. . .": Franz Kafka and the Well-tempered Reader', *Modern Language Studies*, 17 (1987), 60–75.

sense of mastery' which is undermined by Klamm's strained and awkward posture.[11] In any case, we learn later that Klamm looks different at different times: when entering the village, when leaving it, before and after drinking beer, alone and in conversation; and these differences are not due to magic, but arise 'from the mood of the moment, the degree of excitement, the countless nuances of hope or despair felt by those who are privileged to see Klamm' (p. 156).

Thus Klamm and the castle are the object of intense emotions. The complex emotional appeal of the castle is captured in the sound of the great bell, 'with a lively, cheerful note, although the sound was painful too, and made his heart quail momentarily as if threatened with getting what it vaguely desired' (p. 18). The villagers regard the castle and its officials with reverence. K. is forbidden to utter the name of Count Westwest before children. The landlady of the Bridge Inn, Klamm's ex-lover Gardena, asks him not to mention Klamm by name. The formula 'in the name of Klamm' is used repeatedly to reinforce an order. On seeing a letter from Klamm, the mayor's wife folds her hands as though in prayer.

Communication with the castle is generally misleading. K. telephones the castle, only to learn that what one normally hears at the other end, a humming like children's voices, is the sound of the constant telephoning that goes on *within* the castle. If a human voice answers, it is only a bored official who has lifted the receiver for a joke. Even pictures are untrustworthy: Gardena shows K. a photograph of the messenger who summoned her to Klamm, and at first it seems to show a young man stretched out on a bed, but in fact it shows him in a horizontal position doing the high jump.[12] K. receives two letters from Klamm, both of which are hard to interpret. The first encourages K. by promising to watch over him, but K. learns from the village mayor that the letter has no official status; the second urges him to keep up the good work, and K., interpreting it over-literally, is disappointed because as yet he has done no land-surveying work at all.[13]

Castle officials, like Greek gods, use or abuse their authority to have sexual affairs with village women. Gardena had three encounters

[11] Carolin Duttlinger, *Kafka and Photography* (Oxford: Oxford University Press, 2007), 243.

[12] See ibid. 233, for such a photograph: it shows the new high-jumping technique known as the 'Western' or 'Horine' style, developed in 1912.

[13] See the interpretation of this letter by Richard Sheppard, *On Kafka's Castle: A Study* (London: Croom Helm, 1973), 122.

with Klamm, eighteen years previously, and that experience still dominates her life. Frieda is Klamm's mistress when she meets K., but promptly deserts Klamm for K. Amalia has received a crudely expressed sexual summons from the official Sortini and refused to obey it, which has led the entire village to ostracize her and her family.

K., the outsider, is in some respects free from this superstitious reverence. Although, on his first appearance in the village, he seems not to know about the castle, it appears that he has been summoned as a land surveyor, even though most people think that the castle and its community have no need of a land surveyor. He constantly breaches taboos, especially by demanding an interview with Klamm, the official to whom he is responsible. He is able to endure the sight of Klamm, which the landlady thinks impossible; and he breaks a taboo by being friendly with the Barnabas family, whom the landlady hates.

K.'s attitude is that of a rationalist who is prepared to argue against the unreasoned traditional customs of the village. Thus, when the landlady, Klamm's former lover, insists that a meeting with Klamm is impossible, K. gradually induces her to admit that it is actually possible and even persuades her to help to arrange it, though when agreeing she hides her face as if making 'an indecent remark' (p. 78). K. argues with village officials, including the mayor and the schoolteacher. When he is briefly employed as a school janitor, he resists the schoolteacher's petty tyranny. He refuses to accept his dismissal from the schoolteacher on the perfectly reasonable grounds that the teacher did not appoint him. Later, he refuses to allow the castle secretary Momus to subject him to an interrogation. When he hears about the obscene summons issued by Sortini to Amalia, he asserts that Amalia's father ought to have made an official complaint on her behalf.

To some extent, therefore, K. is a force for sense and enlightenment in a community trapped by its unreasoning reverence for tradition. As a land surveyor, his business is to check and, if necessary, correct the boundaries of people's lands: he might therefore change property relations in the village, and it is hinted that the alleged malcontent Brunswick wanted a land surveyor to be summoned for that reason. The village needs to be liberated. Its material poverty and emotional misery are constantly apparent. K. unkindly throws a snowball at Gerstäcker, and only then becomes aware of 'the man's bent form, as if physically mistreated' (p. 18). The peasants are described with features 'contorted into an expression of pain', looking as though their skulls had been beaten flat (p. 23). Women, such as the landladies of the two inns, the barmaid Frieda, and the chambermaid Pepi who briefly succeeds her, are prematurely worn out by hard work. Yet the villagers confirm their own subjection by the quasi-religious awe in which they hold castle officials. Hannah Arendt may well have been right when, in 1944, she offered a political reading of *The Castle* in which the villagers, passively dependent on the castle authorities, are confronted by K. who insists on human rights and thus 'reveals himself to be the only one who still grasps, quite simply, what human life on earth is all about'.[14]

There are two striking examples of villagers making themselves gratuitously miserable. One is the landlady Gardena, who tells K. her life-story. After being abandoned by Klamm, she found sympathy from Hans, a stable-boy; one day, as the then landlord of the inn saw them sitting in Gardena's father's garden, he stopped and offered to lease his inn to them, whereupon they married, and have been running the business ever since. Since they soon made enough money to buy the inn, they are now prosperous. Yet she would still drop everything and return to Klamm if he gave her a sign. K. chides her, arguing that Klamm actually helped her attain her present situation: it was when abandoned by Klamm that she was ready for Hans, and the prestige of having been Klamm's mistress made her more marriageable: 'The blessing of that lucky star was yours, but they didn't know how to make the most of it' (p. 77). It may be right to see in Gardena's attitude, as Elizabeth Boa does, an implicit critique of the destructive effects of romantic love.[15] If Gardena could have overcome her futile hankering after Klamm, and accepted the limitations of ordinary life, she might have been happy.

The other example of self-induced misery is the Barnabas family. Since Amalia refused Sortini's summons, the family believe they are under a curse; all their neighbours despise and avoid them; they are reduced to poverty; the parents, before being overtaken by premature decrepitude, beg for mercy from the castle and even spend days standing by the roadside in the hope of catching the attention of an

[14] Arendt, 'Franz Kafka, Appreciated Anew', in *Reflections on Literature and Culture*, 94–109 (p. 99); originally published as 'Franz Kafka: A Revaluation', *Partisan Review*, 11 (1944), 412–22.

[15] Elizabeth Boa, *Kafka: Gender, Class, and Race in the Letters and Fictions* (Oxford: Clarendon Press, 1996), 262.

official passing in a carriage, even though they know such an event to be impossible. Amalia's sister Olga spends several nights every week being gang-raped by the bestial servants of castle officials, in the hope that she might meet the messenger who brought Sortini's summons. Their submission to the castle is abject. They regard it as a sign of hope when their brother Barnabas is employed as a castle messenger, even though he is hardly ever asked to carry a message and, by hanging about vainly in castle offices, neglects the cobbler's trade on which his family's income depends. Yet the castle has not acted against the family in any way. It seems entirely indifferent, just as Klamm seems indifferent to the loss of his lover Frieda to K. Public opinion in the village reprehends Amalia's refusal, and since the Barnabas family share the common reverence for the castle, they have internalized the contempt in which they are held.

Amalia's refusal has provoked much critical debate. Kafka's friend Max Brod, who understood the castle as the abode of divine grace, thought that Sortini's invitation was a divine command which ought to have overridden ordinary morality. He compared it to God's inexplicable instruction to Abraham to sacrifice his son Isaac, which Kierkegaard in *Fear and Trembling*, a book well known to Kafka, took to illustrate the 'teleological suspension of the ethical'. Writing in the 1970s, Richard Sheppard questioned this interpretation but argued instead that Amalia was refusing 'to live by the life forces within her personality'.[16] Hence she becomes hard, cold, and reserved. But a more complex interpretation is possible. Amalia's rejection of Sortini's crude summons was indeed heroic, as her sister Olga says. It was a blow against the arrogant sexual exploitation practised by the castle officials and sanctioned by tradition. But it was of limited value, because it was only negative. She still accepts the authority of the castle; having disobeyed that authority, she has nowhere left to go. She remains emotionally frozen, with nothing to do but tend her decrepit parents. Her refusal may have been an act of dignified self-assertion; but it is futile so long as her resistance to authority holds her trapped within the structures of authority. 'Anyone who fights with monsters', says Nietzsche, 'should take care that he does not in the process become a monster.'[17]

---

[16] Sheppard, *On Kafka's Castle*, 157. I put forward a partially similar interpretation in *Kafka: Judaism, Politics, and Literature* (Oxford: Clarendon Press, 1985), 260, which I now doubt.

[17] Friedrich Nietzsche, *Beyond Good and Evil*, tr. Marion Faber, Oxford World's Classics (Oxford: Oxford University Press, 1998), 68.

Amalia's story is a partial analogue to K.'s. By the time he hears it from her sister Olga, K. has himself become obsessed with the castle. When his lover Frieda reproaches him for neglect, he listens to nothing but her mention of Klamm's name. He spends many hours in the Barnabas house listening to stories about the castle, with the result that Frieda gets fed up, leaves him, and returns to her old job as a barmaid. Yet it is not clear why he is so obsessed, or why it is so important to him to meet Klamm. He admits: 'it's difficult to say just what I want of him' (p. 78).

And yet K. fails to learn from his repeated experiences of disappointment. The castle, seen by daylight, looks mean and ramshackle. Barnabas the messenger is at first an attractive figure, wearing a white coat that resembles silk, and with an encouraging smile. But when Barnabas brings K. to his own house instead of to the castle, K. feels he has been misled: 'He had let himself be captivated by the silken gleam of Barnabas's close-fitting jacket, which he now unbuttoned, revealing a coarse, grey, much-mended shirt over a powerful broad chest like a labourer's' (p. 30). In Klamm's sleigh, K. finds a bottle of cognac with a delightful aroma: 'the smell was as sweet and delightful as hearing praise and kind words from someone you love' (p. 92); but when he drinks it, it is a warming but coarse drink fit only for coachmen. Such episodes have been interpreted as indicating a Gnostic conception of the world, in which the purity of spiritual things must always be degraded by their translation into material reality.[18] But they could also be interpreted as revealing the human propensity to look for spiritual fulfilment where it is not to be had.

K. is also betrayed by his own aggressive temperament. From the outset he is convinced, for no apparent reason, that the castle is engaged in a conflict with him. He has been seen as a twentieth-century Faust, constantly striving for an ever-receding goal, and as an embodiment of Schopenhauer's conception of humanity as perpetually driven onwards by the metaphysical force that Schopenhauer called the Will.[19] Although he suffers under the bullying of the schoolteacher, he also bullies his childish assistants, and resorts to violence by giving one a blow with his fist (perhaps significantly, a *Faustschlag*—*Faust* means a literal 'fist', as well as being the name of Goethe's hero). Although we learn little about his past, we are told

---

[18] See Heller, 'World of Franz Kafka', 178.
[19] See Sheppard, *On Kafka's Castle*, 127–40.

of an important memory: as a child he climbed the churchyard wall and planted a flag on top of it: 'He rammed the flag into the wall, it flapped in the wind, he looked down and all around him, glancing back over his shoulder at the crosses sunk in the ground. Here and now he was greater than anyone' (p. 29).[20] This reads like a triumph of the will, and even a symbolic triumph over death. It anticipates a crucial event in the novel, when K. tries to force a meeting with Klamm by waiting beside Klamm's sleigh. This proves futile: Klamm will not leave the inn so long as K. is outside, so the coachman unharnesses the horses, leaving K. in possession of an empty triumph:

It seemed to K. as if all contact with him had been cut, and he was more of a free agent than ever. He could wait here, in a place usually forbidden to him, as long as he liked, and he also felt as if he had won that freedom with more effort than most people could manage to make, and no one could touch him or drive him away, why, they hardly had a right even to address him. But at the same time—and this feeling was at least as strong—he felt as if there were nothing more meaningless and more desperate than this freedom, this waiting, this invulnerability. (p. 95)

Such freedom is meaningless precisely because it results from cutting off contact with other people.

However, K. is also, even if briefly and faintly, capable of love. Frieda, the barmaid of the Castle Inn, boasts to him that she is Klamm's lover, yet conceals K. in the bar, where they spend the night making love among the beer-puddles on the floor. In this unpromising venue, K. has an experience of self-surrender which is described lyrically:

Hours passed as they lay there, hours while they breathed together and their hearts beat in unison, hours in which K. kept feeling that he had lost himself, or was further away in a strange land than anyone had ever been before, a distant country where even the air was unlike the air at home, where you were likely to stifle in the strangeness of it, yet such were its senseless lures that you could only go on, losing your way even more. (p. 40)

But since Frieda promptly tells Klamm that she has abandoned him for K., K. falls into despair, since his hopes of using Frieda to approach Klamm have been dashed. Instead of a woman he can use, he has found a woman who loves him. Although they plan to get married, their romance founders on K.'s obsession with the castle

[20] For a perceptive reading of this and the associated episodes, see Markus Kohl, 'Struggle and Victory in Kafka's *Das Schloß*', *Modern Language Review*, 101 (2006), 1035–43.

and also on the mundane difficulties of life. K. gets a job as school janitor; he, Frieda, and his two childish assistants have to live in the school, moving out of the classroom when it is needed for teaching. Needless to say, everything goes farcically wrong; this episode is a triumph of Kafka's often underrated humour. As a result, Frieda gives up on K. Yet even after they have separated, she still says poignantly: 'Oh, how I need to have you close, how lost I have felt when I am without you ever since we met. Being close to you, believe me, is my dream, that and only that' (p. 222). At the same time there is something clinging and deathly in Frieda's love, which finds expression in a necrophiliac fantasy of their lying together in a grave, clasped together as though with pincers.

The assistants, two identical young men called Artur and Jeremias, have an important bearing on K.'s character. Although he seems prepared to accept that they are his old assistants, he has never seen them before, and they know nothing about land surveying. Their main activity is clowning about. But there is more to them. It turns out that they were present all the time K. and Frieda were making love on the bar-room floor, and their unseen presence must have had a good effect, for later, when K. and Frieda try to make love in the assistants' absence, they cannot repeat the earlier experience but merely scrabble together like two dogs. The assistants' function becomes clearer when Jeremias explains to K. that they were sent to him by the official Galater in order to cheer him up, since he is inclined to take things very hard and cannot take a joke.

Another side of K. which he represses is his mildly homosexual attraction to young men. This is very apparent in his attachment to Barnabas, who is first described as follows:

He greatly resembled the assistants; he was as slender as they were, his clothes too were close-fitting, he was nimble and spry, and yet he was quite different. K. would far rather have had him as his assistant! The man reminded him a little of the woman with the baby whom he had seen in the master tanner's house. His clothing was almost white and was probably not silk, but an ordinary winter-weight fabric, but it had the fine look of a silk suit worn for special occasions. His face was clear and open, his eyes very large. His smile was extraordinarily cheering, and although he passed a hand over his face, as if to wipe that smile away, he did not succeed. (p. 23)

While there is no reason to suppose that Kafka was a practising homosexual, he was aware of his own homoerotic impulses and confessed them unabashedly in his diary and in letters to close friends.[21] His references to homosexuality never contain the disgust which is part of his feelings about heterosexual intercourse. In the meeting with the secretary Bürgel, two conflicting sides of K.'s character—his aggressive hypermasculinity and his gentler, homosexual side—find expression. Bürgel is a secretary who is competent to deal with K.'s case. Normally the secretaries go to great lengths to make themselves unavailable to the public. It is just possible, however, that a member of the public can catch a secretary off guard by entering his room in the middle of the night, and then the secretary feels so helpless that he will grant any request. K., having been summoned by another secretary, stumbles into Bürgel's room by mistake, but is so exhausted that even as Bürgel tells him about his lucky chance, K. is already asleep on Bürgel's bed. There he dreams of a victory being celebrated— the successful conclusion of his struggle against the castle. But the struggle is directed against a naked male secretary who resembles the statue of a Greek god, and who, in response to K.'s pressure, squeaks like a girl being tickled. K. then finds himself ready for a fight but without an opponent—a repetition of his futile victory in the snow-covered courtyard—and on waking he feels like a child. Strangely, the officials too appear as childlike. K. witnesses the early-morning distribution of documents, in which the officials concealed in their rooms behave like naughty children: one empties a basinful of water over the servant's head, another imitates the crowing of a cock.

This descent into the unconscious brings about a change in K.: 'he wakes up a new person, freed from the control of obsessive fictions and deriving his identity from sources of his personality which lie below the threshold of his will.'[22] When he sees the servant tearing up a scrap of paper which no official wants, K. wonders if that is the file referring to him, a sign of humility that was not present before. Thenceforth he is milder and gentler in his behaviour towards others. But there is little for him to live for, and the suggestions of death which haunt the novel become more intense: the little room where Pepi invites him to spend the winter, for example, sounds disturbingly like the grave.[23]

[21] See Mark Anderson, 'Kafka, Homosexuality and the Aesthetics of "Male Culture"', *Austrian Studies*, 7 (1996), 79–99.

[22] Sheppard, *On Kafka's Castle*, 81.

[23] See W. G. Sebald, 'The Undiscover'd Country: The Death Motif in Kafka's Castle', *Journal of European Studies*, 2 (1972), 22–34.

The narrative, then, follows an emotional trajectory involving love, loss, and a breakthrough into self-understanding, at least on the unconscious level, which tragically comes too late to help K. to rebuild his life. According to Brod, Kafka said that the story was to end as follows: 'The alleged land-surveyor gains at least partial satisfaction. He does not slacken in his struggle, but dies of exhaustion. The community gathers round his death-bed, and just then the decision comes down from the Castle that although he has no legal claim to live in the village, nevertheless, in the light of certain circumstances, he is allowed to live and work there.'[24] So the novel would have ended with a success that was also a failure.

Along the way, however, the novel keeps offering alternatives to K.'s solitary struggle. Involvement in a community is offered him through Frieda's love, which he wears out by neglecting her. Another possibility of human contact is revealed when the normally withdrawn and sombre Amalia, in conversation with K., breaks into a smile: 'Amalia smiled, and that smile, although a sad one, lit up her sombre face, made her silence eloquent and her strangeness familiar. It was like the telling of a secret, a hitherto closely guarded possession that could be taken back again, but never taken back entirely' (p. 149). This luminous breach in the wall of personal isolation is cited by Stephen Dowden as an example of Kafka's sublime. For classical aesthetics, the sublime is a mode of experience that gives us thrilling glimpses of 'a sort of infinity' outside everyday life.[25] Kafka, however, locates the sublime not in magnificent landscapes, but in the mystery of another person: 'Kafkan sublimity has to do with human identity, a bond that is individual and common. Amalia's smile breaks through the hard shell of ice that surrounds her, and it gives off a light that clarifies her face and establishes a humane contact with K. that exceeds words.'[26]

The novel shows a repeated narrative pattern whereby K., thinking he is on his way to the castle, in fact finds himself in a domestic and hence communal setting. Thus Barnabas leads him not to the castle, but to the family home; and when K. finds that the village

---

[24] Brod, 'Nachwort', 493.

[25] Edmund Burke, *A Philosophical Enquiry into the Origin of our Ideas of the Sublime and Beautiful*, ed. Adam Phillips, Oxford World's Classics (Oxford: Oxford University Press, 1990), 71.

[26] Dowden, 137.

street does not lead to the castle, he rests briefly in the Lasemann household, where it is washing-day.

This washing, in which the Brunswick family also share, deserves a closer look, for it contrasts with a ceremony involving water and fire that later plays a crucial part in the narrative. 'This seemed to be wash-day for everyone' (p. 14): not only are clothes being washed in a corner, but in the centre of the room there is a huge tub, as big as two beds, where two men are bathing. The comparison with beds points forward to Bürgel's bed which is the site of K.'s healing dream, and the washing itself suggests purification. The ritual bath is an important feature of Judaism.

Though superficially similar, the washing-day contrasts with a ceremony described later by Olga, the fire-brigade festival held in summer, after which Sortini issued his fateful invitation to Amalia. On that occasion the castle donated a new hosepipe, and many castle officials were present. In contrast to the family atmosphere of the washing-day, the fire-brigade festival is riotous. Firemen blow trumpets with a hideous noise. Everyone gets drunk on sweet castle wine. Officials observe the village girls, sizing them up; Sortini fixes his gaze on Amalia. The sense of male dominance is reinforced by the phallic hosepipe and the *double entendre* whereby *spritzen* can mean both to emit a jet of water and to ejaculate. Richard Sheppard sees the occasion as 'a festival of procreation and renewal',[27] but it seems more like a scene of sexual predation. And if the bath evoked aspects of Judaism, the fire-brigade festival sounds like a pagan or Dionysiac orgy. That would imply not that Amalia is 'guilty of a sin' by refusing to 'participate in the great festival of procreation around the phallic fire-pump',[28] but rather that she is asserting her dignity, somewhat in the manner of early Christian women who, as Peter Brown has shown, valued virginity as a way of preserving the integrity and autonomy of their own bodies.[29]

Although Amalia's resistance to the castle may in the end be incomplete and damaging, just as K.'s resistance is undone by a fatal obsession with the castle, both show that one need not simply submit

[27] Sheppard, *On Kafka's Castle*, 105.

[28] Ibid. 155.

[29] See Peter Brown, *The Body and Society: Men, Women and Sexual Renunciation in Early Christianity* (New York: Columbia University Press, 1988). Kafka had read the contrasts drawn among various religions by Max Brod in *Heidentum, Christentum, Judentum* (1921): see Robertson, *Kafka: Judaism, Politics, and Literature*, 259, 262.

to an abusive and oppressive authority. But the novel also suggests that a more effective form of resistance, if one could manage it, would be not to fight against the authority—for a struggle is ultimately self-defeating—but to ignore it. It may well be that the castle contains no secret and has no power, except the power that the villagers bestow on it by treating its representatives with servile reverence and by projecting on to it their own hopes and desires. If one withdraws one's desires from the castle, and attaches them instead to everyday tasks and family relationships, one has a far better chance of leading a fully human life. Kafka liked to quote the remark that Flaubert, one of his favourite writers, made after visiting a family with many children: 'Il sont dans le vrai', 'They are in the right'.[30] Kafka's protagonist, of course, fails in this endeavour; but his story enables Kafka to strike a range of new and poignant emotional notes that one might not expect to find in his fiction. *The Castle* needs to be read with fresh eyes and ears, and without the customary associations of the 'Kafkaesque'.

[30] Quoted in Max Brod, *Über Franz Kafka* (Frankfurt a.M.: Fischer, 1966), 89.

NOTE ON THE TEXT

The Castle was prepared for publication after Kafka's death by his friend Max Brod, and published by the Kurt Wolff Verlag in Munich in 1926. This text stops at the point where K. leaves Frieda nursing Jeremias in the Herrenhof. Brod summarized the subsequent events, notably the encounter between K. and Bürgel, in his Afterword, but maintained that these episodes were too sketchy and inconclusive to be published as part of the novel. The first English translation, made by Willa and Edwin Muir and published in 1930, was therefore also incomplete. Brod supplied the remaining chapters, stopping at the end of K.'s conversation with the landlady about clothes, in the second edition (1935). He also presented in an appendix a number of passages which Kafka had stroked out.[1]

The present translation is based on the text of *The Castle* in the Critical Edition of Kafka's works, edited by Malcolm Pasley and published by S. Fischer Verlag in 1982. This edition follows the manuscript of *The Castle* held in the Bodleian Library at Oxford. Cancelled passages are printed in an accompanying volume of critical apparatus and have not been included in the present translation, though they are mentioned in the notes where relevant.

The apparatus in the Critical Edition makes it possible to follow in detail how Kafka wrote the novel. As usual, he did not make plans or drafts, but he did make many small alterations as he went along. Mark Harman, in an illuminating essay on Kafka's textual variants, has shown that his changes tended to make the novel more opaque. Suggestions of allegory were toned down: thus, a reference to Klamm's 'dear name' was removed. K.'s motives are made less explicit: his reflection, 'In this way I was not fighting against the others, but against myself', is removed, leaving the reader to work out that his aggression is futile. K. is also made somewhat less aggressive: Kafka erased his statement 'I'm here for a fight', and removed such actions as threatening the rustics with his walking-stick and snatching Amalia's knitting.[2]

---

[1] The complicated history of successive editions of *The Castle* (before the Critical Edition) is presented most clearly by Richard Sheppard in his contribution to the *Kafka-Handbuch*, ed. Hartmut Binder, 2 vols. (Stuttgart: Kröner, 1979), ii. 441–70 (pp. 444–5).

[2] Mark Harman, 'Making Everything "a little uncanny": Kafka's Deletions in the Manuscript of *Das Schloß* and What They Can Tell Us About his Writing Process', in

From the apparatus we can also see that Kafka began the novel in the first person. In the third chapter, immediately before the sex scene between K. and Frieda, he decided to switch to the third person, and went back through the manuscript changing all the first-person pronouns to 'K.'. An obvious reason for this change is that the love-making scene is the first episode in which K.'s alert consciousness becomes blurred and he makes contact with unconscious feelings: he could hardly, therefore, have reported this experience consciously. It is noteworthy that all three of Kafka's novels are in the third person, as are many of his stories. Where a first-person narrator is present, it is usually as an onlooker and commentator rather than as a participant in the action. In such exceptions as 'A Report for an Academy' and 'A Country Doctor' the narrator is recounting past experiences. The initial use of the first person in *The Castle* was an experiment which proved unsustainable.

James Rolleston (ed.), *A Companion to the Works of Franz Kafka* (Rochester, NY: Camden House, 2002), 325–46.

NOTE ON THE TRANSLATION

KAFKA's *The Castle* was never completed, and when the author died, breaking off in mid-sentence, it had not been edited in the modern manner. A translator of the novel therefore has to face some unresolved problems of terminology. The first problem arises in the second paragraph of the book, where at the Bridge Inn 'einige Bauern saßen noch beim Bier' (were still sitting over their beer). Look up the word *Bauer* in a German-to-English dictionary, and you find that on the face of it the choice is between 'peasant' and 'farmer'. Neither term appealed to me in context. In English, 'peasants' have a rather medieval sound to them, while 'farmers' suggest, to me at least, the modern National Farmers' Union of the British Isles, and in any case many of the people thus described by Kafka are not farmers but small tradesmen: a carrier, a tanner, a couple of shoemakers. What is clear is that *die Bauern* are, so to speak, the working class of the strange world of *The Castle*, whereas the bureaucratic officials of the castle itself are the upper class, and have their own pecking order within the larger social hierarchy. For that first instance *of Bauern* I have therefore translated as 'the local rustics', and subsequently either in the same way, or simply as 'the locals' or 'the rustics' or, where it seemed to fit better, as 'the villagers'.

One of them who, in discussion of land boundaries with K. the land surveyor, does seem to be a farmer is also *der Vorsteher* or, in full, *Gemeindevorsteher*, the top man in the local government of the village and answerable to the castle, although his mousy wife does all the real work of the post. All available terms for him seem to me to have been used already by other translators, and I have nothing new to offer here. I settled for 'village mayor' as the term conveying the most graphic idea of his position, combining it on first occurrence with 'chairman of the parish council'.

Another problematic term is *die Knechte*. In modern parlance *Knecht*, the singular of this noun, is usually a farm labourer or, in US English, a farmhand. But it is pointed out at once that the people thus described, and first called *Bauern* like the drinkers in the Bridge Inn whom we meet in the first chapter, are not exactly the same as those 'local rustics'. They frequent the village's other inn, and turn out to be the servants of the 'gentlemen', the officials who come down from the castle to stay there or regulate local affairs on the spot. They are also referred to as *Diener*, servants, and only later as *Knechte*. In fact the switch between *Diener* and *Knechte*, the latter word being often but not always used for them thereafter, occurs in the middle of a paragraph, making it obvious that they are exactly the same people. *Knecht* was earlier used as a term for a servant in general, sometimes occurring as part of a compound—a *Stallknecht*, for instance, a 'stable servant', is a groom—and while aware that I was exchanging two terms in German for a single term in English, I have called *die Knechte* 'servants' throughout.

The inn to which they and their masters resort is, in German, *der Herrenhof*. The *Herren* are the gentlemen from the castle, while *Hof* (primary English meanings are yard, courtyard, farm, court as in a royal court) is very often found in German as the second element of a compound in the names of inns and hotels, as here. I have called this place the Castle Inn, since it is frequented by the gentlemen from the castle, and the name balances the Bridge Inn where the locals drink, and about the translation of which, mercifully, there is no difficulty.

Finally, another term which comes up very frequently in the closing chapters of the book as we have it, although it does not occur at all earlier on, is *die Parteien*, the plural of *die Partei*, primary sense 'party' in the sense of someone representing a certain side or shade of opinion, as in a political party, someone who is party to a dispute, a conversation, a legal case, and so on. Again, all that is really clear is that 'the parties', who come from the village, are under the authority of the bureaucrats from the castle, to whom they apply for the settlement of various matters, the granting of permits, and so forth. I owe to the editor, Ritchie Robertson, the idea of calling them 'members of the public' as a general all-embracing term.

I would have liked to set out this translation in the modern English manner, with new dialogue beginning on a new line, if only to illustrate visually what a large proportion of *The Castle* consists of direct speech. Sometimes it is conversation in general, sometimes a duologue, and often a monologue of an obsessive or near-deranged nature, but still direct speech. Setting it out in that way would not, however, have been in accord with the usual tradition of Kafka translation, or the style within the present series which is to follow the layout of Kafka's manuscript. However, I do think it is useful to remember how much of *The Castle* is told through the mouths of the characters, who in the process may inadvertently reveal their own feelings, misconceptions, and ulterior motives: a satisfyingly useful function of dialogue in fiction and drama.

A.B.

SELECT BIBLIOGRAPHY

(CONFINED TO WORKS IN ENGLISH)

Translations

The Collected Aphorisms, tr. Malcolm Pasley (London: Penguin, 1994).

The Diaries, tr. Joseph Kresh (Harmondsworth: Penguin, 1972).

Letters to Friends, Family and Editors, tr. Richard and Clara Winston (New York: Schocken, 1988).

Letters to Felice, tr. James Stern and Elizabeth Duckworth (London: Vintage, 1992).

Letters to Milena, expanded edn., tr. Philip Boehm (New York: Schocken, 1990).

Letters to Ottla and the Family, tr. Richard and Clara Winston (New York: Schocken, 1988).

Biographies

Adler, Jeremy, *Franz Kafka* (London: Penguin, 2001).

Brod, Max, *Franz Kafka: A Biography*, tr. G. Humphreys Roberts and Richard Winston (New York: Schocken, 1960).

Diamant, Kathi, *Kafka's Last Love: The Mystery of Dora Diamant* (London: Secker & Warburg, 2003).

Hayman, Ronald, *K: A Biography of Kafka* (London: Weidenfeld & Nicolson, 1981).

Hockaday, Mary, *Kafka, Love and Courage: The Life of Milena Jesenská* (London: Deutsch, 1995).

Murray, Nicholas, *Kafka* (London: Little, Brown, 2004).

Northey, Anthony, *Kafka's Relatives: Their Lives and His Writing* (New Haven and London: Yale University Press, 1991).

Storr, Anthony, 'Kafka's Sense of Identity', in *Churchill's Black Dog and Other Phenomena of the Human Mind* (London: Collins, 1989), 52–82.

Unseld, Joachim, *Franz Kafka: A Writer's Life*, tr. Paul F. Dvorak (Riverside, Calif.: Ariadne Press, 1997).

Introductions

Preece, Julian (ed.), *The Cambridge Companion to Kafka* (Cambridge: Cambridge University Press, 2002).

Robertson, Ritchie, *Kafka: A Very Short Introduction* (Oxford: Oxford University Press, 2004).

Rolleston, James (ed.), *A Companion to the Works of Franz Kafka* (Rochester, NY: Camden House, 2002).

Speirs, Ronald, and Beatrice Sandberg, *Franz Kafka*, Macmillan Modern Novelists (London: Macmillan, 1997).

Critical Studies

Alter, Robert, *Necessary Angels: Tradition and Modernity in Kafka, Benjamin and Scholem* (Cambridge, Mass.: Harvard University Press, 1991).

Anderson, Mark, *Kafka's Clothes: Ornament and Aestheticism in the Habsburg Fin de Siècle* (Oxford: Clarendon Press, 1992).

—— 'Kafka, homosexuality and the Aesthetics of "Male Culture"', *Austrian Studies*, 7 (1996), 79–99.

Boa, Elizabeth, *Kafka: Gender, Class and Race in the Letters and Fictions* (Oxford: Clarendon Press, 1996).

Corngold, Stanley, *Lambent Traces: Franz Kafka* (Princeton: Princeton University Press, 2004).

Dodd, W. J., *Kafka and Dostoyevsky: The Shaping of Influence* (London: Macmillan, 1992).

—— (ed.), *Kafka: The Metamorphosis, The Trial and The Castle*, Modern Literatures in Perspective (London and New York: Longman, 1995).

Duttlinger, Carolin, *Kafka and Photography* (Oxford: Oxford University Press, 2007).

Flores, Angel (ed.), *The Kafka Debate* (New York: Gordian Press, 1977).

Gilman, Sander L., *Franz Kafka, the Jewish Patient* (London and New York: Routledge, 1995).

Goebel, Rolf J., *Constructing China: Kafka's Orientalist Discourse* (Columbia, SC: Camden House, 1997).

Heidsieck, Arnold, *The Intellectual Contexts of Kafka's Fiction: Philosophy, Law, Religion* (Columbia, SC: Camden House, 1994).

Koelb, Clayton, *Kafka's Rhetoric: The Passion of Reading* (Ithaca and London: Cornell University Press, 1989).

Politzer, Heinz, *Franz Kafka: Parable and Paradox* (Ithaca, NY: Cornell University Press, 1962).

Robertson, Ritchie, *Kafka: Judaism, Politics and Literature* (Oxford: Clarendon Press, 1985).

Sokel, Walter H., *The Myth of Power and the Self: Essays on Franz Kafka* (Detroit: Wayne State University Press, 2002).

Zilcosky, John, *Kafka's Travels: Exoticism, Colonialism, and the Traffic of Writing* (Basingstoke and New York: Palgrave Macmillan, 2003).

Zischler, Hanns, *Kafka Goes To the Movies*, tr. Susan H. Gillespie (Chicago and London: University of Chicago Press, 2003).

Historical Context

Anderson, Mark (ed.), *Reading Kafka: Prague, Politics, and the Fin de Siècle* (New York: Schocken, 1989).

Beck, Evelyn Torton, *Kafka and the Yiddish Theater* (Madison, Wisc.: University of Wisconsin Press, 1971).

Bruce, Iris, *Kafka and Cultural Zionism: Dates in Palestine* (Madison, Wisc.: University of Wisconsin Press, 2007).

Gelber, Mark H. (ed.), *Kafka, Zionism, and Beyond* (Tübingen: Niemeyer, 2004).

Kieval, Hillel J., *The Making of Czech Jewry: National Conflict and Jewish Society in Bohemia, 1870–1918* (New York: Oxford University Press, 1988).

Robertson, Ritchie, *The 'Jewish Question' in German Literature, 1749–1939* (Oxford: Oxford University Press, 1999).

Spector, Scott, *Prague Territories: National Conflict and Cultural Innovation in Franz Kafka's Fin de Siècle* (Berkeley, Los Angeles, and London: University of California Press, 2000).

The Castle

Boa, Elizabeth, '*The Castle*', in Julian Preece (ed.), *The Cambridge Companion to Kafka* (Cambridge: Cambridge University Press, 2002), 61–79.

Dowden, Stephen D., *Kafka's Castle and the Critical Imagination* (Columbia, SC: Camden House, 1995).

Friederich, Reinhard H., 'K.'s "bitteres Kraut" and *Exodus*', *German Quarterly*, 48 (1975), 355–7.

Harman, Mark, 'Making Everything "a little uncanny": Kafka's Deletions in the Manuscript of *Das Schloß* and What They Can Tell Us About his Writing Process', in James Rolleston (ed.), *A Companion to the Works of Franz Kafka* (Rochester, NY: Camden House, 2002), 325–46.

Heller, Erich, 'The World of Franz Kafka', in *The Disinherited Mind: Essays in Modern German Literature and Thought* (Cambridge: Bowes & Bowes, 1951), 157–81.

Kohl, Markus, 'Struggle and Victory in Kafka's *Das Schloß*', *Modern Language Review*, 101 (2006), 1035–43.

Krauss, Karoline, *Kafka's K. versus the Castle: The Self and the Other* (New York: Peter Lang, 1996).

Robertson, Ritchie, 'Mothers and Lovers in Some Novels by Kafka and Brod', *German Life and Letters*, 50 (1997), 475–90.

—— 'The Creative Dialogue Between Brod and Kafka', in Mark H. Gelber (ed.), *Kafka, Zionism, and Beyond* (Tübingen: Niemeyer, 2004), 283–96.

Sebald, W. G., 'The Undiscover'd Country: The Death Motif in Kafka's *Castle*', *Journal of European Studies*, 2 (1972), 22–34.

—— 'The Law of Ignominy: Authority, Messianism and Exile in *The Castle*', in Franz Kuna (ed.), *Franz Kafka: Semi-Centenary Perspectives* (London: Elek, 1976), 42–58.

Sheppard, Richard W., *On Kafka's Castle: A Study* (London: Croom Helm, 1973).

—— '*The Trial/The Castle*: Towards an Analytical Comparison', in Angel Flores (ed.), *The Kafka Debate* (New York: Gordian Press, 1977), 396–417.

Smetana, Ron, 'The Peasantry and the Castle: Kafka's Social Psychology', *Twentieth Century Literature*, 37 (1991), 54–8.

Vincent, Deirdre, ' "I'm the King of the Castle. . .": Franz Kafka and the Well-tempered Reader', *Modern Language Studies*, 17 (1987), 60–75.

Zilcosky, John, 'Kafka Approaches Schopenhauer's Castle', *German Life and Letters*, 44 (1990–1), 353–69.

—— 'Surveying the Castle: Kafka's Colonial Visions', in James Rolleston (ed.), *A Companion to the Works of Franz Kafka* (Rochester, NY: Camden House, 2002), 281–324.

Further Reading in Oxford World's Classics

Kafka, Franz, *The Metamorphosis and Other Stories*, tr. Joyce Crick, ed. Ritchie Robertson.

—— *The Trial*, tr. Mike Mitchell, ed. Ritchie Robertson.

A CHRONOLOGY OF FRANZ KAFKA

1883   3 July: Franz Kafka born in Prague, son of Hermann Kafka (1852–1931) and his wife Julie, née Löwy (1856–1934).

1885   Birth of FK's brother Georg, who died at the age of fifteen months.

1887   Birth of FK's brother Heinrich, who died at the age of six months.

1889   Birth of FK's sister Gabriele ('Elli') (d. 1941).

1890   Birth of FK's sister Valerie ('Valli') (d. 1942).

1892   Birth of FK's sister Ottilie ('Ottla') (d. 1943).

1901   FK begins studying law in the German-language section of the Charles University, Prague.

1906   Gains his doctorate in law and begins a year of professional experience in the Prague courts.

1907   Begins working for the Prague branch of the insurance company Assicurazioni Generali, based in Trieste.

1908   Moves to the state-run Workers' Accident Insurance Company for the Kingdom of Bohemia. First publication: eight prose pieces (later included in the volume *Meditation*) appear in the Munich journal *Hyperion*.

1909   Holiday with Max and Otto Brod at Riva on Lake Garda; they attend a display of aircraft, about which FK writes 'The Aeroplanes at Brescia'.

1910   Holiday with Max and Otto Brod in Paris.

1911   Holiday with Max Brod in Northern Italy, Switzerland, and Paris. Attends many performaances by Yiddish actors visiting Prague, and becomes friendly with the actor Isaak Löwy (Jitskhok Levi).

1912   Holiday with Max Brod in Weimar, after which FK spends three weeks in the nudist sanatorium 'Jungborn' in the Harz Mountains. Works on *The Man Who Disappeared*. 13 August: first meeting with Felice Bauer (1887–1960) from Berlin. 22–3 September: writes *The Judgement* in a single night. November–December: works on *The Metamorphosis*. December: *Meditation*, a collection of short prose pieces, published by Kurt Wolff in Leipzig.

1913   Visits Felice Bauer three times in Berlin. September: attends a conference on accident prevention in Vienna, where he also looks in on the Eleventh Zionist Congress. Stays in a sanatorium in Riva. Publishes *The Stoker* (= the first chapter of *The Man Who Disappeared*) in Wolff's series of avant-garde prose texts 'The Last Judgement'.

1914 1 June: officially engaged to Felice Bauer in Berlin. 12 July: engagement dissolved. Holiday with the Prague novelist Ernst Weiss in the Danish resort of Marielyst. August–December: writes most of *The Trial*; October: *In the Penal Colony*.

1915 The dramatist Carl Sternheim, awarded the Fontane Prize for literature, transfers the prize money to Kafka. *The Metamorphosis* published by Wolff.

1916 Reconciliation with Felice Bauer; they spend ten days together in the Bohemian resort of Marienbad (Mariánské Lázně). *The Judgement* published by Wolff. FK works on the stories later collected in *A Country Doctor*.

1917 July: FK and Felice visit the latter's sister in Budapest, and become engaged again. 9–10 August: FK suffers a haemorrhage which is diagnosed as tubercular. To convalesce, he stays with his sister Ottla on a farm at Zürau (Siřem) in the Bohemian countryside. December: visit from Felice Bauer; engagement dissolved.

1918 March: FK resumes work. November: given health leave, stays till March 1919 in a hotel in Schelesen (Železná).

1919 Back in Prague, briefly engaged to Julie Wohryzek (1891–1944). *In the Penal Colony* published by Wolff.

1920 Intense relationship with his Czech translator Milena Polak, née Jesenská (1896–1944). July: ends relationship with Julie Wohryzek. Publication of *A Country Doctor: Little Stories*. December: again granted health leave, FK stays in a sanatorium in Matliary, in the Tatra Mountains, till August 1921.

1921 September: returns to work, but his worsening health requires him to take three months' further leave from October.

1922 January: has his leave extended till April; stays in mountain hotel in Spindlermühle (Špindlerův Mlýn). January–August: writes most of *The Castle*. 1 July: retires from the Insurance Company on a pension.

1923 July: visits Müritz on the Baltic and meets Dora Diamant (1898–1952). September: moves to Berlin and lives with Dora.

1924 March: his declining health obliges FK to return to Prague and, in April, to enter a sanatorium outside Vienna. Writes and publishes 'Josefine the Singer or the Mouse Folk'. 3 June: dies. August: *A Hunger Artist: Four Stories* published by Die Schmiede.

1925 *The Trial*, edited by Max Brod, published by Die Schmiede.

1926 *The Castle*, edited by Max Brod, published by Wolff.

1927 *Amerika* (now known by Kafka's title, *The Man Who Disappeared*), edited by Max Brod, published by Wolff.

1930 *The Castle*, translated by Willa and Edwin Muir, published by Martin Secker (London), the first English translation of Kafka.

1939 Max Brod leaves Prague just before the German invasion, taking Kafka's manuscripts in a suitcase, and reaches Palestine.

1956 Brod transfers the manuscripts (except that of *The Trial*) to Switzerland for safe keeping.

1961 The Oxford scholar Malcolm Pasley, with the permission of Kafka's heirs, transports the manuscripts to the Bodleian Library.

THE CASTLE

CONTENTS

I

Arrival

It was late evening when K. arrived. The village lay deep in snow. There was nothing to be seen of Castle Mount, for mist and darkness surrounded it, and not the faintest glimmer of light showed where the great castle lay. K. stood on the wooden bridge leading from the road to the village for a long time, looking up at what seemed to be a void.

Then he went in search of somewhere to stay the night. People were still awake at the inn. The landlord had no room available, but although greatly surprised and confused by the arrival of a guest so late at night, he was willing to let K. sleep on a straw mattress in the saloon bar. K. agreed to that. Several of the local rustics were still sitting over their beer, but he didn't feel like talking to anyone. He fetched the straw mattress down from the attic himself, and lay down near the stove. It was warm, the locals were silent, his weary eyes gave them a cursory inspection, and then he fell asleep.

But soon afterwards he was woken again. A young man in town clothes, with a face like an actor's—narrowed eyes, strongly marked eyebrows—was standing beside him with the landlord. The rustics were still there too, and some of them had turned their chairs round so that they could see and hear better. The young man apologized very civilly for having woken K., introduced himself as the son of the castle warden, and added: 'This village belongs to the castle, so anyone who stays or spends the night here is, so to speak, staying or spending the night at the castle. And no one's allowed to do that without a permit from the count. However, you don't have any such permit, or at least you haven't shown one.'

K. had half sat up, had smoothed down his hair, and was now looking up at the two men. 'What village have I come to, then?' he asked. 'Is there a castle in these parts?'

'There most certainly is,' said the young man slowly, as some of those present shook their heads at K.'s ignorance. 'Count Westwest's* castle.'

'And I need this permit to spend the night here?' asked K., as if to convince himself that he had not, by any chance, dreamed the earlier information.

'Yes, you need a permit,' was the reply, and there was downright derision at K.'s expense in the young man's voice as, with arm outstretched, he asked the landlord and the guests: 'Or am I wrong? Doesn't he need a permit?'

'Well, I'll have to go and get a permit, then,' said K., yawning, and throwing off his blanket as if to rise to his feet.

'Oh yes? Who from?' asked the young man.

'Why, from the count,' said K. 'I suppose there's nothing else for it.'

'What, go and get a permit from the count himself at midnight?' cried the young man, retreating a step.

'Is that impossible?' asked K., unruffled. 'If so, why did you wake me up?'

At this the young man was positively beside himself. 'The manners of a vagrant!' he cried. 'I demand respect for the count's authority! I woke you up to tell you that you must leave the count's land immediately.'

'That's enough of this farce,' said K. in a noticeably quiet voice. He lay down and pulled the blanket over him. 'Young man, you're going rather too far, and I'll have something to say about your conduct tomorrow. The landlord and these gentlemen are my witnesses, if I need any. As for the rest of it, let me tell you that I'm the land surveyor,* and the count sent for me. My assistants will be coming tomorrow by carriage with our surveying instruments. I didn't want to deprive myself of a good walk here through the snow, but unfortunately I did lose my way several times, and that's why I arrived so late. I myself was well aware, even before you delivered your lecture, that it was too late to present myself at the castle. That's why I contented myself with sleeping the night here, and you have been—to put it mildly—uncivil enough to disturb my slumbers. And that's all the explanation I'm making. Goodnight, gentlemen.' And K. turned to the stove.

'Land surveyor?' he heard someone ask hesitantly behind his back, and then everyone fell silent. But the young man soon pulled himself together and told the landlord, in a tone just muted enough to sound as if he were showing consideration for the sleeping K., but loud enough for him to hear what was said: 'I'll telephone and ask.' Oh, so there was a telephone in this village inn, was there? They were very well equipped here. As a detail that surprised K., but on the whole he had expected this. It turned out that the telephone was installed almost right above his head, but drowsy as he was, he had failed to notice it. If the young man really had to make a telephone call, then with the best will in the world he could not fail to disturb K.'s sleep. The only point at issue was whether K. would let him use the telephone, and he decided that he would. In which case, however, there was no point in making out that he was asleep, so he turned over on his back again. He saw the locals clustering nervously together and conferring; well, the arrival of a land surveyor was no small matter. The kitchen door had opened and there, filling the whole doorway, stood the monumental figure of the landlady. The landlord approached on tiptoe to let her know what was going on. And now the telephone conversation began. The warden was asleep, but a deputy warden, or one of several such deputies, a certain Mr Fritz, was on the line. The young man, who identified himself as Schwarzer, told Mr Fritz how he had found K., a man of very ragged appearance in his thirties, sleeping peacefully on a straw mattress, with a tiny rucksack as a pillow and a gnarled walking-stick within reach. He had naturally felt suspicious, said the young man, and as the landlord had clearly neglected to do his duty it had been up to him to investigate the matter. K., he added, had acted very churlishly on being woken, questioned, and threatened in due form with expulsion from the county, although, as it finally turned out, perhaps with some reason, for he claimed to be a land surveyor and said his lordship the count had sent for him. Of course it was at least their formal duty to check this claim, so he, Schwarzer, would like Fritz to enquire in Central Office, find out whether any such surveyor was really expected, and telephone back with the answer at once.

Then all was quiet. Fritz went to make his enquiries, and here at the inn they waited for the answer, K. staying where he was, not even turning round, not appearing at all curious, but looking straight ahead of him. The way Schwarzer told his tale, with a mingling of malice and caution, gave him an idea of what might be called the diplomatic training of which even such insignificant figures in the castle as Schwarzer had a command. There was no lack of industry there either; Central Office was working even at night, and clearly it answered questions quickly, for Fritz soon rang back. His report, however, seemed to be a very short one, for Schwarzer immediately slammed the receiver down in anger. 'I said as much!' he cried. 'There's no record of any land surveyor; this is a common, lying vagabond and probably worse.' For a moment K. thought all of them—Schwarzer, the local rustics, the landlord and landlady—were going to fall on him, and to avoid at least the first onslaught he crawled under the blanket entirely. Then—he slowly put his head out—the telephone rang again and, so it seemed to K., with particular force. Although it was unlikely that this call too could be about K., they all stopped short, and Schwarzer went back to the phone. He listened to an explanation of some length, and then said quietly, 'A mistake, then? This is very awkward for me. You say the office manager himself telephoned? Strange, strange. But how am I to explain it to the land surveyor now?'*

K. pricked up his ears. So the castle had described him as 'the land surveyor'. In one way this was unfortunate, since it showed that they knew all they needed to know about him at the castle, they had weighed up the balance of power, and were cheerfully accepting his challenge. In another way, however, it was fortunate, for it confirmed his opinion that he was being underestimated, and would have more freedom than he had dared to hope from the outset. And if they thought they could keep him in a constant state of terror by recognizing his qualifications as a land surveyor in this intellectually supercilious way, as it certainly was, then they were wrong. He felt a slight frisson, yes, but that was all.

K. waved away Schwarzer, who was timidly approaching; he declined to move into the landlord's room, as he was now urged to do, merely accepting a nightcap from the landlord and the use of a washbasin, with soap and a towel, from the landlady, and he didn't even have to ask for the saloon to be cleared, since all present were hurrying out with their faces averted, perhaps to keep him from identifying them in the morning. The light was put out, and he was left alone at last. He slept soundly through until morning, scarcely disturbed once or twice by rats scurrying past.

After breakfast, which like K.'s entire board and lodging, so the landlord told him, was to be paid for by the castle, he thought he would go straight into the village. But when the landlord, to whom, remembering his behaviour yesterday, he had said only the bare minimum, kept hovering around him with a silent plea in his eyes, he took pity on the man and asked him to sit down and keep him company for a while.

'I haven't met the count yet,' said K., 'but they say he pays well for good work. Is that so? If you're travelling as far from your wife and child* as I am, you want to bring something worthwhile home.'

'No need to worry about that, sir. There've never been any complaints of poor pay.'

'Well,' said K., 'I'm not the timid sort myself, and I can speak my mind even to a count, but of course it's far better to be on friendly terms with such gentlemen.'

The landlord was perched opposite K. on the edge of the window-sill, not daring to sit anywhere more comfortable, and he kept looking at K. with his large, brown, anxious eyes. To begin with he had moved close to his guest, but now he seemed to want to run away. Was he afraid of being interrogated about the count? Did he fear that, although he was now calling his guest 'sir', K. was not to be relied on? K. thought he had better distract the man's mind. Looking at his watch, he said: 'Well, my assistants will soon be arriving. Will you be able to accommodate them here?'

'Of course, sir,' said the landlord. 'But won't they be staying with you up at the castle?'

Was he so easily and cheerfully giving up the prospect of guests, and in particular the custom of K., whom he seemed anxious to send off to the castle?

'That's not decided yet,' said K. 'First I must find out what kind of work they want me to do. For instance, if I'm to work down here, then it would be more sensible for me to stay down here too. And in addition, I'm afraid that living up in the castle wouldn't agree with me. I always prefer to be a free agent.'

'You don't know what the castle is like,' said the landlord quietly.

'True,' said K. 'One ought not to judge too early. At the moment all I know about the castle is that up there they know how to pick a good land surveyor. And perhaps there are other advantages there as well.' And he rose to his feet, to allow the landlord, who was uneasily biting his lip, a chance to be rid of his company. It wasn't easy to win this man's trust.

As K. was walking away, he noticed a dark portrait in a dark frame on the wall. He had seen it even from where he lay last night, but at that distance he hadn't been able to make out the details, and had thought that the real picture had been removed from the frame, leaving only a dark backing. But there was indeed a picture, as he now saw, the head and shoulders of a man of about fifty. The sitter's head was bent so low on his chest that you could hardly see his eyes, and the reason why he held it like that seemed to be the weight of his high, heavy forehead and large hooked nose. The man's beard, which was squashed in at his throat by the angle of his head, stood out below his chin. His left hand was spread and he was running it through his thick hair, but he could raise his head no higher. 'Who's that?' asked K. 'The count?' He was standing in front of the portrait, and did not even look at the landlord. 'Oh no,' said the landlord, 'that's the castle warden.' 'Well, they have a fine warden at the castle, to be sure,' said K. 'A pity his son has turned out so badly.' 'No, no,' said the landlord, drawing K. slightly down to him and whispering in his ear. 'Schwarzer was putting on airs yesterday; his father is only a deputy warden, and one of the most junior of them.' At this moment the landlord seemed like a child to K. 'What a rascal!' he said, laughing. However, the landlord did not join in his laughter, but said, '*His* father is powerful too.' 'Oh, come along!' said K. 'You think everyone is powerful. Including me, I wonder?' 'No,' said the man, diffidently but gravely, 'I don't think you are powerful.' 'You're a very good observer, then,' said K. 'The fact is, and just between you and me, I really am not powerful. As a result I probably feel no less respect for the powerful than you do, but I am not as honest as you and won't always admit it.' And to cheer the landlord and show his own good-will, he tapped him lightly on the cheek. At this the man did smile a little. He was only a boy really, with a soft and almost beardless face. How had he come to marry his stout, elderly wife, who could be seen through a hatch bustling about the kitchen next door, hands on her hips, elbows jutting? But K. did not want to probe the man any further now, or wipe the smile he had finally won from him off his face; he just signed to him to open the door and stepped out into the fine winter morning.

Now he could see the castle above, distinctly outlined in the clear air, and standing out even more distinctly because of the thin covering of snow lying everywhere and changing the shape of everything. In fact, much less snow seemed to have fallen up on Castle Mount than here in the village, where K. found it as difficult to make his way along the road as it had been yesterday. Here the snow came up to the cottage windows and weighed down on the low rooftops, while on the mountain everything rose into the air, free and light, or at least that was how it looked from here.

Altogether the castle, as seen in the distance, lived up to K.'s expectations. It was neither an old knightly castle from the days of chivalry, nor a showy new structure, but an extensive complex of buildings, a few of them with two storeys, but many of them lower and crowded close together. If you hadn't known it was a castle you might have taken it for a small town. K. saw only a single tower, and could not make out whether it was a dwelling or belonged to a church. Flocks of crows were circling around it.

His eyes fixed on the castle, K. went on, paying no attention to anything else. But as he came closer he thought the castle disappointing; after all, it was only a poor kind of collection of cottages assembled into a little town, and distinguished only by the fact that, while it might all be built of stone, the paint had flaked off long ago, and the stone itself seemed to be crumbling away. K. thought fleetingly of his own home town, which was hardly inferior to this castle. If he had come here only to see the place, he would have made a long journey for nothing much, and he would have done better to revisit the old home that he hadn't seen for so long. In his mind, he compared the church tower of his childhood home with the tower up above. The former, tapering into a spire and coming down to a broad, red-tiled roof, was certainly an earthly building—what else can we build?—but it had been erected for a higher purpose than these huddled, low-built houses and made a clearer statement than the dull, workaday world of this place did. The tower up here—the only visible one—now turned out to belong to a dwelling, perhaps the main part of the castle. It was a simple, round building, partly covered with ivy, and it had small windows, now shining in the sun—there was something crazed about the sight—and was built into the shape of a balcony at the top, with insecure, irregular battlements, crumbling as if drawn by an anxious or careless child as they stood out, zigzag fashion, against the blue sky. It was as if some melancholy inhabitant of the place, who should really have stayed locked up in the most remote room in the house, had broken through the roof and was standing erect to show himself to the world.

Once again K. stopped, as if standing still improved his powers of judgement. But his attention was distracted. Beyond the village church where he now was—in fact it was only a chapel, extended like a barn so that it could hold the whole congregation—lay the school. It was a long, low building, curiously combining the character of something temporary and something very old, and it stood in a fenced garden that was now covered with snow. The children were just coming out, with their teacher. They crowded around him, all eyes were fixed on him, and they were talking away the whole time, so fast that K. couldn't make out what they were saying. The teacher, a small, narrow-shouldered young man who held himself very upright, but without appearing ridiculous, had already seen K. from a distance—after all, apart from his own little flock K. was the only living soul to be seen far and wide. K., as the stranger here, greeted him first, noticing that despite his small stature he was used to being in command. 'Good morning, sir,' he said. All at once the children fell silent, and the teacher probably appreciated this sudden silence in anticipation of his remarks. 'Looking at the castle, are you?' he asked, more gently than K. had expected, but in a tone suggesting that he didn't like what K. was doing. 'Yes,' said K. 'I'm a stranger here; I arrived in the village only yesterday evening.' 'Don't you like the castle?' the teacher was quick to ask. 'What?' K. asked in return, slightly surprised. He repeated the question in a milder tone. 'Do I like the castle? What makes you think that I don't?' 'Strangers never do,' said the teacher. Here K. changed the subject, to avoid saying anything the teacher didn't like, and asked, 'I expect you know the count?' 'No,' said the teacher, and he was about to turn away, but K. wasn't giving up, and asked again: 'What? You don't know the count?' 'What makes you think I would?' asked the teacher very quietly, and he added in a louder voice, speaking French: 'Kindly recollect that we're in the company of innocent children.' This made K. think he might properly ask: 'Could I visit you one day, sir? I shall be here for some time, and feel rather isolated; I don't fit in with the local rustics here, and I don't suppose I shall fit in at the castle either.' 'There's no distinction between the local people and the castle,' said the teacher. 'Maybe not,' said K., 'but that makes no difference to my situation. May I visit you some time?' 'I lodge in Swan Alley, at the butcher's house.' This was more of a statement than an invitation, but all the same K. said: 'Good, then I'll come.' The teacher nodded, and went on with the crowd of children, who all started shouting again. They soon disappeared along a street that ran steeply downhill.

But K. was distracted, fretting at this conversation. For the first time since his arrival he felt real weariness. At first the long journey here had not seemed to affect him at all—and he had walked for days, step after step, on and on!—but now all that physical strain was claiming its due, and at just the wrong time. He was irresistibly drawn to seek new acquaintances, but every new acquaintance left him wearier than ever. If he forced himself to walk at least as far as the entrance to the castle, that was more than enough in his present state.

So he walked on, but it was a long way. For he was in the main street of the village, and it did not lead to Castle Mount but merely passed close to it before turning aside, as if on purpose, and although it moved no further away from the castle, it came no closer either. K. kept thinking that the road must finally bring him to the castle, and, if only because of that expectation, he went on. Because of his weariness he naturally shrank from leaving the road, and he was surprised by the extent of the village, which seemed as if it would never end, with more and more little houses, their window-panes covered by frost-flowers, and with the snow and the absence of any human beings—so at last he tore himself away from the road on which he had persisted and struck out down a narrow alley where the snow lay even deeper. Pulling his feet out of it as they kept sinking in again was hard work. He broke out in a sweat, and suddenly he stopped and could go no further.

But he wasn't entirely alone after all, there were cottages to his right and his left. He made a snowball and threw it at a window. The front door opened at once—the first door he had seen opening on his entire walk all the way through the village—and he saw an old man in a brown fur jacket, his head on one side, looking both frail and friendly. 'May I come into your house for a little while?' asked K. 'I'm very tired.' He did not hear what the old man was saying, but gratefully he realized that a plank was being pushed his way. This got him clear of the snow straight away, and a few more paces took him into the parlour of the cottage.

It was a large, dimly lit room. Coming in from outside, he could see nothing at first. K. staggered and nearly fell over a washing-trough; a woman's hand caught him. He heard a number of children shouting in one corner. Steam billowed out of another, turning the twilight into darkness. K. might have been surrounded by clouds. 'He's drunk,' someone said. 'Who are you?' cried a peremptory voice, and added, probably turning to the old man: 'Why did you let him in? Are we to let in everyone who goes slinking around the streets?' 'I'm the count's land surveyor,' said K., by way of justifying himself to the still–invisible speaker. 'Oh, it's the land surveyor,' said a woman's voice, and then there was total silence. 'You know me?' asked K. 'Yes, indeed,' was all the first voice said again, briefly. Knowing who K. was didn't seem to recommend him to these people.

At last some of the steam drifted away, and gradually K. was able to get his bearings. This seemed to be wash-day for everyone. Clothes were being washed near the door. But the vapour came from the left-hand corner, where two men were having a bath in steaming water in a wooden tub larger than any K. had ever seen before; it was about the size of two beds. But even more surprising, although it was hard to say just why, was the right-hand corner of the room. Through a large hatch, the only opening in the back wall of the parlour, pale snowy light came in, no doubt from the yard, and cast a sheen like silk* on the dress of a woman almost lying, for she looked so tired, in a tall armchair far back in that corner. She had a baby at her breast. A few children were playing around her, obviously village children, although she did not look like a villager herself, but sickness and weariness will make even rustics appear refined.

'Sit down,' said one of the men, a bearded, moustached fellow who kept his mouth open all the time under his moustache, breathing noisily. Raising his hand above the side of the tub, a comical sight, he pointed to a chest, and in doing so splashed hot water all over K.'s face. The old man who had let K. in was sitting on the chest too, lost in thought. K. was glad of the chance to sit down at last. No one bothered about him any more. The woman at the washing-trough, who was blonde, young, and buxom, was singing softly at her work, the men in the tub were stamping their feet and turning this way and that, the children were trying to get closer to them, but were always chased away by great jets of water which did not spare K. either, the woman in the armchair lay as if lifeless, not even looking down at the child at her breast, but gazing vaguely upwards.

K. had probably been watching this unchanging, sad, and beautiful scene for some time, but then he must have fallen asleep, for when a loud voice hailed him he woke with a start and found that his head was resting on the shoulder of the old man beside him. The men had finished bathing in the tub—the children were now splashing about in it, with the blonde woman watching over them—and were standing fully clothed in front of K. The bearded man with the loud voice turned out to be the less important of the two. The other man, no taller than his friend and with a much sparser beard, was a quiet, slow-thinking fellow, sturdy of stature and broad of face, and held his head bent. 'Mr Land Surveyor, sir,' he said, 'forgive the incivility, but you can't stay here.' 'I didn't want to stay,' said K., 'only to rest for a little while. I feel rested now, and I'll be on my way.' 'You're probably surprised to find us so inhospitable,' said the man, 'but hospitality isn't a custom here, and we don't need any visitors.' Slightly refreshed by sleep, and listening a little more attentively than before, K. was glad to hear him speak so frankly. He was moving more easily by this time and, placing his walking-stick now here, now there, he approached the woman in the armchair. He himself was physically the largest person in the room.

'To be sure,' said K. 'Why would you need visitors? But a visitor or so *is* needed now and then, for instance me, as a land surveyor.' 'I don't know about that,' said the man slowly. 'If they sent for you, then they probably do need you, but that's an exception. As for us ordinary folk, we stick to the rules, and you can't hold that against us.' 'No, no,' said K. 'I owe you thanks, you and everyone here.' And when none of them expected it, he suddenly swung round to stand in front of the woman. She looked at K. from tired blue eyes; a translucent silk headscarf came halfway down her forehead, and the baby was sleeping at her breast. 'Who are you?' asked K. Dismissively—and it was not clear whether her disdain was meant for K. or her own answer—she said: 'I'm from the castle.'

All this had taken only a moment, but already the two men were one on each side of K., forcibly frogmarching him to the door, as if there were no other means of communication. The old man, watching, seemed pleased about something, and clapped his hands. The washerwoman too laughed as she stood among the children, who were suddenly romping noisily.

As for K., he was soon out in the alley, with the two men watching him from the doorway. Snow was falling again, but it seemed a little brighter than before. The bearded man called impatiently: 'Where do you want to go? This is the way to the castle, that's the way to the village.' K. did not answer, but said to the other man, who despite his superior status seemed more approachable: 'Who are you? To whom do I owe thanks for my rest here?' 'I am Lasemann,* the master tanner,' was the reply, 'and you owe no one any thanks.' 'Very well,' said K. 'Perhaps we'll meet again.' 'I shouldn't think so,' said the man. At this moment the bearded man, raising a hand, called out: 'Good day, Artur; good day, Jeremias!' K. turned. So there were people out and about on the village streets after all! Two young men were coming along the road from the castle. They were of medium height, very lean, in close-fitting clothes, and their faces too were very much alike, with dark brown complexions setting off their very black goatee beards. They were walking remarkably fast, considering the present state of the roads, swinging their long legs in time. 'What's going on?' called the bearded man. He had to raise his voice to communicate with them, they were walking so fast, and didn't stop. 'We have business here,' they called back, laughing. 'Where?' 'At the inn.' 'I'm going there too,' shouted K., his voice suddenly rising above all the others. He very much wanted the two men to take him with them. Striking up an acquaintance with them didn't seem as if it would lead anywhere much, but they would obviously be good, cheerful companions on a walk. However, although they heard what K. said, they simply nodded, walked on, and were gone in a moment.

K. was left standing in the snow, feeling disinclined to haul his foot out of it only to have it sink in again a little further on. The master tanner and his friend, happy to be rid of K. at last, made their way slowly back through the door of the house, which was only standing ajar, still keeping an eye on him. K. was left alone in the all-enveloping snow. 'If I'd come here by chance and not on purpose,' he thought, 'I might fall into despair at this point.'

Then a tiny window opened in a cottage on his left. Closed, it had looked dark blue, perhaps reflecting the snow, and it was so very tiny that, now it had been opened, you couldn't see the whole face of the person behind it, only that person's eyes: they were old, brown eyes. 'There he is,' K. heard a quavering female voice say. 'It's the land surveyor,' said a male voice. The man came to the window and asked, in not-unfriendly tones, but as if anxious to make sure that all was well with the street outside his house: 'Who are you waiting for?' 'I'm waiting for a sleigh that will give me a lift,' said K. 'There won't be any sleighs coming this way,' said the man. 'We don't have traffic here.' 'But this is the road to the castle,' K. objected. 'All the same,' said the man, with a certain implacable note in his voice, 'we don't have traffic here.' Then they both fell silent. But the man was obviously thinking something over, for the window was still open and smoke was pouring out of it. 'It's a bad road,' said K., to help the conversation along. However, all the man said was: 'Yes, to be sure.' After a while, however, he did add: 'I'll take you in my own sleigh if you like.' 'Yes, please do,' said K., delighted to hear it. 'How much will you ask?' 'Nothing,' said the man, to K.'s great surprise. 'Well, you're the land surveyor,' he explained, 'and you belong at the castle. Where do you want to go?' 'Why, to the castle,' K. was quick to say. 'Oh, then I'm not going,' the man said at once. 'But I belong at the castle,' K. said, repeating the man's own words. 'Maybe,' said the man coldly. 'Take me to the inn, then,' said K. 'Very well,' said the man. 'I'll bring the sleigh round in a minute.' None of this exchange sounded particularly friendly; it was more like a kind of self-interested, anxious, pettily meticulous attempt to get K. away from where he was standing in front of the man's house.

The yard gate opened, and a small, flat-bottomed sleigh appeared. It was for carrying light loads, had no seat of any kind, and was drawn by a feeble little horse, behind which the man came into view. Although he wasn't old he seemed feeble himself, he stooped and walked with a limp, and his face was red, as if he had a cold. It seemed particularly small because of a woollen scarf wrapped tightly around his neck. The man was obviously sick, and had come out of the house only to get K. away from here. K. said something to that effect, but the man dismissed it. All K. learned was that he was Gerstäcker* the carrier, he had brought this uncomfortable sleigh because it happened to be standing ready, and getting another one would have taken too much time. 'Sit down,' he said, pointing to the back of the sleigh with his whip. 'I'll sit beside you,' said K. 'I'm going to walk,' said Gerstäcker. 'But why?' asked K. 'I'm going to walk,' repeated Gerstäcker, and then succumbed to a fit of coughing which shook him so badly that he had to brace his legs in the snow and hold on to the side of the sleigh. K. said no more, but sat down at the back of the sleigh, the man's coughing gradually subsided, and they started to move.

The castle up above, now curiously dark, the place that K. had hoped to reach today, was retreating into the distance again. As if suggesting that this was only a temporary farewell, however, a bell rang there with a lively, cheerful note, although the sound was painful too, and made his heart quail momentarily as if threatened with getting what it vaguely desired. But soon the clang of this great bell died away, to be succeeded by the faint, monotonous sound of a smaller bell, perhaps also up at the castle or perhaps in the village. Its note was certainly a more suitable accompaniment to their slow progress with the feeble but implacable driver.

'You know,' cried K. suddenly—they were already near the church, the road to the inn was not far away, and K. thought he might venture this remark—'I'm very surprised to find you willing to drive me on your own responsibility. Is it allowed?' Gerstäcker took no notice, and continued to walk along beside the horse. 'Hey!' cried K., making a snowball from the snow on the sleigh and throwing it. It hit Gerstäcker right on the ear. At this he did stop and turned, but when K. saw him so close—the sleigh had moved a little further on—when he saw the man's bent form, as if physically mistreated, the red, narrow face with cheeks that somehow looked lopsided, one smooth and the other fallen in, the almost toothless mouth constantly open as if to help him listen better, he found he had to repeat what he had just said in malice but this time with compassion, asking whether Gerstäcker might be punished for giving K. a lift in his sleigh. 'What are you getting at?' asked Gerstäcker blankly, but waiting for no further explanation he called to the little horse and they moved on.

When they had almost reached the inn, which K. recognized by a bend in the road, he saw to his surprise that the place was already entirely dark. Had he been out so long? Only one or two hours, by his calculations. And he had left in the morning, and had not felt hungry since. Again, it had been full daylight until a little while ago, and only now was it dark. 'Short days, short days,' he said to himself, slipping off the sleigh and going towards the inn.

On the small flight of steps up to the house he saw a welcome sight: the landlord raising a lantern in the air and shining it in his direction. Fleetingly remembering the carrier, K. stopped. There was a cough somewhere in the darkness; that was him. Well, he'd probably be seeing him again soon. Only when he reached the top of the steps, to be respectfully greeted by the landlord, did he see two men, one on each side of the door. Taking the lantern from the landlord's hand, he shone it on the pair of them; they were the men he had already met and who had been addressed as Artur and Jeremias. They saluted him. Reminded of the happy days of his military service, he laughed. 'Well, so who are you?' he asked, looking from one to the other. 'Your assistants,' they replied. 'That's right, they're the assistants,' the landlord quietly confirmed. 'What?' asked K. 'Do you say you're my old assistants who were coming on after me and whom I'm expecting?' They assured him that they were. 'Just as well, then,' said K. after a little while. 'It's a good thing you've come. What's more,' he added after another moment's thought, 'you're extremely late. That's very remiss of you.' 'It was a long way,' said one of them. 'A long way?' K. repeated. 'But I saw you coming down from the castle.' 'Yes,' they agreed, without further explanation. 'What have you done with the instruments?' asked K. 'We don't have any,' they said. 'I mean the surveying instruments that I entrusted to you,' said K. 'We don't have any of those,' they repeated. 'What a couple you are!' said K. 'Do you know anything about land surveying?' 'No,' they said. 'But if you claim to be my old assistants, then you must know something about it,' said K. They remained silent. 'Oh, come along, then,' said K., pushing them into the house ahead of him.

2

Barnabas

THE three of them were sitting rather silently at a small table in the saloon bar of the inn over their beer, K. in the middle, his assistants to right and left of him. Otherwise there was only a table where some of the local rustics sat, just as they had yesterday evening. 'I'm going to have a hard time with you two,' said K., comparing their faces yet again. 'How am I to know which of you is which? The only difference between you is your names, and apart from that'—he hesitated— 'apart from that you're as like as two snakes.' They smiled. 'Oh, other people find it easy to tell us apart,' they said. 'I believe you,' said K. 'I've seen that for myself, but then I have only my own eyes, and I can't distinguish between you with those. So I shall treat you as a single man, and call you both Artur, which is the name of one of you— you, perhaps?' K. asked one of the assistants. 'No,' he said, 'my name is Jeremias.' 'Well, never mind that,' said K, 'I shall call you both Artur. If I send Artur somewhere you'll both go, if I give Artur a job to do you'll both do it, which from my point of view will be a disadvantage in that I can't employ you on separate tasks, but also an advantage because then I can hold you jointly responsible for everything I ask you to do. How you divide the work between you is all the same to me, only you can't make separate excuses. To me you'll be just one man.' They thought this over and said: 'We wouldn't like that at all.' 'Of course not,' said K. 'Naturally you're bound to dislike it, but that's how it's going to be.' For some time, he had been watching one of the local rustics prowling around the table, and at last the man made up his mind, went over to one of the assistants, and was about to whisper something in his ear. 'Excuse me,' said K., slamming his hand down on the table and standing up, 'these are my assistants and we are in the middle of a discussion. No one has any right to disturb us.' 'Oh, I see, I see,' said the local man in some alarm, walking backwards to rejoin his company. 'I want you two to take particular note of this,' said K., sitting down again. 'You may not speak to anyone without my permission. I'm a stranger here, and if you're my old assistants then you are strangers here too. So we three strangers must stick together. Let's shake hands on it.' They offered K. their hands only too willingly. 'Well, never mind about those great paws of yours,' he said, 'but my orders stand. I'm going to get some sleep now, and I advise you to do the same. We've missed out on one working day already, and work must start early tomorrow. You'd better find a sleigh to go up to the castle and be here outside the inn with it at six in the morning, ready to leave.' 'Very well,' said one of the assistants. But the other objected. 'Why say "very well", when you know it can't be done?' 'Be quiet,' said K. 'I think you're trying to start distinguishing yourselves from each other.' Now, however, the assistant who had spoken first said: 'He's right, it's impossible. No stranger may go up to the castle without a permit.' 'So where do we have to apply for a permit?' 'I don't know. Maybe to the castle warden.' 'Then we'll apply by telephone. Go and telephone the castle warden at once, both of you.' They went to the telephone, made the connection, crowding together eagerly and showing that outwardly they were ridiculously ready to oblige, and asked whether K. might come up to the castle with them next day. The reply was a 'No' that K. could hear all the way over to his table, but the answer went on. It ran: 'Not tomorrow nor any other time either.' 'I'll telephone myself,' said K., rising to his feet. So far, apart from the incident with that one local rustic, no one had taken much notice of K. and his assistants, but this last remark of his aroused general attention. The whole company stood up with K., and although the landlord tried to fend them off, they crowded around him in a semicircle close to the telephone. Most of them seemed to be of the opinion that K. wouldn't get an answer. K. had to ask them to keep quiet, telling them he didn't want to hear their views.

A humming, such as K. had never before heard on the telephone, emerged from the receiver. It was as if the murmur of countless childish voices—not that it was really a murmur, it was more like the singing of voices, very very far away—as if that sound were forming, unlikely as that might be, into a single high, strong voice, striking the ear as if trying to penetrate further than into the mere human sense of hearing. K. heard it and said nothing; he had propped his left arm on the telephone stand, and listened like that.

He didn't know just how long he stood there, but after a while the landlord plucked at his coat and told him that someone had come with a message for him. 'Go away!' cried K., angrily, perhaps into the telephone, for now someone was answering at the other end, and the following conversation took place. 'Oswald speaking—who's there?' asked the speaker in a stern, haughty voice with a small speech defect for which, as it seemed to K., he tried to compensate by dint of extra severity. K. hesitated to give his name; he was powerless against the telephone, leaving the other man free to shout at him and put down the receiver. If that happened, K. would have cut himself off from what might be a not-unimportant means of getting somewhere. K.'s hesitation made the man impatient. 'Who's there?' he repeated, add-ing, 'I really would rather you lot down there didn't do so much telephoning. We had a call only a minute ago.' Taking no notice of this remark, K. came to a sudden decision and announced: 'This is the land surveyor's assistant speaking.' 'What assistant? What land surveyor?' K. remembered yesterday's conversation. 'Ask Fritz,' he said briefly. To his surprise, this worked. But over and beyond that, he marvelled at the consistency among the people up there, for the answer was: 'Yes, yes, I know. That eternal land surveyor!* Yes, yes, so what else? What assistant?' 'Josef,' said K. He was slightly taken aback by the way the locals were muttering behind him; obviously they didn't like to hear him giving a false name. But K. had no time to bother about them, for the conversation called for all his attention. 'Josef?' came the answer. 'No, the assistants are called'—here there was a pause, while someone else was obviously consulted—'are called Artur and Jeremias.' 'Those are the new assistants,' said K. 'No, they're the old ones.' 'They are the new assistants, but I'm the old one, and I came on later than the land surveyor and got here today.' 'No,' the other man replied, shouting now. 'Who am I, then?' asked K., still keeping calm. And after a pause the same voice, with the same speech defect, yet sounding like another and deeper voice, commanding more respect, agreed: 'You are the old assistant.'

K. was listening to the sound of the voice, and almost missed hear-ing the next question: 'What do you want?' He felt like slamming the receiver down, expecting no more to come of this conversation. But he was forced to reply at once: 'When may my boss come up to the castle?' 'Never,' was the reply. 'I see,' said K., and he hung up.

The locals behind him had come very close now, and the assistants, with many surreptitious glances at him, were busy keeping them back. However, it seemed to be just for show, and the locals, satisfied by the outcome of the conversation, slowly gave way. Then a man

walked through the group from behind it, dividing it in two, bowed
to K., and gave him a letter. Holding the letter in his hand, K. looked
at the messenger, who just now seemed to him more important than
the message itself. He greatly resembled the assistants; he was as
slender as they were, his clothes too were close-fitting, he was nimble
and spry, and yet he was quite different. K. would far rather have had
him as his assistant! The man reminded him a little of the woman
with the baby whom he had seen in the master tanner's house. His
clothing was almost white and was probably not silk, but an ordinary
winter-weight fabric, yet it had the fine look of a silk suit worn for
special occasions. His face was clear and open, his eyes very large.
His smile was extraordinarily cheering, and although he passed a
hand over his face, as if to wipe that smile away, he did not succeed.
'Who are you?' asked K. 'My name is Barnabas,'* he said, 'and I am
a messenger.'* His lips moved in a manly yet gentle way as he spoke.
'How do you like it here?' asked K., indicating the rustics, who were
still taking an interest in him. They were watching him with their
positively tormented faces—their skulls looked as if they had been
beaten flat on top, and their features had contorted into an expression
of pain in the process—they were watching him with their thick-
lipped mouths open, and yet not watching either, for sometimes their
eyes wandered, lingering for a long time on some ordinary object
before returning to him. Then K. also pointed to the assistants, who
were holding each other close, cheek to cheek and smiling, whether
humbly or in derision it was hard to say. He indicated all these people
as if to introduce a retinue forced on him by special circumstances,
expecting—which implied familiarity, and that mattered to K. just
now—that Barnabas would see the difference between him and them.
But Barnabas did not respond to the question—although, as could
easily be seen, in all innocence—and let it pass him by, like a well-
trained servant hearing his master say something that is only apparently addressed to him. He merely looked around as the question
required, greeting acquaintances among the locals with a wave of his
hand, and exchanged a few words with the assistants, all easily and as
a matter of course, without actually mixing with them. K., warned
off the subject but undeterred, turned back to the letter in his hand
and opened it. It ran as follows: 'Dear Sir, you are, as you know,
taken into the count's service. Your immediate superior is the village
mayor as chairman of the parish council, who will communicate to

you all further details concerning your work and your remuneration, and to whom you will be answerable. Nonetheless, I will keep an eye on you myself. Barnabas, the messenger who brings this letter, will make enquiries of you from time to time, find out what your requirements are, and impart them to me. You will find me always ready to oblige you as far as possible. I am anxious to have contented workers.' The signature was illegible, but printed beside it were the words: 'Chief Executive, Office X.' 'Wait a minute!' said K. to Barnabas, who was bowing to him, and he called to the landlord to show him his room, saying he wanted to spend a little time alone studying this letter. As he did so, he remembered that although he had taken to Barnabas so much, he was only a messenger, and ordered him a beer. He watched to see how he would take this; he was obviously pleased, and drank it at once. Then K. went with the landlord. They had been able to give him only a little attic room at the inn, which was a small place, and even that had been difficult, for two maids who had been sleeping there before had to be accommodated elsewhere. In fact all that had been done was to clear the maids out of the room, which otherwise appeared unchanged, with no linen on the only bed and just a couple of bolsters and a horse-blanket, left in the state it had been in after last night, with a few pictures of saints and photographs of soldiers on the walls. The room hadn't even been aired; obviously they hoped that the new guest would not stay long, and they were doing nothing to keep him. But K. didn't mind; he wrapped himself in the blanket and began rereading the letter by the light of a candle.

It was not all of a piece; there were passages where he was addressed as a free agent whose autonomy was recognized, for instance in the opening greeting and the part about his requirements. But then again, there were passages in the letter where he was openly or by implication addressed as a common labourer, hardly worthy even to be noticed by the chief executive of Office X, who obviously felt he must make an effort 'to keep an eye on him', while his superior, to whom he was actually 'answerable', was only the village mayor, and perhaps his sole colleague would be the village policeman. These contradictions were certainly so blatant that they must be intentional. Considering that the letter came from such an authority, K. scarcely even entertained the crazy idea that any indecision might have entered into it. Rather, he saw himself offered a choice: it was left to him to make what he liked of the arrangements in this letter, and decide whether he wanted to be a village worker who seemed, but only seemed, to have the distinction of a link to the castle, or apparently a village worker but one whose conditions of work were really determined entirely by the message that Barnabas had brought. K. did not hesitate to choose, nor would he have done so even without his experiences so far. Only as a village worker as far as possible from the gentlemen in the castle could he get anywhere with the castle itself. These villagers, who were still so suspicious of him, would start talking to him once he was, if not their friend, at least one of them, indistinguishable from, say, Gerstäcker and Lasemann—that must be brought about very soon, everything depended on it—and then, he was sure, all paths would be open to him, paths that would have been closed to him for ever, and not only closed but invisible, if it had depended solely on the good graces of the gentlemen up above. Of course there was a danger, and it was sufficiently emphasized in the letter, even represented with a certain pleasure as if it were inevitable. It was that his was the status of a labourer. 'Service', 'superior', 'work', 'conditions of remuneration', 'answerable', 'workmen': the letter was full of such terms, and even when something else and more personal was said, it was written from the same point of view. If K. wanted to work here then he could, but if so it must be in deadly earnest, without so much as glancing elsewhere. K. knew that no real compulsion threatened him, he wasn't afraid of that, least of all here, but he did fear the force of his discouraging surroundings, he feared getting used to disappointment, he feared the imperceptible influence of every passing moment—but he must contend with that danger. The letter did not, after all, gloss over the fact that if there were any disagreements it would be the fault of K.'s recklessness—it was said with delicacy, and only an uneasy conscience (uneasy, not guilty) would have noticed it in those three words 'as you know', referring to his entering the employment of the castle. K. had applied for the post, and now he knew that, as the letter put it, he had been accepted into the count's service.

K. took a picture off the wall and hung up the letter on the nail instead. He would be living in this room, so this was where the letter should hang.

Then he went down to the saloon bar of the inn. Barnabas and the assistants were sitting at a little table. 'Oh, there you are,' said K. for no special reason, just because he was glad to see Barnabas, who got to his feet at once. No sooner had K. entered the room than the rustics rose to come closer to him; it had become a habit of theirs to follow him around. 'What is it you keep wanting from me?' cried K. They did not take offence, but turned slowly back to their places. One said, by way of explanation as he turned away, but with an inscrutable smile copied by some of the others in the saloon bar: 'We're always hearing something new,' and he licked his lips as if the 'new' was something delicious to eat. K. said not a word to smooth things over; it would be good for them to feel a little respect for him, but no sooner was he sitting beside Barnabas than he felt one of the locals breathing down the back of his neck; the man said he had come to fetch the salt-cellar, but K. stamped his foot angrily and he went away without it. It was really easy to irritate K.; you would only have to set the rustics against him, for instance, for the persistent attention of some of them bothered him more than the reserve of others. But the attitude of the former showed reserve too, for if K. had sat down at their table, they would certainly have left it. Only the presence of Barnabas kept him from making a scene. But still he turned to them menacingly, and they had also turned to him. However, when he saw them sitting like that, each in his place, without talking, without any visible connection with each other, the only thing they had in common being that they were all staring at him, it struck him that it might not be malice at all that made them pester him, perhaps they really did want something from him but simply could not say it, or then again it could be just childishness. This seemed to be a great place for childishness. Wasn't the landlord himself child-like as he held a glass of beer in both hands, taking it to one of the guests? He stood still, looked at K., and failed to hear something that the landlady had called out to him from the kitchen hatch.

Feeling calmer, K. turned to Barnabas; he would have liked to get the assistants out of the way, but could find no pretext for ridding himself of them, and in any case they were staring in silence at their beer. 'I've read the letter,' said K. 'Do you know what it says?' 'No,' replied Barnabas. His glance seemed to convey more than his words. Perhaps K. was mistaken in detecting goodwill in him as well as malice in the rustics, but the messenger's presence still made him feel better. 'The letter mentions you too. It says you are to carry messages between me and the chief executive, so that's why I thought you would know what was in it.' 'My orders', said Barnabas, 'were simply to carry the letter, wait until it had been read, and if you think it necessary take back an answer either oral or written.' 'Good', said K. 'There's no need to write; just tell the chief executive—what's his name, by the way? I couldn't read the signature.' 'Klamm,'* said Barnabas. 'Then thank Mr Klamm on my behalf for my acceptance and his particular kindness, which I know how to value as I ought, not having proved my merits here yet. I will act entirely in accordance with his plans, and I have no particular requirements today.' Barnabas, who had been listening attentively, asked if he could run through that message out loud. K. said yes, Barnabas recited everything word for word. Then he rose to leave.

All this while K. had been scrutinizing his face, and now he did so for the last time. Although Barnabas was about the same height as K., he seemed to be looking down at him from above, but almost humbly, although it was impossible to imagine him causing awkwardness to anyone. To be sure, he was only a messenger and did not know the contents of the letter he had delivered, but his eyes, his smile, his carriage seemed to be a message in themselves, even if he didn't know it. And K. offered his hand, which clearly surprised Barnabas, who had intended only to bow.

As soon as he had gone—before opening the door he had leaned against it for a moment and looked around the room, with a glance that was not meant for any particular person—as soon as he was gone, K. told the assistants: 'I'm going to fetch my drawings from my room, and then we'll discuss our first job of work.' They moved to accompany him. 'No, stay here,' said K. They still wanted to go with him, and K. had to repeat his order more sternly. Barnabas was no longer out in the front hall, but he had only just left, for K. did not see him outside the house, where new snow was falling. 'Barnabas?' he called. No answer. Could he still be inside the inn? There seemed to be no other possibility. All the same, K. shouted his name at the top of his voice, and it echoed through the night. At last a faint answer came back from the distance—Barnabas was so far away already. K. called him back, at the same time going towards him. They met where they were out of sight of the inn.

'Barnabas,' said K., unable to keep a quiver out of his voice, 'there's something else I wanted to say to you. I'll just point out that it's a poor arrangement if I have to rely on your coming by chance when I need something from the castle. It's not by chance that I've found you now—and what speed you make; I thought you must still be in the house!—but who knows how long I'd have had to wait for your next appearance.' 'You can ask the chief executive for me always to come at times of your choice,' said Barnabas. 'That wouldn't do either,' said K. 'Perhaps I might go for as long as a year without wanting to send a message, and then there'd be something urgent only quarter of an hour after you'd left.' 'Well, in that case,' said Barnabas, 'shall I tell the chief executive that there should be some other kind of link between him and you, not involving me?' 'No, no,' said K., 'definitely not, I just mention the matter in passing. This time, fortunately, I was able to reach you.' 'Shall we go back to the inn so that you can give me your new message there?' said Barnabas. He had already taken another step towards the building. 'That's not necessary, Barnabas,' said K. 'I'll walk part of the way with you.' 'Why don't you want to go to the inn?' asked Barnabas. 'The people there bother me,' said K. 'You saw for yourself how importunate those rustics are.' 'We can go to your room,' said Barnabas. 'It's the maids' room,' said K., 'dirty and dismal; I wanted to walk a little way with you so as not to have to stay there. Let's link arms,' added K. to overcome his hesitation, 'and then you'll walk more securely.' And K. took his arm. It was quite dark, K. could not see his face, his figure was indistinct, and he had already tried to touch his arm a little while before.

Barnabas did as he wished, and they moved away from the inn. Hard as he tried, K. found it difficult to keep up with Barnabas, he was impeding the other man's freedom of movement, and in ordinary circumstances this little detail would surely lead to failure, especially in the side-streets like the one where K. had sunk in the snow that morning, and where he was only able to get along now with the support of Barnabas. But he fended off such anxieties, and it cheered him that Barnabas said nothing; if they went along in silence, perhaps Barnabas too felt that just walking might be the point of their keeping company.

And they were indeed walking on, but K. didn't know where they were going; he could make out nothing, and did not even know whether they had passed the church yet. The difficulty he had in simply walking meant that he could not command his thoughts. Instead of remaining fixed on his goal, they became confused. Images of his home kept coming back to him, and memories of it filled his mind.

There was a church in the main square there too, partly surrounded by an old graveyard, which in turn was surrounded by a high wall. Only a few boys had ever climbed that wall, and K. had so far failed to do so. It was not curiosity that made them want to climb it; the graveyard had no secrets from them, and they had often gone into it through the little wrought-iron gate; it was just that they wanted to conquer that smooth, high wall. Then one morning—the quiet, empty square was flooded with light; when had K. ever seen it like that before or since?—he succeeded surprisingly easily. He climbed the wall at the first attempt, at a place where he had often failed to get any further before, with a small flag clenched between his teeth. Little stones crumbled and rolled away below him as he reached the top. He rammed the flag into the wall, it flapped in the wind, he looked down and all around him, glancing back over his shoulder at the crosses sunk in the ground. Here and now he was greater than anyone. Then, by chance, the schoolteacher came by and, with an angry look, made K. get down from the wall. As he jumped he hurt his knee, and it was only with some difficulty that he got home, but still he had been on top of the wall, and the sense of victory seemed to him, at the time, something to cling to all his life. It had not been entirely a foolish idea, for now, on this snowy night many years later, it came to his aid as he walked on, holding Barnabas's arm.

He held that arm more firmly; Barnabas was almost pulling him along, and they preserved an unbroken silence. All K. knew about the way they were going was that, judging by the state of the road surface, they had turned into another side-alley. He resolved not to be deterred from going on by any difficulty on the road, or indeed by anxiety about finding his own way back; his strength would surely hold out. And could this walk go on for ever? By day the castle had seemed an easy place to reach, and a messenger from it was sure to know the shortest way.

Then Barnabas stopped. Where were they? Didn't their path go any further? Was Barnabas going to say goodbye to him now? He would not succeed. K. held Barnabas by the arm so tightly that it almost hurt his own fingers. Or could the incredible have happened, and they were already in the castle or at its gates? But so far as K. was aware they had not gone up any hill. Or had Barnabas led him along a way that climbed only imperceptibly? 'Where are we?' K. asked quietly, more to himself than his companion. 'Home,' said Barnabas just as quietly. 'Home?' 'Take care now, sir, mind you don't slip. This path goes downhill.' Downhill? 'It's only a few steps,' Barnabas added, and he was already knocking at a door.

A girl opened it. They were standing in the doorway of a large room, which was almost dark, for only one tiny oil-lamp hung over a table to the left at the back of the room. 'Who's this with you, Barnabas?' asked the girl. 'The land surveyor,' he said. 'The land surveyor?' repeated the girl in a louder voice, looking at the table. Two old people sitting there rose to their feet, a man and a woman, and so did another girl. They greeted K. Barnabas introduced them all to him: they were his parents and his sisters Olga and Amalia. K. hardly looked at them. They took his wet coat from him to dry it by the stove, and K. let them do as they liked.

So they weren't home, or rather only Barnabas was. But why were they here? K. took Barnabas aside and asked: 'Why did you come here to your home? Or do you live in the castle precincts?' 'In the castle precincts?' repeated Barnabas, as if he didn't understand K. 'Barnabas,' said K., 'you were leaving the inn to go up to the castle.' 'Oh no, sir,' said Barnabas, 'I was going home, I don't go up to the castle until morning. I never sleep there.' 'I see,' said K. 'You weren't going to the castle, only here.' He felt that his smile was wearier and he himself more insignificant. 'Why didn't you tell me so?' 'You didn't ask, sir,' said Barnabas. 'You only wanted to give me another message, but not in the saloon bar at the inn or in your room there, so I thought you could give me the message here, at your leisure, at home with my parents—they'll all go away at once if you say so—and if you like it better here with us you could spend the night. Did I do wrong?' K. could not reply. So it had been a misunderstanding, a stupid, ordinary misunderstanding, and K. had swallowed it hook, line, and sinker. He had let himself be captivated by the silken gleam of Barnabas's close-fitting jacket, which he now unbuttoned, revealing a coarse, grey, much-mended shirt over a powerful broad chest like a labourer's. And everything around him was not only in harmony with this sight but went further: the gouty old father who made his way forward, more with the help of his groping hands than his slow, stiff legs; the mother with her arms crossed over her breast, so stout that she too could take only the tiniest of steps. Both of them, father and mother, had left their corner when K. entered the room, moving towards him, and they were nowhere near him yet. The sisters, two blondes, resembling both each other and Barnabas, but with harsher features than their brother, were tall, strong girls. They stood near the two new arrivals, expecting some kind of greeting from K., but he couldn't get out a word. He had been thinking that everyone here in the village would matter to him, and no doubt that was so, but he wasn't interested in these particular people. If he had been able to make his way back to the inn on his own, he would have set off at once. Even the chance of getting into the castle with Barnabas in the morning didn't entice him.* He had wanted to get into the castle now, by night and unnoticed, guided by Barnabas, but by Barnabas as he had appeared to K. until now, a man more congenial to him than anyone else he had yet seen here, and who, so he had also thought, was closely connected with the castle, far more so than his visible status might suggest. But it was impossible, a hopelessly ridiculous plan, to try going up to the castle in full daylight arm in arm with the son of this family, a family of which he, Barnabas, was entirely a part, sitting with them now at their table, a man who, significantly enough, might not even sleep at the castle.

K. sat down on a window-seat, determined to spend the night there and accept no further favours from the family. The villagers who sent him away or seemed to fear him struck him as less dangerous, for basically they were rejecting only his person while helping him to concentrate his forces. Such apparent helpers as these, however, putting on a little masquerade so as to take him to the bosom of their family rather than the castle, were distracting him whether or not they meant to, working to destroy his powers. He ignored a call inviting him to the family table and stayed where he was, his head bent. Then Olga, the gentler of the two sisters and the one who showed a touch of girlish awkwardness, came over to K. and again invited him to join them; there was bread and bacon, she said, and she would go to fetch some beer. 'Where from?' asked K. 'Why, the inn,' she said. This was welcome news to K. He asked her to accompany him to the inn, where he said he had left some important work, instead of going to fetch beer. However, now it turned out that she didn't intend to go as far as the inn where he was staying, but to another and much closer one, the Castle Inn. All the same, K. asked her to let him be her companion; perhaps, he thought, there'll be a bed for me there. Whatever it was like, he'd have preferred it to the best bed in this house. Olga did not reply at once, but looked at the table. Her brother, standing there, nodded readily, and said: 'Oh yes, if that's what the gentleman wants.' This consent almost brought K. to withdraw his request; if the man agreed to it, the idea must be worthless. But when they discussed the question of whether K. would be allowed into the inn, and everyone present doubted it, he insisted on going with Olga, although without taking the trouble to invent some reasonable pretext for his request. This family must take him as he was, and it was a fact that he felt no sense of shame in front of them. He was slightly put off only by Amalia with her grave, direct gaze. Her expression was unimpressed, but perhaps a little stupid too.

On the short walk to the inn—K. had taken Olga's arm and, despite himself, found that she was pulling him along very much as her brother had done earlier—he learned that this inn was really meant only for gentlemen from the castle, who ate and sometimes even spent the night there when they had business in the village. Olga spoke to K. quietly and as if she knew him well. It was pleasant to walk with her, just as it had been pleasant with her brother. K. fought against this sense of pleasure, but it was there.

Outwardly, the inn resembled the one where K. was staying. There were probably no great outward differences in the whole village, but he noticed small ones at once: the front steps had a handrail, there was a handsome lantern over the door, and as they entered something fluttered overhead: a banner in the count's colours. They were greeted at once in the front hall by the landlord, who was obviously on his rounds keeping an eye on the place. His small eyes, enquiring or sleepy, examined K. in passing, and he said: 'The land surveyor's not allowed anywhere but the bar.' 'Of course,' said Olga, answering for K. 'He's just keeping me company.' The ungrateful K., however, let go of Olga's arm and took the landlord aside, while Olga waited patiently at the other end of the hall. 'I'd like to spend the night here,' said K. 'I'm afraid that's impossible,' replied the landlord. 'You don't seem to know that this inn is exclusively for the use of the gentlemen from the castle.' 'Those may be the rules,' said K., 'but surely you can find me a corner to sleep in somewhere.' 'I'd be very glad to oblige you,' said the landlord, 'but even apart from the strict nature of the rules—and you speak of them very much like a stranger— another reason why it's impossible is that the gentlemen are extremely sensitive, and I am sure they couldn't tolerate the sight of a stranger, or not without being prepared for it in advance. So if I were to let you spend the night here, and by some chance—and chance is always on the gentlemen's side—you were discovered, not only would I be finished but so would you. It may sound ridiculous, but it's the truth.' This tall man, his coat tightly buttoned up, one hand leaning on the wall, the other on his hip, his legs crossed, bending down to K. slightly and speaking to him in a familiar tone, hardly seemed to be one of the villagers, even if his dark clothes looked no better than a local farmer's Sunday best. 'I believe every word you say,' said K., 'and I don't underestimate the importance of the rules, even if I may have expressed myself clumsily. Let me just point out one thing: I have valuable connections in the castle, and shall have some that are even more valuable, and they will secure you against any risk you might incur by my staying here, and guarantee that I'm in a position to render all due thanks for a small favour.' 'I know that,' said the landlord, and he repeated it. 'Yes, I know that.' At this point K. might have put his request more forcefully, but the landlord's answer took his mind off it, so he asked only: 'Are there many gentlemen from the castle staying here tonight?' 'As far as that goes, this is our lucky day,' said the landlord, almost as if tempting him. 'We have just the one gentleman staying here.' K. still felt he couldn't press the landlord, but he hoped he was almost accepted, so he asked the gentleman's name. 'Klamm,' said the landlord casually, as he turned to look for his wife, who came hurrying up in curiously shabby, old-fashioned, but fine city clothes, laden with pleats and frills. She had come to fetch the landlord, saying the chief executive wanted something. But before the landlord left he turned to K. again, as if not he himself but K. must now decide whether he should spend the night here. However, K. could say nothing; in particular, he was surprised to discover that his own superior was staying here, and without being able to explain it entirely to himself, he didn't feel he could be as free with Klamm as with the castle as a whole. Being found here by Klamm would not have deterred K. in the way that the landlord meant, but it would have been an embarrassing impropriety, rather as if he were thoughtlessly planning to upset someone to whom he owed gratitude. He was sorry, however, to see that such thoughts obviously showed how he feared the consequences of being regarded as an inferior, a common workman, and how he couldn't dismiss his fears even here, where they showed so clearly. So he stood where he was, biting his lip and saying nothing. Once, before the landlord disappeared through a doorway, he looked back at K., and K. looked at him, and did not move from the spot until Olga came and led him away. 'What did you want to ask the landlord?' asked Olga. 'I wanted to spend the night here,' said K. 'But you are spending the night with us,' said Olga in surprise. 'Yes, of course,' said K., leaving her to take that whatever way she liked.

3

Frieda

IN the bar, a large room entirely empty in the middle, several men were sitting around the walls, near and on casks, but they looked different from the local rustics in K.'s inn. They were more neatly dressed, all of them wearing clothes of the same coarse, greyish-yellow fabric, their jackets flared out, their trousers fitted closely. They were small men, very like each other at first sight, with flat, bony, and yet round-cheeked faces. They were all quiet and hardly moved, only their eyes followed the new arrivals in the room, but slowly and with an expression of indifference. All the same, they made a certain impression on K., perhaps because there were so many of them and it was so quiet. He took Olga's arm again, by way of explaining his presence here to these people. A man in one corner, evidently an acquaintance of Olga's, rose to his feet and was going to approach them, but K., who was arm in arm with her, turned her away in a different direction. No one but Olga herself could have noticed, and she allowed it with a smiling sideways glance at him.

The beer was poured by a young woman called Frieda.* She was a small blonde, rather insignificant, with a sad face and thin cheeks, but with a surprising expression of conscious superiority in her eyes. When they fell on K. it seemed to him that they had already discovered things about him of which he knew nothing, although that gaze convinced him that they existed. K. kept on looking sideways at Frieda, and still did so as she spoke to Olga. Olga and Frieda did not seem to be great friends; they exchanged only a few cool words. K. decided to help the conversation along, so he asked suddenly: 'Do you know Mr Klamm?' Olga laughed out loud. 'Why do you laugh?' asked K., rather annoyed. 'I'm not laughing,' she said, but she still laughed all the same. 'Olga is a very childish girl,' said K., leaning over the bar counter to make Frieda look at him again. But she kept her eyes lowered, and said quietly: 'Would you like to see Mr Klamm?' K. said he would, and she pointed to a door on her left. 'There's a little peephole there; you can look through that.' 'And what about these people?' asked K. She pouted, thrusting out her lower lip, and led K. over to the door with a hand that was very soft. Through the small hole, which had obviously been made in it for purposes of observation, he could see almost the whole of the next room. Mr Klamm was sitting at a desk in the middle of the room, in a comfortable round armchair, brightly illuminated by an electric light-bulb hanging in front of him. He was a stout, ponderous man of middle height. His face was still smooth, but his cheeks drooped slightly with the weight of advancing age. He had a long, black moustache, and a pair of pince-nez, set on his nose at a crooked angle and reflecting the light, covered his eyes. If Mr Klamm had been sitting upright at the desk K. would have seen only his profile, but as he was turning away from it K. saw him full-face. Klamm was resting his left elbow on the desk, and his right hand, holding a Virginia cigarette, lay on his knee. A beer glass stood on the desktop; as the desk had a raised rim K. couldn't see if there were papers of any kind on it, but he rather thought it was empty. To make sure, he asked Frieda to look through the hole and tell him. However, she had been in that room herself only a little while ago, so she could assure K. without more ado that there were no papers there. K. asked Frieda if he had to leave the peephole now, but she said he could look through it as long as he liked. Now K. was alone with Frieda, for Olga, as he soon saw, had made her way over to her acquaintance and was perched on a cask, swinging her feet in the air. 'Frieda,' said K. in a whisper, 'do you know Mr Klamm very well?' 'Oh yes,' she said. 'Very well.' She leaned close to K., and playfully adjusted her cream-coloured blouse, which, as K. only now saw, was cut rather low at the neck; it was a neckline which didn't quite suit her meagre body. Then she said: 'Don't you remember how Olga laughed?' 'Yes, she's ill-mannered,' said K. 'Well,' she said soothingly, 'there really was something to laugh about. You were asking if I knew Klamm, and as it happens I am'—here she instinctively stood a little straighter, and K. once again felt the force of her triumphant expression, which did not seem to connect at all with what she was saying—'as it happens I am his lover.' 'Klamm's lover,' said K. She nodded. 'Then,' said K., smiling, so as to keep their talk from getting too serious, 'as far as I am concerned you are someone worthy of respect.' 'And not just as far as you're concerned,' said Frieda in friendly tones, but without responding to his smile. However, K. had a weapon to use against her pride, and he brought it to bear by saying: 'And have you ever been in the castle?' But that did not have the desired effect, for she replied: 'No, but isn't it enough that I'm here in the bar?' She obviously had a raging thirst for praise, and she seemed to want to slake it on K. 'To be sure,' said K., 'here in the bar you're doing the landlord's work for him.' 'So I am,' she said, 'and I began as a dairymaid at the Bridge Inn.' 'With those soft hands,' said K., half questioning, and not sure himself whether he was merely flattering her or she had really made a conquest of him. 'No one ever noticed them at the time,' she said, 'and even now—' K. looked enquiringly at her, but she shook her head and would say no more. 'Of course you have your secrets,' said K., 'and you won't discuss them with someone you've known for only half an hour, and who has had no chance to tell you anything about himself yet.' But that, it turned out, was the wrong thing to say; it was as if he had woken Frieda from a slumber in which she liked him, for she took a small piece of wood out of the leather bag that hung from her belt, stopped up the peephole with it, and said to K., visibly forcing herself not to let him see how her mood had changed: 'As for you, I know everything about you. You are the land surveyor.' And she added: 'But now I must get on with my work,' and went back behind the counter, while now and then one of the men here rose to have his empty glass refilled. K. wanted another quiet word with her, so he took an empty glass from a stand and went over to her. 'One more thing, Miss Frieda,' he said, 'it's extraordinary, and takes great strength of mind, to work your way up from dairymaid to barmaid, but is that the height of ambition for a person like you? No, what a silly question. Your eyes—don't laugh at me, Miss Frieda—speak not so much of past struggles as of struggles yet to come. But there are great obstacles in the world, they become greater the greater your goals, and there's nothing to be ashamed of in making sure you have the help of a man who may be small and uninfluential, but is none the less ready to fight. Perhaps we could talk quietly some time, without so many eyes watching us.' 'I don't know what you're after,' she said, and this time, against her will, her tone of voice spoke not of the triumphs of her life but of its endless disappointments. 'Are you by any chance trying to take me away from Klamm? Good heavens!' And she struck her hands together. 'You see right through me,' said K., as if worn out by such distrust. 'Yes, I secretly intended to do that very thing. I wanted you to leave Klamm and become my lover instead. Well, now I can go. Olga!' cried K. 'We're going home.'

Olga obediently slid down from the cask, but she couldn't get away at once from her friends, as they surrounded her. Now Frieda said quietly, with a dark glance at K.: 'When can I speak to you?' 'Can I stay the night here?' asked K. 'Yes,' said Frieda. 'Can I stay here now?' 'You'd better go out with Olga so that I can get the men here to leave. Then you can come back in a little while.' 'Good,' said K., and waited impatiently for Olga. But the men here weren't letting her go; they had invented a dance with Olga at its centre. They danced in a circle, and whenever they all uttered a shout in unison one of them went up to her, put one hand firmly around her waist, and whirled her about several times. The round dance became faster and faster, the raucous, avid shouting gradually merged into what was almost a single cry. Olga, who had tried to break through the circle earlier, smiling, was now staggering from one man to another, with her hair coming down. 'The kind of people they send me here!' said Frieda, biting her thin lips in annoyance. 'Who are they?' asked K. 'Klamm's servants,' said Frieda. 'He always brings them with him, and their presence upsets me. I hardly know what I was discussing with you just now, Mr Land Surveyor, and if there was anything wrong in it you must forgive me. I blame it on the company here, they are the most contemptible and repulsive people I know, and here am I, obliged to fill up their beer glasses. How often I've asked Klamm to leave them behind! I have to put up with other gentlemen's servants too—he might think of me for once, but whatever I say it's no use, an hour before he arrives they come barging in like cattle into the cowshed. And now they really must go to the stables where they belong. If you weren't here I'd open that door and Klamm himself would have to drive them out.' 'Doesn't he hear them, then?' asked K. 'No,' said Frieda. 'He's asleep.' 'What!' cried K. 'Asleep? When I looked into the room he was awake and sitting at the desk.' 'He's still sitting there like that,' said Frieda. 'He was already asleep when you saw him—would I have let you look in otherwise? That's the position he sleeps in, the gentlemen sleep a great deal, it's hard to understand. Then again, if he didn't sleep so much, how could he stand those men? Well, I'll have to chase them out myself.' And picking up a whip* from the corner, she took a single awkward leap high into the air, rather like a lamb gambolling, and made for the dancers. At first they turned to her as if she were a new dancer joining them, and indeed, for a moment it looked as if Frieda would drop the whip, but then she raised it again. 'In the name of Klamm,' she cried, 'out into the stables, all of you, out into the stables.' Now they saw that she was serious, and in a kind of terror that K. couldn't understand, they began crowding away to the back of the room. A door was pushed open by the first to get there, night air blew in, and they all disappeared with Frieda, who was obviously driving them across the yard to the stables. However, in the sudden silence K. heard footsteps in the corridor. For the sake of his own safety he went round behind the bar counter. The only possible place to hide was underneath it. He had not, to be sure, been forbidden to stay in the bar, but as he was planning to spend the night here he didn't want to be seen now. So when the door really was opened, he got under the counter. Of course there was a danger of being discovered there too, but he could always say he had hidden from the boisterous servants, which was a not improbable excuse. It was the landlord who came in. 'Frieda!' he called, pacing up and down the room several times. Luckily Frieda soon came back and did not mention K., but just complained of the common people here, and went round behind the bar in her attempt to find K., who managed to touch her foot. Now he felt sure of himself. Since Frieda did not mention K., in the end the landlord had to. 'So where's the land surveyor?' he asked. In fact he was a courteous man, whose manners had benefited by constant and relatively free intercourse with those of much higher rank than himself, but he spoke to Frieda with particular respect, which was all the more noticeable because during their conversation he was still very much an employer talking to a member of his staff, and a very impertinent one at that. 'I'd quite forgotten the land surveyor,' said Frieda, planting her small foot on K.'s chest. 'He must have left long ago.' 'But I never saw him,' said the landlord, 'and I was out in the front hall almost all the time.' 'Well, he isn't here,' said Frieda coolly, pressing her foot down harder on K. There was something cheerful and easygoing in her demeanour which K. hadn't noticed at all before, and now, improbably, it gained the upper hand as she suddenly bent down to K., smiling and saying: 'Maybe he's hidden down here.' She quickly kissed him and then popped up again, saying regretfully: 'No, he isn't here.' The landlord too sprang a surprise by saying: 'I don't like it at all, I wish I knew for certain whether he's gone. It's not just because of Mr Klamm, it's because of the rules. And the rules apply to you, Miss Frieda, just as they do to me. You stay here in the bar, I'll search the rest of the house. Goodnight, and sleep well!' He had hardly left the room when Frieda turned off the electric light and joined K. under the bar. 'My darling! My sweet darling!' she whispered, but she did not touch K. She lay on her back as if swooning with desire, and spread her arms wide. Time must have seemed endless to her in her amorous bliss, and she sighed rather than sang a little song of some kind.* Then she took alarm, for K. remained quiet, lost in thought, and she began tugging at him like a child. 'Come on, I'm stifling down here.' They embraced one another, her little body burned in K.'s hands, they rolled, in a semi-conscious state from which K. tried constantly but unsuccessfully to surface, a little way on, bumped into Klamm's door with a hollow thud, then lay there in the puddles of beer and the rubbish* covering the floor. Hours passed as they lay there, hours while they breathed together and their hearts beat in unison, hours in which K. kept feeling that he had lost himself, or was further away in a strange land than anyone had ever been before, a distant country where even the air was unlike the air at home, where you were likely to stifle in the strangeness of it, yet such were its senseless lures that you could only go on, losing your way even more. So it was not a shock to him, at least at first, but a cheering sign of dawn when a voice from Klamm's room called for Frieda in a deep, commanding, but indifferent tone. 'Frieda,' said K. in Frieda's ear, alerting her to the summons. In what seemed like instinctive obedience, Frieda was about to jump up, but then she remembered where she was, stretched, laughed quietly, and said: 'I won't go, I'm never going back to him.' K. was about to argue and urge her to go to Klamm, and he began to look for what remained of her blouse, but he couldn't get the words out, he was too happy to have Frieda in his hands, happy but fearful too, for it seemed to him that if Frieda left him he would lose all he possessed. And as if K.'s consent had given her strength, Frieda clenched her fist, knocked on the door with it, and called: 'I'm with the land surveyor! I'm with the land surveyor!' At this Klamm fell silent. But K. got up, knelt down beside Frieda, and looked around him in the dim light that comes before dawn. What had happened? Where were his hopes? What could he expect of Frieda now that all was revealed? Instead of making very cautious progress, with his rival's stature and the greatness of his own goal in mind, he had spent a whole night here rolling about in puddles of beer. The smell of the beer dazed him. 'What have you done?' he asked quietly. 'We're both lost.' 'No,' said Frieda, 'I'm the one who's lost, but I've gained you. Calm down, see how those two are laughing.' 'Who?' asked K., and turned. On the bar counter sat his two assistants, looking as if they hadn't slept well but were still cheerful. It was the cheerfulness that comes from doing your duty punctiliously. 'What do you want here?' cried K., as if they were to blame for everything, and he looked round for the whip that Frieda had used yesterday evening. 'We had to go looking for you,' said the assistants, 'and since you didn't come back to us at the inn we tried Barnabas's house and finally found you here. We've been sitting here all night. Being your assistants isn't an easy job.' 'I need you by day, not by night,' said K. 'Go away!' 'It's day now,' they said, and stayed put. In fact it really was day, the doors into the yard were opened and the servants came pouring in with Olga, whom K. had quite forgotten. Olga was as lively as she had been yesterday evening, untidy as her hair and clothes were, and even in the doorway her eyes sought K. 'Why didn't you take me home?' she asked, almost in tears. 'For the sake of a woman like that!' she answered herself, repeating it several times. Frieda, who had disappeared for a moment, came back with a small bundle of clothes, and Olga stepped sadly aside. 'We can go now,' said Frieda, and it was obvious that she meant they should go to the Bridge Inn. They formed a little procession, K. leading the way with Frieda and the assistants following. The gentleman's servants showed evidence of great dislike for Frieda, understandably, since she had been so stern and domineering with them earlier. One even took his stick and acted as if he wasn't going to let her pass unless she jumped over it, but a glance from her was enough to deter him. Out in the snow, K. breathed a sigh of relief. The pleasure of being out of doors was so great that it made the difficulty of the path tolerable this time, and if K. had been alone it would have been even better. On reaching the inn he went straight to his room and lay down on the bed, Frieda made herself a bed on the floor beside it, and the assistants, who had come in with them, were turned out, but then they came back through the window. K. was too tired to send them away again. The landlady came up specially to welcome Frieda, who called her 'dear little mother', and their meeting was a bafflingly warm affair, with much kissing and hugging. There was certainly little peace and quiet in the small room, and the maids often came trudging in, wearing men's boots, to fetch or remove something.

If they needed some item of theirs from the bed, which was stuffed full of all sorts of things, they unceremoniously pulled it out from under K. They spoke to Frieda as one of themselves. In spite of all this bustle, K. stayed in bed all day and all night. Frieda did him various small services. When he finally got up the next morning, feeling very much refreshed, it was already the fourth day* since he had arrived in the village.

4

First Conversation with the Landlady

HE would have liked to speak to Frieda in private about the assistants. She laughed and joked with them now and then, but their mere intrusive presence troubled him. Not that they were demanding; they had settled down on the floor in a corner of the room, lying on two old skirts; their aim, as they often assured Frieda, was to avoid disturbing their boss the land surveyor, and to take up as little room as possible. They made various attempts to achieve that end, although with much chuckling and whispering, by folding their arms and legs and huddling together, so that in the twilight all you could see in their corner was a large and indeterminate tangled mass. None the less, K.'s daylight experiences showed him that they were observing him very attentively and constantly staring at him, whether they made telescopes of their hands in an apparently childish game and played similar nonsensical tricks, or just looked his way while they devoted most of their attention to the care of their beards, of which they thought a great deal, each comparing his with the other's time and again for length and profusion, and getting Frieda to judge between them. K. often watched the three of them with complete indifference from his bed.

When he felt strong enough to leave it, they all came hurrying to serve him. Much as he might defend himself against their attentions, he had not yet recovered entirely. He noticed that when he realized that he was to some extent dependent on them, so he had to let them do as they pleased. And it was not so very unpleasant to drink the good coffee that Frieda had brought to his table, or to warm himself by the stove that Frieda had lit, to make the eager, if clumsy, assistants run up and down stairs ten times to fetch water for washing, soap, a comb and a mirror, and finally, because K. had expressed a quiet wish that might possibly indicate that he wanted it, a small glass of rum.

In the middle of all this ordering them about and being served, K. said, more in an easygoing mood than with any real hope of success: 'Go away, you two, I don't need anything more just now, and I'd like to talk to Miss Frieda alone.' And on seeing no actual opposition to this idea in their faces, he added, to make it up to them: 'And then the three of us will go and see the village mayor. Wait for me in the saloon downstairs.' Curiously enough, they obeyed, except that before leaving the room they said: 'We could always wait here.' To which K. replied: 'I know, but I don't want you to.'

It was annoying, and yet in a way K. was also glad of it, that when Frieda came to sit on his lap as soon as the assistants had gone, she said: 'What do you have against the assistants, darling? We needn't keep any secrets from them. They're good, faithful souls.' 'Oh, faithful!' said K. 'Watching me all the time. It's pointless, it's horrible.' 'I think I understand you,' she said, putting her arms around his neck, and she was about to say something else but could not go on. The chair on which they were sitting was close to the bed, and they staggered over to the bed and fell on it. There they lay, although not as absorbed in each other as on their first night together. She was in search of something and so was he, they tried to get at it almost angrily, grimacing, butting each other's breasts with their heads, and their embraces and writhing bodies did not bring oblivion but reminded them of their duty to go on searching. Like dogs desperately scraping at the ground, they worked away at one another's bodies, helplessly disappointed as they tried to retrieve the last of their bliss, sometimes licking each other's faces with their tongues. Only weariness brought them to lie still, feeling gratitude to each other. Then the maids came upstairs. 'Oh, just look at them lying here,' said one of the maids, and in her kindness threw a length of cloth over them.

When K. freed himself from the cloth later and looked around, the assistants were back in their corner, which did not surprise him, and were warning each other to preserve a serious demeanour, pointing to K. and saluting—but in addition the landlady was sitting beside the bed knitting a stocking. The fiddly little job didn't seem to suit her huge figure, which almost blotted out the light. 'I've been waiting a long time,' she said, and raised her broad face, which had many of the lines of old age on it, but in its vast size was still smooth and might once have been beautiful. Her words sounded like an accusation, which was unfair, for K. hadn't asked her to come. So he merely nodded his head in acknowledgement, and sat up. Frieda got up too, left K., and went to lean against the landlady's armchair. 'Madam,' said

K. fretfully, 'couldn't you put off whatever it is you want to say until I come back from seeing the village mayor? I have an important meeting with him.' 'Mr Land Surveyor, this is more important, take my word for it,' said the landlady. 'Your meeting is probably just about some job or other to be done, but I'm concerned with a human being, my dear maid Frieda here.' 'Oh,' said K., 'well then, yes, though I don't know why you can't leave our own affairs to the two of us.' 'Out of love, out of concern, that's why,' said the landlady, drawing Frieda's head to her. As the girl stood there, she came only up to the seated landlady's shoulder. 'Since Frieda has such faith in you,' said K., 'there's nothing I can do about that. And as Frieda only recently called my assistants faithful, then we're all friends together. So I can tell you, madam, that I think the best thing would be for Frieda and me to get married, and very soon too. Sad to say, very sad to say, I won't be able to compensate Frieda for what she has lost through me: her position at the Castle Inn and the friendship of Klamm.' Frieda looked up. Her eyes were full of tears, and there was no expression of triumph in them. 'Why me? Why was I chosen?' 'Why?' asked K. and the landlady at the same time. 'She's confused, poor child,' said the landlady. 'Bewildered by too much happiness and unhappiness coming all at once.' And as if to confirm what the landlady had said, Frieda now ran to K., kissed him wildly as if there were no one else in the room, and then fell on her knees in front of him weeping, and still embracing him. As K. stroked Frieda's hair with both his hands, he said to the landlady: 'You seem to agree with me?' 'You're an honourable man,' said the landlady, and her own voice sounded tearful. She looked a little weary, and was breathing heavily, but she found the strength to say: 'Now, there are certain assurances that you must give Frieda, for much as I respect you, you're a stranger here, you can't call on anyone to vouch for you, we don't know your domestic circumstances, so assurances are necessary, as I am sure you will realize, my dear sir. You yourself have pointed out how much Frieda stands to lose by throwing in her lot with yours.' 'Of course, assurances, naturally,' said K. 'They'd better be made in front of a notary, I expect, but perhaps some of the count's authorities will want to be involved as well. What's more, there is something else I absolutely must do before the marriage. I must speak to Klamm.' 'That's impossible,' said Frieda, straightening up slightly and pressing close to K. 'What an idea!' 'But it must be done,' said K. 'If it's impossible for me to arrange it, then you must.' 'I can't, K., I can't,' said Frieda. 'Klamm will never speak to you. How can you imagine that Klamm would speak to you?' 'Well, would he speak to you?' asked K. 'He wouldn't speak to me either,' said Frieda. 'He wouldn't speak to either you or me, it's downright impossible.' She turned to the landlady with her arms outspread. 'There, ma'am, you see what he asks.' 'You're a strange man, sir,' said the landlady, and she looked rather alarming as she sat there very upright, with her legs spread and her mighty knees showing beneath her flimsy skirt. 'You want the impossible.' 'Why is it impossible?' asked K. 'I'll explain,' said the landlady, in a tone suggesting that by explaining she was not doing K. a final favour but inflicting his first punishment on him. 'I will be happy to explain to you. I do not belong to the castle, to be sure, I am only a woman, I am only the landlady of the lowest kind of inn—well, not quite the lowest kind, but not so very far from it—so maybe you won't set much store by my explanation, but I have kept my eyes open all my life, I have met a great many people, and I have borne the whole burden of running this inn on my own, for my husband may be a good young fellow, but he's no landlord, and he will never understand the meaning of responsibility. You, for instance, owe it only to his carelessness—I was tired to death the other evening—that you are here in the village at all, sitting on that bed in peace and comfort.' 'What do you mean?' cried K., emerging from a certain mood of abstraction, but aroused from it more by curiosity than by anger. 'You owe it only to his carelessness,' repeated the landlady, pointing her forefinger at K. Frieda tried to mollify her. 'What do you expect?' the landlady asked Frieda, with a swift turn of her whole body. 'The land surveyor here has asked me a question, and I must answer him. How else is he to understand what we ourselves take for granted, which is that Mr Klamm will never speak to him—and why do I say "will"? He never *can* speak to him. Listen, sir, Mr Klamm is a gentleman from the castle, which in itself, quite apart from Klamm's position in any other respect, means that he is of high rank. But what about you, whose agreement to marry Frieda we are so humbly soliciting here? You're not from the castle, you're not from the village, you're nothing. Unfortunately, however, you *are* a stranger, a superfluous person getting in everyone's way, a man who is always causing trouble—why, the maids have had to move out of their room on your account—a man whose intentions are unknown, a man who has seduced dear little Frieda and whom, unfortunately, we must allow to marry her. Basically I don't blame you for all this; you are what you are. I've seen too much in the course of my life to be unable to tolerate this sight too. But think what you are really asking. You expect a man like Klamm to speak to you. I was sorry to hear that Frieda let you look through the peephole; you'd already seduced her when she did that. Tell me, how did you bear the sight of Klamm? You needn't answer that, I know, you bore it very well. You are in no position to see Klamm properly, and that's not arrogance on my part, because I am in no position to do so either. You want Klamm to speak to you, but he doesn't even speak to the villagers, he himself has never spoken to anyone from the village. It was Frieda's greatest distinction, a distinction that will be my pride to my dying day, that at least he used to call her by name, and she could speak to him as she liked, and had permission to use the peephole, although he never really *spoke* to her either. And the fact that he sometimes called for Frieda doesn't necessarily have the importance with which you might wish to endow it, he simply called Frieda by name—who knows his intentions?—and the fact that Frieda, of course, came hurrying up was her own business. Well, it was due to Klamm's kindness that she was allowed in to see him without any trouble, but you couldn't say he actually summoned her to him. And what's gone is certainly gone for ever. Perhaps Klamm will call for Frieda by name again, yes, that's possible, but she certainly won't be allowed in to see him any more—not a girl who has given herself to you. And there's one thing, just one thing that I can't get my poor head around, which is how a girl said to be Klamm's lover—although personally I consider that a greatly exaggerated description—would so much as let you touch her.'

'Remarkable, to be sure,' said K., and he took Frieda, who complied at once, although lowering her head, to sit on his lap. 'But I think it shows that not everything is exactly as you think. For instance, yes, I am sure you're right when you say that I am nothing compared to Klamm, and if I now demand to speak to Klamm and even your explanation does not dissuade me, it doesn't mean that I am in a position to bear the sight of Klamm without so much as a door between us, or that I might not run out of the room when he appeared. But as I see it, such a fear, though it might be justified, is no reason not even to try the venture. If I succeed in standing up to him, then it's not necessary for

him to speak to me; I will be satisfied by seeing what impression my
words make on him, and if they make none, or he doesn't listen at all,
then it's to my advantage to have spoken freely in front of a powerful
man. But you, madam, with all your knowledge of life and human
nature, and Frieda here, who was still Klamm's lover yesterday—I see
no reason to avoid that word myself—can surely get me an opportunity to speak to Klamm easily enough. If it's not possible in any other
way, then at the Castle Inn. Perhaps he may still be there today.'

'It is not possible,' said the landlady, 'and I see that you lack the
ability to understand that. But tell me, what do you want to speak to
Klamm about?'

'Why, Frieda, of course,' said K.

'Frieda?' asked the landlady, baffled, and turned to Frieda herself.
'Did you hear that, Frieda? He—this man—he wants to speak to
Klamm, Klamm of all people, about you.'

'Oh dear,' said K. 'You are such a clever woman, madam, and so
awe-inspiring too, yet every little thing frightens you. Well, if I want
to speak to him about Frieda that's not such a monstrous idea, it is
perfectly natural. For you are certainly mistaken if you think that
from the moment when I appeared Frieda became of no importance
to Klamm. You underestimate him if you believe that. I realize that
it is presumptuous of me to try putting you right there, but I must
do it. I can't have caused any change in Klamm's relationship with
Frieda. Either there was no real relationship—as those who would
deprive Frieda of the honourable title of being his lover say—in
which case there is none now, or there was such a relationship, but if
so how could it be wrecked by me, a man who, as you rightly say, is
nothing in Klamm's eyes? Such things may be believed in the first
moment of shock, but even the slightest reflection is sure to put that
right. Why don't we let Frieda say what she thinks about it?'

With her eyes looking into the distance, her cheek against K.'s
breast, Frieda said: 'I am sure it is just as my little mother says:
Klamm won't want to know any more about me. But not because you
turned up, darling, nothing of that kind could have troubled him. In
fact I think it is his doing that we came together under the bar—
blessings and not curses on that hour.' 'If that's the case—' said K.
slowly, for Frieda's words were sweet, and he closed his eyes for a
few seconds to let them sink in: 'if that's the case there is even less
reason to fear an interview with Klamm.'

'Really,' said the landlady, as if looking down at K. from above, 'you sometimes remind me of my husband, you're just as contrary and childish. You spend a few days here, and already you think you know better than those who were born in the village, better than me, old woman that I am, better than Frieda who has seen and heard so much at the Castle Inn. I don't deny that it may be possible to do something that transgresses the rules and the good old customs, I have never known anything of the kind myself, but there are said to be instances, although it certainly isn't done in the way you would set about it, by saying no, no, all the time, relying on your own mind and ignoring advice, however well intended. Do you think I'm anxious on your behalf? Did I bother about you while you were on your own? Although if I had, it might have been a good idea, and much of this might have been avoided. All I said to my husband about you at the time was: "Keep well away from him." And I would have felt the same today if Frieda hadn't been dragged into your own fate. It's to her, whether you like it or not, that you owe my concern, even my consideration for you. And you can't simply dismiss me, because you are strictly responsible to me, as the only person who watches over little Frieda with maternal care. It's possible that Frieda is right and everything that has happened is what Klamm wants, but I don't know anything about Klamm, I will never speak to him, he is entirely beyond my reach. But you sit here, keeping your hold on my Frieda, and—why deny it?—you will be kept here by me. Yes, kept by me, for young man, if I turn you out of this house, you just try finding accommodation anywhere in the village, even in a dog kennel.'

'Well, thank you very much,' said K., 'this is plain speaking indeed, and I believe every word you say. Then my position is extremely insecure, and so is Frieda's too.'

'No,' cried the landlady furiously. 'In that respect Frieda's position has nothing to do with yours. Frieda belongs to my household, and no one has any right to call her position here insecure.'

'Very well, very well,' said K. 'I'll agree that you are right in that too, especially since, for reasons unknown to me, Frieda seems too much afraid of you to join in our discussion. So let's stick to me for the time being. My position is very insecure, you don't deny that, indeed you go to great lengths to prove it. However, as with everything you say, that statement is largely but not entirely correct. For instance, I know where I could have a very good bed for the night.'

'Where? Where?' cried Frieda and the landlady at the same time, as avidly as if they had the same reasons for asking.

'At Barnabas's house,' said K.

'With those villains!'* cried the landlady. 'Those infernal villains! At Barnabas's house! Did you hear that?' she asked, turning to the assistants' corner, but they had left it long ago and were standing arm in arm behind the landlady, who now seized the hand of one of them as if she needed support. 'Did you hear where this gentleman goes? To Barnabas and his family! Yes, I'm sure he can have a bed for the night there—oh, if only he'd preferred it to the Castle Inn. But where were you two?'

'Madam,' said K. before the assistants could answer, 'these are my assistants. You treat them as if they were my guards instead, and *your* assistants. I'm prepared at least to discuss your opinions civilly in all other respects, but not when it comes to my assistants, where the situation is only too clear. So I will request you not to speak to my assistants, and if my request to you is not enough, then I will forbid my assistants to answer you.'

'So I'm not allowed to speak to you!' said the landlady to the assistants, and they all three laughed, the landlady with derision but much more quietly than K. had expected, the assistants as they usually did, in a meaningful kind of way yet meaning nothing, just disclaiming any responsibility.

'Oh, don't be angry,' said Frieda. 'You must understand our alarm. We owe it all to Barnabas, if you like, that you and I belong to each other now. When I first saw you in the bar—you arrived arm in arm with Olga—I knew a little about you, but on the whole you were a matter of perfect indifference to me. And not just you; everything, everything was a matter of indifference to me. I was dissatisfied with a good deal at the time, and there was a good deal that annoyed me too, but what kind of dissatisfaction and annoyance was that? For instance, one of the guests in the bar insulted me—they were always after me, you saw those fellows, but then much worse came in too, Klamm's servants weren't the worst of them—well, one of them did insult me, but what did I care for that? I felt as if it had happened years ago, or as if it hadn't happened at all, or as if I had only heard tell of it, or had already forgotten it. But oh, I can't describe it, I can't even imagine it, that's how everything has changed since Klamm left me.'

And Frieda broke off her story, bowed her head sadly, and folded her hands in her lap.

'There, you see,' cried the landlady, as if she were not speaking herself but merely lending her voice to Frieda, to whom she now moved closer until she was sitting right beside her, 'there, Mr Land Surveyor, you see the consequences of your actions, and your assistants, whom I'm not allowed to speak to, may see them too and learn from them. You have torn Frieda away from the happiest situation she was ever in, and it happened mainly because, going too far in her childish pity for you, Frieda couldn't bear to see you arm in arm with Olga, delivered up to Barnabas's family. She saved you, sacrificing herself in the process. And now that it's done, and Frieda has exchanged all she had for the happiness of sitting on your knee, now you come along and play your great trump card, which is the fact that you once had the opportunity of spending the night at Barnabas's house. I suppose you're trying to prove that you are independent of me. To be sure, if you really *had* spent the night with Barnabas, you would be so independent of me that you'd have to leave my house this minute, and in a great hurry too.'

'I don't know what sins Barnabas and his family have committed,' said K., while he carefully raised Frieda, who seemed almost lifeless, placed her slowly on the bed, and rose to his feet. 'Perhaps you're right there, but certainly I was right when I asked you to leave our business, Frieda's and mine, to the two of us alone. You mentioned just now something about love and concern, but I haven't seen a lot of either of those; instead I've heard words of dislike and disdain and threats to turn me out of the house. If you had it in mind to part Frieda from me or me from Frieda, it was very cleverly done, but all the same I don't think you'll succeed, and if you do succeed then—forgive me a veiled threat of my own for once—if you do succeed you will regret it bitterly. As for the room you have given me—by which you can only mean this repellent hole—it is not at all certain that you're doing it of your own free will. I'm more inclined to think that instructions came from the count's authorities. I will let them know that I have been given notice here, and if they find me some other lodging I expect you'll breathe a deep sigh of relief, but my own will be even deeper. And now I'm going to see the village mayor about this and various other matters, so please take care of Frieda, to whom you have done enough harm with what you describe as your maternal advice.'

Then he turned to the assistants. 'Come along,' he said, taking Klamm's letter off the nail and making for the door. The landlady had been watching him in silence, and only when he had his hand on the door knob did she say: 'Mr Land Surveyor, I will give you a piece of information to take with you, for whatever you may say and whatever insults you may offer me, poor old woman that I am, you are Frieda's future husband. It's only on that account that I tell you how shockingly ignorant you are of circumstances here, a person's head fairly spins just listening to you, comparing what you say and think with the situation as it really is. Such ignorance can't be put right all at once, perhaps not at all, but there can be a good deal of improvement if you will only believe some of what I say, and keep in mind your ignorance all the time. Then, for instance, you will immediately do me far more justice and begin to glean some idea of what a shock it was to me—and the consequences of that shock still affect me— when I realized that my dear little girl had, so to speak, deserted the eagle* to ally herself to the slow-worm, but the real situation is far, far worse, and I keep trying to forget it or I couldn't speak a calm word to you. Oh, now you're angry again. No, don't go yet, just listen to my request: wherever you go, always remember that you know less than anyone here, and mind you proceed carefully. Here, where Frieda's presence protects you from harm, you may talk your heart out; here, if you like, you can tell us what you intend to say to Klamm. But don't, I beg you, don't do it in reality.'

She rose to her feet, swaying slightly in her agitation, went over to K., and looked imploringly at him. 'Madam,' said K., 'I don't understand why you demean yourself to beg me for anything with such small cause. If, as you say, it is impossible for me to speak to Klamm, then I won't be able to come near him whether I'm asked to or not. But if it were to be possible, why shouldn't I do it, particularly as then your other fears would become very questionable once your main objection was seen to be invalid? I am certainly ignorant, but facts are facts, which is very sad for me but also advantageous, since an ignorant man will dare to do more, so I will happily go about in my ignorance with what I am sure are its unfortunate consequences for a little longer, as long as my strength allows. In essence, however, those consequences affect only me, and so I really don't understand why you should beg me for anything. I am sure you will always care for Frieda, and if I vanish entirely from Frieda's view that, as you see it, can only be a good thing. So what are you afraid of? I suppose you don't—for to the ignorant anything seems possible—' and here K. opened the door—'I suppose you don't fear for Klamm?' The landlady watched in silence as he hurried down the stairs, with the assistants following him.

5

The Village Mayor

To his own surprise, K.'s conversation with the village mayor went smoothly. He accounted for that by telling himself that, in his experience so far, official dealings with the count's authorities had been very simple. One reason was that a definite decision on his own affairs had obviously been made once and for all, apparently in his favour, and another was the admirable consistency of the offices involved, which you could sense was particularly good in cases where no such thing appeared to be present. When K. thought about all this he was not far from considering his situation satisfactory, although after such cheering moments he always told himself that this was just where the danger lay. Direct communication with the authorities was not too difficult, for well-organized as they might be, those authorities had only to defend something remote, in the name of remote and indeed invisible gentlemen, whereas K. was fighting for something very close to him, for himself, and doing so, at least at first, of his own free will, for he was the one on the attack. And not only was he fighting for himself, so too, it seemed, were other powers unknown to him, although the measures taken by the authorities allowed him to believe in them. However, the fact that from the first the authorities had met K.'s wishes in minor matters—and so far nothing more had been involved—meant that they deprived him of the chance of winning small, easy victories and of the satisfaction that went with them and the well-justified confidence that he would then derive from them for embarking on other and larger battles. Instead, the authorities allowed K. to go anywhere he liked, although only inside the village, thus indulging him but weakening his position, ruling out any possibility of a struggle, and leaving him living a non-official, unpredictable, troubled, and strange kind of life. If he wasn't always on his guard, then, it could be that, despite the amiability of the authorities, and his own performance of all his extremely light official duties to everyone's satisfaction, he might, deceived by the favour apparently shown him, conduct the rest of his life so incautiously that he failed in this place, and the authorities, still in their gentle and kindly way, and as if it were against their will but in the name of some official decree unknown to him, would have to get rid of him. And what actually was the rest of his life here to be? Nowhere before had K. ever seen official duties and life so closely interwoven, so much so that sometimes it almost seemed as if life and official duties had changed places. What was the meaning, for instance, of the power, so far only formal, that Klamm had over K.'s services compared with the power that Klamm really did exert in K.'s bedroom? It just showed how any carelessness in procedure or easygoing attitude was appropriate only in direct contact with the authorities, while elsewhere great caution was necessary, and you had to look round on all sides before taking any step.

At first K. found his idea of the authorities here fully confirmed by the village mayor. A friendly, stout, clean-shaven man, the mayor was ill with a severe attack of gout, and received K. in bed. 'Ah, so this is our land surveyor!' he said, trying to sit up straight to greet the visitor, but he couldn't manage it, and pointing apologetically to his legs he leaned back on the pillows again. A quiet woman, looking almost shadowy in the dimly lit room, where the small windows were also veiled by curtains, brought a chair for K. and placed it by the bed. 'Sit down, Mr Land Surveyor, sit down,' said the mayor, 'and tell me what you want.' K. read Klamm's letter aloud and made a few comments on it. Once again, he felt how very easy it was to communicate with the authorities. They would bear absolutely any burden, you could hand them anything to deal with and remain unaffected and a free agent yourself. As if the mayor felt the same thing in his own way, he shifted uneasily in his bed. Finally he said: 'As you'll have noticed, Mr Land Surveyor, I knew all about this affair. I haven't done anything about it myself, first because of my illness, and then because it took you so long to arrive that I was beginning to think you'd abandoned the whole business. But now that you have been kind enough to come and see me yourself, I have to tell you the whole, if unwelcome, truth. You have been engaged, you say, as a land surveyor, but unfortunately we don't need a land surveyor. There wouldn't be any work for you here at all. The boundary markings of our little farms are all established, everything has been duly recorded. Property hardly ever changes hands, and we settle any little arguments about the boundaries ourselves. So why would we need a land surveyor?' Without actually having thought about it in advance,

K. felt firmly convinced that he had expected some such information. For that very reason he was able to say instantly: 'Well, that does surprise me a great deal. It throws out all my calculations. I can only hope there's some misunderstanding.' 'I'm afraid not,' said the mayor. 'It's exactly as I say.' 'But how can that be possible?' cried K. 'I didn't make such an endless journey just to be sent back again now.' 'Oh, that's another question,' said the mayor, 'and it's not for me to decide, but I can explain how the misunderstanding may have come about. In such a large authority as the count's, it sometimes happens that one department will arrange this matter, another that, and neither hears about it from the other. A higher supervisory department checks everything, and very closely too, but of its nature such supervision comes too late, and so a little confusion can still arise. To be sure, that is only in the tiniest of minor details, such as your own case, and to the best of my knowledge no mistake of the kind has ever been made in matters of real importance, but the minor ones often give trouble enough. And as for your case, I will tell you—I'm not giving any official secrets away, I'm not enough of an official for that, I'm a farmer and that's that—as for your case, I'll tell you straight out what happened. Long ago—I'd been village mayor for only a few months at the time—a decree came from I forget which department, saying in the categorical terms typical of the gentlemen there that a land surveyor was to be appointed, and the village was directed to have all the plans and sketches necessary for his work ready. That decree can't in fact have had anything to do with you personally, because it was many years ago, and I wouldn't have remembered it but for being sick just now, with plenty of time to lie in bed and think about the most ridiculous incidents. Mizzi,' he added, suddenly interrupting his account to address his wife, who was still scurrying about the room busy with something, though K. couldn't make out just what, 'please look in the cupboard there and perhaps you'll find the decree. The fact is,' he said in an explanatory tone, turning to K., 'it dates back to my early days as village mayor, when I used to keep everything.' The woman opened the cupboard at once, while K. and the mayor watched. It was stuffed with papers, and when it was opened two large bundles of files fell out, tied up as you might tie up bundles of firewood. The woman flinched in alarm. 'Try lower down, lower down,' said the mayor, directing operations from his bed. The woman, gathering up the files in her arms, obediently cleared everything out of the cupboard to get to the papers at the bottom. The room was already half full of papers. 'Oh, there's been a lot of work done,' said the mayor, nodding, 'and this is only a small part of it. I keep the larger part of what I have here in the barn, but most of it has been lost. How can anyone keep all this together? But there's still plenty in the barn. Will you be able to find the decree?' he asked, turning to his wife again. 'You must look for a file with the words *Land Surveyor* underlined in blue on it.' 'It's too dark in here,' said his wife. 'I'll fetch a candle.' And she walked over the papers and out of the room. 'My wife is a great help to me,' said the village mayor, 'with the burden of all this official stuff, which I have to do as a sideline. I do have another assistant for the written work, that's the schoolteacher, but all the same no one can ever get through it, there's always a great deal left undone, and it's in that cupboard.' He pointed to another cupboard. 'And when I'm ill, as I am now, it really gets the upper hand,' he said, lying back wearily, but with an expression of pride on his face. 'Couldn't I help your wife to search?' asked K., when the woman had come back with the candle and was kneeling in front of the cupboard, looking for the decree. Smiling, the mayor shook his head. 'As I said just now, I'm keeping no official secrets from you, but I can't go so far as to let you search the files yourself.' All was still in the room now, only the rustle of the papers was to be heard, and the mayor may even have dropped off to sleep for a moment. A soft knock at the door made K. turn. Inevitably, it was his assistants. But at least they had learned to behave a little better, and didn't burst straight into the room but began by whispering through the door, which stood slightly ajar. 'It's too cold for us out there,' they said. 'Who's that?' asked the mayor, waking with a start. 'Only my assistants,' said K. 'I don't know where to leave them to wait for me; it's too cold outside, and they'll be in the way in here.' 'They won't bother me,' said the mayor in kindly tones, 'let them come in. Anyway, I know them. We're old acquaintances.' 'Well, they bother *me*,' said K. frankly, letting his gaze wander from the assistants to the mayor and back to the assistants, and finding it impossible to tell their three smiles apart. 'However, since you're here,' he suggested tentatively, 'you can stay and help the lady look for a file with the words *Land Surveyor* on it underlined in blue.' The mayor did not object to that; while K. wasn't allowed to search the papers the assistants were, and they flung themselves on the files immediately, but just churning up the heaps rather than searching properly, and while one of them was spelling out the words on a piece of paper the other kept snatching it from his hand. As for the mayor's wife, she was kneeling in front of the empty cupboard and no longer seemed to be searching at all, or at least the candle was a long way away from her.

'So your assistants bother you, do they?' said the mayor, with a satisfied smile, as if it was all due to his own arrangements, but no one was in a position even to suspect as much. 'But they're your own assistants.' 'No,' said K. coolly, 'they didn't latch on to me until I got here.' 'Latch on to you?' said the mayor. 'I suppose you mean they were allocated to you.' 'Very well, then, they were allocated to me,' said K., 'but they might just as well have fallen like snow from the sky, so little thought went into choosing them.' 'Oh, nothing happens here without thought,' said the mayor, forgetting the pain in his foot and even sitting up in bed. 'Nothing?' said K. 'What about my appointment?' 'Your appointment will have been carefully considered too,' said the mayor. 'But collateral circumstances entered into it and confused things. I can show you how it all happened from the files.' 'I don't think the files are going to be found,' said K. 'Not found?' cried the mayor. 'Mizzi, please search a little faster! For a start, however, I can tell you the story without files. We replied to the decree I was talking about by sending our thanks, but pointing out that we didn't need a land surveyor. However, that reply doesn't seem to have reached the original department, let's call it A, but by mistake went to another department, B. So Department A received no answer, but unfortunately Department B didn't get our full answer either. Whether the contents of the file were left behind here or were lost in transit— they weren't lost in the department itself, I can vouch for that—well, anyway Department B also received the cover of a file bearing only the remark that the enclosed file (which in fact, unfortunately, was not enclosed) dealt with the appointment of a land surveyor. Department A, meanwhile, was waiting for our answer; it did have some preliminary notes on the matter, but as often and understandably happens, and indeed *should* happen, in view of the meticulous nature of all the official work done, the head of department was relying on us to send an answer, whereupon he would either appoint the land surveyor or, if necessary, correspond with us on the subject further. As a result, he neglected to look at the preliminary notes and let the whole affair lapse into oblivion. In Department B, however, the cover of the file reached an official well known for his conscientiousness, Sordini* by name, an Italian. Even to me, and I'm in the know, it's hard to understand why a man of his abilities is left languishing in one of the lowest-ranking positions of all. Well, this Sordini naturally sent us back the empty cover of the file, asking for the rest of it. But many months, if not years, had passed since those first documents were drawn up for Department A, which is understandable, for when, as generally happens, a file is sent in the proper way it reaches the right department within a day at the latest, and is dealt with that same day. However, if it gets lost—and considering the excellence of the organization it really has to try very hard to get lost or it will never succeed in doing so—then it can indeed take a very long time. So when we received Sordini's note we had only the vaguest memory of the affair; there were only the two of us doing the work at the time, Mizzi and me, they hadn't given me the teacher to assist me yet. We kept copies only of the most important documents—in short, all we could reply, very uncertainly, was that we didn't know anything about any such appointment, and there was no need for a land surveyor here.

'However,' said the mayor, interrupting himself as if, in his eagerness to tell the tale, he had gone too far, or as if it were at least possible that he had gone too far, 'I do hope this story isn't boring you?'

'Not at all,' said K. 'It's entertaining me.'

'I'm not telling it to entertain you,' said the mayor.

'The only reason why it entertains me,' said K., 'is the insight it gives me into the ridiculous confusion which, in some circumstances, can determine the course of a man's life.'

'You haven't been given any such insight yet,' said the mayor gravely, 'and I can go on with the story. Naturally a man of Sordini's calibre wasn't going to be satisfied with our reply. I admire him, even though he's a thorn in my flesh. The fact is, he distrusts everyone, even when, say, he has come to recognize a person on countless occasions as the most trustworthy man alive—he distrusts him on the *next* occasion as if he didn't know him at all, or more correctly, as if he knew him to be a rogue. I think that's quite right, that's the way an official ought to proceed, but unfortunately I can't seem to follow that basic principle. It's on account of my own nature. You see how frankly I am telling you, a stranger, all this, I just can't help it. Sordini, on the other hand, distrusted our answer at once. And then a long correspondence ensued. Sordini asked why it had suddenly occurred to me that no land surveyor ought to be appointed, and I replied, with the help of Mizzi's excellent memory, that the first idea had come from the authorities themselves (of course we had long ago forgotten that it came from a different department of the castle authorities). Sordini then asked why I mentioned the official letter only now, to which I said that it was because I had only just remembered it. That, said Sordini, was very remarkable. To which I replied that it wasn't at all remarkable in an affair that had dragged on so long. Sordini said no, it *was* remarkable, because the letter I had remembered did not exist. Of course it didn't exist, I said, since the whole file had been lost. Here Sordini said that there must, surely, have been a preliminary note regarding that first letter, the one that didn't exist. Here I hesitated, for I didn't like to claim that a mistake had been made, or say I believed that it had been made, in Sordini's department. In your mind, Mr Land Surveyor, perhaps you are blaming Sordini and thinking that reflection on my claim should at least have caused him to enquire about the case in other departments. But that wouldn't have been right; I don't want any blame imputed to the man even in your mind. It is a working principle of the authorities that they do not even consider the possibility of mistakes being made. The excellent organization of the whole thing justifies that principle, which is necessary if tasks are to be performed with the utmost celerity. Sordini therefore could not enquire in other departments; moreover, those departments would not have responded to his enquiries, because they would have noticed at once that they were being asked to look into the possibility of some mistake.'

'Mr Mayor, may I interrupt you with a question?' said K. 'Didn't you mention a supervisory authority checking everything? From what you say, the organization is of such a kind that one feels quite ill at the mere idea of these supervisory checks failing.'

'You are very severe,' said the mayor, 'but if you multiplied your severity a thousand times, it would still be as nothing compared to the severity of the authorities' attitude to themselves. Only a complete stranger would ask your question. Are there supervisory authorities? There are *only* supervising authorities. To be sure, they're not intended to detect mistakes in the vulgar sense of the word, since there are no mistakes, and even if there is a mistake, as in your own case, who's to say that it's really a mistake in the long run?'

'That strikes me as an entirely new idea,' cried K.

'It's a very old one to me,' said the mayor. 'I am no less convinced than you that there has been a mistake, and as a result of his despair Sordini has fallen very ill, and the first supervisory authorities to check the case, those to which we owe the discovery of the source of the mistake, also acknowledge its existence. But who can claim that the second set of supervisory authorities will come to the same conclusion, and then the third set, and so on with all the others?'

'Maybe,' said K., 'but I'd rather not indulge in such reflections, and anyway this is the first time I've heard of these supervisory authorities, so of course I can't understand them yet. Only, I do think that we have to distinguish between two things here: first, what goes on within the authorities, and what is then official or can be taken as official; and second, my own person, outside the orbit of all these official authorities as I am, and threatened by them with such pointless restrictions that I still can't believe the danger is serious. As for the first point, what you, Mr Mayor, describe with such astonishing and extraordinary command of the subject is probably true. Only I wouldn't mind hearing a word about myself as well.'

'I'm coming to that,' said the mayor, 'but you couldn't understand it without a little more preamble. I even mentioned the supervisory authorities too soon. So I'll go back to my argument with Sordini. As I said, my defences gradually came down. But if Sordini can gain even the slightest advantage over someone else, he has already won the day, because then his close attention, energy, and presence of mind are all the greater, and to the man he is attacking he is a fearsome sight, although a welcome one to that man's enemies. It's because I've had this experience in other cases that I can speak of him as I do. By the way, I've never yet managed to set eyes on him myself, he can't come down here, he is so overworked. As his office has been described to me, all the walls are hidden behind towers of huge bundles of files stacked one above another, and these are only the files on which Sordini is working at present. Since files are always being taken out of the bundles or put back into them, and it's all done in a great hurry, the towers are always collapsing, and the sound of them constantly crashing to the floor has become typical of Sordini's office. Well, Sordini is a real worker, and he devotes the same attention to both the smallest cases and the largest.'

'Mr Mayor,' said K., 'you keep calling my case one of the smallest, yet a great many officials have put their minds to it, and while it may have been very small at first, the zeal of officials like Mr Sordini has made it into a major one. That is unfortunate, and not at all what I want, since I have no ambition to see towers of files about me rise in the air and come crashing down, I just want to work at a little drawing-board in peace as a humble land surveyor.'

'No,' said the mayor, 'it's not a major case, you have no grounds for complaint there. It is one of the smallest of small cases. The status of the case is not determined by the amount of work done on it, and if that's what you think you are still very far from understanding the authorities. But even if it did depend on the amount of work, your case would be one of the slightest. There are far more normal cases, I mean cases where no so-called mistakes creep in, and indeed much more rewarding work is done on them. Anyway, you know nothing at all about the real work your case has entailed, and I will now tell you about it. At first Sordini left me right out of it, but then his officials arrived, and there were daily hearings of highly regarded members of this parish at the Castle Inn, all taken down for the records. Most of the villagers backed me, and only a few expressed distrust, saying that the question of land surveying concerns a farmer's interests closely, and thinking that they detected secret deals of some kind and instances of injustice. Furthermore, they found a leader, and Sordini was bound to be convinced, from what they said, that if I had raised the question at the parish council, not all its members would have been against the appointment of a land surveyor. So something obvious—I mean the fact that no land surveyor was needed—was at least questioned. A man called Brunswick was particularly active here—you probably don't know him. He may not be a bad fellow, but he is stupid and has a wild imagination. He's the brother-in-law of Lasemann.'

'Lasemann the master tanner?' said K., and he described the bearded man he had seen at Lasemann's house.

'Yes, that's him,' said the mayor.

'I know his wife as well,' said K., trying a shot at random.

'Quite possibly,' said the mayor, and fell silent.

'She's beautiful,' said K., 'but rather pale, and ailing. I suppose she comes from the castle?' This was said half as a question.

The mayor looked at the time, poured medicine into a small spoon, and quickly swallowed it.

'I suppose all you know of the castle is the offices?' asked K. brusquely.

'Yes,' agreed the mayor, with an ironic yet grateful smile, 'and they're the most important part of it. As for Brunswick: if we could keep him out of the parish council we'd nearly all of us be glad, not least Lasemann. But at that time Brunswick gained some influence. He's not a good speaker, but he shouts, and that's enough for many people. That's how it happened that I was obliged to lay the whole affair before the parish council, which in fact was Brunswick's sole success at first, for of course the great majority of the parish council wouldn't hear of appointing a land surveyor. That was all years ago too, but the case has never really been settled all this time, partly because of the conscientious approach of Sordini, who was trying to discover the motives of both the majority and the opposition through the most careful investigation, and partly because of the stupidity and ambition of Brunswick (who has various personal links with the authorities), which set his imagination to work thinking up more and more new ideas. Sordini, however, was not to be deceived by Brunswick (and how, indeed, *could* Brunswick deceive Sordini?), but if he was not to be deceived new enquiries were necessary, and even before they were dealt with Brunswick had come up with something fresh. Oh yes, his mind is very quick, it's all of a piece with his stupidity. And now I come to a particular feature of our official mechanism. When an affair has been under consideration for a very long time, and even before assessment of it is complete, it can happen that something occurs to settle it, like a sudden flash of lightning at some unforeseeable point, and you can't pinpoint it later. The case is thus brought to an arbitrary, if usually quite correct, conclusion. It's as if the official mechanism could no longer stand up to the tension and the years of attrition caused by the same factor, which in itself may be slight, and has made the decision of its own accord with no need for the officials to take a hand. Of course there has not been any miracle, and certainly some official or other made a note of the matter concluding the case, or came to an unwritten decision, but at least we here can't find out, even from the authority, which official made the decision in this case and why. The supervisory authorities will discover that much later, but we ourselves never do, and by then hardly anyone would be interested. Well, as I was saying, these decisions are generally excellent, and the only disruptive aspect of them is that, as it usually turns out, we learn about them too late, so passionate discussion of an affair that was settled long ago still goes on. I don't know whether such a decision has been taken in your case—there is much to suggest that it has and much to suggest that it hasn't—but if it had, then a note of your appointment would have been sent to you, and you would have set out on your long journey here. Meanwhile a lot of time would have passed, and Sordini would still have been working himself to exhaustion on the same case, Brunswick would have been plotting and intriguing, and I'd have been plagued by the pair of them. I merely suggest this possibility, but I do know the following for certain: meanwhile a supervisory authority discovered that many years ago Department A had sent an enquiry to the parish about a land surveyor, and no answer ever came back. I was asked about it recently, and then of course the whole matter was cleared up. Department A was satisfied with my answer, to the effect that no land surveyor was needed, and Sordini was obliged to realize that he had not been the person competent to deal with this case and, through no fault of his own, had done a great deal of unnecessary and nerve-racking work. If new work hadn't been coming in from all sides, as usual, and if yours had not, after all, been a very small case—we might almost say the smallest of the small—then we would probably all have breathed a sigh of relief, all of us including even Sordini himself, with only Brunswick still feeling ridiculously rancorous. And now, Mr Land Surveyor, imagine my dismay when, after the happy conclusion of the whole affair—and a great deal of time has passed since then too—you suddenly turn up, and it looks as if the whole thing is going to begin again. I am firmly determined not to allow this, so far as in me lies, as I am sure you will understand.'

'To be sure,' said K., 'but I understand even better that I and perhaps the law too have been shockingly abused. Personally, I will know how to defend myself.'

'How are you going to do that?' asked the mayor.

'I can't tell you,' said K.

'I don't wish to impose on you,' said the mayor, 'but I suggest you consider me as—well, I won't say a friend, since we are total strangers—but to some extent an associate. I can't allow you to be accepted as a land surveyor here, but otherwise you can turn to me with confidence, although only within the limits of my power, which is not large.'

'You keep talking', said K., 'about the possibility of my being accepted as a land surveyor, but I have already been appointed in that capacity. Here is Klamm's letter.'

'Klamm's letter', said the mayor, 'is valuable and deserves respect for the sake of Klamm's signature, which does seem to be genuine, but otherwise—no, I dare not even tell you my opinion. Mizzi!' he called, adding: 'What on earth are you all doing?'

The assistants, who had been out of sight for some time, and Mizzi had obviously failed to find the file they were looking for, and had then tried to shut everything up in the cupboard again, but had failed in that too because of the disorganized and exorbitantly large number of files. So the assistants had thought of a plan that they were now putting into practice. They had laid the cupboard down on the floor, stuffed all the files into it, and they and Mizzi sat on the cupboard doors, thus trying to squeeze them slowly shut.

'So the file hasn't been found,' said the mayor. 'Well, that's a pity, but you know the story now, so we don't really need the file any more. Anyway it's sure to be found some time, it's probably at the teacher's place. He has a great many files there. Now, bring the candle over here, Mizzi, and read this letter with me.'

Mizzi came over, looking even more grey and insignificant than before as she sat down on the edge of the bed close to her strong, vigorous husband, who put his arms around her. Only her little face showed now in the candlelight, its clear, stern features softened by the ravages of age. No sooner had she looked at the letter than she clasped her hands and said: 'From Klamm.' Then they read the letter together, whispering to each other from time to time, and finally, just as the assistants were cheering because they had finally managed to close the cupboard doors, and Mizzi was looking at them in quiet gratitude, the mayor said:

'Mizzi thinks just as I do, and now I can venture to speak my mind. This is not an official communication at all, but a private letter. That's clear enough even from the salutation, "Dear Sir". What's more, there isn't a word in it about your being accepted as a land surveyor, it just deals in general terms with service to the castle, and even that says nothing binding, only that you have been appointed "as you know", that is to say, the burden of proof of the fact that you have been appointed lies on you. Finally, you are officially referred to me, the village mayor, as your immediate superior, who will tell you everything else, and I've done most of that already. This is all as clear as day to anyone who is accustomed to reading official communications, and as a consequence reads unofficial letters even better.

But I'm not surprised that you, a stranger, don't understand that. Altogether, the letter means nothing but that Klamm personally intends to concern himself with you should you be accepted into the service of the castle.'

'You interpret the letter so well, Mr Mayor,' said K., 'that in the end there's nothing left of it but the signature on a blank sheet of paper. Don't you think that in doing so you are belittling Klamm's name, which you claim to respect?'

'You misunderstand me,' said the mayor. 'I don't mistake the meaning of the letter, I don't belittle it with my interpretation, quite the contrary. A private letter from Klamm naturally means much more than an official communication. It just doesn't mean what *you* think it means.'

'Do you know Schwarzer?' asked K.

'No,' said the mayor. 'Do you, Mizzi? No, she doesn't either. We don't know him.'

'That's strange,' said K. 'He's the son of one of the deputy wardens.'

'My dear sir,' said the mayor, 'how can I be expected to know all the sons of all the deputy wardens?'

'Very well,' said K., 'then you'll just have to believe me when I tell you that he is. I had a difference of opinion with this man Schwarzer on the day of my arrival. He then spoke on the telephone to a deputy warden called Fritz and was told that I had indeed been appointed land surveyor. How do you explain that, Mr Mayor?'

'Very easily,' said the mayor. 'You have never really been in contact with our authorities. All your contacts are only apparent, but as a result of your ignorance you think that they are real. And as for the telephone: look, there's no telephone here in my house, and I certainly have plenty to do with the authorities. Telephones may come in useful at inns and so on, rather like a musical box, but that's all. Have you ever telephoned anyone here? Well, then perhaps you'll see what I mean. The telephone obviously works very well in the castle, I've been told that they are telephoning all the time there, which of course speeds the work up a great deal. Down here, we hear that constant telephoning as a rushing, singing sound on the line, and I'm sure you've heard it too. But that rushing, singing sound is the only real, trustworthy information that the telephone conveys to us down here, and everything else is just an illusion. There is no telephone connection to the castle, there's no switchboard passing on our calls; if we call someone in the castle from here, the telephones ring in all the lower departments, or perhaps they would if, as I know for a fact, the sound was not turned off on nearly all of them. Now and then a tired official feels the need to amuse himself a little—especially in the evening or at night—and switches the sound back on, and then we get an answer, but an answer that is only a joke. It's very understandable. Who has the right to disturb such important work, always going full steam ahead, with his own little private worries? I really don't understand how even a stranger can believe that if he calls, say, Sordini, it will really be Sordini who answers him. More likely it will be some little clerk in quite a different department. Although then again, a wonderful moment might come when you call the little clerk and Sordini himself answers. In that case, of course, it's advisable to hurry away from the telephone before the first sound is heard.'

'Well, that's not how I saw it,' said K. 'I wasn't to know these details, but it's true that I didn't have much confidence in those telephone calls. I was always aware that only something experienced or achieved in the castle itself has any real significance.'

'You're wrong,' said the mayor, pouncing on one part of this, 'of course these telephone calls have real significance, why not? How could a message passed on from the castle by an official be insignificant? I said so just now, in connection with Klamm's letter. None of what it says has any official meaning, if you ascribe official meaning to it you are wrong; on the other hand its private significance, whether friendly or hostile, is very great, generally greater than an official meaning can ever be.'

'Very well,' said K. 'Assuming it's all as you say, then I must have a number of good friends in the castle; in fact look at it properly, and when that department thought, many years ago, of sending for a land surveyor it was an act of friendship to me, and act after act of friendship followed, until at last I was enticed here to no good purpose and then threatened with expulsion.'

'There's something in what you say,' said the mayor. 'You're right to think that communications from the castle mustn't be taken literally. But caution is necessary in general, not just here, and the more important the communication concerned, the more necessary it is to be cautious. I don't understand what you say about being enticed here. If you had followed what I was saying better, you would surely realize that the question of your appointment is far too difficult for us to be able to answer it in the course of a little conversation.'

'So the outcome is', said K., 'that everything is very confused and nothing can be solved, and I'm being thrown out.'

'Who would venture to throw you out, my dear sir?' said the mayor. 'The very lack of clarity in the earlier questions assures you of the most civil treatment, but you appear to be over-sensitive. No one is keeping you here, but that doesn't amount to being thrown out.'

'Oh, Mr Mayor, sir,' said K., 'now you're the one seeing all this too clearly again. Let me tell you some of the things that keep me here: the sacrifices I made to leave my home; my long and difficult journey; my well-founded hopes of my appointment here; my complete lack of means; the impossibility of finding suitable work at home now; and last but not least my fiancée, who comes from this village.'

'Ah, yes, Frieda!' said the mayor, not surprised. 'I know about that. But Frieda will follow you anywhere. As for the rest of it, certain considerations will be necessary, and I will speak to the castle about that. Should a decision come, or should it be necessary to question you again first, I'll send for you. Does that suit you?'

'No, not at all,' said K. 'I don't want any tokens of favour from the castle, I want my rights.'

'Mizzi,' said the mayor to his wife, who was still sitting close to him toying dreamily with Klamm's letter, which she had folded into a paper boat. In alarm, K. took it from her. 'Mizzi, my leg is beginning to hurt badly again, we'll have to change the compress.'

K. rose to his feet. 'Then I'll say goodbye,' he said. 'Yes, do,' said Mizzi, who was already preparing some ointment, 'there's a nasty draught.' K. turned. The assistants, in their ever-inappropriate readiness to make themselves useful, had opened both sides of the double door as soon as they heard K.'s remark. If he was to keep the penetrating cold out of the sickroom, K. could only bow fleetingly to the mayor. Then, taking the assistants with him, he went out of the room and was quick to close the door.

6

Second Conversation with the Landlady

THE landlord was waiting outside the inn for him. He would not have ventured to speak without being asked first, so K. asked what he wanted. 'Have you found new lodgings?' asked the landlord, his eyes bent on the ground. 'I think you must be asking on behalf of your wife,' said K. 'You seem to be extremely dependent on her.' 'No,' said the landlord, 'I'm not asking on her behalf. But she is very upset and unhappy about you, she can't work, she lies in bed sighing and complaining all the time.' 'Shall I go and see her?' asked K. 'I wish you would,' said the landlord. 'I came to fetch you from the village mayor's house, but listening at the door I heard the two of you in conversation and didn't like to disturb you. I was worried about my wife too, so I came straight back, but she wouldn't let me in to see her, so all I could do was wait for you.' 'Come along then, let's be quick about it,' said K. 'I'll soon set her mind at rest.'

'I only hope so,' said the landlord.

They went through the well-lit kitchen, where three or four maids, all keeping some distance from each other, positively froze in the midst of whatever they were doing at the sight of K. The land-lady's sighs could be heard even here in the kitchen. She was lying in a little room without any windows, divided from the kitchen by a thin wooden partition. There was space only for a big double bed and a wardrobe. The bed was placed so that its occupant could keep an eye on the entire kitchen and what was going on there. On the other hand, hardly anything of the little room could be seen from the kitchen; it was dark inside, and only the red-and-white bedclothes stood out a little. You couldn't make out any details until you had gone in and your eyes became used to the dim light.

'Here you are at last,' said the landlady faintly. She lay stretched full-length on her back, and obviously had some difficulty in breathing; she had thrown back the eiderdown. In bed she looked much younger than when she was fully dressed, but all the same the lacy nightcap she wore was too small for her, and perched unsteadily on top of her head, making her worn face look pitiable. 'How could

I have come?' asked K. gently. 'You didn't send for me.' 'You shouldn't have kept me waiting so long,' said the landlady, with the fretful persistence of an invalid. 'Well, sit down,' she said, pointing to the edge of the bed. 'And you others go away.' For not only K.'s assistants but also the maids had now come in as well. 'Do you want me to go too, Gardena?'* asked the landlord, and for the first time K. heard his wife's name. 'Of course,' she said slowly, and as if her thoughts were elsewhere she added, distractedly: 'Why should you of all people stay?' But when all the others had withdrawn to the kitchen—and this time even the assistants went at once, though the fact was that they were chasing one of the maids—Gardena was obviously paying enough attention to realize that everything said here could be heard from there, for the little room had no door, so she ordered everyone to leave the kitchen too. They obeyed at once. 'Now, Mr Land Surveyor,' Gardena said, 'there's a shawl hanging at the front of the wardrobe. Please will you give it to me? I want to cover myself with it, I can't bear the weight of this eiderdown, I'm breathing with such difficulty.' And when K. had brought her the shawl, she said: 'See this, fine fabric, isn't it?' It looked to K. like perfectly ordinary woollen fabric, and he felt it, simply to please her, but made no comment. 'Yes, very fine fabric,' said Gardena, wrapping it around her. Now she lay there peacefully, and did not seem to be suffering any longer. She even noticed that her hair was untidy from the way she had been lying on it, and sitting up for a little while she rearranged it round the nightcap. She had thick hair.

K. was getting impatient, and said: 'Ma'am, you sent to ask if I had found other lodgings.' 'I sent to ask you that?' asked the landlady. 'No, you're mistaken.' 'But your husband has just asked me.' 'I can believe that,' said the landlady. 'I've been at daggers drawn with him. When I didn't want to have you staying here, he let you stay; now that I'm happy to have you here he's driving you away. He's always doing that kind of thing.' 'Have you changed your mind about me so much,' said K., 'in just a couple of hours?' 'I haven't changed my mind,' said the landlady, sounding weaker again. 'Give me your hand. There. And now promise to be perfectly frank with me, and I will be frank with you.' 'Good,' said K. 'Which of us is going to begin?' 'I will,' said the landlady. She did not give the impression that she was ready to oblige K., but just seemed eager to speak first.

She took a photograph out from under her pillow and handed it to K. 'Look at that picture,' she asked earnestly. To get a better view of it, K. stepped into the kitchen, but even there it wasn't easy to make anything out, for the photograph had faded with age, and was cracked, crumpled, and stained in many places. 'It's not in very good condition,' said K. 'I'm afraid not, I'm afraid not,' said the landlady. 'That's what happens when you carry something on your person over the years. But if you look at it closely I'm sure you'll be able to see everything. I can help you out; just tell me what you see. I like to hear about that picture. What do you see in it, then?' 'A young man,' said K. 'Quite right,' said the landlady, 'and what is he doing?' 'I think he's lying on a plank, stretching and yawning.' The landlady laughed. 'That's quite wrong,' she said. 'But here's the plank, and there he is lying on it,' said K., sticking to his own opinion. 'Look more closely,' said the landlady, annoyed. 'Is he really lying down?' 'Why, no,' said K. now. 'He's not lying down, he is in the air, and now I see it isn't a plank, it's probably a cord, and the young man is doing the high jump.' 'There you are, then,' said the landlady, pleased. 'He's jumping, yes. That's how the official messengers practise. I knew you'd see what it was. Can you see his face too?' 'Very little of it,' said K. 'He's obviously making a great effort, his mouth is open, his eyes are narrowed, and his hair is flying in the air.' 'Very good,' said the landlady approvingly. 'As you never saw him in person you can't make out any more. But he was a handsome lad. I saw him only once, briefly, and I shall never forget him.' 'Who was he, then?' asked K. 'He was the messenger,' said the landlady, 'the messenger who was first sent by Klamm to summon me to see him.'

K. wasn't listening closely; the sound of something tapping on glass distracted his attention. He soon found out the cause of the disturbance. The assistants were standing in the yard, shifting from foot to foot in the snow. They looked pleased to see K. again, cheerfully pointed him out to each other, and kept on tapping at the kitchen window. At a menacing movement from K. they stopped that at once, trying to push one another back, but each kept escaping the other, and soon they were back at the window. K. hurried into the little room, where the assistants couldn't see him from outside and he didn't have to see them. But that soft and imploring tapping on the windowpane still followed him.

'It's those assistants again,' he told the landlady by way of apology, pointing to the yard outside. However, she took no notice of him; she had taken the picture back, and now she looked at it, smoothed it out, and pushed it under the pillow again. Her movements were slower now, but not from weariness, they were slow under the burden of memory. She had wanted K. to talk to her, and as he did so she had forgotten about him. She was playing with the fringe of her shawl. Only after a little while did she look up, pass her hand over her eyes, and say: 'This shawl came from Klamm too. And so did this night-cap. The photograph, the shawl, and the nightcap, they're my three mementoes of him. I'm not young like Frieda, I don't aim as high as she does, nor am I so tender-hearted, she's very tender-hearted. In short, I know what's right and proper, but I have to confess that without those three things I could probably never have borne it here for so long, probably not even for a day. These three mementoes may perhaps appear small things to you, but then, you see, Frieda was intimate with Klamm for so long, but she has no memento of him at all. I asked her; she is so impassioned and so insatiable, while I, on the other hand, who was with Klamm only those three times—he didn't send for me any more after that, I don't know why—I took those mementoes away with me, guessing how short my time would be. Well, you have to look after yourself. Klamm never gives any-thing away of his own accord, but if you see something suitable lying about there, you can ask for it.'

K. felt uncomfortable listening to these stories, much as they also affected him. 'How long ago is all this?' he asked with a sigh.

'Over twenty years,' said the landlady, 'well over twenty years ago.'

'And you've been faithful to Klamm so long?' said K. 'But ma'am, do you realize that when you make such confessions you are causing me severe anxiety when I think of my forthcoming marriage?'

The landlady thought it unseemly for K. to bring up his own affairs, and cast him an angry sideways glance.

'Don't look so cross, ma'am,' said K. 'I'm not saying a word against Klamm, but through the force of circumstance I do have a certain connection with him; Klamm's greatest admirer couldn't deny that. Well then. As a result of what you say, I can't help think-ing of myself at the mention of Klamm, there's no altering that. Moreover, ma'am,' and here K. took her faltering hand, 'remember how badly our last conversation turned out, and recollect that this time we want to part on good terms.'

'You are right,' said the landlady, bowing her head, 'but spare me. I am no more sensitive than anyone else, far from it, but we all have our sensitive spots, and this is mine—my only one.'

'Unfortunately it is also mine,' said K. 'But I will certainly control myself. However, tell me, ma'am, how am I to bear this terrible fidelity to Klamm in my own marriage, always supposing that Frieda is like you in this point?'

'Terrible fidelity,' repeated the landlady suddenly. 'Is it fidelity? I am faithful to my husband, but Klamm? Klamm once made me his mistress, can I ever lose that rank? And you ask how you are to bear it in Frieda? Oh, Mr Land Surveyor, who are you to dare to ask such a question?'

'Madam!' said K. in a tone of warning.

'I know,' said the landlady, caving in, 'but my husband has never asked me such questions. I don't know which of us is to be called more unhappy, I then or Frieda now. Frieda, who wilfully left Klamm, or I, whom he never summoned again. Perhaps Frieda is the unhappier one after all, even if she doesn't yet seem to know the full extent of it. But my thoughts then dominated my unhappiness more exclusively, for I kept on asking myself, and at heart I still haven't stopped asking: why did it happen? Why did Klamm summon me three times and not a fourth time, never again a fourth time? What else could I think about at the time? What else could I speak about to my husband, whom I married soon after it happened? We had no time by day, this inn was in a wretched state when we took it over and had to try to bring it up to scratch, but by night? For years on end, our conversations at night turned only on Klamm and the reasons why he changed his mind. And if my husband fell asleep while we were talking I woke him up, and we went on.'

'Now, if you will permit me,' said K., 'I am going to ask you a very forthright question.'

The landlady said nothing to that.

'So I see you will not permit me,' said K. 'Very well, that is enough for me.'

'Indeed it is,' said the landlady, 'that in particular. You take everything the wrong way, even a silence. You can't help it. I'll allow you to ask.'

'If I take everything the wrong way,' said K., 'perhaps I'm wrong about my question too, and it isn't so forthright after all. I just wanted to know how you came to know your husband, and how this inn came into your hands.'

The landlady frowned, but said equably enough: 'It's a very simple story. My father was the blacksmith here, and Hans, my present husband, was groom to a gentleman farmer and often visited my father. That was after my last meeting with Klamm, I was very unhappy, although I shouldn't have been, for it was all in order, and the fact that I wasn't allowed near Klamm again was Klamm's own decision, so that was in order too, only the reasons for it were obscure, and I might well wonder about those, but I ought not to have been unhappy. However, I was, and I couldn't work, but sat in our front garden all day. Hans saw me there and sometimes sat down with me. I didn't tell him my troubles, but he knew what it was all about, and because he's a good lad he would sometimes shed tears in sympathy with me. And when the landlord of that time, whose wife had died, so that he had to give up the business, besides being an old man already, well, when he passed our little garden one day he saw the two of us sitting there, stopped, and without more ado, offered to lease us the inn. He trusted us, so he didn't want any money in advance, and he set the rent very low as well. I didn't want to be a burden to my father, I was indifferent to everything else, and so, thinking of the inn and the new work there that might perhaps help me to forget a little, I gave Hans my hand in marriage. And that's my story.'

There was silence for a while, and then K. said: 'The old landlord acted generously, if rashly—or did he have special reasons to trust you both?'

'Oh, he knew Hans well,' said the landlady. 'He was Hans's uncle.'

'Then, to be sure,' said K., 'Hans's family must have been greatly in favour of his marriage to you?'

'Perhaps,' said the landlady. 'I don't know, I never troubled to think about it.'

'But it must have been so,' said K., 'if his family was ready to make such a sacrifice and simply hand the inn over to you without security.'

'He wasn't being rash, as it turned out later,' said the landlady. 'I threw myself into the work, I was strong, I was the blacksmith's daughter, I didn't need a maid or a manservant about the place, I was everywhere: in the saloon bar, in the kitchen, in the stables, in the yard.

I cooked so well that guests were even enticed away from the Castle Inn. You haven't been in the saloon bar at midday, you don't know our guests at lunchtime, at that time there were even more of them, although since then many have stopped coming. As a result we could not only pay the rent properly, we were able to buy the whole place after a few years, and we owe almost nothing on it today. To be sure, another result was that I undermined my health with all this, I developed a serious heart condition, and now I am an old woman. You may think that I am much older than Hans, but in reality he is only two or three years younger than me, and you can be sure he will never age, for his kind of work—smoking a pipe, listening to the guests, knocking out his pipe again, sometimes fetching a beer—his kind of work doesn't age anyone.'

'Your achievements are remarkable,' said K., 'no doubt about that, but we were speaking of the time before your marriage, and then it really would have been amazing for Hans's family to urge the two of you to marry, when it meant financial sacrifice, or at least shouldering such a great risk as handing over the inn trusting only in your own capacity for work, which they couldn't have known at the time, and Hans's capacity for work, the total absence of which they must have noticed.'

'Yes, well,' said the landlady wearily, 'I can see what you're getting at, and how wide you are of the mark. Klamm had no hand in any of this. Why would he have thought he should do anything for me, or more accurately, how could he have thought of doing so anyway? He knew nothing about me. The fact that he never summoned me again showed that he had forgotten me. When he doesn't summon anyone any more, he forgets her entirely. I didn't want to say so in front of Frieda. But it's not just that he forgets; it's more than that. For if you have forgotten someone, you can get to know her again. With Klamm, however, that's impossible. When he stops summoning someone he's forgotten her entirely, not just in the past, but for the future too, once and for all. If I go to a great deal of trouble I can think myself into your mind and your ideas, which make no sense here, however much to the point they may be wherever it is you come from. Perhaps your foolish fancies are wild enough to imagine that Klamm gave me in marriage to a man like Hans so that I would have no trouble in coming to him again, should he summon me at some time in the future. Well, folly can go no further. Where is the man who could keep me from going to Klamm if Klamm were to give me a sign? Nonsense, utter nonsense, nothing but confusion comes of playing about with such nonsensical ideas.'

'No,' said K., 'let's not confuse ourselves. My thoughts had gone nowhere near as far as you assume, although to tell you the truth they were on their way there. For the time being, however, I was simply marvelling that Hans's family hoped for so much from his marriage to you, and their hopes were indeed fulfilled, although at the cost of your own heart and your health. The idea of connecting those facts with Klamm was, indeed, forcing itself upon me, but not—or not yet—in the crude way in which you presented it, obviously solely for the purpose of allowing you to snap at me again, which you seem to enjoy. I wish you joy of that! But I was thinking: first, Klamm is obviously the reason for your marriage. If not for Klamm you wouldn't have been unhappy, you wouldn't have been sitting idle in the front garden; if not for Klamm Hans wouldn't have seen you there, and were it not for your grief Hans, who is shy, would never have ventured to speak to you. If not for Klamm you and Hans would never have found yourselves in tears; if not for Klamm Hans's kind old uncle the landlord would never have seen you and his nephew sitting amicably together; if not for Klamm you would not have been indifferent to life, so you wouldn't have married Hans. Well, I would say that Klamm features prominently in all this. But it goes further. If you hadn't been trying to forget, you certainly wouldn't have worked so hard, with no thought for yourself, and given the inn such a good reputation. So I detect Klamm again here too. But quite apart from that, Klamm is the cause of your illness, for your heart was exhausted with unhappy passion even before your marriage. There remains only the question of what induced Hans's family to favour the marriage so much. You mentioned once that to have been Klamm's mistress means a rise in rank for a woman that she can never lose, so I suppose that may have tempted them. But in addition, I think, it was the hope that the lucky star which led you to Klamm—always supposing it was a lucky star, but you say so—was still yours, that is to say, luck was bound to stay with you, and would not abandon you as suddenly and abruptly as Klamm did.'

'Do you mean all that seriously?' asked the landlady.

'I do mean it seriously,' K. was quick to say, 'only I think that Hans's family were neither entirely right nor entirely wrong in their hopes, and I also think I see the mistake you made. Outwardly it all seems to have been successful: Hans is well off, his wife is a fine, capable woman, he enjoys high regard, no money is owed on the inn. But it wasn't really successful: Hans would certainly have been much happier with a simple girl whose first great love he was. If, as you say reproachfully, he sometimes stands there in the saloon bar looking lost, it may be because he really does feel lost—without being unhappy about it, to be sure, as far as I know him by now—but it is equally sure that this handsome, intelligent young man would have been happier with another wife, by which I mean he would have been more independent, hard-working, and virile. And you yourself certainly are not happy. As you said, you wouldn't want to go on living without those three mementoes, and you have a weak heart as well. So were Hans's family wrong in their hopes? No, I don't think so. The blessing of that lucky star was yours, but they didn't know how to make the most of it.'

'What did they fail to do, then?' asked the landlady. She was now lying full-length on her back, looking up at the ceiling.

'They didn't ask Klamm,' said K.

'Ah, so we're back with your own affairs,' said the landlady.

'Or yours,' said K. 'Our affairs run parallel.'

'What do you want of Klamm, then?' asked the landlady. She had now shaken up the pillows so that she could lean back on them sitting upright, and was looking K. full in the face. 'I have told you frankly about my case, from which you might have learnt something. Now, tell me equally frankly what you want to ask Klamm. It was only with difficulty that I persuaded Frieda to go up to your room and stay there. I was afraid you wouldn't speak frankly enough in front of her.'

'I have nothing to hide,' said K. 'But first let me point something out to you. Klamm forgets at once, you said. First, that seems to me most unlikely, and second, it can't be proved and is obviously nothing but a legend invented by the girlish minds of those who have been in favour with Klamm. I am surprised that you believe such a downright invention.'

'It isn't a legend,' said the landlady. 'It derives from general experience.'

'But it can also be countered by a new experience,' said K. 'There's a difference between your case and Frieda's. Klamm didn't stop summoning Frieda; one might say, he did summon her but she didn't comply. It's even possible that he is still waiting for her.'

The landlady fell silent and merely let her eyes wander over K., observing him. Then she said: 'I will listen calmly to everything you have to say. I would rather you spoke openly than think you were sparing me. I have only one request. Do not mention Klamm's name. Call him "he", or something else, but don't call him by his name.'

'I'm happy to oblige you,' said K., 'but it's difficult to say just what I want of him. First I want to see him at close quarters, then I want to hear his voice, and then I want to know from the man himself how he feels about our marriage. Anything else I may ask him depends on the course of the conversation. There could be a good many subjects for discussion, but what matters most to me is to see him face to face. I have never yet spoken directly to any of the real officials here. It seems harder to achieve that than I expected. But now it's my duty to speak to him as a private person, and as I see it that's much more easily done; I can speak to him as an official only in his office, which may be inaccessible, in the castle or—and I'm not sure about that— at the Castle Inn, but I can speak to him as a private person anywhere, indoors or in the street, wherever I happen to meet him. If I then find I have the official facing me instead, I'm happy with that, but it is not my prime aim.'

'Very well,' said the landlady, pressing her face down into the pillows as if venturing to make an indecent remark, 'if I can get your request for a conversation with Klamm passed on through my connections, then promise me to do nothing on your own account* until the answer comes down from the castle.'

'Much as I'd like to do as you ask or humour your whim,' said K., 'I can't promise that. This is urgent, particularly after the unfortunate outcome of my conversation with the village mayor.'

'We can dismiss that objection,' said the landlady. 'The mayor is a man of no importance at all. Didn't you notice? He wouldn't keep his job for a day if it weren't for his wife. She's in charge of everything.'

'Mizzi?' asked K. The landlady nodded. 'She was there, yes,' K. said.

'Did she give an opinion on anything?' asked the landlady.

'No,' said K. 'And I didn't get any impression that she could.'

'Ah, well,' said the landlady, 'you have the wrong idea of everything here. At least, whatever the mayor has decided about you is of no significance. I'll have a word with his wife some time. And if I also promise you that Klamm's answer will come in a week at the latest, you have no reason not to do as I say.'

'None of this is the deciding factor,' said K. 'I've made my decision, and I would try to act by it even if a negative answer came. But if that's what I mean to do all along, I can't request an interview first. What might still be a daring but honestly meant venture without such a request would be downright insubordination after an answer rejecting it. Surely that would be much worse.'

'Worse?' said the landlady. 'It's insubordination in any case. And now do as you like. Hand me my dress.'

Taking no more notice of K., she put on her dress and hurried into the kitchen. A commotion in the saloon had been audible for some time. Someone had knocked on the hatch in the partition. The assistants had pushed it open and called in that they were hungry. Then other faces had appeared there. You could even hear several voices singing in harmony.

It was true that K.'s conversation with the landlady had considerably delayed the cooking of the midday meal, which was not ready yet, but the customers were assembled, although no one had dared to break the landlady's ban on entering the kitchen. However, now that the watchers at the hatch were calling for the landlady to hurry up, the maids came running into the kitchen, and when K. entered the saloon bar the remarkably large company, over twenty people, both men and women, dressed in provincial but not rustic fashion, left the window where they had been assembled and streamed towards the small tables to make sure of their places. A married couple and several children were already sitting at one little table in a corner: the husband, a friendly, blue-eyed gentleman with ruffled grey hair and a beard, was standing up and bending over towards the children, beating time with a knife to their song, which he kept trying to quieten down. Perhaps he hoped that singing would make them forget they were hungry. The landlady apologized to the company in a few words, perfunctorily spoken, and no one reproached her. She looked round for the landlord, but in view of the awkwardness of the situation he had probably made his escape long ago. Then she went slowly into the kitchen, without another glance at K., who hurried up to his room and Frieda.

7

The Teacher

K. FOUND the teacher up there. It was good to see that the room could hardly be recognized, Frieda had been so busy. It had been well aired, the stove heated with plenty of fuel, the floor washed, the bed made, while the maids' things, mostly nasty and tawdry, had gone, and so finally had their pictures. The table, where the encrusted dirt on top of it had previously positively stared you in the face wherever you turned, was now covered with a white crochet-work tablecloth. It was possible to receive guests here now, and the fact that K.'s small stock of underwear, which Frieda had obviously washed earlier, was hanging near the stove to dry was not obtrusive. The schoolteacher and Frieda were sitting at the table and rose to their feet when K. came in. Frieda greeted K. with a kiss, the teacher bowed slightly. K., distracted and still agitated after his conversation with the landlady, began to apologize for not having visited the teacher yet, sounding as if he assumed that the teacher, impatient over his failure to turn up, had now himself come to visit him. However, in his measured way the teacher seemed to recollect only after a while that he and K. had made an appointment to meet at some time. 'So, Mr Land Surveyor,' he said slowly, 'you're the stranger I spoke to a few days ago outside the church.' 'Yes,' replied K. briefly; here in his own room he didn't have to put up with what he had tolerated there when he was feeling so desolate. He turned to Frieda and told her that he had to pay an important call at once, one for which he must be as well dressed as possible. Without asking K. any further questions Frieda immediately called the assistants, who were busy investigating the new tablecloth, and told them to take K.'s clothes, and the boots he began to pull off at once, down to the yard and clean them carefully. She herself took a shirt off the washing-line and went down to the kitchen to iron it.

Now K. was alone with the teacher, who was still sitting at the table in silence, and he made him wait a little longer as he took off the shirt he was wearing and began washing at the basin. Only now, with his back to the teacher, did he wonder why the man had come.

'I have come on behalf of the village mayor with a message,' said the teacher. K. was ready to listen to what the mayor wanted, but as it was difficult to make himself heard through the sound of splashing water, the teacher had to come closer and lean against the wall beside K., who excused himself for washing and for his state of agitation by the urgency of the call he intended to pay. The teacher ignored this, and remarked: 'You were uncivil to the village mayor, that meritorious, experienced, and highly esteemed old man.' 'I didn't know I had been uncivil,' said K., drying himself. 'But it's true that I had something other than elegant manners to think about, something of importance to my very existence, which is threatened by a disgraceful official organization the details of which I need not describe to you, since you yourself work actively for the authorities. Has the village mayor complained of me?' 'In what quarter would he have complained?' said the teacher. 'Even if he knew where to turn, would he ever complain? I have simply drawn up, at his dictation, a small memorandum about your conversation, from which I learned quite enough about the mayor's kindness and the way you answered him back.' As K. was looking for his comb, which Frieda must have tidied away somewhere, he said: 'What? A memorandum? Drawn up after the event, and in my absence, by someone who wasn't present during the conversation? Not bad, I must say. And why a memorandum? Was it something official?' 'No,' said the teacher, 'semi-official, and the memorandum itself is only semi-official. It was written down solely because we must observe strict protocol in everything. At least it's down on paper now, and it does you no credit.' K., who had finally found the comb, which had slipped into the bed, said more calmly: 'Well, so it's down on paper. Did you come just to tell me that?' 'No,' said the teacher, 'but I am not an automaton, and must tell you my opinion. The message I bring, on the other hand, is further proof of the mayor's kindness, which I'd like to point out is beyond my own comprehension, and only under the pressure of my position and out of respect for the mayor do I deliver it.' K., now washed and with his hair combed, sat at the table waiting for the shirt and his other clothes; he was not even curious about what the teacher was telling him, and he was also influenced by the landlady's low opinion of the mayor. 'I suppose it's after midday?' he said, thinking of the long way he had to go, and then, catching himself up, added: 'But you wanted to tell me something about the mayor.' 'Very well,' said the teacher, shrugging his shoulders as if disclaiming any responsibility of his own. 'The village mayor fears that, if the decision on your affairs is too long in coming, you may do something thoughtless of your own accord. For my part, I don't know why he fears that; my own view is that you might as well do what you like. We are not your guardian angels, we're not obliged to chase after you wherever you go. Well then. The village mayor does not share my opinion. To be sure, he cannot hasten the decision itself, that's a matter for the count's authorities. But he is ready to make a provisional and truly generous decision within his own competence, and now it remains only for you to accept it: he offers you the temporary post of school janitor.' At first K. hardly noticed exactly what he was being offered, but the mere fact that there was an offer of any kind seemed to him not insignificant. It indicated that in the mayor's view he was in a position to do things in his own defence which justified the parish council in going to some trouble to protect itself. And how seriously everyone took all this! The teacher, who had been waiting here for some time after writing out the memorandum, must have been positively driven to come here by the mayor.

When the teacher saw that he had made K. thoughtful after all, he went on: 'I put forward my own objections. I pointed out that so far no school janitor had been necessary, the sexton's wife tidies up from time to time, supervised by my assistant teacher Miss Gisa, and I have quite enough trouble with the children, I really don't want a janitor giving me more. But the mayor said that in fact it was very dirty in the school. I replied, truthfully, that it wasn't so very bad. And, I added, will it be any better if we take this man on as janitor? Certainly not. Apart from the fact that he knows nothing about such work, the schoolhouse has only two large classrooms, and no extra rooms, so the school janitor and his family would have to live in one of the classrooms, sleep in it, perhaps even cook in it, which would hardly leave the place any cleaner. But the mayor pointed out that this position was a haven for you in your time of need, and so you would do your utmost to fill it well, and in addition, said the mayor, we would also be obtaining your wife and your assistants to work for us, so that it would be possible to keep not only the school itself but the school garden in perfect order. I was easily able to disprove all this. At last there was no more the mayor could plead in your favour, so he laughed and just said well, after all you are a land surveyor, so you'd be able to tend the beds in the school garden particularly well. No one can take exception to a joke, and so I came to see you with this offer.' 'You have gone to unnecessary trouble, sir,' said K. 'I have no intention of accepting the position.' 'Excellent,' said the teacher, 'excellent. You decline it out of hand.' And he took his hat, bowed, and left.

In a moment Frieda came up, looking anxious; she brought back the shirt un-ironed, and wouldn't answer any questions. To divert her mind, K. told her about the teacher and his offer, but she was hardly listening. She threw the shirt down on the bed and hurried away again. Soon she came back, but with the teacher, who looked morose and gave not a word of greeting. Frieda begged him for a little patience—obviously she had done so already on the way here—and then took K. through a side door which he had not previously noticed into the attic next to his room, where she finally, out of breath and in great agitation, told him what had happened. The landlady, angry that she had lowered herself to make certain confessions to K., and what was even worse had condescended, yielding as her nature was, to promote the idea of a conversation between Klamm and K., and now, having achieved nothing but, as she said, a cold and moreover insincere rejection, was determined not to have K. in the house any longer. If he had connections with the castle, she said, he had better make use of them very quickly, because he must leave the inn today, this very hour, and she would not take him back except by direct order of the authorities and under coercion; but she hoped it wouldn't come to that, for she too had connections with the castle and would make use of them. Furthermore, he was in the house now as a result of the landlord's negligence, and was not in any other distress at all, for this very morning he had boasted of having a bed for the night available to him elsewhere. Frieda was of course to stay here; if Frieda were to move out with K. she, the landlady, would be very unhappy, in fact she had collapsed beside the stove in the kitchen shedding tears at the mere thought of it, that poor woman with her heart trouble, but what else could she do, said Frieda, now that, as the landlady saw it anyway, the honour of Klamm's memory and his mementoes was at stake. That was the landlady's attitude. Frieda would indeed follow him, K., wherever he went, she said, through snow and ice, of course there was no question of that, but they were both in a terrible situation. So she had been very happy to hear about the mayor's offer, and even if it wasn't a suitable post for K., after all it was only temporary, as had been expressly pointed out. They would gain time and would easily find other possibilities, even if the final decision were not to turn out well. 'If need be,' cried Frieda finally, clinging round K.'s neck, 'we can go away; what is there to keep us here in the village? But just for the moment, my dear, let's accept the offer, shall we? I have brought the teacher back, you just have to tell him, "I accept," no more, and we'll move to the school.'

'This is a poor state of things,' said K., but without meaning it entirely seriously, for he didn't much mind where he stayed, and here in the attic, which had no walls and windows on two sides, while a cold draught blew keenly through it, he was freezing in his under-wear. 'You've made the room so nice, and now we have to move out. I'd be very, very unwilling to accept the position; it's embarrassing to be instantly humiliated in front of this petty little teacher, and now he is to be my superior. If we could only stay here a little longer, perhaps my situation may change this very afternoon. If at least you were to stay, we could wait and put the teacher off. I can always find a place to spend the night, in the bar if needs must—' But here Frieda put her hand over his mouth. 'Not that,' she said anxiously, 'please don't say that again. However, I'll do as you say in everything else. If you want me to stay here on my own then I will, sad as it would be for me. If you like we'll reject the offer, although I do think it would be the wrong thing to do. Because listen, if you find any-thing else, even this afternoon, well, naturally we'll give up the place at the school at once then, no one will try to stop us. And as for your humiliation in front of the teacher, trust me to make sure it's no such thing. I'll speak to him myself, you will just have to stand there in silence, and it will be the same later. You'll never have to speak to him yourself if you don't want to. I and I alone will probably be his servant, and not even that, for I know his weaknesses. So all is not lost if we accept the post, but a great deal is lost if we refuse it. Above all, if you don't hear anything from the castle today, you are really unlikely to find a bed for the night anywhere in the village of which I myself, as your future wife, would not be ashamed. And if you don't get a bed for the night, are you going to expect me to sleep here in this warm room, while I know that you are wandering outside in the dark and the cold?' K., who all this time had been standing with his arms folded, slapping his back with his hands to warm himself up a bit, said: 'Then I see there's nothing for it but to accept. Come along!'

Back in the room he went straight to the stove, ignoring the teacher, who was sitting at the table, took out his watch, and said: 'It's getting late.' 'But now we are agreed, sir,' said Frieda. 'We'll take the post.' 'Very well,' said the teacher, 'but the post is offered to the land surveyor here. He must speak for himself.' Frieda came to K.'s aid. 'Really,' she said, 'he does accept the post, don't you, K.?' So K. was able to limit his declaration to a simple: 'Yes,' not even directed at the teacher but at Frieda. 'Then', said the teacher, 'all that remains is for me to tell you what your duties will be, so that we're agreed on that once and for all. You, Mr Land Surveyor, are to clean and heat both classrooms every day, do small repairs about the place, clear the path through the garden of snow, run errands for me and my assistant teacher, and do all the gardening in the warmer seasons of the year. In return you have the right to live in one of the classrooms, whichever you choose, but if the children are not being taught in both rooms at the same time, and you happen to be in the room where they *are* being taught, you must of course move into the other room. You may not cook in the school building, but you and your household will be given board here at the inn at the expense of the parish. I mention only in passing, for as an educated man you will know such things for yourself, that you must strictly uphold the dignity of the school, and in particular the children must never, for instance, have to witness any unpleasant scenes in your domestic life during lessons. In that respect, let me just mention that we must insist on your putting your relationship with Miss Frieda on a legal footing as soon as possible.' All this seemed to K. unimportant, as if it did not concern him, or at least did not bind him in any way, but the teacher's arrogant manner annoyed him, and he said casually: 'Well, I suppose these are the usual obligations.' To cover up a little for this remark, Frieda asked about the salary. 'Whether or not any salary is paid,' said the teacher, 'will be considered only after a month's service on probation.' 'But that's going to be difficult for us,' said Frieda. 'We're to get married almost penniless and set up household on nothing. Sir, couldn't we lodge a petition with the parish asking for a small salary at once? Would you advise that?' 'No,' said the teacher, still speaking to K. 'Such a petition would be answered as you wish only if I were to recommend it, and I wouldn't. I have offered the post only as a favour to you, and favours mustn't go too far if a man's to maintain his awareness of his public responsibility.' Here K. did intervene, almost against his will. 'As for favours, sir,' he said, 'I think you are wrong. Perhaps I'm the one doing you the favour.' 'Oh no,' said the teacher, smiling, for now he had forced K. to speak directly to him after all, 'I have precise instructions on that point. We need a school janitor about as much as we need a land surveyor. Janitor or land surveyor, you're a millstone around our necks. I shall have to think hard to find a way of justifying the expense to the parish council; it would be best, and more in line with the facts, just to put the demand on the table and not try justifying it at all.' 'That's exactly what I mean,' said K. 'You have to take me on against your will, and although you have many reservations about it you have to accept me. But if someone is forced to accept another person, and that other person allows himself to be accepted, he is the one doing the favour.' 'Strange,' said the teacher. 'What, I ask, could force us to take you? Why, only the village mayor's good, over-generous heart. I see very well, Mr Land Surveyor, that you'll have to abandon many of your fanciful notions before you are any use as a school janitor. Naturally such remarks as that won't make anyone feel inclined to pay you a salary. I am afraid I must also remark that your conduct will give me a great deal of trouble; all this time you are trying to negotiate with me, as I can't help seeing, and I can hardly credit it, in your shirt and underpants.' 'So I am,' said K., laughing and clapping his hands. 'What's become of those dreadful assistants of mine?' Frieda hurried to the door. The teacher, realizing that K. was not going to respond to him any more, asked Frieda when they would be moving into the school. 'Today,' said Frieda. 'Then I'll come to check on you first thing tomorrow,' said the teacher, raising a hand in farewell. He was about to go through the door, which Frieda had opened for him, but collided with the maids coming back with their things to settle into the room again. He had to slip past them, for they made way for nobody. Frieda followed him. 'You're in a hurry,' said K. to the maids, very pleased with them this time. 'We're still here, and you have to move in at once?' They did not reply, but merely fiddled awkwardly with their bundles, from which K. saw the familiar grubby rags hanging out. 'I don't think you can ever have washed your things,' said K., not angrily but with a certain liking for them. They noticed it, opened their unyielding mouths at the same time to display fine, strong teeth, like the teeth of animals, and laughed without a sound. 'Come along then,' said K. 'Settle in; it's your room, after all.' But when they still hesitated—perhaps their room struck them as changed too much—K. took one of them by the arm to lead her further in. However, he let her go again at once, for the glance that, after coming to a brief mutual understanding, they both bent on K. was so surprised. 'Well, you've stared at me long enough,' said K., fending off a certain uncomfortable feeling. He took his shoes and boots, which Frieda, followed timidly by the assistants, had just brought, and dressed. It was still a mystery to him how Frieda could be so patient with the assistants. They had been supposed to be cleaning his clothes down in the yard, but after a long search she had found them sitting happily downstairs at their midday meal, the clothes bundled together on their laps. She had had to clean them all herself, and yet, although she was used to giving orders to menials, she did not scold them, but told him, and in their presence too, of their shocking negligence as if it were a little joke, and even tapped one of them lightly, almost flatteringly, on the cheek. K. would reprove her for that in the near future, he thought, but now it was high time to leave. 'The assistants can stay here and help you with moving our things,' said K. to Frieda. But they were not happy with that; cheerful and well fed as they were, they liked the idea of a little exercise. Only when Frieda said: 'That's right, you stay here,' did they agree. 'Do you know where I'm going now?' asked K. 'Yes,' said Frieda. 'And you're not trying to stop me any more?' asked K. 'You'll find so many obstacles in your way,' said she, 'what would anything I say mean?' She kissed K. goodbye, gave him a package of bread and sausage that she had brought up for him, since he had had no lunch, reminded him that he was to go to the school later and not come back here, and with her hand on his shoulder went down to the front door with him.

8

Waiting for Klamm

AT first K. was glad to have escaped the warm room, crowded as it was with the maids and the assistants. It was freezing a little outside, the snow was firmer and walking easier. However, it was beginning to grow dark, so he quickened his pace.

The castle, its outline already beginning to blur, lay as still as always. K. had never seen the slightest sign of life there. Perhaps it wasn't possible to make anything out from this distance, yet his eyes kept trying and wouldn't accept that it could lie so still. When K. looked at the castle he sometimes thought he saw someone sitting quietly there, looking into space, not lost in thought and thus cut off from everything else, but free and at ease, as if he were alone and no one was observing him. He must notice that he himself was under observation, but that didn't disturb him in the slightest, and indeed—it was hard to tell whether this was cause or effect—the observer's eyes could find nothing to fasten on, and slipped away from the figure. This impression was reinforced today by the early coming of darkness. The longer he looked, the less he could make out, and the further everything receded into the twilight.

Just as K. reached the Castle Inn, which still had no lights on, a window on the first floor opened, a stout, clean-shaven young gentleman in a fur coat leaned out and stayed where he was at the window, appearing not to respond to K., who hailed him, with even the slightest nod of his head. K. met no one in either the entrance hall or the bar, where the smell of stale beer was even stronger than before. That sort of thing didn't happen at the Bridge Inn. K. immediately went to the door through which he had seen Klamm last time he was here and carefully pressed the handle down, but the door was locked. Then he tried feeling about for the peephole, but presumably the catch over it was so well fitted that he couldn't find it by touch, and so he struck a match. Then he was alarmed by a cry. A young girl was sitting huddled by the stove in the corner between the door and the sideboard, staring at him as the match flared up and struggling to open her drowsy eyes properly. This was obviously Frieda's successor.

She soon pulled herself together and turned on the electric light, the expression on her face still unfriendly, but then she recognized K. 'Ah, it's you, Mr Land Surveyor,' she said with a smile, and offered him her hand, introducing herself: 'My name is Pepi.'* She was small, red-cheeked, and healthy in appearance, her profuse sandy hair was plaited into a big braid, and curls had escaped it to surround her face. She wore a dress that didn't suit her at all, made of some shiny grey fabric, falling straight but drawn together at the hem with childish clumsiness by a silk ribbon tied in a bow, which kept her from moving freely. She asked how Frieda was, and whether she wasn't going to come back here soon. There was almost a touch of malice in her question. 'I was sent for in a hurry as soon as Frieda had left,' she added, 'because they can't have just any girl working here. I've been a chambermaid until now, and I can't say I've done well out of my change of job. There's a lot of work here in the evenings and at night, which is very tiring, I'll hardly be able to stand it, and I don't wonder that Frieda gave it up.' 'Frieda was very well satisfied with the job here,' said K., to make Pepi aware of the difference between her and Frieda, which she seemed to ignore. 'Don't you believe her,' said Pepi. 'Frieda can control herself better than most people. What she doesn't want to admit she won't admit, so that you don't even notice she has something to admit. I've been working here with her for several years, we always shared a bed, but I can't say I was close friends with her, and I'm sure she doesn't give me a thought any more. Her one woman friend, maybe, is the old landlady of the Bridge Inn, which is typical of her.' 'Frieda is my fiancée,' said K., looking for the peephole in the door as he spoke. 'I know,' said Pepi, 'that's why I'm telling you. If she wasn't your fiancée, then it wouldn't be of any importance to you.' 'I understand,' said K. 'You mean I can be proud of having won myself such a reserved girl.' 'Yes,' she said, and laughed, sounding pleased, as if she had induced K. to come to some secret understanding with her about Frieda.

But it wasn't really anything she said that occupied K.'s mind and distracted him a little from what he was looking for; it was her appearance and her presence here. To be sure, she was much younger than Frieda, almost a child still, and her clothes were ridiculous; she had obviously dressed in line with her own ideas of a barmaid's importance. And in her way she was right, since the position, for which she wasn't yet in the least suited, had presumably come to her unexpectedly, undeserved, and only on a trial basis. Even the little leather bag that Frieda always used to carry at her belt had not been entrusted to her. As for her alleged dissatisfaction with the job, she was simply showing off. Yet in spite of her childlike foolishness, she too probably had connections with the castle. If she wasn't lying, she had been a chambermaid, she slept away the days here without knowing the value of what she had, and if he embraced her small, plump, rather round-shouldered body he couldn't deprive her of that, but proximity to it might encourage him for the difficult task ahead. Then perhaps she was not so very different from Frieda after all? Oh yes, she was. He had only to think of Frieda's glance to be sure of that. No, K. would never have touched Pepi. Yet he had to cover his eyes for a while, he was looking at her so avidly.

'We don't need the light on,' said Pepi, turning it off again. 'I only turned it on because you gave me such a fright. What do you want here, anyway? Has Frieda left something behind?' 'Yes,' said K., pointing to the door. 'Here, in the next room, a tablecloth, a white crochet-work cloth.' 'Oh yes, that's right, her tablecloth,' said Pepi. 'I remember, a fine piece of work, I helped her with it, but it's not in that room.' 'Frieda thinks it is. Who's staying in there?' asked K. 'No one,' said Pepi, 'it's the gentlemen's dining-room, it's where they eat and drink, or rather it's meant for that, but most of the gentlemen stay up in their own rooms.' 'If I could be sure', said K., 'that there was no one in the room next door just now, I'd really like to go in and look for that tablecloth. But I can't be sure, can I? Klamm for one often sits in that room.' 'Klamm certainly isn't there now,' said Pepi. 'He's just going out. The sleigh is waiting for him in the yard.'

K. left the bar immediately, without a word of explanation, and in the entrance hall turned not to the way out but to the interior of the house. A few more steps brought him to the yard. How quiet and beautiful it was here! The yard was rectangular, enclosed on three sides by the inn building and on the other side, where the road lay—a side-street that K. didn't know—by a high white wall. A large, heavy gate in the wall now stood open. Seen from here, the inn looked higher on the side facing the yard than in front, or at least the first floor was greatly extended and seemed larger, for it had a wooden gallery running around it, closed except for a small gap at eye level. Diagonally opposite K., in the central part of the building but at the corner where the side wing adjoined it, there was an open way into the house without any door. In front of it stood a dark, closed sleigh with two horses harnessed to it. There was no one in sight but the driver, whose presence at this distance and in the dark K. guessed at rather than actually seeing him.

Hands in his pockets, looking cautiously around him, and keeping close to the wall, K. skirted two sides of the yard until he had reached the sleigh. The driver, one of those rustics who had been in the bar the other day, was sitting there wrapped in furs and had watched him approaching without interest, much as your eyes might idly follow a cat prowling along. When K. had reached him and said good evening, and even the horses became a little uneasy at the sight of a man emerging from the darkness, he still showed no interest at all. K. welcomed that. Leaning against the wall, he unpacked his sandwich, thought gratefully of Frieda who had provided for him so well, and as he did so peered inside the house. A staircase turning at right angles led up, and a low-ceilinged but apparently long passage crossed it at the bottom of the stairs. Everything was clean, white-washed, neatly delineated.

The wait was longer than K. had expected. He had finished his sandwich long ago, the cold was biting, the twilight had become full darkness, and still there was no sign of Klamm. 'Could be a long time yet,' said a hoarse voice suddenly, so close to K. that he jumped. It was the driver, stretching and yawning loudly as if he had just woken up. 'What could be a long time yet?' asked K., not displeased by the interruption, for the continuing silence and suspense had become oppressive. 'Could be a long time before you leave,' said the driver. K. didn't understand him, but asked no further questions, thinking that was the best way to get this unsociable man talking. Here in the darkness, returning no answer was almost provocative. And indeed, after a while the driver asked him: 'Like a cognac?' 'Yes,' said K., without stopping to think and much tempted by the offer, because he was shivering with cold. 'Open up the sleigh door, then,' said the driver. 'There are several bottles in the side pocket. Take one out, have a drink, and then hand it to me. It's too difficult for me to climb down myself wearing this fur.' K. did not much care for lending a hand in this way, but he had let himself in for conversation with the driver, so he complied, even at the risk of being found by Klamm beside the sleigh. He opened the big door and could have taken the bottle straight out of the pocket fitted inside it, but now that the door was open he felt an irresistible urge to get into the sleigh; he would sit there just for a moment. He quickly climbed in. The warmth inside the sleigh was extraordinary, and it stayed warm even though the door, which K. dared not close, was wide open. You didn't know if you were sitting on a seat or not as you half-lay there so comfortably among rugs, cushions, and furs; you could turn and stretch on all sides, and everywhere you sank into the soft warmth. Arms outstretched, head supported on the cushions ready in place for it, K. looked out of the sleigh at the dark building. Why was it taking Klamm so long to come down? As if numbed by the warmth after standing in the snow for so long, K. wished that Klamm really would arrive at last. The idea that it would be better not to be found by Klamm in his present position did occur to him, but not very clearly, just as a faint anxiety. He was encouraged in this oblivious state by the behaviour of the driver, who must know that he was inside the sleigh and was letting him stay there without even demanding the cognac. That was considerate of him, but K. wanted to do the man some little service, so moving slowly and without changing his position he reached for the side pocket, but not the one in the open door, which was too far away; instead he reached for the closed door behind him, and it came to the same thing, for there were bottles in the side pocket there too. He took one out, unscrewed the top, and sniffed it. Instinctively he smiled; the smell was as sweet and delightful as hearing praise and kind words from someone you love, and you don't know why, nor do you want to know, you are just happy to hear the beloved person uttering them. Can this really be cognac? K. wondered, tasting it out of curiosity. Yes, it was cognac, remarkably enough, burning and warming him. But as he drank it, it turned from something that was little more than the vehicle of sweet perfumes into a drink more suitable for a driver. Is it possible? K. wondered again, as if reproving himself, and he drank once more.

Then—K. was just in the middle of taking a long draught—it was suddenly bright, electric light had been switched on indoors on the staircase, in the corridor, in the entrance hall, and outside above the entrance itself. Steps were heard coming downstairs, the bottle dropped from K.'s hand, cognac was spilt over a fur, and K. jumped out of the sleigh. He just had time to close the door, which made a loud bang, and next moment a gentleman came slowly out of the building.

The one consolation seemed to be that it wasn't Klamm—or was that in fact to be regretted? It was the gentleman whom K. had already seen at the first-floor window. A young gentleman, very good-looking, with a pink-and-white complexion, but extremely grave. K. looked at him gloomily, but the gloom was on his own behalf. If only he had sent his assistants here instead; they too might have behaved as he had. Facing him, the gentleman remained silent, as if there wasn't enough breath in his broad barrel of a chest for what had to be said. 'This is terrible,' he remarked at last, pushing his hat a little way back from his forehead. What was this? It wasn't likely that the gentleman knew K. had been in the sleigh, but he thought something or other was terrible. Perhaps it was K.'s making his way into the yard? 'How do you come to be here?' asked the gentleman in a softer voice, breathing out with a sigh of resignation. What questions! What answers! Was K. to speak up himself and expressly confirm to this gentleman that the errand on which he had set out so full of hope had been for nothing? Instead of replying, K. turned to the sleigh, opened it, and retrieved his cap, which he had left inside. He noticed, to his chagrin, that cognac was dripping over the running-board.

Then he turned back to the gentleman; he had no scruples now about showing that he had been in the sleigh. After all, it wasn't the end of the world. If he were asked, but only then, he would not conceal the fact that the driver himself had at least encouraged him to open the sleigh door. The worst of it, however, was that the gentleman had taken him by surprise and there hadn't been time to hide from him so that he could go on waiting for Klamm undisturbed, or that he hadn't had the presence of mind to stay in the sleigh, close the door, and wait for Klamm lying on the furs there, or at least stay in it until this gentleman was close. Of course, he couldn't know whether Klamm himself might not now turn up, in which case it would naturally have been much better to encounter him outside the sleigh. Yes, there was a good deal to think about in all this, but not now, for this particular venture of his was over.

'Come with me,' said the gentleman, not really in a commanding tone; the sense of command lay not in his words but in the brief and intentionally indifferent gesture that accompanied them. 'I'm waiting for someone,' said K., just on principle rather than hoping for any success now. 'Come with me,' repeated the gentleman, undeterred, as if to show he had never doubted that K. was waiting for someone. 'But then I'll miss the man I'm waiting for,' said K., shrugging. In spite of what had happened, he felt that something had so far been gained, something that he only apparently possessed, to be sure, but he didn't have to give up at anyone's request. 'Go or stay, you'll miss him anyway,' said the gentleman, giving his opinion rather brusquely, but showing striking forbearance for K.'s train of thought. 'Then I'd rather wait here and miss him,' said K. defiantly. He wasn't going to be driven from this place by mere words from this young gentleman. Thereupon the gentleman, with an expression of superiority on his face, closed his eyes for a while as he put his head back, as if returning from K.'s foolishness to his own good sense, ran the tip of the tongue over his lips with his mouth slightly open, and then told the driver: 'Unharness the horses.'

The driver, obeying the gentleman but giving K. a nasty look, had to climb down in his heavy fur, and very hesitantly, as if expecting not a change of orders from his master but a change of mind on K.'s part, he began leading the horses and the sleigh backwards, closer to the side wing where the stables and carriage-house obviously lay behind a large gate. K. found himself left alone; on one side the sleigh was moving away and so, on the other side, was the young man, going back the way that K. had come, although they both went very slowly, as if to show K. that it was still in his power to fetch them back.

Perhaps he did have that power, but it would have been no use to him; fetching the sleigh back meant banishment for himself. So he stayed put, the only claimant to occupation of this place still left here, but it was a joyless victory. He looked alternately at the gentleman and the driver as they went away. The gentleman had already reached the door through which K. had entered the yard in the first place, and he glanced back once more. K. thought he saw him shake his head at such obstinacy. Then he turned away with a last brief and determined movement and stepped into the entrance hall, disappearing at once. The driver stayed in the yard a little longer; he had a lot of work to do with the sleigh. He had to open the heavy gate to the stable, get the sleigh backwards through it to its proper place, unharness the horses and lead them to their manger, and he did all this very gravely, entirely absorbed in himself, since he had no prospect now of driving away soon. All this busy, silent activity, done without so much as a look askance at K., seemed to K. himself far more of a reproach than the gentleman's behaviour. And when, having finished his work in the stables, the driver crossed the yard with his slow, swaying gait, opened the big gate, then came back, all the time moving with slow formality and keeping his eyes bent on his own tracks in the snow, shut himself into the stable, and put out all the electric lights—why would they be left on for anyone now?—and the only remaining light came through the gap in the wooden gallery above, catching the wandering eye for a moment, it seemed to K. as if all contact with him had been cut, and he was more of a free agent than ever. He could wait here, in a place usually forbidden to him, as long as he liked, and he also felt as if he had won that freedom with more effort than most people could manage to make, and no one could touch him or drive him away, why, they hardly had a right even to address him. But at the same time—and this feeling was at least as strong—he felt as if there were nothing more meaningless and more desperate than this freedom, this waiting, this invulnerability.

9

Opposition to Questioning

HE tore himself away and went back into the building, not along the wall this time, but through the middle of the snow. In the entrance hall he met the landlord, who greeted him in silence and pointed to the door of the bar, and followed the direction in which he was pointed, because he was freezing and wanted to see other human beings; but he was very disappointed when he saw the young gentleman sitting at a little table which had probably been put there specially for him, because usually casks were used for seating. In front of the gentleman—a sight that dismayed K.—stood the landlady of the Bridge Inn. Pepi, looking proud with her head thrown back, her smile always the same and standing very much on her dignity, her braid shaking whenever she turned, was hurrying back and forth bringing beer and then pen and ink, for the gentleman had spread papers out in front of him, was comparing what he found now in one of them, then in another at the far end of the table, and then he set about writing. Looking down from her full height, and with her lips slightly pursed as if at rest, the landlady was keeping an eye on the gentleman and his papers, as if she had already said all she needed to say, and it had been well received. 'Ah, Mr Land Surveyor,' said the gentleman, looking up for a moment when K. came in, and then he immersed himself in his papers again. The landlady too just glanced at K. with an indifferent expression, showing no surprise at all. However, Pepi seemed to notice K. only when he stepped up to the bar counter and ordered a cognac.

K. leaned on the counter, put his hand to his eyes, and took no more notice of anything. Then he sipped the cognac, and pushed it away; it was undrinkable. 'All the gentlemen drink it,' said Pepi briefly, poured the rest away, washed the little glass, and put it back in the cupboard. 'The gentlemen must have better cognac too,' said K. 'Maybe,' said Pepi, 'but I don't.' K. had no answer to that, and she went back to serving the young gentleman, but he needed nothing. She could only keep walking up and down behind him, respectfully trying to catch a glimpse of the papers over his shoulders, but it was just silly curiosity and showing off, and the landlady expressed her disapproval by frowning.

Suddenly, however, the landlady pricked up her ears and stared into space, listening with great concentration. K. turned. He could hear nothing special, and no one else seemed to either, but the landlady, striding out on tiptoe, went to the door at the back leading into the yard, looked through the keyhole, then turned to the others with her eyes wide and her face flushed, crooked a finger, and beckoned them over. Now they too looked through the keyhole in turn, although the landlady still had the lion's share. But Pepi too had a turn; the gentleman, relatively speaking, was the least interested. Pepi and the gentleman soon came back, only the landlady kept looking, bending low, practically kneeling, you almost felt as if she were adjuring the keyhole to let her through, for there could be nothing left to see any more. When she finally straightened up, passed her hands over her face, tidied her hair and took a deep breath, apparently obliged to accustom her eyes to the room and the people here again and reluctant to do so, K. asked: 'Has Klamm left, then?' He said it not to have what he already knew confirmed but to anticipate an attack, for he rather feared he was vulnerable now. The landlady walked past him in silence, but the gentleman said, from his little table: 'Yes, to be sure. Once you had left the place where you were standing guard, Klamm was able to go out. But it's amazing what a sensitive gentleman he is. Did you notice, ma'am,' he asked the landlady, 'how nervously Klamm looked around?' The landlady did not seem to have noticed, but the gentleman went on: 'Well, luckily there was nothing left to be seen. The driver had covered up the tracks in the snow.' 'The landlady here didn't notice anything,' said K., but not hopefully, only annoyed by the gentleman's remark, which was meant to sound so final and conclusive. 'Perhaps I wasn't at the keyhole just then,' said the landlady at first, showing that she was on the gentleman's side, but she wanted to do Klamm justice too, and added: 'Although I don't believe Klamm is so very sensitive. We are anxious about him, to be sure, we try to protect him, so we start by assuming Klamm's extreme sensitivity. That is good, and certainly what Klamm wants. But how matters really are we don't know. To be sure, Klamm will never speak to someone he doesn't want to speak to, however much trouble that person may take and however insufferably intrusive he is, but the mere fact that Klamm will never speak to him or give him an interview is enough. And why shouldn't he be able to stand the sight of someone? Well, that can't be proved, for it will never be put to the test.' The gentleman nodded eagerly. 'Of course, in principle that's my own opinion,' he said. 'If I didn't put it quite like that, it was so that the land surveyor here would understand me. It's a fact, however, that when Klamm stepped out of doors he turned in a semicircle several times, looking around him.' 'Perhaps he was looking for me,' said K. 'Possibly,' said the gentleman, 'but somehow I never hit upon that idea.' Everyone laughed, Pepi loudest of all, although she understood hardly any of what was going on.

'As we are all so merry together now,' said the gentleman, 'I would like to ask you, Mr Land Surveyor, to help me complete my files by giving me some facts.' 'There's been a lot of writing here,' said K., looking at the files from a distance. 'Yes, a bad habit,' said the gentleman, laughing again. 'But perhaps you don't yet know who I am. I am Momus,* Klamm's village secretary.' At these words the whole room turned very serious; although the landlady and Pepi of course knew the gentleman well, they were still impressed by the mention of his name and dignified office. And the gentleman buried himself in the files and began writing, as if he had said too much even for himself to take in and wanted to avoid any extra solemnity implied by his words, so there was nothing to be heard in the room but the scratching of his pen. 'What does village secretary mean?' K. asked after a while. Speaking for Momus, who didn't think it appropriate to give such explanations after introducing himself, the landlady said: 'Mr Momus is a secretary to Klamm like any of Klamm's other secretaries, but his office, and if I am not wrong also his official sphere of influence—' here Momus shook his head vigorously as he wrote, and the landlady corrected herself—'well, only his office and not his official sphere of influence is restricted to the village. Mr Momus deals with all Klamm's written work that may be necessary in the village, and is the first to receive all petitions to Klamm coming from the village.' And as K., still not much impressed by all this, looked blankly at the landlady, she added, almost awkwardly: 'That's the way it's organized; all the gentlemen from the castle have their village secretaries.' Momus, who in fact had been listening much more attentively than K., added, to the landlady: 'Most of the village secretaries work only for one master, but I work for two,

Klamm and Vallabene.' 'Yes,' said the landlady now, also remembering, and turned to K. 'Mr Momus works for two masters, for Klamm
and for Vallabene, so he is village secretary twice over.' 'Twice
over—fancy that,' said K., nodding as you might nod to a child
whom you have just heard praised and addressing Momus, who now,
leaning forward, looked up at him. If there was a certain disdain in
that nod, it either went unnoticed or actually seemed requisite. The
merits of a man from Klamm's close circle were being presented at
length to K. of all people, deemed unworthy even to have Klamm set
eyes on him by chance, and it was done with the unconcealed intention of demanding K.'s recognition and praise. Yet K. was not in the
mood for it; having tried with all his might to get a glimpse of
Klamm, he did not rate the position of a man like Momus who could
always see Klamm particularly highly, and admiration, even envy,
were far from his mind. Klamm's proximity in itself was not so very
much worth striving for; the point was that he, K., he alone and no
one else, was trying to get to Klamm with his own requests, not for
the sake of lingering with him but in order to get past him and go on
into the castle.

So he looked at his watch and said: 'Well, I must be going home
now.' Immediately the footing they were on changed in favour of
Momus. 'Yes, indeed,' he said. 'Your duties as school janitor call
you. But you must give me a moment longer. Just a few brief questions.' 'I don't feel like it,' said K., moving towards the door. Momus
slammed a file down on the table and stood up. 'In Klamm's name,
I command you to answer my questions.' 'In Klamm's name?'
repeated K. 'Why, is he interested in my affairs, then?' 'On that
point,' said Momus, 'I have no authority to judge, and I suppose you
have much less. We will both of us leave that to him. However, I command you, in the position entrusted to me by Klamm, to stay here
and answer me.' 'Mr Land Surveyor,' said the landlady, joining in,
'I won't advise you any further. You have rejected my advice so far,
the best-meant advice that could ever be given, in the most outrageous manner, and I came here to see this gentleman, Mr Secretary
Momus—I have nothing to hide—only to inform his office in a
fitting manner of your conduct and your intentions, and to protect
myself forever from any possibility of your being lodged with me
again. That's how matters stand between us, and nothing about it
will change now. If I tell you my opinion at this point, it is not to help

you but to give Mr Secretary Momus here some slight assistance in the onerous task of dealing with a man like you. All the same, on account of my total candour—and I cannot be other than candid with you, reluctant as I am to talk to you at all—all the same, you may derive some benefit from my remarks if you like. I will therefore point out that the only way leading you to Klamm will be through Secretary Momus's records here. However, I don't want to exaggerate; perhaps the path does not lead to Klamm at all, perhaps it will come to an end long before reaching him, it all depends on the good-will of Mr Secretary Momus. But in any case it's the only way leading in the direction of Klamm, for you at least. And are you going to refrain from taking that one and only path solely out of defiance?' 'Oh, madam,' said K., 'it is not the only way to Klamm, nor is it worth more than any other. So do you, Mr Secretary, decide whether what I choose to say here may come to Klamm's ears or not?' 'Yes, indeed I do,' said Momus, lowering his eyes proudly and looking to left and to right, where there was nothing to be seen. 'Why else would I be his secretary?' 'There, you see, madam,' said K. 'I don't need a way to Klamm, only to Mr Secretary Momus.' 'I was going to open that way up for you,' said the landlady. 'Didn't I offer, yesterday afternoon, to see that your request reached Klamm? That would have been done through Mr Momus. But you turned my offer down, and yet there won't be any other way for you, only that one. To be sure, after your performance today, after your attempt to accost Klamm, you'll have even less chance of success. But this last small, vanishingly small, almost non-existent hope is the only hope you have.' 'How is it, madam,' said K., 'that at first you tried so hard to keep me away from Klamm, and now you take my request seriously, and seem to consider me lost, so to speak, if my plans fail? If you could once advise me not to try seeing Klamm at all, and do so honestly, how can you now, and equally honestly, positively urge me forward on the path to Klamm, even if admittedly it may not lead to him?' 'Urge you forward?' said the landlady. 'Is it urging you forward if I say that your attempts are hopeless? How brazen you would be to go palming off the responsibility on me like that! Is it by any chance the presence of Mr Secretary Momus that makes you want to do it? No, Mr Land Surveyor, I am not urging you to do anything. I can confess to only one thing, that when I first saw you I may have overestimated you a little. Your swift conquest of Frieda alarmed me; I didn't know what else you might be capable of. I wanted to prevent further harm, and thought the only way to do it was for me to try deterring you by dint of requests and threats. But now I have learned to think about the whole affair more calmly. You may do as you wish. Perhaps you may leave deep footprints in the snow out in the yard, but that will be the only result of your actions.' 'The contradiction doesn't seem to me entirely explained,' said K., 'but I will be satisfied with having pointed it out to you. However, now, Mr Secretary, I'll ask you to tell me whether the landlady is right, I mean in saying that the records you want me to help you complete could result in my getting an interview with Klamm. If that is the case, then I'm prepared to answer all your questions at once. Yes, if it comes down to that I am ready for anything.' 'No,' said Momus, 'there's no such connection. My business is only to get a precise account of this afternoon's events down on paper for Klamm's village registry. The account is drawn up already, there are just two or three gaps I want you to fill in to make sure it's all in order. There is no other purpose, nor can any other purpose be achieved.' K. looked at the landlady in silence. 'Why are you looking at me?' asked the landlady. 'Isn't that what I said myself? He's always like that, Mr Secretary, he's always like that. Falsifies the information he's given, and then claims to have been wrongly informed. I've been telling him forever, I tell him today and I always will, that he hasn't the slightest prospect of an interview with Klamm, and if there isn't any prospect of it then he won't get one through your records. Can anything be clearer? What's more, let me say that those records are the only real official connection he can have with Klamm. That's clear enough too, it's beyond all doubt. But if he doesn't believe me and goes on and on hoping, don't ask me why, that he will be able to see Klamm, then in view of the way his mind works nothing can help him but that one and only real official connection with Klamm, namely these records. That's all I said, and anyone who claims anything different is maliciously distorting my words.' 'If that's the case, madam,' said K., 'then I must apologize to you, and I've misunderstood you, for I thought, mistakenly as it now turns out, I had gathered from your earlier remarks that there was in fact some kind of hope for me, however small.' 'Exactly,' said the landlady, 'just as I was saying. You're twisting my words again, only this time in the opposite direction. In my view such a hope for you does exist, and it is indeed to be found solely in these records. But it is not the case that you can simply ask Mr Secretary Momus aggressively: "If I answer your questions, can I see Klamm?" If a child says something like that we laugh at it; if an adult does so, it is an insult to Klamm's office, and the secretary kindly covered up for the insult with the elegance of his reply. However, the hope I mean lies in the fact that through the records you have, or perhaps you may have, a kind of connection with Klamm. Isn't that hope enough? If you were asked what merits you possess to make you worthy of the gift of such a hope, could you come up with the slightest thing? To be sure, nothing more precise can be said about that hope, and Mr Secretary Momus in particular will never be able to give the faintest hint of such a thing in his official capacity. For him, as he said, it is merely a matter of an account of this afternoon, to make sure that everything's in order, and he will say no more even if you ask him here and now about it with reference to my remarks.' 'Very well, Mr Secretary,' said K., 'will Klamm read these records?' 'No,' said Momus, 'why would he? Klamm can't read all the records, in fact he never reads any of them. "Oh, don't come pestering me with your records!" he often says.' 'Mr Land Surveyor,' wailed the landlady, 'you really are exhausting me with such questions. Is it necessary, is it even desirable, for Klamm to read the records and have a word-by-word account of the petty details of your life? Would you not rather beg humbly for the records to be kept from Klamm, although that request would be as unreasonable as the first, for who can keep anything from Klamm, but at least it would be evidence of a change of heart in you? And is it necessary for what you call your hope? Haven't you said yourself that you would be happy if you just had a chance to speak in front of Klamm, even if he didn't look at you or listen to you? And will you not at least achieve that through these records, and perhaps much more?' 'Much more?' asked K. 'How?' 'If only', cried the landlady, 'you weren't forever wanting to have everything presented to you ready on a plate, like a child! Who can answer such questions? The records go into Klamm's village registry, as you've heard, no more can be said about the matter for certain. I mean, do you know the whole significance of the records, of Mr Secretary Momus, of the village registry? Do you know what it means for Mr Secretary Momus to question you? It's possible, even probable, that he doesn't know himself. He sits quietly here doing his duty to make sure, as he said, that everything is in order. You should remember that Klamm has appointed him, that he works in Klamm's name, that what he does, even if it never reaches Klamm, is approved by Klamm from the first. And how can something be approved by Klamm from the first if it isn't imbued with his own spirit? Far be it from me to offer Mr Secretary Momus blatant flattery, he himself would deplore it, I am not talking of his individual personality but of what he is when acting with Klamm's approval, as he is now. He is a tool in Klamm's hand, and if someone won't do as he wants, well, that's just too bad.'

K. was not afraid of the landlady's threats, and he was tired of the hopes in which she was trying to entangle him. Klamm was far away; the landlady had once compared Klamm to an eagle, which had struck K. as ridiculous at the time, but not any more; he thought of Klamm's remote distance, his impregnable residence, his silence, perhaps interrupted only by such screams as K. had never heard. He thought of Klamm's piercing glance from on high that would brook no contradiction and couldn't be tested either, of the immutable circles in which he soared, free from any interference by the likes of K. down below, moving by inscrutable laws and visible only for brief moments—Klamm and the eagle had all this in common. It was a fact, however, that the records over which Momus was crumbling a salted pretzel at this moment had nothing to do with any of this. He was enjoying the pretzel with his beer, scattering salt and crumbs all over the papers.

'Well, good night,' said K. 'I have a rooted dislike of any kind of questioning.' And he was on his way to the door. 'Is he going, then?' Momus asked the landlady, almost anxiously. 'He'll never dare,' said the landlady. But K. heard no more; he was already out in the entrance hall. It was cold, and there was a strong wind blowing. The landlord, who seemed to have been keeping watch on the hall through some peephole, came through a doorway. Even here in the front hall the wind was tearing so hard at his coat-tails that he had to clutch them tightly around him. 'So you're off already, Mr Land Surveyor?' he said. 'Are you surprised?' asked K. 'Well, yes,' said the landlord. 'Haven't you been questioned?' 'No,' said K. 'I wasn't letting anyone question me.' 'Why not?' asked the landlord. 'I really don't know why I should let myself be questioned,' said K., 'why I should go along with a joke or some official whim. And perhaps I'd have dismissed it as just a joke or a whim another time, but not today.'

'Why no, to be sure,' said the landlord, but he was agreeing only out of civility, not from conviction. 'Well, I must let the servants into the bar now,' he added. 'They were supposed to start serving there long ago, I just didn't want to disturb the hearing.' 'You thought it so important?' asked K. 'Oh yes,' said the landlord. 'Then you think I ought not to have refused to answer questions?' asked K. 'No,' said the landlord, 'you ought not.' And as K. said nothing, he added, whether to console K. or to get on with the work in the bar more quickly: 'Well, well, that doesn't mean we'll necessarily see fire and brimstone* raining down from the sky.' 'No, to be sure,' K. agreed. 'The weather doesn't look like that at all.' And they parted, laughing.

10

On the Road

K. WENT out on the steps up to the inn, where the wind was blowing wildly, and peered into the darkness. It was appalling weather. The thought of that somehow made him remember how hard the land-lady had tried to make him comply and help to complete the records, and how he had stood up to her. She hadn't, of course, been making an honest effort; secretly she had been dissuading him at the same time, so after all he didn't really know whether he had stood firm or given in. Hers was a nature made for intrigue, apparently working for no purpose, like the wind, according to strange and distant orders of which no one ever got a sight.

No sooner had he taken a few steps along the road than he saw two lights swaying in the distance. This sign of life cheered him, and he hurried towards the lights, which themselves were moving towards him. He didn't know why he was so disappointed when he recognized the assistants; however, there they were coming his way, probably sent by Frieda, and he supposed the lanterns that freed him from the darkness in which the wind roared all around him were his own property. All the same, he was disappointed, for he had expected someone new, not these old acquaintances who were such a nuisance to him. But the assistants were not on their own; walking between them, Barnabas emerged from the darkness. 'Barnabas,' cried K., offering his hand. 'Were you coming to find me?' The surprise of this meeting at first made K. forget all the trouble that Barnabas had caused him. 'Yes, indeed I was coming to find you,' said Barnabas, with his old friendly manner, 'with a letter from Klamm.' 'A letter from Klamm!' said K., putting his head back and taking it swiftly from Barnabas's hand. 'Give me some light!' he told the assistants, who came close to him on his right and left and raised their lanterns. K. had to fold the large sheet of notepaper very small to protect it from the wind. Then he read: 'To the Land Surveyor at the Bridge Inn. I appreciate the surveys you have carried out so far. The work of your assistants is praiseworthy too; you know how to keep them busy. Do not desist from your zealous labours! Bring the work to a happy conclusion! Any interruption would be irksome to me. Furthermore, rest assured that the matter of your remuneration will be decided very soon. I am keeping an eye on you.' K. did not look up from the letter until the assistants, who had been reading much more slowly than he did, gave three loud cheers to celebrate the good news. 'Calm down,' he told them, and added, to Barnabas: 'This is a misunderstanding.' Barnabas didn't know what he meant. 'It's a misunderstanding,' repeated K., and all this afternoon's weariness came back to him. The way to the schoolhouse seemed so long, Barnabas's whole family loomed in the background, and the assistants were still crowding K. so close that he elbowed them out of the way. How could Frieda have sent them to meet him when he had ordered them to stay with her? He would have found the way home by himself, and more easily than in this company. What was more, one of the assistants had wound a scarf around his neck, its free ends were fluttering in the wind and had blown into K.'s face several times. The other assistant kept removing the scarf from K.'s face at once with his long, pointed, nimble fingers, but that did nothing to improve matters. Both of them actually seemed to have enjoyed this going back and forth, and they were all worked up by the wind and the wild night. 'Go away!' shouted K. 'If you were going to come and meet me, why didn't you bring my stick? What am I going to use now to drive you home?' They ducked behind Barnabas, but they were not so frightened that they didn't first place their lanterns on their protector's shoulders to right and left. He shook them off at once. 'Barnabas,' said K., and it depressed him to see that Barnabas clearly didn't understand him, and that while at times of calm his jacket might look very smart there was no help to be found in him when matters were serious, only mute resistance, and there was no resisting that resistance either, for Barnabas himself was defenceless, only his smile shone, but that was as little help as the stars up there against the stormy wind down here below. 'See what the gentleman says to me,' said K., holding the letter in front of Barnabas's face. 'The gentleman has been misinformed. I have not carried out any surveys, and you can see for yourself what my assistants are worth. I clearly can't interrupt work that I am not doing, I can't even be irksome to the gentleman, so how could I have earned his appreciation? And I feel I can never rest assured of anything.' 'I'll go and pass that message on,' said Barnabas, who had been looking past the letter all this time.

He couldn't have read it anyway, for K. was holding it very close to his face. 'Oh yes?' said K. 'You promise to pass on what I tell you, but can I really believe you? I need a trustworthy messenger so much—now more than ever!' And K. bit his lip impatiently. 'Sir,' said Barnabas, bending his neck slightly in a way that almost tempted K. to believe in him again, 'sir, I will certainly pass on what you say, and I will certainly deliver that last message you gave me too.' 'What?' cried K. 'You mean you haven't delivered it yet? Didn't you go up to the castle next day?' 'No,' said Barnabas, 'my dear father is an old man, you've seen him yourself, and there was a lot of work at home, I had to help him, but I'll soon be going up to the castle again.' 'But what are you thinking of, you extraordinary fellow?' cried K., clapping a hand to his forehead. 'Doesn't Klamm's business come before everything else? You hold the high office of a messenger, and is this how you fill it? Who cares about your father's work? Klamm is waiting for news, and instead you prefer to muck out the stable!' 'My father is a shoemaker,' said Barnabas, undeterred. 'He had orders from Brunswick, and I'm my father's journeyman.' 'Shoemaker—orders—Brunswick,' cried K. grimly, as if conclusively dismissing each of those words for ever. 'So who here needs boots on roads that are always empty? And what do I care for all this stuff about shoemakers? I didn't give you a message to be consigned to oblivion and confusion on the shoemaker's bench, but so that you could deliver it to the gentleman straight away.' Here K. calmed down a little, for it occurred to him that all this time Klamm had probably not been in the castle but at the Castle Inn. However, Barnabas aroused his ire again when he began reciting K.'s first message to show how well he remembered it. 'All right, that'll do,' said K. 'Don't be angry, sir,' said Barnabas, and as if unconsciously he meant to punish K. he looked away from him and down, but it was probably in dismay at the way K. was shouting. 'I'm not angry with you,' said K., and indeed, now his anger was turned against himself. 'Not with you personally, but it's not a good thing for me to have no one but such a messenger for my important business.' 'Well, you see,' said Barnabas—and it appeared that in his anxiety to defend his honour as a messenger he was saying more than he ought to—'it's like this. Klamm doesn't wait for messages, in fact he's quite cross when I bring them. "More messages again," he says, and when he sees me coming in the distance he usually stands up, goes into the

next room, and won't receive me. And it's not a settled thing that I'm
to come at once with every message—if it was a settled thing of
course I'd go there at once, but it's not settled, and if I never came
with a message no one would remind me to. If I bring a message I do
it of my own free will.' 'Very well,' said K., observing Barnabas and
deliberately looking away from the assistants, who slowly took turns
to rise as if from the depths behind Barnabas's shoulders, and then
bob quickly down again with a slight whistle imitating the wind, as if
alarmed by the sight of K. They amused themselves like that for
some time. 'Very well, I don't know how Klamm may feel, but I
doubt whether you can know about everything up there in detail, and
even if you could there'd be nothing we could do to improve matters.
But you can carry a message, and that's what I ask you to do. A very
short message. Can you take it tomorrow, and bring me the answer
tomorrow too, or at least tell me how you were received? Can you
and will you do that? It would be of great value to me. And perhaps
I'll get a chance yet to thank you properly, or perhaps you already
have a wish that I can grant.' 'I will certainly take your message,' said
Barnabas. 'And will you try to carry it as well as possible, to give it
to Klamm himself, to get the answer from Klamm himself and do it
all tomorrow, tomorrow morning. Will you do that?' 'I'll do my
best,' said Barnabas. 'I always do.' 'Well, we won't quarrel about it
any more,' said K. 'This is the message: K. the land surveyor asks the
chief executive, Office X, to allow him to speak to him in person; he
undertakes from the outset to accept any condition attached to such
permission. He is forced to make this request because so far all inter-
mediaries have failed entirely, and as proof of this he would like to
mention that he has not yet carried out any surveys at all, and from
what the village mayor says he never will; it was therefore with
despair and shame that he read the last letter from the chief executive, and only a personal interview with the chief executive can
help him here. The land surveyor knows how much he is asking,
but he will do all he can to cause the chief executive as little trouble
as possible, he will agree to any restriction on the time of an interview, and if it is thought necessary he will agree to use only a set
number of words in it. He thinks he could manage with ten words.
With deep respect and the greatest impatience, he awaits the decision.' Forgetting himself, K. had spoken as if he were at Klamm's
own door and addressing the doorkeeper. 'Well, it came out a lot

longer than I meant,' he added, 'but you must carry it orally, I won't write a letter which would only set out on a never-ending journey into the files.' So K. scribbled it all on a piece of paper, for the benefit of Barnabas alone, leaning the paper on the back of one of the assistants, while the other held a light for him. However, K. was able to write it straight out as dictated back to him by Barnabas, who had remembered every word and recited it as meticulously as a schoolboy, taking no notice of the way the assistants were saying it all wrong. 'Your memory is remarkable,' said K., giving him the paper, 'so please show yourself remarkable in other respects too. And what about your own wishes? Don't you have any? I'll say frankly, it would reassure me a little about the fate of my message if you did want something'. At first Barnabas was silent, but then he said: 'My sisters send their regards.' 'Your sisters,' said K. 'Ah yes, those tall, strong girls.' 'They both send you their regards, but particularly Amalia,' said Barnabas. 'And she brought me this letter from the castle for you today too.' Seizing upon this piece of information above all, K. asked: 'Then couldn't she take my message to the castle as well? Or couldn't you both go and try your luck separately?' 'Amalia isn't allowed into the offices,' said Barnabas. 'Otherwise I'm sure she'd be happy to do it.' 'I may visit you tomorrow,' said K., 'but come to see me yourself first with the answer. I'll expect you at the school. And give my regards to your sisters too.' K.'s words seemed to make Barnabas very happy, and after they had shaken hands he touched K. briefly on the shoulder. As if everything was back the way it had been when Barnabas, in all his finery, first appeared among the locals in the bar of the inn, K. felt that this touch, although given with a smile, was a mark of distinction. He was less upset now, and let the assistants do as they liked on their way back.

11

At the School

HE reached home frozen. It was dark everywhere, the candles in the lanterns had burned down, and he made his way into one of the classrooms with the help of the assistants, who knew their way around the place—'Your first praiseworthy job done,' he told them, remembering Klamm's letter. Frieda, still half asleep, called from a corner of the room: 'Let K. sleep! Don't disturb him!' For K. occupied her mind even when she was so overcome by drowsiness that she hadn't been able to wait up for him. Now a lamp was lit, although it couldn't be turned up very far, for there was very little paraffin. Their new household still lacked a number of things. There was heating, but the large room, which was also used as the school gymnasium—the gymnastic apparatus stood around and hung from the ceiling—had already used up all the wood for the stove. K. was assured that it had been nice and warm, but unfortunately it had now cooled down again entirely. There was a large supply of wood in a shed, but the shed was locked and the teacher, who would allow firewood to be taken to heat the rooms only during school hours, had the key. They could have put up with that if there had been beds where they could take refuge. However, there was nothing but a single straw mattress, neatly covered with a woollen shawl of Frieda's in a way that did her credit, but there was no eiderdown, and just two stiff, coarse blankets that gave hardly any warmth. The assistants were looking covetously even at this wretched straw mattress, but of course they had no hope of ever lying on it. Frieda looked anxiously at K.; she had shown at the Bridge Inn that she could make even the most miserable room fit to live in, but she hadn't been able to do much here, entirely without any means. 'The gymnastic apparatus is all we have to decorate our room,' she said, trying to smile through her tears. As for what they needed most, beds to sleep in and fuel to heat the room, she promised K. that she would get something done about it next day, and asked him to wait patiently until then. Not a word, not a hint, not a look on her face suggested that she felt the slightest bitterness in her heart towards K., although as he couldn't help reflecting he had taken her away first from the Castle Inn and now from the Bridge Inn. So K. did his best to seem to find it all tolerable, which was not so hard for him, because in his mind he was with Barnabas, going over his message again word by word, although not exactly as he had given it to Barnabas but as he thought it would sound to Klamm. At the same time, however, he was really glad of the coffee that Frieda made him over a spirit-burner, and leaning against the stove, which was now cooling off, he watched her quick and expert movements as she spread the inevitable white tablecloth on the teacher's desk, which did duty as a table, put a flowered coffee cup on the cloth, and beside it some bread and bacon and even a can of sardines. Now everything was ready. Frieda hadn't eaten yet herself, but had waited for K.'s return. There were two chairs, which K. and Frieda drew up to the table, while the assistants sat on the podium at their feet, but they would never keep still, even when they were eating they were a nuisance. Although they had been served good helpings of everything, and hadn't nearly finished what was on their plates, they rose from time to time to see if there was still plenty left on the table so that they could hope for seconds. K. took no notice of them, and only Frieda's laughter drew his attention to them. He covered her hand on the table affectionately with his own, and asked quietly why she let them get away with so much, even putting up with their bad habits in a friendly way. This way, he pointed out, they would never be rid of the assistants, while a certain amount of stern treatment, such as their conduct deserved, might either enable him to keep them under control or, more probably and even better, make them dislike their position so much that in the end they would run away. The schoolhouse here didn't look like being a pleasant place to live in; well, their stay wouldn't be long, but if the assistants weren't around and the two of them were alone in this quiet house they would hardly mind what was missing. Didn't she notice, he asked, that the assistants were getting more impertinent every day, as if they were actually encouraged by Frieda's presence and the hope that K. would not attack them in front of her, as he otherwise would? What was more, there might be a perfectly simple means of getting rid of them at once, without much ceremony; perhaps Frieda, who knew this place so well, might even know of something. And they'd really be doing the assistants a favour if they drove them away somehow, for the life they were leading here was not very comfortable, and they'd have to give up, at least to some extent, the idleness they had enjoyed so long, because they would have to work, while Frieda must rest after all the upheavals of the last few days, and he, K., would be busy finding a way out of their present plight. However, if the assistants were to go, he said, he would feel so relieved that he would easily be able to take on the duties of a school janitor as well as everything else.

Frieda, who had listened attentively to him, slowly caressed his arm and said that all that was her own opinion too, but perhaps he made too much of the assistants' bad habits; they were young fellows, cheerful and a little simple, taken into a stranger's service for the first time, away from the stern discipline of the castle and so a little surprised and excited all the time, and in that frame of mind, yes, they did sometimes do silly things. Of course it was natural to get annoyed about that, but it would be more sensible to laugh. Sometimes she really couldn't help laughing at them herself. All the same, she entirely agreed with K., she said, that it would be better to send them away, and then there'd be just the two of them. She moved closer to K. and hid her face against his shoulder. And still in that position, she said in a voice so muffled that K. had to bend down to hear her, that no, she didn't know any means of getting rid of the assistants, and she was afraid that none of the ideas K. had suggested would work. As far as she knew, she said, K. himself had asked for his assistants, and now he had them and would have to keep them. It would be a good idea simply to accept them as the lightweight couple they were, that was the best way to put up with them, she said.

K. was not happy with this reply. Half in earnest, half joking, he said that she seemed to be in league with them, or at least to like them very much; well, they were good-looking young fellows, but there was no one you couldn't get rid of if you really put your mind to it, and so he would show her with the assistants.

Frieda said she would be very grateful to him if he succeeded, and promised that from now on she wouldn't laugh at them or say an unnecessary word to them any more. She didn't think there was anything to laugh at in them now, and it was really no joke to be under observation all the time by two men; yes, she said, she had learned to see the pair of them through his eyes. And she did jump slightly when the assistants rose again now, partly to see how much food was left, partly to discover what all this whispering was about.

K. took advantage of this to take Frieda's mind off the assistants; he drew her to him, and they finished their meal sitting close together. It was really time to go to sleep now, and they were all very tired; one of the assistants had actually fallen asleep over his supper, which amused the other very much, and he kept trying to make his master and mistress look at the sleeping man's stupid face, but he didn't succeed, for K. and Frieda were sitting above him and didn't respond. They hesitated to drop off in the cold, which was becoming unbearable, and finally K. said they really must have some heating or it would be impossible to sleep. He looked for some kind of axe. The assistants knew where to find one, and brought it, and now they went out to the woodshed. Its flimsy door was soon broken down, and the assistants, as delighted as if they had never known such fun, began carrying wood into the classroom, chasing and pushing each other about. Soon there was a great heap of it there, the stove was lit, and everyone lay down around it. The assistants were given one of the blankets to wrap themselves in, which was quite enough for them, for it was agreed that one should stay awake and keep the fire going. After a while it was so warm by the stove that the blankets weren't even needed any more. The lamp was put out, and K. and Frieda, happy to be warm and quiet, lay down to sleep.

When a sound of some kind woke K. in the night, and in his first uncertain drowsy movement he groped around for Frieda, he found one of the assistants lying beside him instead. This, probably as a result of his irritable mood on being suddenly woken, was the biggest shock he had yet had in the village. With a cry, he half rose, and in a blind fury punched the assistant so hard with his fist that the man began shedding tears. The whole affair was soon cleared up. Frieda had been woken when some large animal—or so it had seemed to her at least—probably a cat, jumped on her breast and then ran away again. She had risen, and was searching the whole room for the animal with a candle. The assistant had seized his chance to enjoy lying on the straw mattress for a little while, and now paid dearly for it. However, Frieda could find nothing; perhaps she had just imagined it, and now she came back to K. On her way, as if she had forgotten the evening's conversation, she comfortingly stroked the whimpering assistant's hair as he crouched on the ground. K. said nothing about that, but he told the assistant to stop putting fuel in the stove, for almost all the wood they had piled up was burned, and the room was too hot now.

In the morning they none of them woke up until the first of the schoolchildren had arrived and were standing around the place where they lay, full of curiosity. This was awkward, for as a result of the heat, although now it had given way to a cool atmosphere again, they had all undressed to their underclothes, and just as they were beginning to get dressed Miss Gisa the assistant teacher, a tall, blonde, handsome girl with a little stiffness in her manner, appeared at the door. She was obviously prepared for the new school janitor, and the teacher had probably told her how to treat him, for even in the doorway she said: 'I really can't have this. Here's a nice thing! You have permission to sleep in the classroom, but that's all; it's not my duty to teach the children in your bedroom. A school janitor and his family lying in bed until the middle of the morning! Shame on you!'

Well, K. thought he could have said a thing or two about that, particularly on the subject of beds and his family, as he and Frieda—the assistants were useless here, and were lying on the floor staring at the teacher and the children—quickly pushed the parallel bars and the vaulting-horse together, draped the blankets over them, and so created a small room in which they could at least get dressed away from the children's eyes. Not that they had a moment's peace; first the assistant teacher was cross because there was no fresh water in the washbasin—K. had just been thinking of fetching the wash-basin for Frieda and himself, but he gave that idea up for the time being so as not to annoy the assistant teacher still more. However, abandoning the notion did not help, for soon there was a great crash. Unfortunately they had forgotten to clear away the remains of their supper, and now Miss Gisa was sweeping it all off the teacher's desk with her ruler. Everything fell on the floor. The teacher wasn't going to bother about the fact that the oil from the sardines and the remains of the coffee were spilt on the floor, and the coffee-pot had broken to pieces; after all, the school janitor would clear it up. Still not fully dressed, K. and Frieda, leaning against the gymnastic appa-ratus, watched the destruction of their few household goods. The assistants, who clearly had no idea of getting dressed, peered out from under the blankets, much to the children's amusement. What upset Frieda most, of course, was the loss of the coffee-pot, and only when K., to comfort her, assured her that he would go straight to the village mayor, ask for a replacement, and get one, did she pull herself together enough to emerge from their enclosure, still in nothing but her chemise and petticoat, to retrieve the tablecloth at least and keep it from being soiled any further. And she succeeded, although the teacher, trying to alarm her, kept hammering on the desk with the ruler in a nerve-racking way. When K. and Frieda were dressed they not only had to urge the assistants, who seemed quite dazed by these events, to dress too, giving them orders and nudging them, they even had to help with dressing the pair themselves. Then, when they were all ready, K. shared out the next tasks: the assistants were to fetch wood and heat the stoves, going first to the stove in the other class-room, a source of great danger, for the teacher himself was probably there now. Meanwhile Frieda would clean the floor, and K. would fetch water and generally tidy up. They couldn't think of having any breakfast yet. K. wanted to emerge from their shelter first, so as to find out what the assistant teacher's temper was like in general, and the others were to follow only when he called them. One reason why he made this arrangement was that he didn't want to let the situation go straight from bad to worse because of the assistants' silly tricks, and another was to spare Frieda as much as possible; she had high ambitions, he did not; she was sensitive, he was not; she thought only of their present petty discomforts, while he was thinking of Barnabas and the future. Frieda did all he said and hardly took her eyes off him. No sooner had he stepped out into the room than the assistant teacher asked, to the accompaniment of laughter from the children which seemed as if it would never stop: 'Oh, had your sleep out, have you?' When K. ignored this, for it was not a real question, and instead made for the washstand, Miss Gisa asked: 'Whatever have you been doing to my kitty?' For a large, fat old cat lay stretched out on the washstand, and Miss Gisa was examining one paw, which was obviously slightly injured. So Frieda had been right; the cat had not actually jumped on her, for it probably couldn't jump any more, but it had clambered over her, was alarmed to find people in the usually empty schoolhouse, and had hidden in a hurry, hurting itself in its unwonted haste. K. tried to explain all this calmly to Miss Gisa, but she saw only the outcome of this course of events and said: 'You've hurt my kitty, that's how you start your work here. Look at this!' And she called K. up to the desk, showed him the paw, and before he knew what she was about she had run it over the back of his hand, scratching him. The cat's claws were blunt, to be sure, but Miss Gisa, without thought for the cat itself, had pressed them down so hard that they left bloody weals. 'Now, get on with your work,' she said impatiently, bending over the cat again. Frieda, who had been watching with the assistants from behind the apparatus, screamed at the sight of the blood. K. showed the children his hand and said: 'There, just see what a nasty, sneaking cat did to me.' Of course he didn't really mean that for the children, whose screams and laughter had now become so independent of all else that they needed nothing more to set them off, and no words could get through to them or make them do anything. But when Miss Gisa herself answered this retort only with a brief glance at him, and went on tending the cat, having apparently satisfied her first spurt of anger by inflicting the scratch on him, K. called to Frieda and the assistants and they began work.

When K. had taken out the bucket of dirty water, fetched fresh water, and now began sweeping the schoolroom, a boy of about twelve rose from one bench, touched K.'s hand, and in all the noise said something he couldn't make out at all. Then the racket suddenly stopped. K. turned. Here was what he had feared all morning. The teacher, small man that he was, stood in the doorway holding an assistant by the collar with each hand. He had probably caught them fetching firewood, for he thundered in a mighty voice, pausing after every word: 'Who has dared to break into the woodshed? Where is the fellow? Let me crush him as he deserves!' Here Frieda rose from the floor, which she was trying to wash around Miss Gisa's feet, looked at K. as if to draw strength from the sight, and said, with something of her old dignity in her voice and bearing: 'I did, sir. I couldn't think of anything else to do. If the classrooms were to be heated at all this morning, we had to open the shed, and I dared not come to you for the key at night. My fiancé had gone to the Castle Inn, it was possible that he might spend the night there, so I had to make the decision for myself. If I did wrong you must forgive my inexperience. I was scolded hard enough by my fiancé when he saw what had happened. In fact he even forbade me to heat the rooms early, because he thought your locking the woodshed showed that you didn't want them heated until you had arrived yourself. So the fact that they aren't heated is his fault, but breaking into the woodshed is mine.' 'Who broke down the door?' the teacher asked the assistants, who were still trying to shake off his grip, but in vain. 'That gentleman,' they both said, and pointed to K., thus leaving the matter in no doubt. Frieda laughed, and this laughter seemed even more convincing than her words. Then she began to wring out the rag she had been using to wash the floor in the bucket, as if her explanation were the end of the incident, and what the assistants said was just a passing joke. Only when she was kneeling down again to get on with the work did she say: 'Our assistants are like mere children,* and in spite of their years they still belong on those school benches. I broke down the door with the axe by myself yesterday evening. It was perfectly simple, and I didn't need the assistants to help me. They would only have been in the way. But then, in the night, my fiancé came back and went out to see the damage and repair it if possible, and the assistants went with him, probably fearing to stay here on their own; they saw my fiancé working on the broken door, and that's why they say what they do now—as I said, they are just children at heart.' While the assistants kept shaking their heads as Frieda gave her explanation, pointed to K. again, and tried but failed to make Frieda change her mind through mute pantomime, they finally gave in, took Frieda's words as an order, and did not reply to another question from the teacher. 'Well then,' the teacher said to them, 'so you were lying? Or at least, you blamed the school janitor out of carelessness?' They were still silent, but their trembling and their anxious glances seemed to show that they knew they were to blame. 'Then I shall give you a sound thrashing on the spot,' said the teacher, and he sent a child into the other room to fetch his cane. When he raised it, Frieda cried: 'Oh no, the assistants were telling the truth!' and flung her rag desperately into the bucket, making the water splash up. Then she ran behind the apparatus and hid there. 'What a pack of liars,' said Miss Gisa, who had just finished bandaging the cat's paw, and now took the animal on her lap, for which it was almost too large.

'So that leaves us with the school janitor,' said the teacher, pushing the assistants away and turning to K., who had been listening and leaning on his broom all this time. 'The school janitor, who is cowardly enough to let others take the blame for his own shabby tricks.' 'Well,' said K., noticing that Frieda's intervention had in fact moderated the teacher's first fury, 'if the assistants had been given a bit of a thrashing it wouldn't have bothered me; they've been let off scot free a dozen times when they deserved it, so they might as well pay for that with a thrashing on one occasion when they don't. However, there are other reasons why I'd have been glad to avoid a direct clash between you and me, sir. And perhaps you'd have been glad too. But since Frieda has sacrificed me for the sake of the assistants,' said K., pausing—and in the silence Frieda could be heard sobbing behind the blankets—'we must of course have the whole thing out in the open.' 'Outrageous,' said the assistant teacher. 'I entirely agree with you, Miss Gisa,' said the teacher. 'You are of course dismissed as school janitor on the spot for this shameful dereliction of duty. I reserve the right to decide what punishment will follow, but now get out of this house at once, with all your belongings. It will be a great relief to us, and we'll be able to begin lessons at last. So hurry up!' 'I'm not moving from this place,' said K. 'You are my superior here, but it wasn't you who appointed me to this post, that was the mayor, and I'm accepting notice only from him. And nor did he appoint me for my household and me to freeze to death in this place, but—as you yourself have said—to keep me from any rash acts that I might commit in my desperation. So dismissing me now out of hand would directly contravene his intentions, and until I hear otherwise from the mayor himself I won't believe it. What's more, it will probably be very much to your advantage if I don't go along with your thoughtless dismissal of me.' 'You mean you won't go?' said the teacher. K. shook his head. 'Think it over carefully,' said the teacher. 'Your decisions aren't always the wisest; think, for instance, of yesterday afternoon when you declined to answer questions at a hearing.' 'Why do you mention that now?' asked K. 'Because I feel like it,' said the teacher, 'and now, for the last time, I repeat: get out of here!' But when that too had no effect, the teacher went to Miss Gisa's desk and consulted his assistant quietly. She said something about the police, but the teacher wouldn't have that, and finally they came to an agreement. The teacher told the children to go over to his classroom, and they would be taught their lessons with the other set of children, a change which delighted them all. The room was cleared amidst laughter and shouting, with the teacher and his assistant bringing up the rear. Miss Gisa was carrying the class register, with the corpulent and totally apathetic cat lying on it. The teacher himself would rather have left the cat behind, but a suggestion to that effect was rejected so firmly by Miss Gisa, with reference to K.'s cruelty, that to put the lid on his offences K. had now also unloaded Miss Gisa's cat on the teacher, a fact which probably affected the last words spoken to K. by the teacher as he stood in the doorway. 'Miss Gisa is forced to leave this room with the children because you are refractory and refuse to go when I dismiss you, and no one can expect her, a young girl like that, to give lessons in the middle of your squalid household arrangements. You will therefore be left alone, and can do as you like in this room, undisturbed by the aversion of all decent bystanders. But it won't be for long, you mark my words.' And with that he slammed the door.

12

The Assistants

As soon as they had all left K. told the assistants: 'Go away, you two!' Surprised by this unexpected order, they obeyed, but when K. locked the door behind them they tried to get back in, and stood outside whimpering and knocking. 'You're dismissed!' cried K. 'I'm never going to take you back into my service.' They were not at all happy with that, and hammered on the door with their hands and feet. 'Let us back in, sir!' they cried, as if K. were dry land and they were sinking in a river nearby. But K. was ruthless. He waited impatiently for the ghastly noise to force the teacher to intervene, and so he soon did. 'Let your damned assistants in!' he shouted. 'I've dismissed them,' K. shouted back, which had the unintended side-effect of showing the teacher what happened when you were strong enough not just to give people notice but to make sure they actually went. The teacher tried to soothe the assistants by speaking kindly to them, telling them just to wait here—after all, K. would have to let them in again. Then he went away. And all might have remained quiet if K. hadn't started shouting at the assistants again, telling them they were dismissed once and for all, without the slightest hope of being taken back again. Thereupon they began making as much noise as before. Back came the teacher, but he didn't reason with them any more, he drove them out of the house, obviously with that much-feared cane.

Soon they reappeared outside the windows of the school gymnasium, knocking on the panes and shouting, but their words could no longer be made out. They didn't stay there very long, however; they couldn't jump about in the deep snow well enough to express their profound uneasiness. So they hurried to the fence around the school garden, climbed up on its stone base, from which they had a better view into the room, although only from a distance, ran along the base, clinging to the fence, and then stopped again and held their clasped hands out pleadingly to K. They carried on like this for a long time, ignoring the futility of their efforts. As if they'd been struck blind, they probably went on even when K. drew the curtains over the windows to be rid of the sight of them.

In the now dim light of the room, K. went over to the gymnastic apparatus to look for Frieda. Under his eyes she rose to her feet, tidied her hair, dried her face, and in silence put some coffee on to heat. Although she knew it, K. told her formally that he had dismissed the assistants. She just nodded. K. sat down on one of the school benches and observed her weary movements. It had been her sprightliness and determination that lent beauty to her meagre body, and now that beauty was gone. A few days of living with K. had been enough to do it. Her work in the bar of the inn had not been easy, but she had probably liked it better. Or was her removal from Klamm's sphere the real reason for her decline? It was the proximity of Klamm that had made her so ridiculously enticing, and enticed as he was, K. had swept her into his arms, where she was now withering away.

'Frieda,' said K. She immediately put the coffee-mill down and came over to K. on the bench. 'Are you cross with me?' she asked. 'No,' said K. 'I think you can't help it. You were living happily at the Castle Inn. I ought to have left you there.' 'Yes,' said Frieda, looking sadly into space. 'You ought to have left me there. I am not worthy to live with you. Free of me, you might be able to achieve everything you want. It's out of thoughtfulness for me that you submit to that tyrannical teacher, accept this miserable job, go to so much trouble to get an interview with Klamm. All for me, and I repay you so poorly.' 'No, no,' said K., putting his arm round her to console her. 'All these things are petty details that don't hurt me, and it's not just on your account that I want to see Klamm. Think how much you have done for me! Before I met you I was absolutely lost here. No one would take me in, and if I forced myself on people they soon said goodbye. And if I could have found peace with anyone, it would have been with those from whom I fled in my turn, say Barnabas and his family—' 'You did flee from them, didn't you? Oh, my dearest!' cried Frieda, interrupting impulsively, but then, after a hesitant, 'Yes' from K., she lapsed into lethargy again. But K. himself no longer felt enough determination to explain just how things had turned out well for him through his connection with Frieda. He slowly removed his arm from her waist, and they sat for a while in silence, until Frieda, as if K.'s arm had given her a warmth that was essential to her now, said: 'I won't endure this life here any more. If you want to keep me we must go away, emigrate, go anywhere, to the south of France, to Spain.'* 'I can't emigrate,' said K. 'I came to this place meaning to stay here, and stay I will.' And in a spirit of contradiction which he didn't even try to explain he added, as if to himself: 'What could have lured me to this desolate part of the country but a longing to stay here?' Then he added: 'But you must want to stay here too; it's your own country, after all. However, you miss Klamm, and that's what casts you into despair.' 'You think I miss Klamm?' said Frieda. 'There's an excessive amount of Klamm here, there's only too much Klamm. I want to go so that I can get away from him. You're the one I'd miss, not Klamm. It's for your sake I want to go, because I can't get enough of you here where everyone's pulling me in different directions. I'd rather my pretty face were gone, I'd rather my body felt wretched, just so long as I could live in peace with you.' All that K. gathered from this was a single point. 'Klamm is still in touch with you, is he?' he asked at once. 'Does he want you to go back to him?' 'I don't know anything about Klamm,' said Frieda, 'it's other people I'm talking about now, it's the assistants.' 'Oh, the assistants,' said K. in surprise. 'Do they pester you?' 'Haven't you noticed?' asked Frieda. 'No,' said K., and tried in vain to think of any details. 'They're importunate, lecherous young fellows, but no, I hadn't noticed them pestering you.' 'You hadn't?' said Frieda. 'You mean you never noticed how there was no getting them out of our room at the Bridge Inn, or the way they jealously watched what we were doing together, you didn't notice one of them lying down in my place on the straw mattress, you didn't hear the things they said about you just now, hoping to drive you away, ruin you, and be left alone with me. You never noticed any of that?' K. looked at Frieda without replying. No doubt her complaints of the assistants were justified, but in view of their utterly ridiculous, childish, restless, and intemperate nature all that could be seen in a much more innocent light. And didn't the way they had always done their utmost to go everywhere with K. rather than being left alone with Frieda disprove her accusation? K. said something of the kind. 'Hypocrisy,' said Frieda. 'Didn't you see through it? Why did you drive them away if that wasn't the reason?' And she went to the window, moved the curtain a little way aside, looked out, and then called K. over to her. The assistants were still out there by the railings; from time to time, tired as they obviously were, they still summoned up enough strength to raise their arms and point imploringly to the school. One of them had attached himself by his coat to a spike in the fence behind him so that he didn't have to cling to it all the time.

'Poor things! Poor things!' said Frieda. 'You ask why I drove them away?' asked K. 'Well, you were the immediate cause.' 'I was?' asked Frieda, without taking her eyes off the scene outside. 'Your excessively friendly treatment of the assistants,' said K., 'forgiving their naughty tricks, laughing at them, caressing their hair, feeling sorry for them all the time. You've just called them "poor things, poor things" again, and then only a little while ago you were ready to sacrifice me to save the assistants from a thrashing.' 'That's just it,' said Frieda, 'that's what I'm talking about, that's what makes me unhappy and keeps me apart from you, although I know of no greater happiness than to be with you all the time, without interruption, without end, but I feel in my dreams that there is no place on earth where our love can be at peace, not in the village or anywhere else, and I imagine a deep and narrow grave where we lie embracing tightly in each other's arms as if in pincers, I bury my face against you, you bury yours against me, and no one will ever see us again. But here—just look at the assistants! It's not you they're pleading with when they clasp their hands, it's me.' 'Well, I don't see that,' said K., 'even if you do.' 'Indeed I do,' said Frieda almost angrily, 'that's what I keep telling you. Why else would the assistants be after me, even if they are Klamm's envoys—' 'Klamm's envoys?' said K., greatly surprised by this idea, although it instantly seemed to him natural. 'Yes, Klamm's envoys, to be sure,' said Frieda, 'but even if they are, they're also silly young fellows, they need a good thrashing to teach them a lesson. What ugly, grubby lads they are, and how I hate the contrast between their faces, from which anyone might think they were adults or maybe students, and their foolish, childish conduct! Do you think I don't see that? I'm ashamed of them. And that's just it; they don't actually repel me, but I'm ashamed of them. I can't help looking at them all the time. When I ought to be cross with them I can't help laughing. When they should be getting a thrashing I can't help caressing their heads instead. And when I lie beside you at night I can't sleep, and I can't help constantly glancing across you and see-ing one of them asleep, wrapped up in his blanket, and the other kneeling in front of the stove door putting wood on the fire, while I have to bend forward so far that I almost wake you up. It's not the cat that scares me, either—oh, I know about cats—and I know how diffi-cult it was to sleep in the bar, where I was always being disturbed. No, it's not the cat that scares me, it's myself. And it didn't take that monstrous cat to startle me either, I jump at the slightest little sound. Sometimes I'm afraid you'll wake up and it will all be over between us, and then again I jump up and light the candle so that you *will* wake up and you can protect me.' 'I had no idea of any of this,' said K. 'Or, rather, I had a slight presentiment of it, that's why I drove the assistants away. But now they're gone, so perhaps all will be well.' 'Yes, they're gone at last,' said Frieda, but her face was anxious and not happy. 'Only we don't really know who they are. I call them Klamm's envoys in my mind, as a game, but maybe they actually are. Their eyes, so guileless yet sparkling, sometimes remind me of Klamm's. Yes, that's it, those eyes of theirs sometimes look at me as Klamm's did. So it's not quite accurate to say I'm ashamed of them. I only wish I were. I do know that anywhere else, in other people, the same behaviour would be stupid and repellent, but in them it's not. I even watch their silly tricks with respect and admiration. However, if they're Klamm's envoys, then who's going to free us from them, and would that even be a good thing? Don't you think you'd better run after them, catch up with them quickly, and be glad if they came back?' 'You want me to let them in again?' asked K. 'No, no,' said Frieda. 'There's nothing I want less. The sight of them storming in, their delight at seeing me again, the way they'd hop about like children but reach out their arms to me like men, I might not be able to bear any of that. But then again, when I think that by remaining so implacable to them you may be denying Klamm himself access to you, I know I want to protect you from the consequences of that in any way I can. Yes, when I think of that I do want you to let them in. So quick, let's have them in again. Never mind me, what do I matter? I'll defend myself as long as I can, but if I should fail, well, then I'll fail knowing that I did it all for your sake.' 'You only confirm me in what I think of the assistants,' said K. 'They'll never come in here again with my consent. The fact that I threw them out shows that in some circumstances they can be controlled, and what's more, it shows that they have nothing to do with Klamm. Only yesterday evening I received a letter from Klamm which clearly proves that he has been entirely misinformed about the assistants, and from that we must conclude in turn that they are a matter of total indifference to him, for if they were not, he would surely have known the facts about them more accurately. Your thinking you see Klamm in them proves nothing, because I'm sorry to say that you're still under the landlady's influence, so you see Klamm everywhere. You are still more Klamm's lover than my wife. Sometimes that makes me very downcast, and I feel as if I'd lost everything, it's as if I had only just arrived in the village, not full of hope as I really was at that time, but aware that only disappointments await me, and I must suffer them one after another to the very last. But it's only at times I feel like that,' added K., smiling when he saw Frieda sinking under the effect of his words, 'and basically it's good because it shows what you mean to me. And if you're going to ask me to choose between you and the assistants, well, the assistants have lost. What an idea, choosing between you and them! Well, now I'll be finally rid of them. And who knows whether we're not both feeling rather weak just because we haven't had any breakfast yet?' 'That's possible,' said Frieda, with a tired smile, and she set to work. K. himself picked up the broom again.

13

Hans

AFTER a little while there was a quiet knock at the door. 'Barnabas!' cried K., throwing down his broom, and in a few strides he was at the door. Frieda looked at him in alarm, more because of that name than anything else. But K.'s hands were so unsteady that he couldn't undo the old lock of the door at once. 'Just coming, just opening up,' he repeated, instead of asking who was out there knocking. And then, having flung the door wide, he saw not Barnabas coming in but the little boy who had tried to speak to him earlier in the day. Not that K. remembered that with any pleasure. 'What are you doing here?' he asked. 'Lessons are in the classroom next door.' 'That's where I've come from,' said the boy, and looked up calmly at K. with his big brown eyes, standing very upright with his arms at his sides. 'What do you want, then? Quick, out with it!' said K., bending down a little way, because the boy spoke so softly. 'Can I help you?' asked the boy. 'He wants to help us,' K. told Frieda, and then, turning to the boy, asked: 'What's your name?' 'Hans Brunswick,' said the boy. 'I'm in Class Four and my father is Otto Brunswick, the master shoemaker who lives in Madeleine Alley.' 'Well, well, so your name is Brunswick,' said K., sounding friendlier. It turned out that Hans had been so upset to see the bleeding scratch inflicted on K.'s hand by the assistant teacher that he had made up his mind there and then to go over to K.'s side. Now he had come from the schoolroom next door like a deserter, risking severe punishment. Such boyish ideas might well motivate him, but a gravity to match them was evident in all he did. At first, however, shyness had held him back, but soon he felt at ease with K. and Frieda, and when he had been given some good hot coffee he became lively and confiding. He also asked eager questions that were very much to the point, as if he wanted to learn the most important facts as quickly as possible so that then he could decide for himself what was best for K. and Frieda. He was naturally a little overbearing, but that was mingled with childish innocence so that you felt like doing as he said half in earnest, half in jest. At any rate, he claimed all their attention. They had stopped work, and breakfast was going to be a long business. Although Hans sat on the classroom bench, K. at the teacher's desk, and Frieda in a chair near it, it looked as if the boy were the teacher himself, testing them and assessing their answers. A slight smile on his soft mouth seemed to indicate that he knew it was just a game, but he took it very seriously. Or perhaps it was not a smile but the happiness of childhood playing around his lips. It was some time before he admitted to having seen K. before, on the day when K. called at Lasemann's house. K. was pleased. 'You were playing around at that woman's feet, weren't you?' asked K. 'Yes,' said Hans, 'she's my mother.' And now he had to tell them about his mother, but he did it hesitantly, and only after being asked repeatedly, for it turned out that he was a little boy who sometimes seemed to speak almost like a clever, energetic, and far-sighted man, particularly in his questions, and perhaps anticipating what he would be in future, or then again perhaps it was only a trick of the senses if you were listening to him intently. But suddenly, without any apparent transition, he was once again a schoolboy who didn't even understand many of the questions put to him, mistook the meaning of others, spoke too quietly out of childish thoughtlessness, although he had often had this failing pointed out to him, and finally, as if defiantly, said nothing at all in reply to many urgent queries, entirely without embarrassment, as a grown-up man never could be. It was as if he thought he should be the only one allowed to ask questions, while questions asked by other people broke some rule and were a waste of time. Then he could sit still for a long while, his back straight and his head bent, his lower lip thrust out. Frieda rather liked that, so much so that she often asked him questions, hoping that they would make him adopt this silent pose. And she sometimes succeeded, but that irked K. On the whole they learned little: his mother was rather poorly, but it wasn't clear just what ailed her. The child who had been on Mrs Brunswick's lap was Hans's sister and was called Frieda (Hans didn't seem to like it that the woman questioning him had the same name), and they all lived in the village, but not with Lasemann. They had just been visiting his house to take a bath, because Lasemann had that big tub, and the small children, although Hans wasn't one of those, specially enjoyed bathing and playing about in it. Hans spoke of his father with respect or even fear, but only when they weren't also talking about his mother. By comparison with her, his father didn't seem to be so important, and all questions about his family life, however they were phrased, remained unanswered. They did learn that his father was the leading shoemaker in the village, he had no equal, as Hans frequently repeated, even in answer to quite different questions. Why, he even gave work to other shoemakers, such as Barnabas's father, although in that case Brunswick probably did it only as a special favour, or so at least Hans's proud turn of the head suggested. That made Frieda bend down to him quickly and give him a kiss. Asked whether he had ever been in the castle, Hans answered only after many repetitions, and then in the negative, and when asked the same question about his mother, he did not answer at all. Finally K. grew tired of this, for there didn't seem to be any point in the questioning; he thought the boy was right, trying to worm family secrets out of an innocent child by roundabout ways was nothing to be proud of, particularly since they hadn't even learned anything. When K. finally asked the boy just what kind of help he was offering, he was not surprised to hear that Hans meant only help with the work here, so that the teacher and Miss Gisa wouldn't be so cross with K. any more. K. explained that such help wasn't necessary, the teacher was probably naturally bad-tempered, and no one could really protect himself from that however hard he worked. As for the work itself, he said, it wasn't really difficult, and he was behind with it today only as a result of unforeseen circumstances. Anyway, the teacher's bad temper did not affect K. as much as it would a schoolboy, he shook it off easily, he said, he was almost indifferent to it. He also hoped to escape the teacher entirely very soon. However, he thanked Hans very much for offering his help, and said he could go back to the other classroom now, and he hoped he wouldn't be punished. All the same, K. did not emphasize the fact that it was only help against the teacher that he didn't need, he only suggested as much spontaneously, leaving the question of other help open. Hans, clearly picking this hint up, asked if K. might need help of a different kind, saying that he'd be very glad to help him, and if he couldn't do it himself he would ask his mother to, and then he was sure everything would be all right. When his father was in any difficulty he always asked his mother for help, he said. And his mother had already asked after K. once. She herself hardly left the house, she had been visiting Lasemann just that once, he said, but he, Hans, went there quite often to play with the Lasemann children. So his mother had once asked him if the land surveyor had been there again. It wasn't a good idea to ask his mother unnecessary questions, because she was so weak and tired, so he had simply said no, he hadn't seen the land surveyor again, and they didn't discuss it any further. But when Hans had found K. here in the school, he'd had to speak to him so that he could tell his mother about it. What his mother liked best was to have her wishes granted without asking for that openly. In response to this K. said, after a moment's thought, that he didn't need help, he had all he needed, but it was very kind of Hans to want to help him, and he thanked him for his good intentions. After all, it was possible that he might need something later, and then he would turn to Hans; he knew the address. On the other hand, perhaps he, K., could offer a little help. He was sorry to hear that Hans's mother was not well, and obviously no one here knew what the matter with her was; such a case, if neglected, can turn from a mild ailment to something much worse. He, K., had some medical knowledge, and what was even more valuable, he had experience of treating the sick and had been known to succeed where the doctors had failed. At home, he said, he had been nicknamed 'Bitter Rue'* because of his cures. At any rate, he would happily go to see Hans's mother and talk to her. Perhaps he could offer good advice, he'd be glad to do that for Hans's sake. At first Hans's eyes lit up at this offer, which led K. to become more pressing, but the result was unsatisfactory, for in answer to various questions Hans said, and didn't even sound as if he regretted it, that no strangers could visit his mother. She had to be spared any strain, and although K. had hardly exchanged a word with her on that one occasion, she had taken to her bed for several days afterwards. Hans had to say that such things often happened. At the time his father had been very angry with K., and he would certainly never let K. visit his mother, why, his father had wanted to go to see K. to punish him for his conduct, and only Hans's mother had restrained him. Most important, however, his mother herself never wanted to speak to anyone in general, and her question about K. didn't mark any exception to the rule. On the contrary, when he was mentioned she might have expressed a wish to see him, but she hadn't, which clearly showed what she really wanted: to hear about K. but not to speak to him. She didn't suffer from any identifiable illness, Hans added, and sometimes she hinted that it was probably just the air here that she couldn't tolerate, but she didn't want to leave the village because of Hans's father and their children, and anyway her trouble was better than it had once been. This was roughly what K. learned; Hans's intellectual powers increased when it came to shielding his mother from K., whom he had said he would like to help. In fact with the idea of keeping K. away from his mother in view, he contradicted much of what he had said before, for instance about her ailment. All the same, K. realized that Hans was still kindly disposed to him, but in thinking of his mother he forgot everything else, anyone who wanted to see Hans's mother was instantly in the wrong. It was K. this time, another time it could have been Hans's father. K. thought he would broach that subject, and said it was certainly very sensible of Hans's father to protect his wife from any kind of agitation, and if he, K., had so much as guessed at anything of the kind when he met her he certainly wouldn't have ventured to speak to her. Now he would like to apologize, in retrospect, to the family at their home. On the other hand he couldn't quite understand why Hans's father, if the cause of the trouble was as obvious as Hans said, prevented the boy's mother from recovering in healthier air; prevented was the word for it, because it was for the sake of Hans's father and her children that she didn't leave the village. But she could take the children with her, she didn't have to be away for long or go very far. Even up on Castle Mount the air must be quite different. And surely Hans's father didn't have to fear the expense of such a trip. After all, he was the most important shoemaker in the village, and surely either he or Hans's mother had friends or relations at the castle who would willingly take them in. So why didn't he let them go? He shouldn't underestimate such an ailment, said K., who had seen her only fleetingly, but, struck by her pallor and weakness, had been moved to speak to her. Even then he had wondered at the children's father for taking his sick wife into the musty air of the room where so many people were washing clothes and bathing, and failing to keep his loud voice down. He supposed Hans's father didn't know what it was really about, and of course it was true his mother had seemed better recently, such disorders come and go, but if left untreated it might return as strongly as ever, and then nothing could be done. So if he, K., couldn't speak to the boy's mother, perhaps it would be a good idea for him to have a word with Hans's father and point all this out to him.

Hans had listened intently, understanding most of this and much affected by the menace latent in what he didn't understand. All the same, he said no, K. couldn't speak to his father, his father had taken a dislike to him, and would probably treat him as the teacher did. He said this smiling shyly when he spoke of K., and bitterly and sadly when he mentioned his father. However, he added that K. might perhaps be able to speak to his mother after all, but only without his father's knowledge. Then Hans thought for a little while, his eyes fixed, like a woman contemplating something forbidden and looking for a way to do it with impunity, and said it might be possible the day after tomorrow, his father would be going to the Castle Inn that evening, and then he, Hans, would come and take K. to see his mother, always assuming that she agreed, which wasn't very likely. She never did anything against his father's will, she went along with everything he wanted, even if, as Hans could see clearly, it was unreasonable. In fact Hans was now recruiting K. to help him against his father; it was as if he had deceived himself in thinking he wanted to help K., while in reality he had wanted to find out whether, since no one in the neighbourhood had been any help to his mother, this stranger who had suddenly appeared and whom she had even mentioned might be able to do something. Until now it would hardly have been possible to glean from the boy's appearance and words how subconsciously withdrawn and almost crafty he was! You could gather that only from his later admissions, elicited both by chance and intentionally. Now, in the course of his long conversation with K., he was considering the difficulties to be overcome, and with the best will in the world on Hans's part they were all but insuperable. Deep in thought, yet still seeking help, he kept looking at K., and his eyes blinked restlessly. He could say nothing to his mother before his father went out, or his father would learn of it and then it would have been all in vain, so he could mention it only later, but not suddenly and abruptly, out of consideration for his mother, but slowly and at a suitable opportunity. Only then must he ask his mother to agree, only then could he come to fetch K., but wouldn't that be too late, wouldn't the threat of his father's return be looming already? Yes, it was impossible after all. K., on the other hand, showed him that it was not impossible. There was no need to fear there wouldn't be enough time; a short conversation, a brief encounter, would be enough, and Hans wouldn't have to come to fetch K., because K.

would be waiting concealed somewhere near the house, and once Hans gave him a signal he would come at once. Oh no, said Hans, K. mustn't wait near the house—once again he was anxious about his mother's sensitivity—K. mustn't set out without his mother's knowledge, Hans couldn't enter into a secret agreement with K. unknown to his mother, he would have to fetch K. from the school, and not before his mother knew about it and had given permission. Very well, said K., in that case it really was risky; it could be that Hans's father would find him in the family house, and even if he didn't, Hans's mother wouldn't let K. come at all for fear that he would, so everything would fail because of the boy's father. But Hans denied that again, and so the argument went back and forth. Long before this K. had told Hans to leave the bench and come up to the teacher's desk, where he held him between his knees, caressing him soothingly from time to time. This physical closeness meant that, in spite of the occasional reluctance shown by Hans, they did come to an understanding. Finally they agreed on the following plan: first Hans would tell his mother the whole truth, but adding, to make it easier for her to agree, that K. also wanted to speak to Brunswick himself—not about her, though, but on some other business. This was true too, for in the course of the conversation K. had recollected that, however dangerous and unpleasant Brunswick might be in other respects, he really couldn't be his, K.'s, enemy, for Brunswick, at least according to the village mayor, had been the leader of those who had wanted to have a land surveyor appointed, even if for political reasons of their own. So K.'s arrival in the village must be welcome to Brunswick, although it was true that in that case his surly greeting to K. on the first day, and the dislike of which Hans spoke, were hard to understand. But perhaps Brunswick's feelings had been hurt because K. had not turned to him for help in the first place, or perhaps there was some other misunderstanding that could be cleared up in a few words. And once that was done, K. could get Brunswick's support against the teacher, indeed even against the village mayor, and the entire official deception—for what else was it?—through which the village mayor and the teacher were keeping him from the castle authorities and forcing him to take the job of school janitor could be revealed. If it came to a quarrel over K. between Brunswick and the village mayor, then Brunswick would have to get K. on his side, K. would be received as a guest in Brunswick's house,

Brunswick's powers would be at his disposal in defiance of the village mayor, and who knew where all that might get him? And he would often be near the woman anyway—so he played with his dreams, and they with him, while Hans, thinking entirely of his mother, observed K.'s silence with concern, as you observe a doctor lost in thought trying to find a way to treat a severely ill patient. Hans agreed to K.'s suggestion of saying that he wanted to speak to Brunswick about the post of land surveyor, although only because that would protect his mother from his father, and anyway it was just an emergency measure that he hoped wouldn't have to be adopted. He merely asked how K. would explain the late hour of his visit to his father, and finally was satisfied to hear, although he did look a little gloomy, that K. would say his intolerable position as school janitor, and the teacher's humiliating treatment of him, had driven all else out of his mind in a sudden fit of despair.

When they had anticipated all contingencies like this, as far as anyone could tell, and the possibility of success at least needn't be entirely ruled out any longer, Hans became more cheerful, freed of the burden of thought, and he chattered away in childish fashion for a little longer, first with K. and then with Frieda, who had been sitting there for some time with her mind on very different subjects, and who only now began to join in the conversation again. Among other things, she asked Hans what he wanted to be when he grew up. He didn't have to think about that for long, but said he wanted to be a man like K. When asked his reasons he wasn't able to give any, and when asked whether he really wanted to be a school janitor he firmly said no. Only further questions elicited the workings of his mind in expressing such a wish. K.'s present situation was by no means enviable, but dismal and humiliating, Hans himself saw that clearly, and he didn't need to observe other people to see it; he himself would have liked to keep his mother right away from the sight of K. and from anything he said. All the same, he had come to K. asking for help, and was glad when K. agreed to give it, he thought he had seen that other people felt the same, and above all his mother herself had mentioned K. These opposing ideas led to his belief that K. might be in a low, humiliating position at the moment, but in an admittedly almost unimaginably distant future he would still triumph over everyone. And that future, foolish as the idea might be, and K.'s proud rise in it looked alluring to Hans. At that price, he was even ready to accept K. as he now was. The particularly childish and precocious nature of his wish lay in the fact that Hans looked down on K. as if he were a younger boy, with a longer future ahead of him than his own, a small boy's future. It was with almost mournful gravity that, under pressure from Frieda, he spoke of these things. But K. cheered him up again by saying he knew what Hans envied him for—his handsome gnarled walking-stick, which was lying on the table, and with which Hans had been absent-mindedly playing as they talked. Well, said K., he knew how to make such walking-sticks, and if their plan succeeded he would make Hans an even better one. Hans was so pleased by K.'s promise that it wasn't quite clear whether he might not indeed have had the walking-stick in mind all the time, and he said a cheerful goodbye, not without pressing K.'s hand firmly and saying: 'So, I'll see you the day after tomorrow.'

14

Frieda's Grievance

HANS had left none too soon, for next moment the teacher opened the door and cried, on seeing K. and Frieda sitting quietly at the table: 'Oh, pray forgive me for disturbing you! But can you tell me when you are finally going to tidy this place up? We're having to sit all cooped up together over there, and lessons are suffering from it, while you lounge around in the big gymnasium, and you've sent the assistants away so as to have even more room for yourselves. So kindly stand up and get moving!' And he added, to K. alone: 'And you, fellow, go and fetch me my buffet lunch from the Bridge Inn!' All this was said furiously, at the top of his voice, but the words were relatively inoffensive, even the disrespectful address of K. as 'fellow'. K. was ready to do as he was told at once, and it was only to sound the teacher out that he said: 'But I've been dismissed.' 'Dismissed or not, fetch me my lunch,' said the teacher. 'Dismissed or not is what I want to know,' said K. 'What are you going on about?' said the teacher. 'You didn't accept the dismissal.' 'So is that enough to cancel it out?' asked K. 'Not as far as I'm concerned, believe me,' said the teacher. 'But extraordinarily enough, the village mayor won't hear of it. So get moving, or you really will be thrown out.' K. was pleased; so in the interim the teacher had spoken to the village mayor, or perhaps not spoken to him but simply worked out what he expected the village mayor's opinion would be, and it was to K.'s advantage. Now K. started straight off to fetch the buffet lunch, but the teacher called him back again from the corridor, whether because he had just wanted to test K.'s willingness to be of service with this special order, so that he could add more directions to it, or because he felt like giving orders and it pleased him to see K. running busily back and forth like a waiter at his behest. For his part, K. knew that if he gave way too far he would become the teacher's slave and scapegoat, but he would put up with the man's whims within limits, for if the teacher, as it transpired, could not legitimately dismiss him, he could certainly make his job unpleasant to the point of being intolerable. And now K. was much more anxious to keep the job than before.

His conversation with Hans had given him new hope—admittedly improbable hope, and for no good reason at all, but hope not to be forgotten all the same. It almost put even Barnabas out of his mind. If he acted in accordance with it, and he had no alternative, then he must do everything in his power to think of nothing else, not food and lodging, not the village authorities, not even Frieda—and at bottom this was all about Frieda, for everything else concerned him only in relation to her. So he had to try to keep this job, which gave Frieda some security, and with his eye fixed on that purpose he must not shrink from enduring more from the teacher than he could otherwise have brought himself to do. All this was not too painful; it was to be classed with the constant little pinpricks of life, it was nothing by comparison with what K. was striving for, and he had not come here to lead a life of peace in high esteem.

And so, while he had been ready to run straight off to the inn, he was also prepared to obey the new order to tidy up the room first, so that Miss Gisa could move back with her class. But it had to be done very fast, for after that K. was to fetch the lunch anyway, and the teacher said he was very hungry and thirsty. K. assured him that he would do just as he wanted. The teacher watched for a little while as K. made haste to clear away the bedding, put the gymnastic apparatus back in its proper place, and sweep up in haste, while Frieda washed and scoured the podium. All this industry seemed to satisfy the teacher. He pointed out that there was a heap of firewood for the stove outside the door—he wasn't going to let K. have access to the woodshed any more—and then he went away, threatening to be back soon and look in on the children.

After some time spent working in silence, Frieda asked why K. was obeying the teacher so meekly now. She probably meant her question to show sympathetic concern, but K., thinking how little Frieda had succeeded in keeping her original promise to protect him from the teacher's orders and his violence, just said briefly that now he was a school janitor he must fill the post well. Then they were quiet again, until those few words reminded K. that Frieda had been deep in anxious thought for a long time, indeed through almost his entire conversation with Hans, and now, as he was carrying in firewood, he asked straight out what was on her mind. She replied, slowly looking up at him, that it was nothing in particular. She was just thinking of the landlady and how true much of what she said was.

Only when K. pressed her further did she reply at greater length, and after several refusals, but without stopping her work, which she was doing not out of zeal, since she was really getting nowhere with it, but only so as not to be forced to look at K. And now she told him how she had listened calmly to his conversation with Hans at first, but then, startled by some of the things K. said, she had begun to listen more closely, and from that point on had been unable to stop hearing in it confirmation of a warning that the landlady had given her, although she had never wanted to believe it. K., angered by all these generalities, more irritated than moved even by Frieda's tearful voice—and above all because here came the landlady meddling in his life again, at least in his mind, since she hadn't yet had much success in person—dropped the wood he was carrying in his arms on the floor, sat down on it, and speaking seriously, insisted on a full explanation. 'Well,' began Frieda, 'the landlady often tried to make me doubt you, right from the start, she didn't say you were lying, on the contrary, she said you were childishly honest, but your nature was so different from ours that even when you speak frankly we can hardly bring ourselves to believe you, and without a good friend like her to come to our aid we could bring ourselves to believe it only through bitter experience. It had been much the same even for her, she said, despite her keen eye for human nature. But since that last conversation she had with you at the Bridge Inn—I'm only repeating what she said—she had seen through you, you couldn't deceive her any more however hard you tried to conceal your intentions. "Not that he really conceals anything," she kept saying, and then she added: "Do try listening to him properly at every opportunity, not just superficially, listen to what he's actually saying." That was all she said, yet what I read into it was something like this: you'd chatted me up—yes, that was the vulgar term she used—just because I happened to cross your path, you didn't dislike me, and you wrongly thought a barmaid was bound to fall for every guest who put his hand out to her. In addition, as the landlady learned from the landlord of the Castle Inn, you wanted to spend the night there for some reason or other, and whatever that reason was, I was the only way you could achieve that aim. All of this would have been enough for you to make love to me that night in the hope that more would come of it, and that more was Klamm. The landlady doesn't claim to know what you want from Klamm, she says only that you were as anxious to me

Klamm before you knew me as you were later. The only difference was that earlier you had no hope of an interview, but now you thought you could use me as a sure way of actually getting to see Klamm quickly, even of having some advantage over him. How alarmed I was—but at first only momentarily, without any deeper reasons—when you said today that before you knew me you had gone astray here. Those might be the very words the landlady used; she also says that only after you came to know me were you sure of your purpose. That comes of your believing that, in me, you had made a conquest of one of Klamm's lovers, a pledge to be redeemed at the highest price. And she said your sole aim was to negotiate with Klamm over that price. As you thought nothing of me, only of the price, you were ready to make any concessions as far as I was concerned, except over the price. That's why you don't mind my losing my place at the Castle Inn, you don't mind my having to leave the Bridge Inn too, you don't mind my having to do the hard work of a school janitor here, you have no tenderness and not even any time left for me. You leave me to the assistants, you're not jealous, I am valuable only to you because I was Klamm's lover, in your ignorance you try not to let me forget Klamm so that in the end I won't fight back too hard when the crucial moment comes, yet you are also at odds with the landlady, the only person who, you think, could tear me from you, so you quarrel with her in order to be made to leave the Bridge Inn with me; for you never doubt that, so far as it is up to me, I shall be your chattel come what may. You imagine that an interview with Klamm is a matter of ᵗing a deal, cash down for cash down. You reckon on all possibil- ⁱˢ; just so long as you get the price you want you're ready to do ᵗhing; if Klamm wants me, you will give me to him; if he wants to stay with me, you will stay with me; if he wants you to reject ᵒu'll reject me, but you're ready for pretence too if it's to your ᵗntage, you will pretend to love me, you will try to counter his ᶠerence by emphasizing your own low worth, shaming him by ᵃct that you are his successor, or by telling him of my confes- ᵗ of love for him, which I really did make, and asking him to take ᵃck again, after paying the price, of course; and if there is noth- ᵗlse for it, then you will simply beg in the name of Mr and K. But, the landlady concluded, if you then see that you have wrong in every way, in your assumptions and in your hopes, in idea of Klamm and his relationship with me, then my torments will really begin, for then more than ever I will be all you have, something on which you rely although at the same time it has proved worthless, and you will treat me accordingly, since you have no feeling for me but a sense of ownership.'

K. had listened intently, his mouth firmly closed. The wood under him had started shifting so that he almost slipped and fell on the floor, but he took no notice of that. Only now did he stand up, sit down on the podium, take Frieda's hand, which she feebly tried to withdraw from his, and said: 'I wasn't always able to tell your own opinion and the landlady's apart in what you said.' 'It was only the landlady's opinion,' said Frieda. 'I listened to it all because I respect the landlady, but it was the first time in my life that I'd ever entirely dismissed her opinion. Everything she said seemed to me so pitiful, so far from any understanding of how matters really stood between the two of us. In fact the truth seemed to be the complete opposite of what she said. I thought of that gloomy morning after our first night. How you knelt beside me, with a look that seemed to say all was lost. And then it really did turn out that, much as I tried, I didn't help you, I was a hindrance to you. Through me the landlady became your enemy, a powerful enemy and one you still underestimate. It was for my sake, because you have to provide for me, that you had to fight for your job, you were at a disadvantage with the village mayor, you had to submit to the teacher, you were at the mercy of the assistants, and the worst of it is that for my sake you may even have offended Klamm. The fact that you kept wanting to see Klamm was only a useless attempt to be reconciled with him somehow. And I told myself that the landlady, who must know all this much better than I did, was only trying to keep me from reproaching myself too much with her whispered insinuations. It was well-meant but unnecessary trouble. My love for you would have helped me to get over anything, it would finally have buoyed you up too, if not here in the village then somewhere else, it had already given proof of its power in saving you from Barnabas and his family.' 'So that was your opinion at the time,' said K. 'And what has changed since then?' 'I don't know,' said Frieda, looking at K.'s hand holding her own. 'Perhaps nothing has changed; when you are so close to me, and you ask so calmly, I think nothing has changed. But in reality,' she added, withdrawing her hand, sitting up straight opposite him, and shedding tears openly, holding her tear-stained face up to him as if she were not crying over herself and so had nothing to hide, as if she were in tears over K.'s betrayal and the misery of the sight was meant for him, 'in reality everything changed when I heard you talking to that boy. How innocently you began, asking about his life at home, about this, that, and the other, I felt as if you were just coming into the bar, so trusting, so open-hearted, seeking to meet my eyes in such a childlike, eager way. There was no difference between then and now, I only wished the landlady were here listening to you, and I tried to stick to that opinion. But then suddenly, I don't know just how, I noticed why you were talking to the boy like that. Your words of sympathy won his trust, which is not easily given, so that you could make straight for your goal, which I saw more and more clearly. Your goal was that woman. Your apparent concern for her now openly showed that you were thinking only of your own affairs. You are betraying the woman before you've even won her. I heard not only my past but my future in your words, it was as if the landlady were sitting beside me explaining it all, and I was trying to argue against her with all my might, but clearly seeing the hopelessness of any such thing, and yet it was not really I who was being deceived now, it was the other woman. And when I pulled myself together and asked Hans what he wanted to be, and he said a man like you, he was so utterly devoted to you, oh, what a difference was there between him now, that good boy whose trust you have abused so badly, and me then in the bar of the inn?'

'Everything you say,' said K., who had managed to pull himself together as he grew used to her reproachful tone, 'everything you say has something in it, it is not untrue, only hostile. Those are the thoughts of the landlady, my enemy, even if you believe they are your own, and that's a comfort to me. But they are instructive; there's a lot to be learnt from the landlady. She didn't say all this to me herself, although she hasn't spared me otherwise; obviously she handed you this weapon hoping that you would use it at a particularly bad or crucial time for me. If I am abusing your trust, then so is she. But now, think, Frieda: even if it were all exactly as the landlady says, it would be very bad only in one event, which is to say if you don't love me. Then and only then would I really have won your heart by calculation and cunning for the sake of advantage. Perhaps it would even have been part of my plan to make you feel sorry for me, and that was why I appeared in front of you arm in arm with

Olga, and the landlady has simply forgotten to add that to the list of my misdeeds. But if that's not the case, and no cunning beast of prey snatched you away, but instead you came to me as I went to you and we found each other, forgetting ourselves, tell me, Frieda, then what? Then I am backing your cause as well as mine, there's no difference, and only an enemy like the landlady can separate the two. That's true in general, and it also applies to Hans. And in judging my conversation with Hans your tender feelings lead you to exaggerate wildly, for if what Hans and I want is not entirely the same, no actual conflict of interests is involved, and what's more, our own difference of opinion was no secret from Hans. If you think so, then you underestimate that cautious little fellow, and even if he didn't notice anything, I hope no harm would come to anyone because of that.'

'It's so difficult to know what to think, K.,' said Frieda, sighing. 'I certainly didn't feel any distrust of you, and if I caught something of the kind from the landlady I will gladly dismiss it and beg you on my knees to forgive me, which is really what I am doing constantly, even if I say nasty things. But it is still true that you've kept a good deal secret from me. You come and go, and I don't know where to and where from. When Hans knocked on the door you even called out the name of Barnabas. If only you had ever just once uttered my name as lovingly, as for some reason I don't understand you uttered that hated name! If you don't trust me, how can I feel no distrust myself? And then I'm left to the landlady, and your conduct seems to confirm what she says. Not in everything, I don't claim that it confirms her opinion in everything, for didn't you chase the assistants away for my sake? Oh, if only you knew how hard I try to find a kernel of good for myself in all you do and say, even if it torments me.' 'Remember above all, Frieda,' said K., 'that I am not hiding the least little thing from you. But how the landlady hates me, doing all she can to part you from me, and what contemptible means she uses, and you give way to her, Frieda, how you give way to her! Tell me, in exactly what respect am I hiding something from you? You know that I want an interview with Klamm, you also know that you can't help me to get one, so I must try by myself, and you can see that so far I haven't succeeded. I make useless attempts, which humiliate me quite enough as it is, and am I to humiliate myself twice over by telling you about them? Am I to boast of having waited in vain and freezing all through a long afternoon at the door of Klamm's sleigh? Happy to dismiss such thoughts at last, I hurry to you, and now I hear all these accusations of yours. What about Barnabas? Yes, I am certainly expecting him. He is Klamm's messenger, but that wasn't my doing.' 'Barnabas again,' cried Frieda. 'I can't believe he is a good messenger.' 'You may be right,' said K., 'but he's the only messenger who's been sent to me.' 'That makes it all the worse,' said Frieda. 'You should beware of him all the more.' 'I'm afraid he has given me no reason to beware of him yet,' said K., smiling. 'He seldom comes, and what he brings is of no importance; only the fact that it comes directly from Klamm gives it any value.' 'But look,' said Frieda, 'you aren't even making Klamm your business any more, and perhaps that's what worries me most. The way you were always wanting to go and see Klamm, overriding me, was bad enough, but now you seem to want to avoid Klamm, which is much worse, and something that even the landlady didn't foresee. According to the landlady my happiness, precarious yet very real as it was, ended on the day when you finally saw that your hopes of Klamm were in vain. But now you aren't even waiting for such a day any more; all of a sudden a little boy comes along, and you begin quarrelling with him over his mother as if you were fighting for the very air you breathe.' 'You have the right idea of my conversation with Hans,' said K. 'Yes, that's how it really was. But is all your earlier life really so remote from you (except, of course, for the landlady, and there's no getting rid of her) that you no longer know how one must fight to make any progress, particularly when you start from so far below? How any method offering any kind of hope must be used? And this woman comes from the castle, she told me so herself when I lost my way and visited Lasemann's house on my first day here. What would be more natural than to ask her for advice, or even aid? If the landlady knows about all the obstacles keeping people from Klamm, then that woman probably knows the way to find him; after all, she came the same way herself.' 'The way to Klamm?' asked Frieda. 'To Klamm, yes, of course, where else?' asked K. Then he jumped up. 'But now it's high time I went to fetch that buffet lunch.' Frieda earnestly begged him to stay, pleading far harder than the situation required, as if only his staying would prove all the consoling things he had said to her. But K. remembered the teacher, pointed to the door that might be flung open at any moment with a crash like thunder, and promised to come back quickly, saying she wouldn't even have to heat the stove, he would do it himself. And finally, in silence, Frieda agreed. As K. trudged through the snow outside—the path ought to have been shovelled clear a long time ago; it was strange how slowly all this work went—he saw one of the assistants still clinging to the barred fence, worn out. Only one; where was the other? Had K. at least broken the spirit of one of them? The remaining assistant was certainly still eager to carry on as before, you could see that when, enlivened by the sight of K., he immediately began stretching out his arms and rolling his eyes imploringly. I must say, K. told himself, he's a model of intransigence, but immediately he couldn't help adding: it could freeze him to that fence. However, outwardly K. had nothing to offer the assistant but a threat, shaking his fist in a manner calculated to deter him from any approach, and indeed the assistant anxiously moved some way backwards. Frieda was just opening a window to air the room before the stove was lit, as she and K. had agreed. At that the assistant left K. alone and stole up to the window, irresistibly drawn to it. Her expression one of mingled kind feelings for the assistant and helpless pleading when she looked at K., she waved her hand slightly out of the window. It wasn't even clear whether that was to fend the assistant off or to welcome him, but it didn't keep him from coming closer. Then Frieda quickly opened the outer window, but stayed behind it, her hand on the latch, her head on one side, her eyes wide, and a fixed smile on her lips. Did she know that she was enticing rather than deterring the assistant? But K. did not look back any more; he wanted to hurry as fast as possible and be back again soon.

15

At Amalia's House

AT last—it was already dark, late in the afternoon—K. had cleared the garden path, piling up the snow and beating it down firmly on both sides of the path, and now he had finished his day's work. He stood at the garden gate, with no one else in sight. He had sent the assistant off hours ago, chasing after him for quite a long way, and then the assistant had gone to hide somewhere among the little gardens and huts, couldn't be seen, and had not emerged since. Frieda was at home, either doing their laundry or still busy bathing Gisa's cat; it was a sign of great confidence on Gisa's part to give Frieda the job of bathing the cat, unpleasant and unsuitable for her as it was, and K. would certainly not have allowed it had it not been advisable, considering his various derelictions of duty, to seize every opportunity of getting into Gisa's good graces. Gisa had watched with pleasure as K. brought down the small child's bathtub from the attic, water was heated, and finally the cat was picked up and carefully placed in the tub. Then Gisa had left the cat entirely to Frieda, for Schwarzer, K.'s acquaintance of that first evening, had arrived, greeted K. with a mixture of timidity—for which the foundations had been laid that evening—and the boundless disdain due to a school janitor, and then went into the other schoolroom with Gisa. K. had been told at the Bridge Inn that Schwarzer, although he was the son of one of the castle wardens, had been living in the village for a long time for love of Gisa, and through his connections had got the parish council to appoint him an assistant teacher, although his work in that capacity was mainly confined to missing hardly any of the lessons given by Gisa herself, sitting either on the school bench with the children, or for preference at Gisa's feet on the podium. By now he was not in the way; the children had long ago become used to him, perhaps more easily because Schwarzer neither liked nor understood children and hardly spoke to them. All he had done was to take over the gymnastics lessons from Gisa, and for the rest he was happy to be near her, to live in the air that Gisa breathed and the warmth of her presence.* His greatest pleasure was to sit beside Gisa and correct the pupils' exercise books with her. They were busy with that today. Schwarzer had brought a large stack of exercise books with him, the teacher gave them his too, and as long as there was still light K. could see the pair of them sitting at a little table by the window, their heads together, never moving. Now all you could see there was the flickering light of two candles. It was a grave and silent love that united the couple. The tone was set by Gisa, whose lethargic nature would nonetheless sometimes break out into wild excess, but who would never have tolerated such conduct in other people at other times, and so the lively Schwarzer had to adapt to her, walk slowly, speak slowly, keep silent a great deal. However, anyone could see that he was richly rewarded for all this by Gisa's mere silent presence. Yet perhaps Gisa did not really love him at all, at least her round, grey eyes, which almost never blinked, although their pupils seemed to roll, gave no answer to such questions. You saw that she tolerated Schwarzer, but she certainly did not understand what an honour it was to be loved by the son of one of the castle wardens, and she carried her full and sensuous body in the same way whether Schwarzer's eyes were following her or not. Schwarzer, for his part, made constant sacrifices for her by staying in the village; when messengers came from his father to fetch him back, as they often did, he dispatched them with as much indignation as if being briefly reminded by them of the castle and his duty as a son was a harsh and irremediable disruption of his happiness. However, he really had plenty of spare time, for in general Gisa would keep him company only during lessons and while they were correcting exercises, not in any spirit of calculation but because she liked her comfort, and therefore being alone, more than anything, and was probably happiest when she could stretch out on the sofa at home at complete liberty beside her cat, who never bothered her at all, since it could hardly even move any more. So Schwarzer drifted around with nothing to do for a large part of the day, but he enjoyed that too, for it always gave him the chance, a chance which he often seized, to go to Lion Alley where Gisa lived, climb up to her little attic room, listen at the door, which was always locked, and then go away again after hearing nothing inside the room but the most complete and strange silence. The consequences of this way of life did show in him sometimes, but never in Gisa's presence, only in ridiculous outbursts at moments when he once more felt wounded in his official pride, which to be sure did not suit his present situation. When such incidents occurred they usually turned out rather badly, as K. had discovered for himself.

The only surprising thing was that Schwarzer was spoken of with a certain respect, at least at the Bridge Inn, even in matters that hardly merited it but were rather ridiculous, and the respect felt for him extended to Gisa. All the same, it was not right for Schwarzer, as an assistant teacher, to feel so vastly superior to K. No such superiority in fact existed; a school janitor is someone of great importance to the teaching staff of a school, certainly to a teacher of Schwarzer's kind; he may not be disdained with impunity, and if such disdain is felt, if someone feels he must show it for reasons of his own status, something suitable should at least be done in recompense. K. liked to think of that now and then, and Schwarzer was still in his debt from that first evening. The debt had not been diminished by the fact that the next few days had shown Schwarzer's reception of him to be correct, for that reception, it must not be forgotten, might have determined the course of all that followed it. Because of Schwarzer, the full attention of the authorities had, nonsensically enough, been drawn to K. that very first hour, when he was still a total stranger in the village, knowing no one, with nowhere to go, worn out by his long journey on foot, helpless as he lay there on the straw mattress, at the mercy of every attack from the authorities on high. Only a night later it might all have gone differently, smoothly, and in some privacy. At least no one would have known anything about him, would have had no suspicion, would at least not have hesitated to let him spend a day with them as a travelling craftsman. They would have seen how useful and reliable he was, word of it would have gone around the neighbourhood, he would probably soon have found a job as a manservant somewhere. Of course he would not have challenged the authorities. But there was a great difference between calling Central Office or someone else to the telephone in the middle of the night on his account, asking an official in Central Office to make an instant decision, and moreover asking him to do this with apparent humility but irritating persistence, especially when the person doing the asking was Schwarzer, who was probably not popular up there, and going to knock on the village mayor's door next day instead. K. could have gone there during working hours, could have said, as the situation required, that he was a stranger here, a travelling journeyman who had found a bed for the night with a certain resident of the parish, and was probably going on in the morning unless he found work here, improbable as that might be, work for only a few days, naturally, on no account would he stay any longer. That, or something like it, was how matters would have gone but for Schwarzer. The authorities would have looked into his case all the same, but at leisure, in the line of business, undisturbed by the impatience of the party pressing them for answers, whom they probably particularly disliked. Well, K. was not to blame for any of this, it was Schwarzer's fault, but Schwarzer was the son of a castle warden, and to outward appearance had behaved perfectly correctly, so it could only be chalked up against K. And what was the ludicrous reason for the whole thing? Perhaps a little spurt of temper on Gisa's part that day, which had left Schwarzer wandering around at night suffering from insomnia, and taking his annoyance out on K. Looking at it from the other side, of course, you could say that K. owed a good deal to Schwarzer's conduct. That alone had made something possible that K. would never have done on his own, would never have dared to try on his own, and for their part the authorities would hardly have allowed it: from the first he had come face to face with those authorities, so far as that was possible, openly and without equivocation. But that was a poor sort of compensation; it might spare K. a good deal of lying and secretiveness, but it also left him almost defenceless, or at least put him at a disadvantage in his struggle, and could have cast him into despair had he not felt obliged to remember the disproportionate balance of power between the authorities and himself. All the lies and cunning of which he might be capable could not have done much against that disproportion, but must have been only a relatively minor factor. However, this was only an idea entertained by K. to console himself. Schwarzer was still indebted to him, all the same, and if he had done K. harm at first, perhaps he could help now, for K. was going to need help in future in the slightest things, in his basic prerequisites, and Barnabas seemed to have failed him once more. For Frieda's sake K. had hesitated all day to go to Barnabas's home, to avoid having to receive him in front of Frieda he had worked out of doors, and after the work was done had stayed outside waiting for Barnabas, but Barnabas did not come. Now there was nothing for it but to visit the sisters, just for a little while; he would simply stand in the doorway to ask his question, and he'd soon be back. So he rammed the shovel into the snow and went off. He arrived at the Barnabas family's house out of breath, knocked briefly, flung the door open, and asked, paying no attention to what the room looked like: 'Hasn't Barnabas come in yet?' Only now did he notice that Olga wasn't there, that once again the two old people were drowsing at the table, which was a long way from K.—they still hadn't taken in the fact of his arrival at the door, and turned their faces to look his way only slowly—and finally that Amalia was lying under some rugs on the bench beside the stove, and in her first fright at K.'s appearance had started up and was holding her hand to her forehead to recover herself. If Olga had been here, then she would have replied at once, and K. would have been able to leave again, but as it was he had to take at least the few steps that would bring him to Amalia. He offered her his hand, which she pressed in silence, and asked her to keep her alarmed parents from wandering off, which she did with a few words. K. learned that Olga was out in the yard chopping wood, the exhausted Amalia—she did not say why she was exhausted—had had to lie down just now, and no, Barnabas was not home yet, but he was sure to come in very soon, for he never stayed at the castle overnight. K. thanked her for the information. Now he was free to go again, but Amalia asked if he wouldn't like to wait for Olga. He was sorry, he said, he had no time just now. Then Amalia asked if he had already spoken to Olga that day. Surprised, he answered in the negative, and asked whether there was anything in particular that Olga wanted to tell him. Amalia curled her lip as if mildly annoyed, nodded silently to K., clearly in farewell, and lay down again. From her reclining position she scrutinized him as if surprised to see that he was still there. Her gaze was cold, clear, fixed as ever, and was not precisely directed at what she was observing, instead passing by it almost imperceptibly, but without any doubt, which was disturbing. It did not seem to be due to weakness, or embarrassment, or dishonesty, but to a constant desire for privacy which dominated every other feeling, and perhaps she herself became aware of it only in this way. K. thought he remembered that this look of hers had occupied his mind on that first evening, indeed probably the entire unattractive impression the family had immediately made on him derived from it. In itself her expression was not ugly, but proud, and showed genuine reserve. 'You are always so sad, Amalia,' said K. 'Is something troubling you?

Can't you tell me? I've never seen a country girl like you before. Only today, only now, has that really occurred to me. Do you come from this village? Were you born here?' Amalia said yes, as if K. had asked only the last question, and then added: 'So you will wait for Olga, then?' 'I don't know why you keep asking the same thing,' said K. 'I can't stay any longer because my fiancée expects me home.' Amalia propped herself on her elbows; she said she didn't know anything about any fiancée. K. told her Frieda's name. Amalia said she didn't know her. She asked if Olga knew about the engagement, and K. said he thought so; after all, Olga had seen him with Frieda, and such news spread quickly in the village. However, Amalia assured him that Olga was unlikely to know about it, and it would make her very unhappy, for she seemed to be in love with K. herself. She hadn't said anything about it openly, for she was very reserved, but she involuntarily betrayed her love. K. was sure, he said, that Amalia was wrong. Amalia smiled, and that smile, although a sad one, lit up her sombre face, made her silence eloquent and her strangeness familiar. It was like the telling of a secret, a hitherto closely guarded possession that could be taken back again, but never taken back entirely. Amalia said she was sure she wasn't wrong, why, she knew even more, she knew that K. liked Olga too, and that his visits, on the pretext of some message or another from Barnabas, were really to see Olga. But now that Amalia knew all about it, he didn't have to be so strictly cautious and could come more often. That was all she'd wanted to tell him, she added. K. shook his head and thought of his engagement. Amalia didn't seem to be giving that engagement much thought; the immediate impression made on her by K., who after all was standing in front of her alone, was what mattered to her. She asked only when K. had met the girl Frieda; he had been in the village only a few days. K. told her about the evening at the Castle Inn, to which Amalia said only, and briefly, that she had been very much against anyone's taking him there. She called on Olga to vouch for that, for her sister was just coming in with an armful of wood, fresh and pink-cheeked from the cold air, lively and strong, as if her usual heavy immobility indoors were transformed by the work outside. She threw the wood down, greeted K. without embarrassment, and immediately asked after Frieda. K. cast Amalia a meaning glance, but she did not seem to think herself refuted yet. A little annoyed by that, K. talked about Frieda at greater length than he would have done otherwise, describing the difficult circumstances in which she was trying to keep house somehow or other in the school, and in the haste of telling his tale—for he wanted to go straight home—he forgot himself so far that, as he took his leave, he invited the sisters to visit him some time. But now he did feel alarm and stopped, while Amalia immediately said, without giving him time to say another word, that she would accept the invitation, so now Olga had to say so too, and she did. K., however, still harried by his feeling that he ought to get away in a hurry, and uneasy under Amalia's gaze, did not hesitate to say bluntly that the invitation had been entirely unconsidered, he had made it only out of personal inclination, but unfortunately he would have to withdraw it, since there was such hostility, although for his own part he didn't know why, between Frieda on the one hand and Barnabas and his family on the other. 'Oh, it's not hostility,' said Amalia, getting up from the bench and dropping the rug behind her, 'it's nothing that looms as large as that, it's just a case of going along with public opinion. Well, off you go to your fiancée, I can see what a hurry you're in. And never fear that we shall come and see you. I said we would at first only as a joke, out of malice. But you can come and see us when you like, there's no difficulty about that. You can always give Barnabas's messages as an excuse. I'll make it still easier for you by saying that even if Barnabas brings you a message from the castle, he can't go to the school to see you. He can't run about like that, poor lad, he's wearing himself out in the service of the castle, you'll have to come to fetch the message yourself.' K. had never heard Amalia make such a long speech, and it did not sound like the usual way she spoke; there was a kind of haughtiness in it felt not only by K. but also, obviously, by her sister Olga, who knew her well. She stood a little to one side, hands held in her lap, once again in her usual attitude, stooping slightly and with legs apart. Her eyes were fixed on Amalia, while Amalia looked only at K. 'This is all a mistake,' said K. 'You are much mistaken if you think I'm not serious about waiting for Barnabas. Getting my affairs with the authorities into order is my dearest, indeed my only, wish. And Barnabas is going to help me achieve it; much of my hope is set on him. To be sure, he has disappointed me badly once, but that was more my own fault than his. It happened in the confusion of my first hours here. I thought at the time I could get everything done on a little evening walk, and then I bore him a grudge because the

impossible proved to be impossible indeed. That has influenced me
even in assessing your family and you yourselves, but that's all over.
I think I know you better now. You are even—' here K. looked for
the right word, did not find it at once, and contented himself by saying something like what he meant: 'You may well be more kindly
disposed than any of the other village people, as far as I yet know
them. But Amalia, you bewilder me again when you make so light, if
not of your brother's job, then of his importance to me. Perhaps you
are not in the know about Barnabas's affairs. If so, very well, and I
will let the matter rest. But perhaps you *are* in the know—indeed,
that's the impression I get—and then it's bad, then it would mean
that your brother is deceiving me.' 'Never fear,' said Amalia. 'I am
not in the know, nothing could induce me to let anyone tell me about
his affairs, nothing, not even consideration for you, and I would do a
good deal for you, for as you said we are kindly disposed people. But
my brother's affairs are his own, I know nothing about them except
what I hear now and then by chance and involuntarily. On the other
hand, Olga can tell you all about it, because she's very close to him.'
And Amalia went away, first to her parents, with whom she had a
whispered conversation, and then into the kitchen. She had left without taking her leave of K., as if she knew he would stay a good deal
longer, and goodbyes were not needed.

16

K. STAYED behind, looking rather surprised; Olga laughed at him and drew him over to the bench by the stove. She seemed to be really happy to be able to sit here alone with him, but it was a peaceable happiness, certainly untroubled by jealousy. And that very lack of jealousy, and thus also of any severity, did K. good. He liked to look into her blue eyes, which were not enticing nor dominating, but shy as they rested on him and held his gaze. It was as if the warnings of Frieda and the landlady had made him not more receptive to all this, but more attentive and alert. And he laughed with Olga when she wondered why he had called Amalia kindly disposed just now. Amalia had all kinds of qualities, but kindness was not among them. To that K. explained that naturally his praise had been intended for her, Olga, but Amalia was so overbearing that she not only applied everything said in her presence to herself, but made you apply it to her of your own free will. 'That's true,' said Olga, growing more serious now. 'Truer than you think. Amalia is younger than me, younger than Barnabas too, but she's the one who makes decisions in the family, for good and for bad, and indeed she has more to bear than any of us, good as well as bad.' K. thought she was exaggerating, for only just now Amalia had said that she didn't concern herself with her brother's affairs. However, Olga knew all about that. 'How am I to explain it?' said Olga. 'Amalia cares neither for Barnabas nor for me, she really cares for no one but our parents, she tends them day and night, she has just asked what they would like for supper and has gone to the kitchen to cook for them, and has brought herself to get up, although she has been feeling unwell since midday and was lying on the bench here. But even if she doesn't care for us we are dependent on her as if she were the eldest, and if she were to give us advice on what to do we'd be certain to take it, but she doesn't; we are not close to her. You have a great deal of experience of human nature, you come from outside this place, doesn't she seem to you too particularly clever?' 'She seems to me particularly unhappy,' said K., 'but how does your respect for her fit the fact that, for instance, Barnabas carries messages, and Amalia disapproves of his job and perhaps even despises it?' 'If he knew what else to do he would stop carrying messages at once. It's not a job that satisfies him at all.' 'Isn't he a trained shoemaker?' asked K. 'Yes, to be sure,' said Olga. 'He does some work on the side for Brunswick, and could have work day and night and earn good money if he wanted.' 'Well then,' said K., 'he'd have something to do instead of working as a messenger.' 'Instead of working as a messenger?' said Olga, astonished. 'Why, do you think he does the job for what he can earn from it?' 'Maybe,' said K., 'but you were just saying it didn't satisfy him.' 'It doesn't satisfy him, for several different reasons,' said Olga, 'but it is service to the castle, after all, a kind of service to the castle, or at least that's what people are meant to think.' 'What?' said K. 'Are you all in doubt even of that?' 'Well,' said Olga, 'not really. Barnabas goes to the offices, mingles with the servants as if he were one of them, even occasionally sees an official in the distance, he is regularly given important letters to carry, why, even oral messages are entrusted to him to be delivered. That's a great deal, and we can be proud of what he has already achieved at such a young age.' K. nodded. There was no thought of going home in his mind now. 'Does he have his own livery too?' he asked. 'The jacket, you mean?' said Olga. 'No, Amalia made that for him even before he was a messenger. But you are close to touching a sore point. For a long time he'd have liked to have, well, not a livery, because there is no such thing at the castle, but an official suit, and he was promised one too, but they are very dilatory about such things at the castle, and the worst of it is that you never know what the delay means. It could mean that the matter is going through official channels, but then again it could mean that the official process hasn't even begun, that—for instance—they want to test Barnabas more first. And finally, it could also mean that the case has already been through official channels, and Barnabas will never get that suit. Nothing can be discovered in more detail, or only after a long time. We have a saying here—maybe you know it—"Official decisions are as elusive as young girls."' 'That's a good observation,' said K., and he took it even more seriously than Olga. 'A good observation, and such decisions may share certain other characteristics with young girls.' 'Perhaps,' said Olga, 'though I really don't know what you mean. Maybe you mean it as a compliment. However, as to the official suit, that's only one of Barnabas's worries, and as we all share our worries it's one of mine too. We ask ourselves in vain: why doesn't he get an official suit? But then none of this is simple. The officials, for instance, don't seem to wear official dress; as far as we know here, and from what Barnabas tells us, no, the officials go about in ordinary clothing, although it is very elegant. And you've seen Klamm. But of course Barnabas is not an official, even an official of the lowest rank, and does not presume to be one. However, even upper servants, not that we get to see those here in the village, have no official dress, according to Barnabas, which you might think on the face of it is some comfort, but a deceptive one, for is Barnabas an upper servant? No, however fond I may be of him I can't say that, he is not an upper servant, and the mere fact that he comes into the village and even lives here proves it; the upper servants are even more reserved than the officials, perhaps rightly so, perhaps in fact they rank higher than many of the officials, and there's something to be said for that view, for they do less work. According to Barnabas it is a wonderful sight to see those remarkably tall, strong men slowly walking down the corridor. Barnabas always steals carefully around them. In short, there can be no question of Barnabas's being an upper servant. So he could be one of the lower servants, but they do have official suits, at least when they come down into the village, not exactly livery, for there are many differences between them, but anyway, you can always tell the servants from the castle at once by their clothes. You've seen such men at the Castle Inn. The most striking thing about those clothes is that they are generally close-fitting. No farmer or craftsman could wear clothing like that. Well, Barnabas doesn't have such a suit, which is not just slightly shameful or humiliating, that could be borne, but it makes us doubt everything—especially when we feel depressed, and sometimes, in fact quite often, Barnabas and I do feel depressed. Then we wonder: is what Barnabas does service to the castle? He certainly goes into the offices, but are the offices really the castle? And even if the castle does have offices, are they the offices which Barnabas is allowed to enter? He goes into offices, yes, but that's only a part of the whole, for there are barriers, and yet more offices beyond them. He is not exactly forbidden to go any further, but he can't go any further once he has found his superiors, and when they have dealt with him they send him away. What's more, you are always being watched there, or at least you think you are. And even if he did go further, what good would that do if he had no official work there and was an intruder? You mustn't imagine those barriers as distinct dividing-lines; Barnabas always impresses that upon me. There are barriers in the offices that he does enter too; there are barriers that he passes, and they look no different from those that he has never crossed, so it can't be assumed from the outset that beyond those last barriers there are offices of an essentially different kind from those into which Barnabas has been. We think so only at those times of depression. And then the doubts continue, there's no dismissing them. Barnabas speaks to officials, Barnabas is given messages. But what kind of officials, what kind of messages are they? Now, he says, he has been assigned to Klamm, and Klamm in person gives him work to do. Well, that would be a great achievement, even upper servants do not get so far, in fact it would be almost too much, and that's cause for concern. Just think of being assigned to Klamm, speaking to him face to face! But is it really all it seems? Well, yes, it is, but then why does Barnabas doubt that the official who is described there as Klamm really is Klamm?' 'Olga,' said K., 'are you joking? How can there be any doubt of Klamm's appearance? It's well known what he looks like; I have seen him myself.' 'Oh, I'm certainly not joking, K.,' said Olga. 'Those are not jokes, they are my gravest anxieties. But I'm not telling you this to relieve my heart and perhaps burden yours, I am telling you because you were asking about Barnabas, Amalia told me to tell you, and I too think it will be useful for you to know more. I am also doing it for the sake of Barnabas, so that you won't hope for too much from him, so that he won't disappoint you, when he himself would suffer from your disappointment. He is very sensitive; for instance, he didn't sleep last night because you were displeased with him yesterday evening, and it seems you said that it was very hard on you to have "only such a messenger" as Barnabas. Those words kept him awake, although I don't suppose that you personally noticed it much, for messengers have to be in control of themselves. But he doesn't have an easy time, not even with you. As you see it, I'm sure you don't think you are asking too much of him; you have certain ideas of a messenger's work in your head, and you judge your own demands by those ideas. But at the castle they have other ideas of a messenger's job, ideas that can't be reconciled with yours, even if Barnabas were to sacrifice himself entirely to his work, which I'm afraid he sometimes does seem inclined to do. We'd have to go along with that, we couldn't object to it, but for the question of whether what he does really is a messenger's work. To you, of course, he can't express any doubt; as he sees it, if he did he would be undermining his own existence, offending severely against the laws which he thinks still govern him, and he doesn't speak freely even to me. I have to cajole and kiss his doubts away, and even then he won't admit that they *are* doubts. There is something of Amalia in him. And of course he doesn't tell me any of this, even though I'm his only confidante. But we do sometimes talk about Klamm. I have never seen Klamm myself, you know, Frieda doesn't much like me, and would never have given me a glimpse of him, but of course it's well known in the village what he looks like, a few people have seen him, everyone has heard of him, and it seems as if a picture of Klamm has been built up out of rumours and certain ulterior motives which distort that picture, yet in outline it is probably correct. But only in outline. Otherwise it is apt to change, perhaps not even so apt to change as Klamm's real appearance. It's said that he looks different when he comes into the village and when he leaves it, different before and after he has drunk a beer, different awake and asleep, different on his own and in conversation, and it is quite understandable, with all this, that he looks almost entirely different up in the castle. Even within the village, quite wide differences are reported: differences of size, bearing, figure, of his beard, it's only when the accounts come to his clothes that luckily they tally; he always wears the same thing, a black coat with long tails. Of course all these differences aren't the result of some magic trick, but they are easy to understand, arising from the mood of the moment, the degree of excitement, the countless nuances of hope or despair felt by those who are privileged to see Klamm, and then again, in general they catch only a brief glimpse of him. I am telling you all this as Barnabas has often explained it to me, and someone who is not personally and directly affected can set his mind at rest with that thought. But we can't, and whether he really speaks to Klamm is a matter of life and death to Barnabas.' 'It's the same for me,' said K., and they moved closer together on the bench by the stove. K. was indeed affected by all this disturbing information from Olga, but he felt it was a considerable compensation to find people here who, at least apparently, had much the same experience as he did, so that he could ally himself with them, striking up an understanding in many points, not just some, as with Frieda. He was in fact gradually abandoning any hope of success through a message brought by Barnabas, but the worse a time Barnabas had up there, the closer he was to him down here. K. would never have thought that any of the villagers themselves could be making such unhappy endeavours as Barnabas and his sister did. To be sure, that had not been fully enough explained yet, and could change to its opposite; he mustn't let himself be led astray by Olga's own nature, which was certainly innocent, into believing in Barnabas's honesty too. 'Barnabas knows the stories of Klamm's appearance,' Olga went on, 'and he has collected and compared many of them, perhaps too many, he himself once even saw Klamm through a carriage window, or thought he saw him, so he was well enough prepared to know who he was, and yet—how would you explain this?—when he went into an office in the castle, and one official among several was pointed out to him, and he was told that was Klamm, he didn't recognize him, and for a long time afterwards he couldn't get used to the idea that the official had been Klamm. But if you ask Barnabas in what way that man was different from the usual idea of Klamm, he can't reply, or rather he does reply and describes the official at the castle, but that description tallies exactly with the description of Klamm that we know. "Well then, Barnabas," I say to him, "why do you doubt it, why torment yourself?" Whereupon, in obvious difficulty, he begins to enumerate distinctive features of the official at the castle, although he seems to be inventing rather than reporting them, and in addition they are so slight—a special way of nodding the head, for instance, or simply his unbuttoned waistcoat—that you can't possibly take them seriously. What seems to me even more important is the way Klamm treats Barnabas. Usually Barnabas is taken into a large room which is an office, but it is not Klamm's office, it is not any one person's office. All down its length this room is divided into two parts by a desk at which people stand, one part of the room being narrow, where two people can only just avoid colliding, and that's the officials' area, and one part broad, the room for members of the public, the spectators, the servants, the messengers. Large books lie open on the desk side by side, with officials standing and reading most of them. But they don't always stick to the same book, and they don't exchange the books, they change places instead, and what surprises Barnabas most is the way they have to squeeze past each other in changing places, because the space is so cramped. In front of the desk and close to it there are low tables at which clerks are seated, taking dictation when the officials want them to. It always surprises Barnabas to see how that is done. There is no express order from an official, and the dictation is not loud, in fact you hardly notice that any dictation is going on. It is more as if the official is reading, as before, only he whispers as he does so, and the clerk is listening. Often the official dictates so quietly that the clerk, sitting down, can't hear him. Then he has to keep jumping up to catch what is being dictated, sit down again quickly, write it down, jump up again quickly, and so on. How strange that is, how almost incomprehensible! Of course, Barnabas has plenty of time to observe all this, for he stands in the viewing area for hours, sometimes days, before Klamm's glance falls on him. And even if Klamm has seen him, and Barnabas stands to attention, nothing is certain yet, for Klamm can turn back from him to the book, and forget him, which often happens. But what kind of a message service is so unimportant? My heart sinks when Barnabas tells me in the morning that he is going to the castle. The journey will probably be futile, the day will probably be wasted, the hope will probably be in vain. What's the point of it? And down here the shoemaking work piles up, no one does it, and Brunswick is pressing for it to be done and delivered.' 'Very well,' said K., 'so Barnabas has to wait a long time before he is given something to do. That's understandable, there seems to be an excessive number of employees there, not everyone can be given work to do every day. You shouldn't complain, it could happen to anyone. After all, Barnabas *is* given work to do; he has already brought me two letters,' 'It's possible', said Olga, 'that we are wrong to complain, particularly me, since I know all this only by hearsay, and as a girl I can't understand it as well as Barnabas, who doesn't tell me by any means everything. But now, let me tell you about the letters, for instance those letters that were brought to you. Barnabas doesn't get them directly from Klamm, he gets them from the clerk. On a random day at a random hour—that's one reason why, easy as it may seem, the work is so tiring, for Barnabas has to be on the alert all the time—the clerk remembers him and signals to him to come over. It doesn't seem to be Klamm's doing; he is quietly reading his book, and sometimes he is cleaning his pince-nez when Barnabas arrives, though he does that often anyway, and then he may look at him, supposing he can see without the pince-nez on, which Barnabas doubts. Klamm's eyes are closed, he seems to be asleep and cleaning his pince-nez in a dream. Meanwhile the clerk takes a letter for you out of the many files and papers under the table, but it isn't a letter for you that has just been written, judging by the look of the envelope it is a very old letter that has been lying there for a long time. But if it is an old letter, why has Barnabas been kept waiting so long? And you as well, probably. And finally the letter too, because by now it is probably ancient. All this gives Barnabas the reputation of being a bad, slow messenger. However, the clerk shrugs it off, gives Barnabas the letter, says: "From Klamm for K.," and with that Barnabas is dismissed. Now and then Barnabas comes home out of breath, with the letter he has at last acquired next to his skin, under his shirt, and we sit down on the bench here, as you and I are sitting now, he tells me about it, and we think hard about every detail, working out what he has achieved. We end up concluding that it is very little, and even that little is questionable, and Barnabas puts the letter away and doesn't feel like delivering it, so he takes up his shoemaking work and spends the night sitting on his stool. That's how it is, K., those are my secrets, and now I suppose you won't be surprised any more that Amalia feels she can do without them.' 'But what about the letter?' asked K. 'The letter?' said Olga. 'Well, after a while, when I have pressed Barnabas enough, and meanwhile days and weeks could have passed, he takes the letter and goes to deliver it. He is very dependent on me in such practical details, because once I have overcome the first impression of what he is telling me, I can understand what it is that he's unable to do, probably because he knows more about it. And so I can keep asking him, for instance: "What do you really want, Barnabas? What kind of career do you dream of, what is your ambition? Do you want to go so far as to abandon us, abandon me, entirely? Is that your aim? I think I should believe that, shouldn't I, because otherwise there'd be no understanding why you are so dreadfully dissatisfied with what you have already achieved. Look around you, see if any of our neighbours has done as well. To be sure, their situation is different from ours, and they have no reason to look for a better way of life, but even without making the comparison anyone can see that all is going very well for you. There are obstacles, there are doubtful factors, there are disappointments, but that means only, as we knew before, that no one gives you anything gratis, you must strive for every little thing yourself—one more reason to be proud and not downcast. And then you are fighting for us too, surely? Does that mean nothing to you?

Doesn't it give you fresh strength? And doesn't the fact that I feel proud, almost arrogant, to know that I have such a brother give you a sense of security? It is true that you disappoint me not in what you have achieved at the castle but in what I have achieved in you. You can go to the castle, you are a constant visitor to the offices, you spend whole days in the same room as Klamm, you are a publicly acknowledged messenger, you carry important messages, you are all that, you can do all those things, and then you come down—and instead of our falling into each other's arms weeping for happiness, all your courage seems to desert you at the sight of me, you doubt everything, nothing but the shoemaker's last seems to tempt you, and you do nothing with the letter which guarantees our future." That's how I talk to him, and after I have repeated it for days on end he sighs, picks up the letter, and goes out. But that's probably not the influence of my remarks, for he is on his way up to the castle again—where else?—and he wouldn't dare to go there without carrying out his errand.' 'Well, you are right in everything you tell him,' said K., 'you have summed it all up extremely well. How remarkably clearly you think!' 'No,' said Olga, 'you're deceived, and perhaps I am deceiving him. For what has he achieved? He can enter an office, but it doesn't even seem to be a real office, more of an anteroom to the offices, perhaps not even that, perhaps a room where all who may not enter the real offices must be detained. He speaks to Klamm, but is it really Klamm? Isn't it more likely someone who simply resembles Klamm? A secretary, perhaps, who at a pinch looks a little like Klamm, and tries to be even more like him, and then puts on airs in Klamm's sleepy, drowsy way. That part of his nature is the easiest to imitate, many try to copy it, although they carefully leave the rest of him alone. And a man like Klamm—in such demand, although it is so difficult to come into his presence—easily takes on different forms in people's minds. For instance, Klamm has a village secretary by the name of Momus. Ah, so you know him? He too keeps his distance, but I have seen him several times. A strong young gentleman, isn't he? And he probably doesn't look at all like Klamm. Yet you can find people in the village who would swear that Momus is Klamm, and that there really is a similarity between the two of them, but it's a similarity that Barnabas always doubts. And there is everything to back up his doubts. Is Klamm going to thrust his way into a common room here among other officials, pencil behind his ear?

That's most unlikely. Barnabas has the slightly childish habit of saying sometimes—but this is when he's in a confident mood—"The official looks very like Klamm; if he were sitting in an office of his own, at a desk of his own, and his name were on the door, well, I'd have no doubts at all." Childish but sensible. It would be even more sensible, however, if when Barnabas is up there he would ask several people how things really stand. After all, from what he says there are plenty of people going around in that room. And wouldn't what they say be much more reliable than the information of the man who showed him Klamm unasked? With so many up there, they must surely come up with points of reference of some kind, points of comparison would at least arise from the sheer number of them. That's not my idea, Barnabas thought of it, but he dares not act on it; he dares not speak to anyone for fear he might lose his job through some kind of unintentional infringement of unknown rules. That shows you how insecure he feels. His insecurity, pitiful as it really is, shows up his position more clearly than any description. How uncertain and menacing everything there must seem if he dares not even open his mouth to ask an innocent question! When I think of that I blame myself for leaving him alone in those unknown rooms where such things go on that even he, who is reckless rather than cowardly, probably trembles for fear there.'

'Now here I think you come to the crucial point,' said K., 'and this is it. From all you have said, I think I now see the situation clearly. Barnabas is too young for his responsibilities. It's impossible to take any of what he says seriously just like that. If he is half dead of fear when he goes up to the offices—well, he can't notice anything there, and if he is forced to talk about it here all the same, you'll only get confused fairy tales. I am not surprised. Awe of the authorities is innate in all of you here, and then it is also dinned into you throughout your lives in all manner of different ways and from all sides, and you yourselves add to it as best you can. I'm saying nothing against that in principle; if authorities are good authorities, why shouldn't people go in awe of them? But an uninformed youth like Barnabas, who has never been far outside the village, ought not to be suddenly sent to the castle and then expected to come back with faithful reports, whereupon everything he says is studied like a revelation, with everyone's own happiness depending on its interpretation. Nothing can be more misguided. To be sure I, like you, let myself be led astray by him, I placed my hopes on him and suffered disappointment through him, both hopes and disappointment founded merely on his words, which is to say that they had hardly any foundation at all.' Olga did not reply. 'It will not be easy for me,' said K. 'to shake your confidence in your brother, for I see how you love him and what you expect of him. But I must do it, not least for the sake of your love and your expectations. Listen: something—I don't know what it is—keeps preventing you from recognizing fully what Barnabas has not in fact achieved himself but has been granted to him. He can go into the offices, or into an anteroom if you like, well, if it is an anteroom there are doors leading further, barriers that can be crossed if you know how to do it. To me, for instance, that anteroom is entirely inaccessible, for the time being anyway. I don't know who Barnabas talks to there, perhaps that clerk is the lowest of the servants, but even if he is the lowest he can go to the next one up, and if he can't go to him he can at least give his name, and if he can't give his name then he can point to someone who *will* be able to give his name. The alleged Klamm may not have anything in common with the real one, the similarity may be visible only to Barnabas, whose eyes are blinded by his excitement, the man may be the lowest of the officials, he may not even be an official at all, but he has some kind of work to do at that desk, he is reading something or other in his big book, he whispers something or other to the clerk, he is thinking something or other when, after a long time, his eye falls on Barnabas, and even if none of that is the case, and the man and what he does mean nothing, then someone has appointed him to be there, and that person has done it with intent of some kind. Given all that, I will say that yes, there's something in it, something is offered to Barnabas, something or other at least, and Barnabas is the only one to blame if he can't get any further than into doubt, fear, and hopelessness. And in saying so I'm setting out by assuming the worst case, which in fact is very unlikely. For we have the letters in our hands, not that I trust them much, but I trust them far more than what Barnabas says. Even if they are old, worthless letters picked at random out of a pile of other equally worthless letters, with no more understanding than the canaries at fairs have, pecking out people's fortunes at random, well, even if that is so, at least those letters bear some relation to my work. They are obviously for me, if perhaps not for my own use, and as the village mayor and his wife have shown, they were written by Klamm himself and, again according to the village mayor, they have only private and rather obscure yet weighty significance.' 'Is that what the village mayor really said?' asked Olga. 'Yes, he did,' replied K. 'Oh, I'll tell Barnabas,' said Olga quickly, 'it will encourage him so much.' 'He doesn't need encouragement,' said K. 'Encouraging him means telling him he's right, he only has to go on as before, but that way he will never get anywhere. You can encourage someone with his eyes blindfolded to see through the blindfold as much as you like, he'll still never see a thing. He can't see until the blindfold is removed. Barnabas needs help, not encouragement. Think about it: up there are the authorities in their unimaginable greatness—I thought I had some approximate idea of them before I came here, but how childish that was!—well, up there are the authorities, and Barnabas comes into contact with them, all on his own, a pitiful sight. That in itself is too much honour for him, if he isn't to spend the rest of his life cast up, adrift, in some dark corner of the offices.' 'Oh, K.,' said Olga, 'don't think that we underestimate the heavy burden of the task that Barnabas has undertaken. We don't fail in our awe of the authorities. You said so yourself.' 'But it is awe gone astray,' said K. 'Awe in the wrong quarters, and that dishonours its object. Is it still worthy to be called awe if Barnabas misuses the privilege of entry to that room to spend idle days there, or if he comes down suspecting and belittling those before whom he has just been trembling? Or if, in despair or weariness, he fails to deliver letters at once, and doesn't come straight back with messages entrusted to him? I don't call that awe any more. But the blame for it goes further, it falls on you too, Olga, I can't spare you that. Although you think you are in awe of the authorities, you sent Barnabas in all his youth and weakness and isolation to the castle, or at least you didn't keep him from going.'

'As for your reproaches,' said Olga, 'I have levelled them against myself for a long time. I am not to blame for sending Barnabas to the castle, I didn't send him, he went of his own accord, but I ought perhaps to have kept him back by all possible means, by persuasion, by cunning, by main force. Yes, I ought to have kept him from it, but if today were that day of decision, if I were to feel the misery of Barnabas and our family then as I do now, if Barnabas were to move away from me again and go, gently and smiling, clearly aware of all the responsibility and danger, then even now I would not stop him, in spite of all we have gone through since then, and I think you yourself couldn't act otherwise in my place. You don't know our miserable situation, and so you do us, and particularly Barnabas, wrong. We had more hope then than we do now, but even then our hope was not great, only our misery, and so it has remained. Hasn't Frieda told you about us?' 'She's only given vague hints,' said K. 'Nothing definite, but even the name of your family upsets her.' 'And the landlady too hasn't said anything?' 'No, nothing.' 'Nobody else either?' 'Nobody.' 'Well, of course not, how could anybody say anything? Everyone knows something about us, either the truth so far as it's available to them, or at least some kind of rumour they've heard or more usually invented themselves, and they all think about us more than is necessary, but no one will tell the story straight out. They're afraid to put these things into words. And they're right too. It's difficult to dredge it all up, even to tell you about it, K., and isn't it possible that when you've heard it you too will go away and won't want to know any more about us, however little it seems to affect you personally? Then we'll have lost you, and now, I confess, you mean almost more to me than all the service that Barnabas has so far rendered to the castle. And yet—this contradiction has been tormenting me all evening—and yet you must know about it, for otherwise you will not be able to get an idea of our situation, you will still be unjust to Barnabas, which would particularly distress me, we would lack the full agreement between ourselves that we need, and you could neither help us nor accept our help, unofficial though it is. But there's still one question. Do you want to know what it is?' 'Why do you ask?' said K. 'If it's necessary, yes, I want to know it, but why do you ask like that?' 'Out of superstition,' said Olga. 'You will be drawn into our affairs in all innocence, and you won't be much more to blame than Barnabas.' 'Go on, quick, tell me,' said K. 'I'm not afraid. Your feminine anxiety makes it seem even worse than it is.'

17

Amalia's Secret

'JUDGE for yourself,' said Olga, 'and by the way, it sounds very simple, so you may not understand at once what great significance it can have. There's an official at the castle called Sortini.'* 'Oh, I've heard of him before,' said K. 'He had something to do with my appointment.' 'I don't think so,' said Olga. 'Sortini hardly ever appears in public. Aren't you mixing him up with Sordini, spelt with a "d"?' 'You're right,' said K. 'It was Sordini.' 'Yes,' said Olga. 'Sordini is very well known, he's one of the most industrious of the officials, and there are many stories about him. Sortini, on the other hand, is extremely reserved and a stranger to most of us. It's over three years ago that I saw him for the first and last time, on 3 July* at a fire-brigade festival. The castle joined in the festivities by donating a new fire engine. Sortini, who was said to be partly involved in the affairs of the fire brigade, or perhaps he was only deputizing for someone else—the officials very commonly deputize for each other, so it's difficult to be sure which of them is responsible for what—anyway, Sortini took part in the presentation of the fire engine, and of course other people from the castle came too, officials and their servants, and Sortini, as suits his character, kept right in the background. He is a small, puny, thoughtful gentleman, and all who saw him noticed the frown on his brow, remarkable because all the lines in it—and there were a great many, although he can't be over forty—fanned out over his forehead to the bridge of his nose. I've never seen anything like it. Well, so the day of the fire-brigade festival came. We, I mean Amalia and I, had been looking forward to it for weeks. We had freshened up our Sunday best, and Amalia's dress in particular was very fine, with her white blouse ruffled in front with row upon row of lace. Our mother had lent Amalia all her own lace. I was envious at the time and cried half the night before the party. Only when the landlady of the Bridge Inn came to look us over in the morning—' 'The landlady of the Bridge Inn?' asked K. 'Yes,' said Olga, 'she was great friends with us, so she dropped in, and she had to admit that Amalia had the advantage over me, and to cheer me up she lent me her own Bohemian garnet necklace. When we were ready to go out, and Amalia was standing there in front of me, we all admired her and Father said: "Amalia will find a sweetheart today, you mark my words," and then, I don't know why, I took off the necklace, though I'd been so proud of it, and put it round Amalia's neck. I wasn't at all envious any more. I acknowledged her triumph, and I thought everyone was sure to pay her tribute. Perhaps we felt surprised that she looked different from usual, because she wasn't really beautiful, but that dark glance of hers, she's kept it ever since, passed right over us, and we instinctively felt like bowing to her and almost did. Everyone noticed, including Lasemann and his wife, who came to fetch us.' 'Lasemann?' asked K. 'Yes, Lasemann,' said Olga. 'We were highly respected at the time, and in fact the party couldn't very well have begun without us, because our father was Trainer Number Three with the fire brigade.' 'Was your father still so robust at the time?' asked K. 'Father?' asked Olga, as if she didn't entirely understand the question. 'Why, three years ago he was still a relatively young man. For instance, during a fire at the Castle Inn he carried out one of the officials on his back at a run, a heavy man called Galater.* I was there myself—there was no danger of a real conflagration, it was the dry wood stacked beside a stove that started smoking, that was all, but Galater took fright and called out of the window for help. So the fire brigade came, and my father had to carry him out even though the fire was extinguished by then. Well, Galater doesn't move easily, so he has to be cautious in such cases. I'm telling you this only on my father's account. But it can't be much more than three years since that day, and now see how he sits there.' Only then did K. see that Amalia was back in the room, but she was some way away from them, at the table with her parents, where she was feeding her mother, who couldn't move her arthritic arms, and talking to her father, asking him to wait patiently for his meal, she would soon get around to feeding him too. But what she said had no effect, for her father, greedily waiting for his soup, overcame his own physical weakness and tried sometimes sipping soup from his spoon, sometimes drinking it straight from the plate, and he grumbled when he couldn't manage either, for the spoon was empty long before it reached his mouth, and when he tried the plate his drooping moustache but not his mouth got into the soup, which sprayed and dripped all over the place, anywhere except into the old man's mouth. 'Is this what three years have done to him?' asked K., but he still felt revulsion rather than pity for the old people at that corner of the family table. 'Three years,' said Olga slowly, 'or rather, just a few hours at a party. The festival was held on a meadow outside the village, by the stream. There was already a large crowd when we arrived, and a great many people had come from the neighbouring villages too, the noise was really bewildering. First of all, of course, our father took us to see the new fire engine, and he laughed with delight at the sight of it. A new fire engine made him a happy man; he began touching it and explaining it to us, he wouldn't let anyone say a word to contradict him or seem cool about it in any way, and if he wanted to point out something underneath the fire engine we all had to bend down and almost crawl under it. Barnabas, who was reluctant to do that, earned himself a slap. Only Amalia took no notice of the fire engine, but stood there very upright in her beautiful dress, and no one dared say anything to her. I sometimes went over to her and took her arm, but she still said nothing. Even today I can't explain to myself how it came about that we stood there so long by the fire engine, and only when our father moved away from it did we notice Sortini, who had obviously been behind the engine all this time, leaning against a lever that operated it. There was certainly a very loud noise, not just the kind you usually hear at parties, because the castle had also sent the fire brigade some trumpets, special instruments on which you could play the wildest of music with very little difficulty or effort, even a child could have done it. Hearing that noise, you'd have thought the Turks* were upon us, and no one could get used to it. We all jumped every time the trumpets sounded. And new as they were, everyone wanted to try playing one, and since it was a public festival one and all were allowed to have a go. There were some of those trumpet-players around us, perhaps attracted by the sight of Amalia, and it was difficult to think straight in such a racket. It was as much as we could do to pay attention to the fire engine as well, as our father demanded, and that was why we failed to notice Sortini, whom we hadn't known at all before, for such an unusually long time. "There's Sortini," Lasemann whispered to our father at last; I was standing close to them. Our father bowed deeply and signed frantically to us to bow too. Without ever meeting him, our father had always respected Sortini as an expert on the fire brigade, and had often mentioned him at home, so now seeing him in person was a great surprise and meant a lot to us. However, Sortini took no notice of us, it wasn't his way to notice people, and in fact most of the officials seemed indifferent to all they saw in public. In addition he was tired; only his official duty kept him down here, and it's not always the worst of the officials who find such duties as representing the castle a severe trial. Now that they were there, other officials and their servants mingled with the people, but Sortini stayed put beside the fire engine, his silence repelling everyone who tried to approach him with some request or flattering remark. So it was that he noticed us only after we had noticed him. It wasn't until we bowed respectfully, and Father began making excuses for us, that he glanced our way, looked wearily from one to another of us, as if he could only sigh to see yet another person standing by the person before—until he came to Amalia, and his eyes lingered on her. He had to look up at her, because she was much taller than he was. Then he gave a start of surprise, and climbed over the shafts of the fire engine to get closer to Amalia. We misunderstood that at first and, led by our father, we all tried to approach him, but he raised a hand to fend us off and then waved us away. That was all. We teased Amalia, saying she really had found a sweetheart, and stupid as we were, we were cracking jokes all afternoon, but Amalia was more silent than ever. "She's head over heels in love with Sortini," said Brunswick, who is always rather coarse and doesn't understand natures like Amalia's, but this time we almost agreed with him. Altogether, we were in a mood for tomfoolery that day, and all of us except Amalia were slightly dazed by the sweet wine from the castle when we came home after midnight.' 'What about Sortini?' asked K. 'Ah yes, Sortini,' said Olga. 'I saw Sortini many times in passing during the festivities, sitting on the shafts of the fire engine with his arms crossed over his chest, and he stayed there until the carriage from the castle came to fetch him. He didn't even stay to see the fire brigade drilling, in which our father distinguished himself more than anyone else of his age, hoping that Sortini was watching.' 'And did you hear no more of him?' asked K. 'You all seem to go in great awe of Sortini.' 'Awe, oh yes,' said Olga, 'and yes, we did hear more of him. Next morning we were woken from our tipsy slumbers by a cry from Amalia. The rest of us went straight back to bed, but I was wide awake now, and ran to Amalia where she stood at the open window, holding a letter that a man had just handed in. The man was waiting for an answer. Amalia had read the letter—it was a short one—and was holding it in her hand, which hung down limply by her side. I always loved her so much when she looked as tired as that! I knelt down beside her and read the letter. As soon as I had finished it, Amalia took it back after a brief glance at me, but she couldn't bring herself to read it again. She tore it up, threw the pieces out into the face of the man waiting outside, and closed the window. That crucial morning was the turning point. I call it crucial, but every moment of the afternoon before had been just as crucial too.' 'And what did the letter say?' asked K. 'Oh yes, I haven't told you yet,' said Olga. 'Well, the letter was from Sortini and addressed to "the girl with the garnet necklace". I can't reproduce the contents, but he was commanding her to go to him at the Castle Inn, and at once too, Sortini said, because he would have to leave again in half-an-hour's time. The letter was written in the most vulgar language, using words I had never heard before—I could only half guess what they meant from the context. Anyone who didn't know Amalia and had read that letter would have thought her dishonoured by the fact that someone could dare to address her in such a way, even though no man had ever touched her. And it wasn't a love letter, there wasn't an affectionate word in it, indeed Sortini was obviously angry to think that the sight of Amalia had affected him so much and had taken his mind off his business. We worked out later that Sortini had probably meant to go back up to the castle on the evening of the festival, but had stayed in the village because of Amalia, and in the morning, feeling angry with himself because he hadn't succeeded in forgetting her overnight, he had written that letter. At first you couldn't help feeling indignant at its language and its cold-blooded tone, but then its harsh threats would probably have inspired fear in anyone but Amalia. Amalia, however, remained indignant; she doesn't know the meaning of fear for herself or for other people. And as I crept back to bed, repeating to myself the unfinished closing sentence of the letter: "You had better come at once, or else—!" Amalia stayed where she was on the window-seat, looking out as if she expected further messengers, and was ready to treat every one of them as she had treated the first.' 'So that's what the officials are like,' said K., his voice faltering. 'To think that there are such characters among them! What did your father do? I hope he complained of Sortini forcefully in the proper quarters, if he didn't decide to go straight to the Castle Inn as the shortest and most certain way. The nastiest part of the story is not the insult to Amalia, which could easily be rectified; I don't know why you make so much of it—how could Sortini really have disgraced Amalia for ever by writing her such a letter? From what you say, one might suppose he had, but that's impossible: it would have been easy to get satisfaction for Amalia, and the incident would have been forgotten in a few days, so it wasn't Amalia whom Sortini disgraced but himself. It's from Sortini that I recoil, from him and the idea that someone can so misuse his power. Well, his abuse of power failed here, because his intentions were stated clearly, were entirely transparent, and he found a stronger opponent in Amalia, but in a thousand other cases where the circumstances were only slightly less favourable it could have succeeded and never been noticed at all, even by the victim of his abuse.' 'Hush,' said Olga. 'Amalia is looking at us.' Amalia had finished feeding her parents, and was now busy undressing her mother; she had just undone her skirt, she placed her mother's arms around her neck, raised them slightly, stripped off the skirt, and then sat quietly down again. Her father, still querulously protesting because she was attending to her mother first—obviously only because the old woman was even more helpless than he was—tried undressing himself, perhaps to punish his daughter because he thought she was dawdling, but all the same he began with the least essential and easiest to remove of his garments, the loose, outsize slippers in which his feet flopped about. But there was no way he could take them off; he had to give up, breathing heavily, and leaned back stiffly in his chair. 'You don't understand what the crucial point was,' said Olga. 'You may be right in all you say, but the crucial point was that Amalia didn't go to the Castle Inn. In itself, the way she treated the messenger might have been glossed over, that could have been hushed up. It was because she didn't go that our family was doomed, and then her treatment of the messenger also became unpardonable, in fact much was made of it for public consumption.' 'What?' cried K., but he immediately lowered his voice when Olga raised her hands pleadingly. 'You, her own sister, are surely not saying that Amalia ought to have obeyed Sortini and gone to the Castle Inn?' 'No,' said Olga, 'heaven forbid, how can you think that? I know no one who is as firmly in the right as Amalia in everything she does. If she had gone to the Castle Inn I would have thought her conduct just as correct; but her refusal to go was heroic. As for me, I'll admit to you frankly, if I had received such a letter I would have gone. I couldn't have borne the fear of the consequences if I hadn't, only Amalia could face them. There were many ways out; another girl would have made her face up prettily, for instance, and made sure it took her some time, and then she would have gone to the Castle Inn to discover that Sortini had already gone, perhaps that he'd left directly after sending the message, which in fact is very likely, for the gentlemen's whims don't last long. But Amalia didn't do that or anything like it, she was too deeply insulted and she returned a forthright answer. If she had only somehow or other appeared to obey, if she had just crossed the threshold of the Castle Inn that day, disaster might have been averted. We have some very clever lawyers here who know how to make anything you like out of almost nothing, but in this case even that helpful nothing wasn't available; on the contrary, we were left with the dishonouring of Sortini's letter and the insult offered to his messenger.' 'But what disaster?' said K. 'And what kind of lawyers? Surely Amalia couldn't be prosecuted or actually punished for Sortini's criminal behaviour?' 'Oh yes, she could,' said Olga. 'Not after a regular trial, of course, and she was not punished directly, but in another way, she and our whole family, and now I suppose you are beginning to understand how harsh that punishment is. It seems to you unjust and monstrous, but that is not the general opinion in the village; your view of the affair is kind to us, and ought to console us, and so it would if it didn't obviously arise from misconceptions. I can easily prove that to you, and forgive me if I mention Frieda here, but apart from its final outcome the relationship between Frieda and Klamm was very like the relationship between Amalia and Sortini. That may shock you at first, but you will find that I am right. And it is not a case of habit, feelings do not become blunted by dint of habit when it's a simple matter of judgement; one just has to abandon one's misconceptions.' 'No, Olga,' said K. 'I don't know why you want to go dragging Frieda into this, it wasn't like that at all with her, so please don't confuse two such fundamentally different cases. But go on with your story.' 'Please,' said Olga, 'don't take offence if I stand by my comparison. You still have some misconceptions about Frieda too if you think you have to defend her against a comparison. She is not to be defended, merely praised. If I compare the cases I don't say they are the same, they are like black and white to each other, and Frieda is white. At the worst people may laugh at Frieda, as I was ill-mannered enough to do in the bar—I was very sorry for that later—but even those who laugh at her, whether out of malice or envy, well, they can still laugh. But Amalia can only be despised by those who aren't her blood relations. That's why they are, as you say, fundamentally different cases, but all the same they are similar.' 'They are not similar,' said K., shaking his head indignantly. 'Leave Frieda out of this. Frieda never received any charming letter such as the one sent to Amalia by Sortini, and Frieda really loved Klamm. Anyone who doubts that can ask her; she still loves him today.' 'Are those such great differences?' asked Olga. 'Do you think Klamm might not have written to Frieda in just the same terms? That's how the gentlemen behave when they get up from their desks; they're ill at ease, in their distraction they will say some very coarse things, not all of them, but many do. In Sortini's mind his letter to Amalia may have been written in total disregard of what he actually set down on the paper. What do we know of the gentlemen's minds? Didn't you hear the tone in which Klamm spoke to Frieda for yourself, or haven't you been told about it? Everyone knows that Klamm is very coarse; I'm told he will say nothing for hours on end, and then suddenly he comes out with something so coarse that it makes you shudder. We don't know anything like that about Sortini, but then we aren't acquainted with him anyway. All we really know of him is that his name is very like Sordini's, and but for that similarity of their names we probably wouldn't know anything at all about him. He probably also gets confused with Sordini as an expert on the fire brigade, because Sordini is the real expert, but he makes use of the similarity of their names to land Sortini with the duty of deputizing for him, so that he himself can go on with his work undisturbed. Well, when a man as unused to the ways of the world as Sortini is suddenly smitten by love for a village girl, naturally it's not like the carpenter's journeyman next door falling in love with a girl. And we must remember that there is a great distance between an official and a shoemaker's daughter, a distance that has to be bridged somehow. Sortini tried it in that way, someone else might try another. Yes, it is said that we all belong to the castle, and there is no distance at all, no gap to be bridged, and in the usual way that may be so, but unfortunately we've had an opportunity of seeing that when it comes to the point it isn't. Anyway, all this will have made it easier for you to understand Sortini's behaviour and see it as less monstrous. In fact, compared with Klamm's it is indeed far easier to understand and far easier to bear, even to someone closely concerned. When Klamm writes an affectionate letter it is more embarrassing than the coarsest letter that Sortini could pen. Don't misunderstand me, I wouldn't venture to judge Klamm, I'm only making the comparison because you won't hear of it. But Klamm acts like a military commander with women, he orders now one of them and now another to come to him, he doesn't keep any of them for long, and then he orders them to leave again in just the same way. Oh, Klamm wouldn't even give himself the trouble of writing a letter at all. And is it, by comparison, still a monstrous thing for Sortini, who keeps himself to himself so much, about whose relationships with women we know nothing, to say the least, to sit down one day and write a letter in his fine official handwriting, even if it is a disgusting letter? And if there is no difference between that and Klamm's favours, but rather the opposite, then will Frieda's love create one? The relationship between the women and the officials, believe me, is very difficult to judge, or perhaps very easy. There is never any lack of love in this place. The officials' love is never unrequited. In that respect it isn't praise to say of a girl—and of course I'm not talking about Frieda—that she gave herself to an official only because she loved him. She loved him and gave herself to him, yes, but there is nothing praiseworthy in it. However, you will say that Amalia did not love Sortini. Well, she didn't love him, or perhaps she did love him after all, who can say? Not even Amalia herself. How can she think she loved him if she rejected him in such strong terms? Very likely no official was ever rejected in those terms before. Barnabas says that she still sometimes trembles with the same emotion as when she closed the window three years ago. That's true too, so there's no need to ask her; she has broken with Sortini, and that's all she knows, she has no idea whether she loves him or not. But we know that women can't help loving officials when the officials turn to them, indeed, they love the officials even before that, much as they may deny it, and Sortini didn't just turn to Amalia, he jumped over the shafts of the fire engine at the sight of her, he jumped over them with his official legs still stiff from sitting working at his desk. But Amalia is an exception, you will say. Yes, she is, she showed it when she refused to go to Sortini, that was exceptional enough. However, to say that in addition she didn't love Sortini would be almost too exceptional, that would be beyond understanding. We were certainly blind that afternoon, but the fact that we thought we saw something of Amalia's lovesick state even through the mists before our eyes showed that we did have some idea of it. Well, put all this together, and what's the difference between Frieda and Amalia then? Only that Frieda did what Amalia wouldn't do.' 'Maybe,' said K., 'but for me the main difference is that Frieda is my fiancée, while fundamentally Amalia matters to me only in being the sister of Barnabas, who is a castle messenger, and perhaps her fate is linked to Barnabas's employment. If an official had done her such a great injustice as it seemed to me at first from your story, it would have weighed on my mind a great deal, but even so, more as a public scandal than because of Amalia's private suffering. Now, after your story, the picture does indeed change into one that I don't entirely understand, but you are the one telling the tale and making it sound plausible enough, so I'll be perfectly happy to drop the subject entirely, I am no fireman, what does Sortini matter to me? Frieda does matter to me, however, and it is strange to me that you, whom I trusted entirely and would like to go on trusting, keep attacking Frieda through Amalia in that roundabout way, trying to make me suspect her. I don't think you are doing it on purpose, let alone with malicious intent, or I would have had to leave long ago. So you aren't doing it on purpose, circumstances make you do it, out of love for Amalia you try to elevate her above all other women, and as you can't find enough that's praiseworthy in Amalia herself for your purpose, you resort to running other women down. What Amalia did is remarkable, but the more you tell me about it, the less anyone can say whether it was a great or a small thing to do, clever or foolish, heroic or cowardly. Amalia keeps her reasons to herself, and no one will worm them out of her. Frieda, on the other hand, has done nothing remarkable, only followed her heart. That's clear to all who look at the situation in the right light, anyone can see that, there's no room for gossip. However, I don't want to run Amalia down myself or defend Frieda, I just want to make my feelings for Frieda clear to you, and point out that any attack on Frieda is also an attack on me. I came here of my own free will, and I have settled here of my own free will, but all that has happened since, and above all my future prospects—sombre as they may be, still, they do exist—all this I owe to Frieda, there's no arguing that away. It is true that I was appointed here as a land surveyor, but that was only for show, people were playing with me, driving me from pillar to post, and they are still playing with me today, but it's so much more involved now, I have gained in stature, so to speak, and that in itself is something. Little as it all may mean, I have a home, a position, and real work; I have a fiancée who, when I have other business, will do my work for me, I am going to marry her and become a member of this community, and outside the official relationship I have a personal one with Klamm, even if so far I admit I have been unable to exploit it. Isn't that something? And when I visit you, who is it you're welcoming in? To whom do you confide your family's story? From whom do you hope for a chance of some kind of help, even if only a tiny, improbable chance? Not from the land surveyor who only a week ago was forcibly expelled from Lasemann's house by the householder himself and Brunswick, no, you hope to get it from a man who already has a certain power, but I owe that power to Frieda, who is so modest that if you were to try asking her about it she would certainly claim to know nothing at all. And yet it seems to me that Frieda in her innocence has done more than Amalia in all her arrogance, because you see, I have the impression that you are looking for help for Amalia. And from whom? In fact from none other than Frieda.' 'Did I really speak so badly of Frieda?' said Olga. 'I certainly didn't mean to, and I didn't think I had, but it is possible, in our situation we are at odds with all the world, and if we begin to complain of our fate we get carried away, we hardly know where. And you are right, there is a great difference now between us and Frieda, and it is as well to emphasize that for once. Three years ago we were well-to-do girls, and Frieda only an orphan who was dairy-maid at the Bridge Inn; we passed her by without a glance, we were certainly too arrogant, but that's how we had been brought up. That evening in the Castle Inn, however, you saw the present state of affairs: Frieda with the whip in her hand, and I among the servants. But it is even worse. Frieda may despise us, that's in line with her position, it's inevitable in the circumstances. However, who does not despise us? Those who decide to despise us join the vast majority of society. Do you know Frieda's successor? Her name is Pepi. I met her only yesterday evening; she used to be a chambermaid. She certainly despises me even more than Frieda does. She saw me from the window as I came to fetch beer, hurried to the door, and locked it. I had to spend a long time begging her to open the door, and before she would let me in she made me promise her the ribbon in my hair. But when I gave it to her she threw it away in a corner. Well, she may despise me, for in part I am dependent on her goodwill, and she is a barmaid at the Castle Inn, although only temporarily, and she certainly doesn't have the qualifications for a permanent appointment there. You have only to hear how the landlord speaks to Pepi, and compare it with the tone he used to adopt in talking to Frieda. But that doesn't keep Pepi from despising Amalia too, Amalia, a glance from whose eyes alone would be enough to send little Pepi with all her braids and bows running out of the room faster than she could go on her fat little legs of her own accord. Yesterday I heard her, yet again, saying such outrageous things about Amalia that finally the guests took my side, although in the same way as you have seen for yourself.' 'How frightened you are,' said K. 'I was only giving Frieda her due, I wasn't trying to run you down, as you now seem to think. Your family seems special to me as well, I have not hidden it, but how that special quality can arouse disdain I don't understand.' 'Oh, K.,' said Olga, 'I'm afraid even you will understand it yet. Can't you see how Amalia's conduct to Sortini was what first caused that disdain?' 'That really would be strange,' said K. 'Amalia may be admired or condemned for her conduct, but why disdained? And if people really feel disdain for Amalia, out of some feeling that I don't understand, why would it be extended to the rest of you, her innocent family? It really is too bad if Pepi despises you, and if I am ever in the Castle Inn again I shall give her a good scolding.' 'But K.,' said Olga, 'if you were to try changing the minds of everyone who despises us it would be hard work, because it all starts with the castle. I still remember the late morning of that same day. Brunswick, who was our assistant at the time, had come as usual; our father had given him work to do and sent him home, and we were sitting at lunch, everyone was very lively except for Amalia and me, our father kept talking about yesterday's festivities. He had all kinds of plans for the fire brigade. The castle, you see, has its own fire brigade and had sent a detachment of it to the party. There had been a great deal of discussion with the castle firemen, the gentlemen from the castle had seen all that our own firemen could do, and the result was very much in our favour; there had been talk of the need to reorganize the castle fire brigade, instructors from the village would be called in, some of them were being considered, and our father hoped that he would be chosen.

He was talking about it now, and as he had a pleasant habit of talking at length at mealtimes he sat there, his arms resting on the table, and as he looked out of the open window and up at the sky his face was so young, so happy and hopeful—and I was never to see him like that again. Then Amalia said, with an air of knowing better that we had not seen in her before, that we ought not to trust the gentlemen very much when they said such things; the gentlemen liked to say something pleasing on such occasions, but it meant very little or nothing at all. No sooner was it said than it was forgotten for ever, but next time people would fall for their tricks again. Our mother reproved her for saying such things, and our father just laughed at her worldly-wise air of experience, but then he stopped short, seemed to be looking for something that he only now noticed was missing, but nothing was gone, and then he said that Brunswick had said something about a messenger and a torn-up letter. He asked if we knew anything about it, who was the letter for or about, what had happened? We girls said nothing. Barnabas, as young as a little lamb at the time, said something particularly silly or bold, we talked of other things, and the matter was forgotten.'

18

Amalia's Punishment

'BUT soon afterwards questions were being fired at us from all sides about that letter. Friends and enemies called to see us, acquaintances and strangers, but no one stayed long. Our best friends were in more of a hurry than anyone to say goodbye. Lasemann, usually slow and solemn in his manner, came in as if he just wanted to examine the size of the room, took a look around the place, and he'd finished. It was like some horrifying children's game when Lasemann fled, and Father excused himself from talking to some other visitors and hurried after him to the front door of the house, where he gave up. Brunswick came and told Father that he wanted to set up in business for himself, he said it straight out—he was a clever fellow, he knew how to seize his moment. Customers went into Father's storeroom looking for the boots they had brought for repair and taking them away. At first Father tried to make them change their minds—and we all backed him up as well as we could—but later he gave up and silently helped them to search. Line after line in the order book was crossed out, the stocks of leather that had been left with us were handed back, debts were paid, it all passed off without any argument. People were glad to be able to cut their links with us quickly and completely; they might suffer a loss, but that wasn't a major consideration. And finally, as anyone could have foreseen, along came Seemann the captain of the fire brigade. I still see the scene before me: Seemann so tall and strong, but slightly stooped and tubercular, always serious, he can't laugh at all, standing in front of my father whom he admired, in private he'd held out the prospect of appointment as deputy fire chief to him, and now he had to tell him that the Association was dismissing him and asking him to return his diploma. The people there in our house stopped what they were doing and crowded into a circle around the two men. Seemann can't say a word, he only claps my father on the shoulder as if knocking out of him the words that he himself ought to say and can't find. As he does so he keeps on laughing, probably in the hope of soothing himself and everyone else a little, but as he can't laugh, no one has ever heard him laugh, it doesn't occur to anyone that he *is* laughing. From then on, however, Father is too tired and despairing to help Seemann out. Indeed, he seems too tired to take in what's going on at all. We were all equally despairing, but as we were young we couldn't believe in such total disaster, we kept thinking that with all these visitors arriving, someone would come at last to stop the process and make everything go back to where it used to be. Seemann, we foolishly thought, was just the man for the part. We waited in suspense for clear words to emerge from his fits of laughter. What was there to laugh about except the stupid injustice being done to us? Oh, fire chief, fire chief, do talk to these people, we thought, and crowded about him, but that just made him turn round and round in a funny way. At last, however, he began—well, not to do as we secretly wished, but to speak after all in response to the encouraging or angry cries of the others. We still had some hope. He began by praising Father, called him an ornament to the fire service, an incomparable example to the next generation, an indispensable member of the fire brigade whose departure must be a heavy blow to it. That was all very well, and if only he had ended there! But he went on. If, none the less, the Fire Service Association had decided to ask our father to resign his post, although only temporarily, everyone would know how serious were the grounds that forced the Association to do so. Yesterday's festivities, he said, would not have been so good without Father's brilliant achievements, but those very achievements had attracted a particular degree of official attention, a spotlight was now turned on the Association, and it must be even more careful of its pure reputation than before. And then there had been the insult to the messenger, the Fire Service Association could find no other way out, and he, Seemann, he said, had assumed the onerous duty of saying so. He hoped Father would not make things even more difficult for him. Seemann was so glad to have got it over and done with that he wasn't even very considerate any more, he pointed to the diploma hanging on the wall and crooked his finger at it. Our father nodded and went to take it down, but his hands were shaking so much that he couldn't get it off the hook, and I climbed on a chair to help him. And from that moment on it was all over; he didn't even take his diploma out of the frame but handed the whole thing to Seemann just as it was. Then he sat down in a corner, did not move, and spoke to no one any more. We had to deal with all those people as best we could by ourselves.'

'And where do you see the influence of the castle in that?' asked K. 'It doesn't seem to have done anything yet. What you have told me about so far was only the unreasoning anxiety of the people, enjoyment of their neighbour's misfortunes, unreliable friendships—things that we meet with every day, and a certain pettiness on your father's part too (or so it seems to me), for what was that diploma? Confirmation of his abilities, and he still had those, they made him all the more indispensable, and he could really have made things difficult for the fire chief only by throwing the diploma on the floor at his feet once the man had spoken the first word. But characteristically, as I see it, you don't mention Amalia at all; Amalia, whose fault it all was, was probably standing calmly in the background watching the devastation.' 'No, no,' said Olga, 'it was no one's fault, no one could act in any other way, it was all the influence of the castle.' 'The influence of the castle,' Amalia repeated. She had come in from the yard, unnoticed; her parents had been in bed for some time. 'Are you telling stories about the castle? Are you still sitting together? Even though you wanted to leave at once, K., and now it's nearly ten. Don't such stories trouble you at all? There are people here who feed on stories like that, they sit together the way you two are sitting here and ply one another with gossip. But you don't seem to me to be one of them yourself.' 'Yes, I am,' said K. 'I am certainly one of them, and I'm not impressed by those who don't care for such stories and leave them to others.' 'Ah, well,' said Amalia, 'people have interests of very different kinds. I once heard of a young man who was busy thinking about the castle day and night, he neglected all else, there were fears for his sanity because his whole mind was up there in the castle. However, in the end it turned out that he wasn't thinking of the castle at all, only of the daughter of a woman who washed the dishes in the offices there. He got his girl and then everything was all right again.' 'I think I'd like that man,' said K. 'I doubt whether you'd like the man,' said Amalia, 'but you might like his wife. Now, don't let me disturb you, I'm going to bed myself, and I'll have to put the light out for my parents' sake; they drop off to sleep at once, but their deep sleep lasts only for an hour, and after that the smallest glimmer of light disturbs them. Goodnight.' And sure enough, the room was darkened at once. Amalia probably made herself a bed somewhere on the floor beside her parents' bed. 'Who is that young man she was talking about?'

asked K. 'I don't know,' said Olga. 'Maybe Brunswick, although it doesn't sound quite like him, maybe someone else. It's not always easy to understand exactly what Amalia means, because you often can't tell whether she is serious or speaking ironically. She's usually serious, but she may be ironic.' 'Never mind the interpretations!' said K. 'How did you come to depend on her so much? Did you feel the same before the great disaster, or only afterwards? And don't you ever feel a wish to be independent of her? Then again, have you any sensible reason for depending on her? She is the youngest, and ought to obey you. Guilty or innocent, she brought misfortune on your family. Instead of asking each of you to forgive her every new day, she carries her head higher than anyone, cares for nothing except your parents—I expect she feels sorry for them—doesn't want to be "in the know" about anything, as she puts it, and when she does at last speak to the rest of you, "she's usually serious, but she may be ironic". Or is it because of her beauty, which you sometimes mention, that she rules the rest of you? Well, you are all three very much alike, but what distinguishes her from you and Barnabas is not in her favour, not at all. Even when I first set eyes on her, her dull, unloving look alarmed me. And although she may be the youngest you wouldn't know it from her outward appearance. She has the look of those women who hardly age at all, but have never been truly young. You see her every day, you don't notice how hard her face is. That's why, when I think about it, I can't even take Sortini's fondness for her very seriously. Perhaps he just meant to punish her with that letter, not summon her to him.' 'I don't want to talk about Sortini,' said Olga. 'Anything is possible with the gentlemen from the castle, whether we're talking about the most beautiful girl or the ugliest. But otherwise you are quite wrong about Amalia. Look, I have no reason in particular to win you over to Amalia's side, and if all the same I am trying to do so, it is only for your own sake. In some way or other Amalia was the cause of our misfortune, that's certain, but even Father, who was worst affected by the disaster, and could never control his tongue very well, certainly not at home, even Father has never spoken a word of reproach to Amalia, not at the worst of times. And that's not because, say, he approved of what Amalia did; how could he, who revered Sortini, have approved of it? He couldn't even remotely understand it, he'd gladly have sacrificed himself and all he had to Sortini, although not in the way he actually did, not in the shadow of Sortini's probable anger. I say probable anger because we never heard any more of Sortini; if he had been reserved before, from then on he might not have existed at all. And you should have seen Amalia at that time. We all knew that no actual punishment would be inflicted. Everyone simply ostracized us, here as well as in the castle. But while of course we noticed the villagers here withdrawing from us, there was no sign from the castle. We hadn't noticed the castle paying us any special attention earlier, so how could we notice any change now? This calm state of affairs was the worst of it, not ostracism by the villagers, not by a long way, they hadn't done it out of any kind of conviction, perhaps they had nothing serious against us, their disdain had not reached its present extent, they had acted only out of fear, and now they were waiting to see what would happen next. We were not yet in want; everyone who owed money had paid us, the final balance had been to our advantage, and as for what we lacked in the way of food, relations helped us out in secret. That was easy, for it was harvest time, although we had no fields ourselves and no one would let us work for them. For the first time in our lives, we were condemned almost to idleness. So there we sat together behind closed windows in the heat of July and August. And nothing happened. No invitation, no news, no visit, nothing.' 'Well,' said K., 'since nothing happened, and you didn't expect any punishment to be inflicted, what were you all frightened of? What strange folk you are!'

'How can I explain it to you?' said Olga. 'We didn't fear anything in the future, we just suffered in the present, we were in the middle of our punishment. The villagers were waiting for us to come back to them, for Father to open his workshop again, for Amalia, whose clever needle could make lovely dresses, although only for the finest people, to be taking orders again, they were all sorry for what they had done. When a highly esteemed family is suddenly entirely excluded from village life, everyone suffers in some way; they had only thought they were doing their duty when they ostracized us, and we would have done just the same in their place. They hadn't even known exactly what it was all about, just that the messenger had returned to the Castle Inn with a handful of scraps of paper; Frieda had seen him go and then come back, had exchanged a couple of words with him, and immediately passed on what she had learnt, but again not out of hostility to us, only because it was her duty, as it

would have been anyone's duty in a similar situation. So now a happy
solution of the whole thing would have been—how shall I put
it?—the most welcome outcome to the people here. If we'd suddenly
turned up with the news that everything was all right again, perhaps
that it had been just a misunderstanding which was now entirely
cleared up, or again that, yes, an offence had been committed but
amends had been made, or—and even this would have satisfied
people here—that through our connections in the castle we had succeeded in getting remission of everything, well, then we would
certainly have been taken back, received with open arms, with kisses
and embraces, people would have thrown parties; I've seen that kind
of thing several times in other cases. But not even such news as that
would have been necessary; if we had only come of our own accord
and offered ourselves, picked up our old connections without another
word about the letter, it would have been enough. Everyone would
happily have stopped mentioning the subject, for as well as fear it
was mainly the embarrassment of the whole business that had separated them from us, they merely wanted not to have to hear about it,
talk about it, think about it, feel it affecting them in any way at all. If
Frieda mentioned it she didn't do so for pleasure, but in defence of
herself and everyone around her, to alert the community to the fact
that something had occurred from which they should keep their
distance most carefully. We as a family weren't at the centre of the
affair, only the incident itself, and we were concerned only because
we had become involved in the incident. So if we had simply come
out in public, leaving the past behind, had shown by our behaviour
that we had got over it, had appeared, so to speak, not to mind about
it, and people in general had thus been convinced that the affair,
whatever its real nature, wouldn't be mentioned again, then again
everything would have been all right, we would have found helpful
people everywhere again, even if we had forgotten the incident only
incompletely they would have understood, they'd have helped us to
forget it entirely. But instead we stayed at home. I don't know what
we were waiting for, maybe for Amalia's decision, for at the time of
the disaster, on that same morning, she had taken the reins as head
of the family and held them firmly, making no particular arrangements, giving no orders, making no requests, she did it almost
entirely through her silence alone. The rest of us, of course, had
much to discuss; we were whispering from morning to evening, and

sometimes my father called me to him in sudden alarm, and I spent half the night at his bedside. Or sometimes we sat together, I and Barnabas, who understood very little of the whole business and kept passionately demanding explanations, always the same explanations; he realized that the carefree years ahead of other boys of his age were no longer for him, so we sat together, K., very much as you and I are sitting now, and forgot that night was falling and morning coming again. My mother was the feeblest of us all, probably because she suffered not just our common affliction but everyone's separate trouble too, and we were horrified to see in her changes such as, we guessed, were in store for our whole family. Her favourite place was the corner of a sofa—we don't have it any more, it is in Brunswick's big living-room—but she sat there and—well, we didn't know exactly what she was doing—she dozed or held long conversations with herself, as the movement of her lips seemed to indicate. It was only natural for us to keep discussing the business of the letter, looking at it this way and that in all its known details and unknown possibilities, and to compete constantly in thinking up ways to bring it all to a happy conclusion. Yes, it was natural and inevitable, but not a good idea; it plunged us ever more deeply into what we wanted to escape. And what use were our ideas, however excellent? None of them could have been put into practice without Amalia, they were all just preliminaries, rendered pointless by the fact that they did not get through to Amalia at all, and even if they had, would have met with nothing but silence. Well, fortunately I understand Amalia better now than I did then. She bore more than any of us, it is incredible how much she has borne, and she still lives here with us today. Our mother perhaps bore the affliction of all of us, she bore it because she suffered its full onslaught, and then she couldn't bear it for long; it can't be said that she still bears it today, and even then her mind was confused. But Amalia not only bore our affliction, she also had the lucidity of mind to see it for what it was; while we saw only the consequences she saw the reason; we hoped for some small means of improvement, whatever it might be; she knew that all was decided, we had to whisper, she had only to keep silent. She faced the truth and lived, and bore her life then as she does now. How much better off the rest of us are, for all our misery, than Amalia. We had to leave our house, of course, and Brunswick moved in; we were given this hovel and brought our belongings here on a handcart, making several journeys. Barnabas and I pulled it, our father and Amalia pushed at the back. Our mother, whom we had brought here first, was there to welcome us, sitting on a crate and moaning quietly all the time. But I remember that we ourselves, during those laborious journeys—which were also very humiliating, for we often met harvest carts with harvesters who fell silent and turned their faces away as we passed—I remember that we, Barnabas and I, could not help talking about our anxieties and plans even on those journeys, that we sometimes stopped in mid-conversation and were reminded of our duty only when our father hailed us. But none of our conversations changed anything in our life, except that now we gradually began to feel the effects of want. Remittances from our relations stopped coming, our financial means were almost used up, and at that of all times the disdain for us as you have seen it began to be felt. People noticed that we didn't have the strength to work our way out of the letter incident, and thought poorly of us for that; they didn't underestimate our sad fate, but all the same they didn't know just what it was like. If we had overcome it they would have respected us for doing so, but as we didn't, they finally made a permanent ostracism out of what had been only temporary before. They knew that in all likelihood they themselves would not have stood the test any better than we did, but that just made it more necessary to cut off all contact with us. Now they no longer spoke of us as human beings, our family name was never mentioned, if they had to say something about us we were merely called "the family of Barnabas", who was the most innocent of us all. Even this hovel fell into disrepute, and if you are honest with yourself you will admit that you too thought you saw how justified the general disdain was when you set foot here. Later, when people sometimes came to see us again, they looked down their noses at unimportant things, for instance that the little oil-lamp there hung above the table. Where else would it hang if not over the table? But to them it seemed intolerable. However, if we hung the lamp anywhere else, they disliked that just as much. Everything we were, everything we had, met with the same disdain.'

19

Petitioning

'AND what were we doing meanwhile? The worst thing we could have done, something for which we might more rightly have been despised than for our real offence—we betrayed Amalia, we broke with her rule of silence, we couldn't go on living like that without any hope at all, and we began petitioning or pestering the castle, each in our own way, with demands for forgiveness. Of course we knew that we were in no position to make good the damage, and we also knew that the one link we had with the castle offering any hope at all, the link with Sortini, the official who liked our father, was beyond our reach because of what had happened, but all the same we set to work. Our father began paying pointless visits to the village mayor, to the secretaries, the attorneys, the clerks, who usually refused to see him, and if by chance or cunning he made his way in after all—how we rejoiced and gleefully rubbed our hands at such news—then he was sent packing very quickly and never received again. It was only too easy to answer him, everything was always so easy for the castle. What did he want, they asked? What had happened to him? What did he want forgiveness for? When had anyone in the castle raised so much as a finger against him, and if someone had, who was it? He was certainly impoverished, he had lost his customers, and so on, but those were the accidents of everyday life, the vicissitudes of his trade and the market, was the castle to take care of everything? It did in fact take care of everything, but it couldn't simply interfere in developments just like that, merely to serve the interests of a single man. Was it supposed to send its officials running after our father's customers and bringing them back to him by force? But, Father would object—we discussed all these things in detail at home both before and after he went, huddled in a corner as if hiding from Amalia, who noticed it all but left us alone—but, our father would object, he wasn't complaining of his destitution, he could easily make good everything he had lost, that was all just incidental, if only he were forgiven. But what was he to be forgiven for? they replied, no one had so far reported any wrongdoing of his, at least it wasn't in the records, or not in the records available to the attorneys, so consequently, and as far as could be discovered, he had not been charged with anything, and there were no proceedings in progress. Could he perhaps name an official order made against him? Father couldn't. Or had there been any intervention by an official agency? Father didn't know of one. Well, if he didn't know of any such thing, and nothing had happened, what did he want, then? What was there to forgive him? At most, the way that he was now pestering the offices to no good purpose, although that in itself was unforgivable. Our father did not desist, he was still a strong man then, and the idleness forced upon him left him plenty of time. 'I will win Amalia's honour back, it won't be long now,' he told Barnabas and me several times a day, but only very quietly, so that Amalia wasn't able to hear it, even though it was said only for Amalia's sake, for in fact he wasn't so much concerned with winning back her honour as with being forgiven. But to be forgiven he must first establish his guilt, and that very thing was denied him in the offices. He began thinking—and this showed that his mind was already failing—that they were keeping his wrongdoing secret because he didn't pay enough money. So far he had paid only the standard taxes, and they were high enough, at least for people in our position. But now he thought he ought to be paying more, which was certainly wrong, in our offices here they do take bribes, for the sake of a quiet life and to avoid unnecessary talk, but you never actually get anywhere that way. However, if that was what Father hoped we weren't going to upset him. We sold what we still had—almost all of it was stuff we really couldn't spare—to get our father the means for making his enquiries, and for a long time we had the satisfaction every morning of knowing that when he set off on his way at least he had a few coins in his pocket. We ourselves went hungry all day, because the only thing we could still do by getting money was to keep our father in a certain state of cheerful hope. This, however, was not much of an advantage. On his way he tormented himself, and a period that without the money would very soon have come to the end it deserved was dragged out at length like this. As there was really nothing much to be achieved in return for the extra payments, sometimes a clerk would at least appear to be doing something, promising to make enquiries, indicating that certain clues had already been found, and they would be followed up not as a duty but just as a favour to Father. And instead of doubting it he became more and more credulous. He would bring one of these obviously empty promises home as if he were restoring every blessing to our household, and it was painful to see him trying to make us understand, always behind Amalia's back, with a twisted smile and widened eyes, pointing at Amalia, that as a result of his efforts her salvation, which would surprise no one more than Amalia herself, was very close, but it was all still a secret and we mustn't say a word. And so it would surely have gone on much longer, if in the end we had not been entirely unable to scrape up any more money for Father. It is true that by now, after many pleas, Brunswick had taken on Barnabas as an assistant, but only if he fetched the work to be done under cover of dark in the evening, and once it was done brought it back under cover of darkness too—it must be admitted that Brunswick was running a certain risk to his business for our sake, although in return he paid Barnabas very little, and Barnabas does flawless work—but his wages were only just enough to keep us from starving to death. With great consideration for our father, and after preparing him for it in all sorts of ways, we broke it to him that we could no longer support him financially, but he took it very calmly. His mind was now unable to see how hopeless his efforts were, but he was worn out all the same by the constant disappointments. He did say—and he no longer spoke as clearly as before, but this he said almost too distinctly—that he would have needed only a very little more money, he'd been going to find out everything today or tomorrow, and now it was all in vain, we had failed only because of the money, and so on and so forth, but the tone in which he said it showed that he didn't really believe it himself. And now he was immediately, all of a sudden, making new plans. As he had not succeeded in proving that he was guilty of anything, and as a result could not achieve anything in the official line, he must turn exclusively to pleading and approach the officials in person. There must be some among them who had kind and sympathetic hearts, to which of course they could not give way in their work, but perhaps they might show kindness outside office hours, if taken by surprise at the right moment.'

Here K., who had so far been listening to Olga deep in thought, interrupted her story by asking: 'And you don't think that was right?' Of course the rest of the story would give him the answer, but he wanted to know it at once.

'No,' said Olga, 'there can be no question of sympathy or anything of the kind. Young and inexperienced as we were, we knew that, and so did our father, of course, but he had forgotten it just as he had forgotten almost everything. His plan was to stand on the road close to the castle, where the officials' carriages drive by, and somehow or other present his petition for forgiveness there. To be honest, it made no sense at all, even if the impossible had happened and his plea really had come to the ear of some official. Can a single official forgive anyone? At the most, it must be a matter for the authorities as a whole, but even the authorities as a whole probably can't forgive, they can only judge. But could an official form an idea of the case anyway from what our father, that poor, tired, ageing man, would mutter to him, even if he were to get out of the carriage and put his mind to the matter? The officials are very well educated, but only in a one-sided way; in his own department, an official will see a whole train of ideas behind a single word, but you can spend hours on end explaining matters from another department to him, and while he may nod politely he doesn't understand a bit of it. Of course that's all perfectly natural, you just have to think of the little official matters affecting yourself, tiny things that an official will deal with merely by shrugging his shoulders, you just have to understand that thoroughly, and then you will have plenty to occupy your mind all your life and never run out of ideas. But even if our father had reached an official responsible for our case, that official could have done nothing without the back files, particularly not on the road, he couldn't forgive anything, he could only act as an official, and to that end he would merely point out the official channels, but our father had already failed entirely to achieve anything by going through those channels. How far gone Father must have been to think that he could get anywhere with this new plan! If any opportunity of that kind had been even remotely possible, the road there by the castle would be swarming with petitioners, but since it's impossible, as the most elementary education will show, there's not a soul on the road. Perhaps that encouraged our father in his hopes, for which he drew nourishment from everywhere and anywhere. And he needed that very much now; a sound mind must not let itself in for such lofty considerations, it must clearly recognize impossibility in the most superficial aspects of the matter. When the officials drive to the village or back to the castle, they are not going on a pleasure excursion, there is work waiting for them both in the village and at the castle, that's why they drive so fast. Nor does it occur to them to look out of the carriage window in search of petitioners standing outside, because anyway their carriages are crammed full of files which they study as they are driven along.'

'Oh,' said K., 'but I've seen the inside of an official sleigh that had no files in it at all.' Such a vast and incredible world was opened up to him in Olga's story that he couldn't refrain from contributing his own mite of experience, thereby convincing himself more clearly of its existence as well as his own.

'That may be so,' said Olga, 'but then it's even worse. It means that the official has such important business that the files are too valuable or too extensive to be taken with him, and then such officials travel at a gallop. At least, they could have no time left for my father. And what's more, there are several ways to the castle. Sometimes one is in fashion, and most of the officials drive that way, sometimes another, and then that one gets crowded by traffic. No one has ever yet discovered the rules governing that change. At times they will all be driving along one road at eight in the morning, then half-an-hour later they will all be on another road, ten minutes later they'll be using yet a third, then half-an-hour later they may go back to the first road and that road will be in use all day, but every moment there is the possibility of a change. It's a fact that all the ways from the castle meet close to the village, but there all the carriages are racing along, while their speed is a little more moderate close to the castle. And just as the order in which the roads are used by the carriages is irregular, and no one can work it out, so is the number of carriages. There are often days when there's not a carriage to be seen, and then there will be crowds of them again. And just imagine our father facing all this. In his best suit, soon his only suit, he leaves the house every morning, accompanied by our blessings and good wishes. He takes with him a small fire-brigade badge, which he was really wrong to keep, and puts it on outside the village because he is afraid to wear it in the village itself, even though it is so small that you can hardly spot it two paces away, but our father really thinks it will mark him out to the officials as they drive by. Not far from the entrance to the castle there is a market garden belonging to a man called Bertuch* who supplies the castle with vegetables, and our father chose a place there on the narrow stone base of the garden fence. Bertuch allowed it, because he used to be friends with our father, and was one of his most faithful customers too; one of his feet is slightly crippled, and he thought only Father could make him a boot to fit it. So Father sat there day after day; it was a gloomy, rainy autumn, but he didn't mind the weather; he had his hand on the doorknob at the appointed time every morning and waved us goodbye, and in the evening he came home wet through, stooping more every day, and flung himself down in a corner. At first he told us about the little things that had happened, for instance how out of pity and for old times' sake Bertuch had thrown a blanket over the fence for him, or how he thought he had recognized this or that official in a carriage driving past, or again how a driver recognized him now and then, and flicked him lightly with the lash of his whip in jest. Later he stopped telling us these things, obviously no longer hoping to achieve anything at all, but he thought it his duty, his dreary vocation, to go up and spend the day there. It was at this time that his rheumatic pains began, winter was coming, snow fell, winter begins early here, well, so he sat there sometimes on stones wet with rain, sometimes in the snow. At night he groaned with pain, in the morning he sometimes wasn't sure whether he ought to go out, but he overcame his feelings and went anyway. Our mother clung to him and didn't want to let him go, and he, probably afraid that his limbs would no longer obey him, allowed her to go with him, and so she became a martyr to the pain too. We were often there with them, we took them food, or just went to see them or try to persuade them to come home—how often we found them there, huddled together on their narrow perch with a thin blanket over them, hardly covering them, and nothing around but the grey of snow and mist far and wide, with not a human being or a carriage to be seen all day long! Oh, what a sight, K., what a sight! Until one morning our father couldn't get his stiff legs out of bed any more. He was in despair, in a fevered fantasy he thought he saw a carriage stopping at Bertuch's market garden at that very moment, an official getting out, looking along the fence for our father, and then, shaking his head with an angry expression, getting back into the carriage again. At that our father uttered such cries that it was as if he wanted to attract the official's attention all the way off up there, explaining how he couldn't help his absence. And it was a long absence, for he never went there again. He had to stay in bed for weeks. Amalia took over his care and nursing, his treatment, everything, and she has done the same until this day with only a few breaks. She knows about healing herbs to soothe his pain, she hardly needs any sleep, she is never alarmed, fears nothing, is never impatient, she did all the work for our parents. And while we, unable to do anything to help, hovered around ineffectually, she remained cool and calm in every way. But when the worst was over, and Father could make his way out of bed again, cautiously and supported on both sides, Amalia immediately withdrew and left him to us.'

20

Olga's Plans

'Now we had to find some occupation for our father that he could
still manage, something that would at least keep him believing that it
helped to lift the blame from our family. Finding anything like that
was not easy, basically everything I thought of was about as useful as
sitting outside Bertuch's market garden, but I did hit upon something that gave even me a little hope. Whenever there had been talk
in the offices or among the clerks or elsewhere about our guilt, only
the insult to Sortini's messenger had ever been mentioned, and no
one dared go any further into it. Well, I said to myself, if public
opinion, even if only on the surface, seems to know only about the
insult to the messenger, everything could be put right, again even if
only on the surface, if we could make things up with the messenger
himself. No complaint has been made, they explain, so no office is
looking into the case, and therefore the messenger is free to be reconciled with us for his own part, and that's what it's all about. None
of this could have any crucial significance, it was just for show and
could lead to nothing more, but it would please our father, and perhaps the many seekers after information who had pestered him so
much could be driven into a corner, which would be very satisfying
to him. First, of course, the messenger must be found. When I told
our father about my plan he was very angry at first—for he had
always been extremely self-willed—partly because he thought, and
this notion had developed during his illness, that we had prevented
his ultimate success all along, first by stopping our financial support
and then by keeping him in bed, and partly because he was no longer
entirely able to take in new ideas. I hadn't finished telling him everything before he had rejected my plan; as he saw it, he ought to go on
waiting outside Bertuch's market garden and, since he was certainly
in no state to go up there daily by himself, we must take him in the
handcart. But I persisted, and gradually he came to terms with the
idea. What upset him was just that in this he must rely entirely on
me, for only I had seen the messenger, and Father didn't know him.
To be sure, any one of the castle servants is much like any other, and

even I couldn't be absolutely certain that I would know this one again. So we began going to the Castle Inn and looking around among the servants there. The man had been a servant of Sortini, and Sortini didn't come into the village any more, but the gentlemen often chopped and changed servants, we might well find him in the group serving another gentleman, and if we couldn't find Sortini's messenger himself, then we might get news of him from the others. But to do that we would have to go to the Castle Inn every evening, and we were not welcome anywhere, certainly not in a place like that. And we couldn't figure as paying customers. However, it turned out that we could be useful there after all; you probably know how the servants pestered Frieda. Most of them are quiet enough in themselves, but spoilt and made slow-witted by having only light work to do. "May you be as well off as a servant," say the officials when wishing each other well, and sure enough, so far as living well goes, the servants are the real masters in the castle. They appreciate that too, and are quiet and dignified in the castle itself, where they live by its rules, as I have been assured many times. Down here too we find traces of that attitude among the servants, but only traces, because otherwise it's as if they were transformed by the fact that the castle regulations don't apply to them so much here in the village, where they are a wild, unruly set, ruled not by the castle regulations but by their own insatiable desires. Their shameless conduct knows no bounds, and it's lucky for the village that they may leave the Castle Inn only when they're told to. However, in the Castle Inn itself we have to try to get along with them; Frieda found that very difficult, so she was extremely glad to turn to me to calm the servants down. I've been spending the night with the servants in the stables at least twice a week for more than two years. Earlier, when Father could still get to the Castle Inn with me, he would sleep somewhere in the bar, waiting for me to bring him any news early in the morning. There wasn't much of it. To this day we haven't found the messenger concerned, although he's said to be still in the service of Sortini, who thinks very highly of him, and when Sortini withdrew to more remote offices they say he went too. In general the servants have gone as long as us without seeing him, and if one of them does claim to have seen him it's probably a mistake. So my plan was likely to fail, and even if it hasn't failed entirely we haven't found the messenger, and unfortunately my father was finished off by walking to the Castle

Inn and spending the night there—and perhaps even by his sympathy for me, in so far as he is still capable of it—and he has been in the condition in which you've seen him for almost two years, although perhaps he is better off than my mother, whose death we expect any day now. Only Amalia's superhuman efforts keep it at bay. But what I have managed to do at the Castle Inn is to establish a certain connection with the castle; please don't despise me when I say that I am not sorry for what I did. You will perhaps be thinking, what kind of close connection with the castle may that be? And you are right, it is not a close connection. I do know many of the servants now, the servants of almost all the gentlemen who have come to the village over the last few years, and if I were ever to get into the castle I wouldn't feel I was a stranger there. To be sure, I know the servants only as they are in the village; in the castle they are quite different and probably don't deign to recognize anyone, certainly not someone they've consorted with in the village, even if they have sworn a hundred times in the stable that they'd be very glad to see me again at the castle. I have enough experience to know how little such promises mean. But that's not the main point. It's not only through the servants themselves that I have a connection with the castle; it may be the case, and I hope it is, that someone up there is observing me and what I do—and the administration of such a large body of servants must be a very important, onerous part of the official work—and whoever is watching me from up there may judge me more leniently than others do. Perhaps he realizes that I am fighting for our family and continuing our father's efforts, if only in rather a pathetic way. If you look at it like that, then perhaps I will also be forgiven for taking money from the servants and using it for our family. And I have achieved something else as well, although perhaps you will be another who blames me for it. I have heard a great deal from the servants about how people can get into the service of the castle without going through the tedious process of public acceptance, which can last years. Then they are not officially acknowledged employees, but they work under cover and are semi-official. They have neither rights nor duties, and the fact that they have no duties is the worst of it, but they do have one advantage, they are close to everything, they can spot good opportunities and use them. You are not an employee if you are one of them, but you may find some work by chance if there's no employee ready to hand, someone calls, you come hurrying up, and now you are employed, which you weren't a moment before. But when does such an opportunity arise? Sometimes quickly, you have hardly arrived, you have hardly looked around you when the opportunity comes, not everyone has the presence of mind to take it at once, but then again it may not come for more years than the procedure of public acceptance takes, and such a semi-official employee cannot be publicly acknowledged in the regular sense. There is plenty to think about here, but no one mentions the fact that very meticulous selection is involved in the process of public acceptance, and any member of a family that seems disreputable in some way or another is ruled out from the first, suppose such a person applies. He may be on tenterhooks for years anticipating the result, and from the first day everyone has been asking him in amazement how he can embark on such a hopeless venture, but he still has hope, how else could he live? Then, after many years, perhaps in old age, he learns of his rejection, he learns that all is lost and his life has been in vain. Here again, of course, there are exceptions, so it is easy to fall prey to temptation. It can happen that even disreputable people are finally accepted, there are officials who like the scent of such game, positively against their will, and then during the acceptance tests they sniff the air, they twist their mouths, they roll their eyes; in some way such a man seems to them extraordinarily appetizing, and they have to stick resolutely to the guidelines in the legal books to resist him. Sometimes, however, that helps the man not to acceptance but to an endlessly protracted acceptance procedure, one that will never come to an end at all, but will be cut short only by his death. So both legal acceptance and the other kind are full of difficulties both overt and covert, and before you let yourself in for anything of that nature it is highly advisable to weigh up the pros and cons carefully. And Barnabas and I did not fail to do so. Whenever I came back from the Castle Inn, we sat down together and I told him the latest news of what I had learnt. We discussed it for days, and Barnabas neglected the work he was doing more often than he should. And here, as you see it, I may be to blame. For I knew that we couldn't rely much on the stories the servants told. I knew that they never wanted to talk to me about the castle, they were always changing the subject, I had to wheedle every word out of them, and then when they did get going they let rip, talked nonsense, boasted, outdid each other in exaggerations and inventions, so that obviously in all that shouting, each vying with the other in the darkness of the stable, there might be at best some few indications of the truth. However, I passed it all on to Barnabas, just as I had memorized it, and he, who was still unable to distinguish between truth and lies, and as a result of our family's situation was almost dying of longing for these things, he drank it all in and was eager for more. And it was on Barnabas that my new plan depended. There was no more to be had from the servants. Sortini's messenger could not be found, and never would be, Sortini seemed to withdraw ever further, and with him so did the messenger. Even their appearance and Sortini's name often seemed to be lapsing into oblivion, and I had to describe them at length, achieving nothing except that, with some difficulty, people did remember them but could say nothing beyond that. And as for my life with the servants, naturally I had no influence on how it was judged, I could only hope that it would be taken as it was meant and that a little of the guilt would be lifted from our family, but I saw no sign of that. Yet I stuck to it, since I saw no other opportunity of doing something for us at the castle. For Barnabas, however, I did see such an opportunity. If I felt like it, and I felt like it very much indeed, I could gather from the servants' stories that a man taken into the service of the castle can do a great deal for his family. Although how much of those stories was credible? It was impossible to find out, but it was clear that it would really be very little. If, for instance, a servant whom I would never see again, or whom I would hardly recognize if I did see him again, assured me solemnly that he could help my brother find a job in the castle, or at least give Barnabas some support if he could get into the castle somehow or other, for instance by providing him with refreshment, since according to the servants' stories it appears that applicants for posts can fall down in a faint or become mentally confused while they wait, and then they are lost if they have no friends to care for them—if I was told such things and more, they were probably well-justified warnings, while the promises that went with them were entirely empty. Not to Barnabas, however, although I warned him against believing them, but the fact that I told him the stories was enough to win him over for my plans. What I said to him myself had little influence on him, he was influenced mainly by the servants' stories. And so I was really thrown entirely on my own resources; no one could communicate with our parents but Amalia, and the more I followed my father's old plans in my own way, the more Amalia cut herself off from me. She will speak to me in front of you or other people, but never now when we are alone; I was only a toy to the servants at the Castle Inn, one that they furiously tried to break, I never spoke a single word with any of them in friendship for two years, it was all underhand or lies or false, so I was left with only Barnabas, and Barnabas was still very young. When I told my stories and saw the gleam in his eyes—it is there to this day—I was alarmed, but I didn't give up; there seemed to be too much at stake. To be sure, I did not have my father's grand if empty plans, I did not have a man's determination, my idea was still to make up for the insult to the messenger, and I even thought this modest wish of mine might be considered meritorious. But what I alone had failed to do, I now hoped to achieve in a different way and more securely through Barnabas. We had insulted a messenger and chased him out of the offices at the front of the castle; what was more obvious than to offer the castle a new messenger in the person of Barnabas, so that Barnabas could do the work of the messenger who had suffered the insult, thus making it possible for him, the messenger, to stay away with an easy mind for as long as he liked, for however long he needed to forget the insult? I did realize that for all the modest nature of this plan there was also presumption in it; it could give the impression that we were dictating to the authorities, telling them how to manage their own staff, or make it look as if we doubted whether the authorities were able to make arrangements for the best of their own accord, or had been doing so long before we even thought of lending them a hand. But then again I thought it was impossible for the authorities to misunderstand me like that, or if they did they would do it on purpose, and then all I did would be rejected from the outset, without more thought. So I persisted, and Barnabas's ambition did the rest. In this time of preparation, Barnabas became so grand in his ideas that he thought shoemaking too dirty a job for someone who was to be an office employee, he even dared to contradict Amalia when she said something to him, which was rare enough, and indeed he contradicted her outright. I did not begrudge him this brief pleasure, for on the first day when he went to the castle, as could easily have been foreseen, there was an end to our joy and grand ideas. And now he began that apparent service which I have already told you about. The way Barnabas first set foot in the castle, or more correctly in that office which has, so to speak, become his place of work, without any difficulty was astonishing. This success almost turned my wits at the time, and when Barnabas whispered his news to me on coming home I ran to Amalia, seized her, led her into a corner, and kissed her fiercely, with my lips and teeth and all, so that she wept with pain and fright. I couldn't speak for excitement, and it was so long since we had talked to each other anyway, I thought I would put it off for a few days. But there was no more to tell over the next few days. We got no further than that first achievement. For two years Barnabas led the same monotonous, oppressive life. The servants failed me entirely; I gave Barnabas a little letter to take with him, in which I recommended him to their attention, at the same time reminding them of their promise, and whenever Barnabas saw one of the servants he took out the letter and showed it to him. Sometimes he came upon servants who didn't know me, and his way of showing the letter in silence, because he dared not speak up there, probably annoyed even those who did, yet it was a shame that no one helped him. Release came in a way that we ourselves could and should have thought of long before, when one servant, on whom the letter had probably been pressed several times, crumpled it up and threw it into a waste-paper basket. He might have been saying, it occurred to me: "Well, that's only the way you treat letters yourselves." Unsuccessful as this whole period was otherwise, however, it had a beneficial effect on Barnabas, if you can call it beneficial that he aged before his time, became a man before his time, and in many ways is more grave and understanding than most grown men. That often makes me look at him very sadly, comparing him with the boy he still was two years ago. And yet I do not have the comfort and support that, as a man, he might be able to provide. Without me he would hardly have got into the castle at all, but now that he is there he is independent of me. I am his one close friend, but I am sure he tells me only a small part of what is on his mind. He tells me a great deal about the castle, but from his stories, from the little things he does tell me, it's hard to understand how it can have changed him so. In particular, it's hard to understand why, when he was so brave as a boy, almost driving us to despair, he has now so entirely lost his courage as a man up there. To be sure, all that pointless standing about and waiting day after day, always starting all over again without any prospect of change, will wear a man down and make him doubtful, and ultimately incapable of anything but that despairing standing about. But why didn't he put up any resistance even at the start? Particularly since he soon realized that I had been right, and there was nothing there to satisfy his ambition, though there might be some prospect of improving our family's situation. For everything is in a very low key there, except for the whims of the servants, ambition seeks its satisfaction in work up there, and as the work itself is what matters ambition is lost entirely, there is no room there for childish wishes. But Barnabas thought, as he told me, that he saw clearly how great was the power and knowledge of even those very dubious officials into whose room he was allowed. How they dictated, fast, with eyes half-closed, brief gestures, how they handled the morose servants just by crooking a forefinger, without a word—and at such moments the servants, breathing heavily, smiled happily—or how they found an important place in their books, struck the page ostentatiously, and then, so far as was possible in the cramped space, the others came hurrying up and craned their necks to look. That and similar things gave Barnabas great ideas of these men, and he had the impression that if he ever rose so high as to be noticed by them, and was able to exchange a few words with them, not as a stranger but as a colleague in the office, although one of the most junior rank, then he could do all sorts of things for our family. But it's never come to that yet, and Barnabas dares not do anything that might bring him within reach of it, although he knows very well that, in spite of his youth, he himself has moved into the responsible position of head of the family on account of the unfortunate circumstances. And now for the last of my confessions; you came here a week ago, I heard someone at the Castle Inn mention it, but took no notice; a land surveyor had arrived—well, I didn't even know what a land surveyor was. However, next evening Barnabas—whom I usually go a little way to meet at a certain time—comes home earlier than usual, sees Amalia in the living-room, and so takes me out into the road, where he puts his face against my shoulder and weeps for minutes on end. He is the little boy of the old days again. Something has happened that is more than he can deal with. It's as if a whole new world had suddenly opened up before him, and he cannot bear the happiness and the anxiety of all that novelty. Yet nothing has really happened except that he has been given a letter to you to deliver. But it is the first letter, the first job of work, that he has ever been given.'

Here Olga stopped short. All was quiet except for the heavy and sometimes stertorous breathing of her parents. K. simply said, in a non-committal tone, as if expanding Olga's story: 'So you've all been pretending to me. Barnabas brought me the letter, acting like a busy, experienced messenger, and both you yourself and Amalia, who was obviously in league with you and Barnabas this time, made out that his work as a messenger and the letters themselves were nothing much to speak of.' 'You must distinguish between us,' said Olga. 'Those two letters made Barnabas a happy child again, in spite of all his doubts about what he is doing. He entertains those doubts only so far as he and I are concerned; in your case his honour requires him to figure as a real messenger, just like his own idea of real messengers. For instance, although his hopes of getting an official suit are now rising, within two hours I had to alter his trousers so that they would at least look like the close-fitting trousers worn by the castle employees, and as of course it's easy to deceive you in such things, he can hold his own in front of you. That's just like Barnabas. Amalia, however, really does despise his work as a messenger, and now that he seems to be having a little success, as she can easily tell from the way Barnabas and I sit together whispering, she despises it even more. She is speaking the truth, never let yourself be so far deceived as to doubt that. But if I have sometimes belittled the work of a messenger, K., it was not with any intention of deceiving you, it was out of fear. Those two letters brought by Barnabas are the only sign of grace, doubtful as it may be, that our family has had in three years. This turn in our fortunes, if it really is a turn in our fortunes and not another deception—for deceptions are more common than such a happy turn of events—is connected with your arrival here, and our fate now depends on you to some extent. Perhaps those two letters are just a start, and Barnabas's activities will extend far beyond carrying messages to you—we'll hope for that as long as we can—but for the time being it all points to you. As for the castle up there, we must content ourselves with what they give us, but down here we may perhaps be able to do something ourselves, that's to say make sure of your favour, or at least preserve ourselves from your dislike, or, and this is the main point, protect you as far as our powers and experience allow, so that you don't lose your connection with the castle, which might be a lifeline to us too. But how best to do that? How to ensure that you would have no suspicion of us when we approach you, because you're a stranger here and so you nurture certain well-justified suspicions of everyone? In addition we are generally disdained, and you are influenced by the general opinion, particularly your fiancée's, so how can we approach you without, for instance, being at odds with your fiancée even if we didn't intend it, and thus hurting your feelings? And the messages, which I read closely before you got them—Barnabas hasn't read them, as a messenger he isn't allowed to—at first sight they don't seem very important, they're old, they diminished any importance of their own by referring you to the village mayor. How are we to behave to you in view of that? If we made much of their importance, we'd be suspect for overestimating something so obviously unimportant, vaunting our merits as the ones who brought those messages to you, pursuing our own ends and not yours. Why, in that way we could belittle the messages themselves in your eyes and deceive you, which is the last thing we want to do. But if we suggest that the messages aren't very important then we're suspect too, because why in that case would we bother about delivering these unimportant letters, why would our actions and our words contradict each other, why would we deceive not only you, to whom they are addressed, but our employer, who certainly didn't give us the letters to have our explanations devalue them in the eyes of the person who received them? And treading the middle line between these extremes, I mean assessing the letters correctly, is impossible because they keep changing their own value, they give rise to endless considerations, and only chance decides where we stop, that's to say, opinion is a matter of chance. Then bring our fear of you into it as well, oh, it all gets so confused, and you mustn't judge what I say too severely. For instance, if as it happened Barnabas came home with the news that you weren't satisfied with his work as a messenger, and in his first alarm, unfortunately showing something of a messenger's sensitivity, offered to resign, I'd be in a position to retrieve his mistake by practising deception, by telling lies, by betrayal, anything bad so long as it will help. Yet then I'd be doing it, or at least I think I would, as much for your sake as for ours.'

There was a knock. Olga went to the door and opened it. A strip of light fell into the darkness from a dark lantern. The late visitor asked whispered questions and was given whispered answers, but he wasn't satisfied with that, and tried coming into the room. It seemed that Olga couldn't stop him, so she called Amalia, obviously hoping that to protect her parents' sound sleep Amalia would do all in her power to make the visitor go away. Sure enough she came hurrying up, pushed Olga aside, stepped out into the road, and closed the door behind her. It took her only a minute, and she was back as soon as she had done what Olga couldn't.

K. then heard from Olga that the visitor had come about him; it had been one of the assistants looking for him on behalf of Frieda. Olga had wanted to protect K. from the attentions of the assistants; if K. was going to tell Frieda about his visit here later, then well and good, but it ought not to be the assistants who found out that he had been to see them, as K. agreed. However, he declined Olga's suggestion that he might stay the night here and wait for Barnabas; so far as he was concerned he might have accepted, for it was late, and it seemed to him that now, whether he liked it or not, he was so bound to this family that even if it might be awkward for other reasons, staying the night here was the most natural thing in the world for him because of the bond between them. However, he still declined, made uneasy by the assistant's visit; he could not understand how Frieda, who knew his mind, and the assistants, who had learnt to fear him, were now so much in league again that Frieda didn't shrink from sending one of the assistants to find him, and only one at that. The other must have stayed with her. He asked Olga if she had a whip; she did not, but she had a good willow switch, which he took. Then he asked if there was another way out of this house. Yes, there was a second way out through the yard, only you had to climb over the garden fence and go through the garden next door before you came to the road. K. decided to do that. While Olga showed him the way across the yard to the fence, K. quickly tried to calm her fears, saying that he was not at all angry with her for giving the story her own little twist, but understood her very well, he thanked her for the confidence in him that she had shown, and proved by telling her story, and told her to send Barnabas to the school as soon as he came home, even if it was still night. It was true that the messages brought by Barnabas were not his only hope, or he would be in a bad way, but he certainly didn't want to try coping without them, he wanted to keep a good hold on them, but at the same time he wasn't going to forget Olga, for with her courage, her circumspection, her clever mind, and the way she sacrificed herself for her family, Olga herself was almost more important to him than the messages. If he had to choose between Olga and Amalia, it wouldn't take him much thought to make the choice. And he pressed her hand with heartfelt emotion as he swung himself up on the fence of the garden next door.

When he was out in the road, as far as the gloomy night would allow he could still see the assistant further along it, pacing up and down outside Barnabas's house. Sometimes he stopped and tried shining his lantern into the living-room through the curtained window. K. called out to him, and without visibly taking alarm he stopped spying on the house and came towards K. 'Who are you looking for?' asked K., testing the flexibility of the willow switch against his thigh. 'You,' said the assistant, coming closer. 'But who are you?' asked K. suddenly, for it didn't seem to be the assistant after all. He seemed older, wearier, his face fuller but more lined, and the way he walked was quite different from the jaunty bearing of the assistants, who looked as if their joints were galvanized. He walked slowly, limping slightly, with a pernickety and sickly air. 'Don't you know me?' asked the man. 'Why, I'm Jeremias, your former assistant.' 'You are?' said K., showing a small length of the willow switch that he had been hiding behind his back. 'But you look quite different.' 'That's because I'm alone,' said Jeremias. 'When I'm on my own my cheerful youthfulness is all gone.' 'Where's Artur, then?' asked K. 'Artur?' said Jeremias. 'Your little favourite? He's left your service. You were rather too harsh with us, and he couldn't put up with it, poor sensitive soul. He's gone back to the castle to complain of you.' 'And what about you?' asked K. 'It was fine for me to stay,' said Jeremias. 'Artur is complaining on my behalf too.' 'What are the pair of you complaining about?' asked K. 'We're complaining,' said Jeremias, 'that you can't take a joke. And what have we done? Cracked a few jokes, laughed a bit, teased your fiancée a little. And all of it, by the way, done to order. When Galater sent us to you—' 'Galater?' asked K. 'Yes, Galater,' said Jeremias. 'He was deputizing for Klamm at the time. When he sent us to you he said—I took particular note of it, because that's what we refer to in our complaint—you two are going to be the land surveyor's assistants, he said. What, we said, us? We don't know the first thing about that kind of work. To which he said: that's not the point; if necessary he'll teach you. But the main thing is that I want you to cheer him up a little. I hear he takes everything very hard. He's come to the village, and to him this is a great event, whereas in fact it's nothing at all, and you're going to show him that.' 'Well,' said K., 'Galater was right there—and did you carry out your task?' 'I don't know,' said Jeremias. 'It wasn't possible in such a short time. All I know is that you were very rough with us, and that's what we're complaining of. I really don't understand how you, only an employee here, and not even employed by the castle, can't see that service of that kind is very hard work, and it's extremely unfair to make a man's work hard for him in such a wilful, almost childish way as you did. Your callous attitude in leaving us freezing outside by the fence, the way you almost struck Artur dead—and he's a sensitive soul who feels pain for days after so much as a cross word—when you brought your fist down on the mattress where he lay like that, the way you hunted me all over the place in the snow in the afternoon—why, I needed an hour to recover! I'm not as young as I was!' 'My dear Jeremias,' said K., 'you're perfectly right, only you should be saying all this to Galater. It was his own idea to send you to me, I never asked him to do it. And as I never asked for you, I was justified in sending you back again, and I would rather have done it peaceably than by force, but you obviously wouldn't have that. Why didn't you come to me at once and speak about it as openly as you do now?' 'Because I was on duty, of course,' said Jeremias. 'That goes without saying.' 'And you're not on duty now?' asked K. 'Not any more,' said Jeremias. 'Artur has given in our notice at the castle, or at least the procedure that will finally take us off the job is in progress.' 'But you still come in search of me as if you *were* on duty,' said K. 'No,' said Jeremias, 'I came in search of you only to set Frieda's mind at rest. When you left her for those girls, Barnabas's sisters, she was very unhappy, not so much because of her loss as because of your betrayal, but then again she'd seen it coming long ago, and it had made her suffer severely. I went back to the school window to see if by any chance you'd come back to your senses. But you weren't there, I saw only Frieda sitting on a school bench crying. So I went in to see her and we came to an agreement. I'm going to be room-service waiter at the Castle Inn, at least until my business at the castle is cleared up, and Frieda will be back behind the bar. That's better for her. There was no sense in marrying you, not for Frieda. What's more, you didn't appreciate the sacrifice she was making for you. And now, good soul, she is still wondering sometimes whether she hasn't done you wrong, whether perhaps you weren't with Barnabas's sisters after all. But of course there could be no doubt where you were, I went to find out once and for all, because after all that agitation Frieda deserves a good night's rest, and so do I. So I went, and not only did I find you, I could see that those girls were doing just as you wanted like puppets on a string. Especially the brunette*—oh, she's a real wild-cat, the way she spoke up for you. Well, each to his own taste. Anyway, you didn't have to go taking the long way round through the garden next door, because I know it myself.'

21

So what could have been foreseen but not prevented had happened. Frieda had left him. That needn't necessarily be final; it wasn't as bad as all that, Frieda could be won back. She was easily influenced by strangers and definitely by those assistants, who thought that Frieda was in the same situation as they were, and that now they had given in their notice Frieda must do the same. But K. had only to appear in person, remind her of all the points in his favour, and she would be remorseful and go back to him, particularly if he could justify his visit to the girls by showing her that he had succeeded in something, and owed it to them. However, although he tried to reassure himself with these reflections when he thought of Frieda, he was not in fact reassured. Only a little while ago he had praised Frieda to Olga, saying that she was his only prop and stay, but she was not a very steady prop and stay; it did not take some powerful man to intervene and rob him of Frieda, only that not very appetizing assistant, a specimen of humanity who sometimes gave the impression of not being properly alive.

Jeremias had already begun moving away, and K. called him back. 'Jeremias,' he said, 'I will be perfectly open with you, so please answer one question honestly yourself. We aren't master and servant any more, and you are not the only one to be glad of it, so am I, which means we have no reason to deceive each other. Here before your eyes I break the switch I had intended for you; I took the way through the garden not for fear of you but to take you by surprise and give you a taste of the switch. Well, don't bear me a grudge, that's all over now. If the authorities hadn't forced you to be my servant, if you'd only been an acquaintance of mine, I am sure we would have got on very well, even if your appearance does bother me a little at times. And now we can make up for our omissions in that respect.' 'Do you think so?' said the assistant, rubbing his tired eyes and yawning. 'I could explain the whole thing to you in more detail, but I don't have the time, I must go to Frieda, the child's waiting for me. She hasn't gone back to work yet—she wanted to immerse herself in work at once, probably to forget you, but I persuaded the landlord to give her a little time to recover, and we will at least spend that time together. As for your idea, I certainly have no reason to lie to you, but I have no reason to confide in you either. I'm not the same as you, you see. As long as I was your servant of course you were a very important person to me, not on account of your own qualities but because of my job as a servant, and I would have done anything you wanted, but now you are a matter of indifference to me. I'm not touched by your breaking that switch either; it only reminds me what a rough master I had, so it's no use trying to win me over that way.'

'You speak to me like that,' said K., 'as if you were perfectly certain you'd never have anything to fear from me again. But that isn't the case. You're probably not free of me yet, things aren't done at such speed here—' 'Sometimes they're done even faster,' protested Jeremias. 'Sometimes,' said K., 'but there's nothing to suggest that this is one of those times. At least, neither you nor I have written notice of the termination of your job in our hands. So the procedure is only just starting, and I haven't yet intervened through my own connections, but I will. If the outcome is not in your favour, well, you didn't do much beforehand to ingratiate yourself with your master, and I may even have been over-hasty in breaking that willow switch. And you may be puffed up with pride after stealing Frieda from me, but in spite of the respect I feel for your person, even if you feel none for mine any more, I know that if I say a few words to Frieda they will be enough to tear apart the web of lies you wove to catch her. For only lies could turn Frieda against me.' 'Those threats don't alarm me,' said Jeremias. 'You don't want me as an assistant, you're afraid of me as an assistant, you're afraid of assistants in general, it was only out of fear that you hit that good soul Artur.' 'Maybe,' said K., 'but did it hurt him any less because of that? Perhaps I'll get many similar chances yet to show how afraid I am of you. I see that you don't enjoy being an assistant, and for my part I really enjoy forcing you to be one, never mind any fear of you I may have. In fact I shall be quite pleased to have you as my assistant on your own this time, without Artur. Then I can devote more attention to you.' 'Do you think,' said Jeremias, 'that I'm in the least afraid of all that?' 'Well,' said K., 'you're certainly a little afraid, and if you have any sense you're very afraid. Why else haven't you gone to Frieda already? Tell me, do you love her?' 'Love?' said Jeremias. 'She's a good, clever girl, a former lover of Klamm's, which makes her someone to be respected anyway.

And if she keeps begging me to free her from you, why shouldn't I do her the favour? Particularly as I'm not even doing you any harm, now that you've found consolation with Barnabas's wretched sisters.' 'Now I see your fear,' said K., 'and a pitiful fear it is too. You're trying to entangle me in your lies. Frieda asked me for just one thing, to set her free from my servile, lascivious assistants who had run so wild. Unfortunately I didn't have time to finish doing as she asked, and now I see the consequences of omitting to do so.'

'Mr Land Surveyor, sir! Mr Land Surveyor!' someone shouted down the road. It was Barnabas. He arrived out of breath, but didn't forget to bow to K. 'I've succeeded,' he said. 'Succeeded in what?' asked K. 'You mean you've delivered my request to Klamm?' 'Not that, no,' said Barnabas. 'I tried hard, but it just couldn't be done. I pushed my way to the front, I stood there all day uninvited, so close to the lectern that once a clerk actually pushed me aside because I was standing in his light, I tried to attract attention, which is strictly forbidden, by raising my hand when Klamm looked up, I stayed in the office longer than anyone. In the end I was alone there with the servants, and then I had the pleasure of seeing Klamm come back again, but it wasn't because of me, he just wanted to look something up in a book, and then he left directly. At last, as I still didn't move, a servant practically swept me out of the doorway with his broom. I'm telling you all this to make sure you aren't dissatisfied with what I've done again.' 'What use is all your industry to me, Barnabas,' said K., 'if you weren't successful?' 'Oh, but I was successful,' said Barnabas. 'When I left my office—well, I call it *my* office—I saw a gentleman coming slowly along, apparently from the corridors further inside the building. Otherwise the place was empty, it was already very late. I decided to wait for him; it was a fine opportunity to stay there, in fact I felt like staying there for ever rather than having to bring you bad news. But it was worth waiting for the gentleman anyway, because he was Erlanger.* Don't you know him? He's one of Klamm's principal secretaries. A slight little gentleman with a bit of a limp. He recognized me at once, he's famous for his memory and his knowledge of human nature; he simply frowns and that's enough for him to recognize anyone, often including people he's never met before, people he's only heard or read about, and he can't very well ever have seen me, for instance. But even though he recognizes everyone at once, he starts by asking questions as if he wasn't sure. "Aren't you Barnabas?" he said to me. Then he asked: "You know the land surveyor, don't you?" And then he said: "This is handy. I'm just going to the Castle Inn. Tell the land surveyor to call and see me there. I'll be in Room 15. But he'll have to come at once. I have only a few hearings to conduct there, and I'll be going back at five in the morning. Tell him I am very anxious to speak to him."'

Suddenly Jeremias set off at a run. Barnabas, who had hardly noticed him before in his excitement, asked: 'What's up with Jeremias?' 'He wants to get to Erlanger ahead of me,' said K., running after Jeremias himself. He caught up with him, took his arm firmly, and said: 'Is it desire for Frieda that's come over you all of a sudden? I feel exactly the same, so we'll go at the same pace.'

A small group of men stood outside the dark Castle Inn, two or three of them carrying lanterns, so that you could make out many of their faces. K. saw only one man he knew, Gerstäcker the carrier. Gerstäcker greeted him with the words: 'So you're still in the village, are you?' 'Yes,' said K. 'I'm here indefinitely.' 'Well, that's nothing to do with me,' said Gerstäcker, coughing hard and turning to the others.

It turned out that they were all waiting for Erlanger. Erlanger had arrived, but he was still talking to Momus before receiving the other members of the public. The general conversation turned on the fact that they weren't allowed to wait inside the inn, but had to stand out here in the snow. To be sure, it wasn't very cold, but all the same it was thoughtless to leave them waiting outside the house in the night, perhaps for hours. Of course, that was not Erlanger's fault, he was said to be very easygoing, he probably hardly knew about it, and would certainly have been very angry if he had been told. It was all the fault of the landlady of the Castle Inn, who in her neurotic striving for refinement didn't want so many members of the public in the Castle Inn all at once. 'If we must have them here, if they really must come,' she was in the habit of saying, 'then for heaven's sake let them come one after another.' And she had carried her point, so the members of the public, who at first just waited in a corridor, had to wait on the stairs later, then in the front hall, finally in the bar, and last of all they were thrown out into the street. Even that wasn't enough for her. She found it intolerable to be 'always under siege', as she put it, in her own house. She couldn't understand why members of the public had to come there at all. 'To make the steps outside the house dirty,' an official had once said in answer to her question. He probably spoke in anger, but she had found the idea very plausible, and liked to quote his remark. She was trying to get a building put up opposite the Castle Inn where members of the public could wait, which in fact would suit their own wishes very well. She would have liked it best of all if discussions with the members of the public and hearings had taken place entirely away from the Castle Inn, but the officials opposed any such idea, and if the officials seriously opposed it then of course the landlady couldn't win, although she did exercise a kind of little tyranny in minor matters, thanks to her tireless yet softly feminine zeal. However, it looked as if the landlady would have to continue putting up with discussions and hearings at the Castle Inn, for the gentlemen from the castle declined to leave the inn to go about their official business when they were in the village. They were always in a hurry, and anyway they came to the village only very much against their will; they had not the faintest desire to prolong the time they spent here beyond what was strictly necessary, so they could not be expected to move temporarily over the street with all their papers, thus losing time, just for the sake of peace and quiet in the Castle Inn. They liked best to do official business in the bar or in their rooms, if possible during a meal, or from their beds either before going to sleep or in the morning, when they felt too tired to get up and wanted to lie in bed a little longer. However, the question of erecting a building where they could wait seemed to be approaching a happy solution, although of course it was a real trial for the landlady—people laughed about that a little—because the building of such a place in itself made many discussions necessary, and the corridors of the inn were hardly ever empty.

The people now waiting were discussing all these things under their breath. It struck K. that while there was plenty of grumbling here, no one had any objection to Erlanger's summoning members of the public in the middle of the night. He asked about that, and was told that in fact they ought to be very grateful to Erlanger. Apparently it was solely his own good nature and his elevated concept of his office that moved him to come down to the village at all. If he had wanted he could have sent some under-secretary to take down statements instead, which in fact might have been more in line with the regulations. But he generally refrained from doing so, he wanted to see and hear everything for himself, although it meant giving up his nights for the purpose, because no time for visits was provided in his official timetable. K. objected that Klamm too came to the village by day, and even spent several days on end here. Was Erlanger, who was only of secretarial rank, more indispensable up at the castle? A few good-natured people laughed, while others preserved an awkward silence, the latter were in the majority, and no one seemed inclined to answer K.'s question. But one man did say, hesitantly, well, of course Klamm was indispensable in the castle and the village alike.

Then the door of the inn opened, and Momus appeared between two servants carrying lamps. 'The first to be admitted to Mr Secretary Erlanger', he said, 'are Gerstäcker and K. Are those two here?' They said they were, but then Jeremias slipped into the house ahead of them, saying: 'I'm the room-service waiter here,' and was greeted by Momus with a pat on the back. 'I see I'll have to keep a closer eye on Jeremias,' said K. to himself, although he was aware that Jeremias was probably far less dangerous than Artur, who was intriguing against him up in the castle. Perhaps it was actually wiser to let the assistants pester him than to allow them to wander around unchecked, free to hatch the plots that they seemed to delight in so much.

When K. passed Momus the latter acted as if he only now recognized him. 'Ah, the land surveyor!' he said. 'The man who was so unwilling to answer questions is now anxious for a hearing. You'd have had an easier time of it with me. Ah, well, it's difficult to choose the right hearing.' And when, at these words, K. was about to stop dead, Momus said: 'Go along, go along in! I could have done with your answers then, I don't need them any more now.' All the same K., nettled by the attitude of Momus, said: 'You none of you think of anything but yourselves. I'm not answering questions just because you're officials, either then or now.' 'Well, who else would we be thinking of?' said Momus. 'Who else matters here? Go along in!'

A servant received them in the front hall and led them the way that K. already knew, across the yard, then through the gate, and into the low corridor that sloped slightly down. Obviously only the higher-ranking officials stayed on the upper floors, while the rooms for the secretaries, even Erlanger, who was one of the most important of them, lay off this corridor. The servant extinguished his lantern, for there was bright electric light here, where everything was built on a small scale but delicately designed. The best possible use was made of the space. You could only just walk upright along the corridor; door after door opened off the sides of it, all the doors close to each other, and the walls did not go all the way up to the ceiling, presumably for ventilation, since there were probably no windows in the little rooms off this low-lying, cellar-like passage. The disadvantage of the gap at the top of the walls was that the corridor and inevitably the rooms too were noisy. Many of the rooms seemed to be occupied, and the occupants of most of these were still awake, for voices, hammer-blows, and the clinking of glasses could be heard. However, there was no impression of any particular merriment. The voices were muted; you could catch a word here and there, and no conversations seemed to be going on; the voices were probably just dictating or reading something aloud. No words were spoken in the rooms where the clink of plates and glasses could be heard, and the hammer-blows reminded K. of something he had once been told: many of the officials, as a means of relaxation after their constant intellectual efforts, liked to go in for hobbies like joinery, precision engineering, and so on. The corridor itself was empty, except for a tall, pale, lean gentleman who was sitting outside one door, wearing a fur coat with his nightclothes showing under it. He had probably found it too stuffy in the room, so he was sitting outside reading a newspaper, but not very attentively. He often stopped reading with a yawn, and then leaned forward to look down the corridor. Perhaps he was expecting a member of the public whom he had asked to come and see him and who was late. When they had passed him the servant said to Gerstäcker, referring to the gentleman: 'That's Pinzgauer!' Gerstäcker nodded. 'He hasn't been down here for a long time,' he said. 'No, indeed, not for a long time,' agreed the servant.

Finally they came to a door that looked no different from the rest, although, as the servant informed them, Erlanger was staying in the room behind it. The servant got K. to raise him on his shoulders and then looked down into the room through the space above the corridor wall. 'He's lying on his bed,' said the servant, clambering back down to the floor, 'fully clothed, but I think he's asleep. Sometimes weariness overcomes him in the village; it's the different way of life here. We'll have to wait. He'll ring the bell when he wakes up. I've known him to sleep away his entire visit to the village, and then have to go back to the castle as soon as he woke again. After all, it's voluntary work he does down here.' 'Let's hope he has his sleep out, then,' said

Gerstäcker, 'because if he has any time left for work after he wakes up he'll be very cross that he fell asleep, he'll try to get everything done in a hurry, and we'll hardly have any chance to say a thing.' 'You've come about a permit for the rights to work as a carrier for the building-site, have you?' asked the servant. Gerstäcker nodded, drew the servant aside, and spoke to him quietly, but the man was hardly listening. He looked beyond Gerstäcker, for he was more than a head taller, and gravely and slowly ran his hand over his hair.

22

THEN, looking aimlessly around, K. saw Frieda in the distance, at a turn in the corridor; she acted as if she didn't recognize him, and just looked blankly at him. She was carrying a tray of empty dishes. He told the servant, although the man didn't seem to be attending to him—the more you spoke to this servant the more his mind appeared to be elsewhere—that he would be back in a minute, and walked towards Frieda. On reaching her, he grasped her by the shoulders as if taking possession of her again, asked a few trivial questions, and looked searchingly into her eyes. But her rigid bearing hardly changed; she absently tried rearranging the china on the tray several times and said: 'What do you want from me? Go back to those—well, you know their names. You've just come from them, I can tell that you have.' K. hastily changed the subject; he didn't want this subject to be broached so suddenly, and to begin in the worst, least promising way possible for him. 'I thought you'd be in the bar,' he said. Frieda looked at him in surprise, and then gently passed her one free hand over his forehead and cheek. It was as if she had forgotten what he looked like, and did that to recall him to her mind. Her eyes too had a veiled look of appearing to remember something with difficulty. 'Yes, I've been taken back to work in the bar,' she said slowly, as if it didn't matter what she said, but beneath the words she spoke she was conducting another and more important conversation with K. 'The work down here isn't fit for me, any girl can do it—anyone who can make a bed and look friendly and doesn't fear the pestering of the guests, but actually invites it, can be a chambermaid. But a barmaid is a different matter. I was taken back at once to work in the bar, although I left the post in circumstances that weren't very creditable, but of course this time I had protection. And the landlord was glad I had protection, which made it easy for him to take me back. It was almost as if they had to press me to take the job, and if you stop to think what the bar reminds me of you'll understand why. But in the end I accepted. I'm just helping out as a chambermaid. Pepi asked them not to shame her by making her leave the bar at once, so since she's been working hard, and done everything as well as she was able, we've given her twenty-four hours' grace.' 'That's all very efficiently arranged,' said K., 'but you once left the bar for my sake, and are you going back there now just before our wedding?' 'There isn't going to be any wedding,' said Frieda. 'Because you think I was unfaithful?' asked K. Frieda nodded. 'Look here, Frieda,' said K., 'we've often talked about this supposed unfaithfulness of mine, and in the end you always had to acknowledge that your suspicions were unjust. Nothing has changed since then so far as I'm concerned, everything is as innocent as ever, and that can't change either. So there must have been some change on your part, because of rumours whispered by other people, or perhaps another reason. You do me wrong anyway, for what do you think my feelings are for those two girls? One of them, the dark one—I am almost ashamed to have to defend myself in such detail, but you make me—I probably find the dark girl's company as awkward as you do; if I can avoid her then I do, and that suits her as well. No one could be more reserved.' 'Yes,' cried Frieda, and the words burst out as if against her will. K. was glad to see her mind diverted from the subject. She wasn't acting as she had intended. 'You may think her reserved, you call that most shameless of all women reserved, and incredible as it may be you mean it; you are not pretending, I know that. The landlady of the Bridge Inn says of you: "I can't stand the man, but I can't leave him to his fate either; when you see a small child who can't walk very well yet venturing too far you can't help yourself, you have to do something about it."' 'Well, take her advice this time, then,' said K., smiling. 'We can leave that girl right out of it—whether she's reserved or shameless, I don't want to know about her.' 'But why do you call her reserved?' Frieda persisted. K. thought this attitude of hers a good sign for him. 'Have you tried making approaches, or do you want to run others down by saying so?' 'Neither,' said K. 'I'm just glad I can describe her as reserved, because she makes it easy for me to ignore her, and if she were to accost me frequently I couldn't bring myself to go back there, which would be unfortunate, since I have to go there on account of our joint future, as you know. That's why I have to talk to the other girl, and while I appreciate her efficiency, circumspection, and lack of egotism, no one can call her a temptress.' 'The servants think otherwise,' said Frieda. 'In that and in much else,' said K. 'Are you going to conclude that I'm unfaithful because the servants give their lust free rein?' Frieda did not reply, and allowed

K. to take the tray from her, put it on the floor, link arms with her, and begin slowly walking up and down the small space in her company. 'You don't know what it means to be faithful,' she said, pulling slightly away from him. 'The way you may behave with those girls isn't the main thing; your going to see that family at all and coming back with the smell of their living-room on your clothes shames me beyond bearing. And then you leave the school without a word. And you stay half the night with them, and when someone comes looking for you, you get the girls to deny that you are there, to deny it passionately, especially the one who's so wonderfully reserved. You slink out of the house by a secret way, perhaps to spare the reputation of those girls. The reputation of those girls, indeed! No, let's not talk about it any more.' 'No, let's not talk about that,' agreed K., 'but about something else. You're right, there's no more to be said on that subject. You know why I have to go there. It isn't easy for me, but I overcome my feelings. You shouldn't make it harder for me than it is already. Today I meant to call just for a minute and ask whether Barnabas was home at last, because for a long time he's been supposed to be bringing me an important message. He hadn't returned, but I was credibly assured that he was bound to be home soon. I didn't want to have him following me back to the school, in order to spare you his presence. Well, the hours passed by, and I'm afraid he didn't come. But someone else did, someone I hate. I didn't want to have him spying on me, so I left through the garden of the house next door, but I wasn't going to hide from him either, and instead I went openly out on the road, carrying, I admit, a very flexible willow switch. That's all, so there's no more to be said about that either, although again there *is* something else to add. What about those assistants, mention of whom I find almost as repellent as mention of that family is to you? Compare your relationship with them and my conduct towards that family. I understand your dislike of the family, and can share it. I visit them only for the sake of our cause, and sometimes I almost feel that I'm exploiting them and doing them wrong. But what about you and the assistants? You don't deny that they are pursuing you, and you've admitted that you are attracted to them. I wasn't angry with you for that, I saw that there are forces beyond your control at work here, I was happy to think that at least you were resisting, I helped to defend you, and just because I neglected to do so for a couple of hours, trusting in your constancy and, moreover, in the hope that the place was firmly locked up and the assistants finally put to flight—I'm afraid I keep underestimating them—just because I neglected our defence for a couple of hours, and that man Jeremias, who when you look at him closely is not very healthy and is getting on in years, had the gall to go up to the window—am I to lose you just for that, Frieda, and be greeted with the news that "there isn't going to be any wedding"? Shouldn't I be the one to feel I might reproach you? But I don't, no, I still don't reproach you.' Once again, it seemed a good idea to K. to take Frieda's mind off the subject, so he asked her to bring him something to eat, since he hadn't eaten anything since midday. Obviously relieved by such a request, Frieda nodded and went off to fetch something, going not further along the corridor in what K. expected to be the direction of the kitchen, but down a couple of steps to one side. She soon brought back a plate of sliced cold meats and a bottle of wine, but these looked like the remains of someone else's supper. The slices of meat had been rearranged in a hurry to disguise the fact, but there were even some sausage-skins left on the plate, and the bottle was three-quarters empty. However, K. said nothing about that, and set about his meal with a hearty appetite. 'Did you go to the kitchen?' he asked. 'No, to my room,' she said. 'I have a room down here.' 'Well, you might have taken me with you,' said K. 'I'll go along there now so that I can sit down while I eat.' 'I'll bring you a chair,' said Frieda, and was on her way again. 'No, thank you,' said K., holding her back. 'I won't go down there after all, nor do I need a chair now.' Frieda bore his grip on her with an expression of defiance, with her head bent and biting her lip. 'Very well, yes, he's down there,' she said. 'What else did you expect? He's lying in my bed, he caught a chill outside, he's freezing, he could hardly eat a thing. Basically it's all your fault. If you hadn't chased the assistants away and gone running after those people, we could be sitting peacefully in the schoolhouse now. You're the one who's destroyed our happiness. Do you think that as long as he was in your service Jeremias would have dared to run off with me? If so, you don't understand the way things work here in the slightest. He wanted to be near me, he was in torments, he lay in wait for me, but that was just a game, like a hungry dog playing about yet not daring to jump on the table. And it was the same with me. I was attracted to him, he was my playmate in our childhood days—we played together on the slopes of Castle Mount, ah, happy days! You've never asked me about my past life. But none of that mattered as long as Jeremias was kept in check by his service to you, for I knew my duty as your future wife. But then you go driving the assistants away and boasting of it too, as if you'd done it all for me, which in a certain sense is true. Your intentions worked with Artur, although only for the time being, he is a sensitive soul, he doesn't have the passion of Jeremias, who fears no difficulty. You almost killed Artur with that blow of your fist in the night—it was a blow struck against our happiness too. He fled to the castle to complain, and although he may be back soon, he's not here now. Jeremias, however, stayed. While he's on duty he fears the merest flicker of his master's eyes, but off duty he fears nothing. He came and took me away when you had abandoned me. Under my old friend's influence I couldn't help myself. I didn't unlock the school door; he broke the window and helped me out. We fled here, the landlord respects him, and the guests will be delighted to have such a good waiter on room service, so we were taken in. He isn't living with me, but we share the same room.' 'In spite of everything,' said K., 'I'm not sorry I drove the assistants away from my service. If the relationship was as you describe it, then it was as well for everything to come to an end. Our happiness wouldn't have been very great, in a marriage where two beasts of prey who duck only under the lash were also present. So I am grateful to that family too, since they unintentionally played their part in separating us.' They fell silent, and went on walking up and down. No one could have said who had begun it. Frieda, beside K., seemed cross that he did not take her arm again. 'So everything would be all right,' K. went on, 'and we could part and go away, you to your new master Jeremias, who probably still has a chill from the school garden—considering that, perhaps you've left him alone too long—I to go back to the school on my own or, since I have no business there without you, somewhere else, anywhere they will take me in. If I hesitate all the same, it's because I still have good reason to doubt what you've told me a little. I get quite the opposite impression of Jeremias. All the time he was in my service he was after you, and I don't think being on duty would have kept him for ever from attacking you in earnest. But now that he thinks his service to me is over, it's different. Forgive me if I put it like this: since you are not his master's fiancée any more, you are not such a temptation to him as you were before. You may be his childhood sweetheart, but in my opinion—although I really know him only from a short conversation last night—he doesn't place much value on such emotions. I don't know why he seems to you passionate. His way of thinking strikes me as particularly cool. As far as I'm concerned, he was given a job by Galater which was not, perhaps, very much to my liking, he tried to carry it out, with a certain devotion to duty, yes, that I will admit—it isn't so very rare here—and part of it was to destroy our relationship. He may have tried that in various ways, one of them being to tempt you by his lustful behaviour, another—and here the landlady supported him—to tell lies about my unfaithfulness. He succeeded in his attempt; some kind of memory of Klamm clinging to him may have helped; he did lose his post, but perhaps at the very moment when he didn't need it any more, and now he harvests the fruits of his labours by helping you out of the school window, but with that his work is over, he's not devoted to duty any more, he feels tired. He'd rather be in Artur's place. Artur is probably not complaining at all but is enjoying praise and new commissions, but someone has to stay behind to see how things develop now. Looking after you is his rather onerous obligation. He doesn't feel a trace of love for you, he told me so openly, as Klamm's former lover you seem to him, naturally, someone to be respected, and settling into your room and feeling like a little Klamm for once must be very nice, but that's all. You yourself mean nothing to him, it is only as a small part of his main task that he has had you taken back here; he's stayed himself so as not to make you uneasy, but only for the time being, until he gets more news from the castle and you have cured him of his chill.' 'How you slander him!' said Frieda, and struck her little fists together. 'Slander him?' said K. 'No, I don't mean to slander him. But I may be doing him wrong, that's always possible. What I have said about him isn't clear for all to see; it may be interpreted otherwise. But slander? The only purpose of slander could be to counter your love for him. If that were necessary, and if slander were a suitable means, I wouldn't hesitate to slander him. No one could blame me for that; the man who sent him gave him such an advantage over me that, alone and relying only on myself, I might well try a little slander. It would be a relatively innocent, if ultimately useless, means of defence. So give those fists of yours a rest.' And K. took Frieda's hand in his; Frieda tried to withdraw it, but smilingly, and not exerting very much strength. 'However, I don't have to slander him,' said K., 'because you don't love him, you only think you do, and you will be grateful to me for opening your eyes to the deception. Look, if someone wanted to separate you from me without force, but by dint of very careful calculation, then it had to be done through the two assistants. Apparently good, childish, amusing, irresponsible lads coming here from on high, from the castle, a little memory of your childhood too, that's all very delightful, particularly if I am the opposite of all this, always out and about on business that you don't entirely understand, that bothers you, that brings me together with people whom you dislike, and for all my innocence perhaps you transfer some of that dislike to me. The whole thing is just a malicious, if very clever, exploitation of the flaws in our relationship. Every relationship has its flaws, and so does ours; we came together out of two entirely different worlds, and since we have known each other both our lives have taken an entirely new turn. We still feel uncertain of ourselves; it is all too new. I am not speaking about myself, that's not so important, basically I have been given gift after gift since you first turned your eyes to mine, and it's not very difficult to get accustomed to gifts. But you, apart from everything else, were torn away from Klamm; I can't judge what that means, but I have gradually gained some notion of it. The ground shakes beneath your feet, you can't find your way, and even if I was always ready to steady you I wasn't always present, and when I was, your attention was sometimes claimed by your reveries, or a more physical presence such as the landlady—there were moments when you looked away from me, longing to be somewhere else, somewhere half-unspecified, poor child, and in such interim periods suitable people had only to be brought in front of your eyes and you were lost to them, a prey to the pretence that what were only brief moments, ghosts, old memories of your past life now passing further and further away, still made up your real life in the present. A mistake, Frieda, nothing but the last obstacle in the way of our final union, and seen in the right light it's a pathetic one. Come to yourself, come to your senses; you may have thought that the assistants were sent by Klamm—which is not true; they come from Galater—and if they could cast such a spell on you with the help of that deception, you may then have thought you saw traces of Klamm even in their dirt and dissolute ways, just as someone may think he sees a lost jewel in a muck-heap, while he couldn't find it there even if it were real. But they are only rough fellows like the servants who sleep in the stables, except that they don't have the same sturdy good health; a little fresh air makes them sick and sends them to bed, although they know how to choose the bed as astutely as any of those servants.' Frieda had laid her head on K.'s shoulder, and they walked up and down in silence, with their arms around one another. 'If only,' said Frieda slowly, calmly, almost contentedly, as if she knew that only a little time of peace against K.'s shoulder was granted her, but she wanted to enjoy it to the last, 'if only we had gone away at once, that very night, we could be somewhere safe now, still together, your hand always close enough for me to take it. How I need to have you close, how lost I have felt when I am without you ever since we met. Being close to you, believe me, is my dream, that and only that.'

Then someone called out in the side corridor. It was Jeremias; he stood there on the bottom step in nothing but his shirt, but with a shawl of Frieda's wrapped around him. As he stood there, hair tousled, his thin beard looking drenched as if with rain, keeping his eyes open with difficulty, pleading and reproachful, his dark cheeks reddened but the flesh of them sagging, his bare legs trembling with cold, so that the long fringe of the shawl trembled too, he looked like a patient escaped from the hospital, and setting eyes on him you could think of nothing but getting him back to bed. That was how Frieda herself saw it. She moved away from K. and was beside him in a minute. Having her near him, the careful way with which she drew the shawl more closely around him, her haste in trying to make him go straight back into the room, seemed to make Jeremias a little stronger already. It was as if only now did he recognize K. 'Ah, the land surveyor,' he said, while Frieda, who didn't want any more talk, patted his cheek soothingly. 'Forgive me for disturbing you, but I don't feel at all well, so you'll excuse me. I think I'm running a temperature, I need an infusion to make me sweat. Those damned railings in the school garden, I still think of them, and now, with a chill already, I've been running around all night. A man sacrifices his health, without even noticing at once, for things that really aren't worth it. But as for you, Mr Land Surveyor, please don't let me disturb you. Come into our room with us, come and visit the sick, and tell Frieda what else you have to say to her in there. If two people who are well known to each other part, of course they have so much to say in those last moments that a third person, even if he is lying in bed waiting for the promised infusion, can't possibly understand it.

But do come in, and I'll keep perfectly quiet.' 'Hush, hush,' said Frieda, pulling at his arm. 'He's feverish and doesn't know what he's saying. But please don't go with him, K. It is my and Jeremias's room, or rather just my room, and I am forbidding you to go into it. You are persecuting me, oh K., why are you persecuting me? I will never, never come back to you; I shudder at the mere thought of it. Go to those girls of yours; they sit on the bench with you beside their stove in nothing but their shifts, as I've been told, and if someone comes looking for you they spit and hiss at him. I'm sure you feel very much at home there if you are so drawn to the place. I have always tried to keep you away from it, with little success, but I did try to keep you from it. Well, that's over now. You are free. You have a fine life before you—you may have to fight the servants a little over one of them, but as for the second girl, no one on earth will grudge her to you. Your union is already blessed. Say nothing against it, I'm sure you'll try to refute it all, but in the end it's not to be denied. Just think, Jeremias, he denied it all!' And they nodded and smiled at each other. 'But,' Frieda went on, 'supposing he had refuted it all, what good would that have done, what do I care? As for what may happen to someone visiting those folk, that's their business and his, not mine. It is my business to nurse you until you're as healthy as you were before K. started tormenting you on my account.' 'So you really won't come with us, Mr Land Surveyor?' asked Jeremias, but Frieda, who wouldn't even turn to look at K. any more, led him away. Down below K. could see a small door, even lower than the doors here in the corridor. Not only Jeremias but Frieda too had to bend her head as she went in. It looked bright and warm inside. There was still a little whispering to be heard, probably Frieda lovingly persuading Jeremias to go back to bed, and then the door was closed.

23

ONLY now did K. notice how quiet it had become in the corridor—not just in this part of the corridor, where he had been standing with Frieda and which seemed to be part of the domestic staff's quarters, but also in the long corridor with the rooms that had earlier sounded so lively leading off it. So the gentlemen had finally gone to sleep. K. himself was very tired, perhaps so weary that he hadn't defended himself against Jeremias as he should have done. It might have been cleverer to take his cue from Jeremias himself, who was obviously exaggerating his chill—his pitiful state was not the result of a chill but was innate in him, not to be cured by any healthy herbal infusion—yes, to take his cue from Jeremias, make a great spectacle of his very real weariness, collapse here in the corridor, which would surely feel good, sleep for a while, and then perhaps enjoy a little nursing. Only it wouldn't have turned out as well as it did for Jeremias, who would certainly and probably rightly have won in any such competition for sympathy, and no doubt any other contest too. K. was so tired that he wondered whether he might not try getting into one of these rooms, many of which must be empty, and have a good long sleep in a fine bed. He thought that might compensate for a good deal. He had a nightcap ready to hand too. There had been a small carafe of rum on the tray of china that Frieda had left lying on the floor. K. did not shrink from the effort of going back to it, and emptied the little flask.

Now at least he felt strong enough to appear before Erlanger. He looked for the door of Erlanger's room, but as the servant and Gerstäcker were no longer to be seen, and all the doors looked the same, he couldn't find it. However, he thought he remembered roughly whereabouts in the corridor the door was, and decided to try opening a door that in his opinion was probably the one he wanted. The venture couldn't be too risky; if the door led to Erlanger's room, he supposed Erlanger would see him now; if it was someone else's room he could apologize and leave again, and if the guest in the room was asleep, which was the most likely outcome, K.'s visit wouldn't even be noticed. It could be unfortunate only if the room was empty, for then K. would hardly be able to resist the temptation of lying down on the bed and getting some sleep at last. He looked to right and left down the corridor again, to see whether, after all, anyone was coming who could give him information and make his daring venture unnecessary, but the long corridor was quiet and empty. Then K. listened at the door, but again there was no noise. He knocked so softly that the sound could not have woken anyone sleeping inside, and when still nothing happened he very cautiously opened the door. However, a slight scream came to his ears. It was a small room, more than half filled by a broad bed, the electric light on the bedside table was on, and there was a small travelling-bag beside it. In the bed, but entirely hidden under the covers, someone moved uneasily and whispered, through a gap between the blanket and the sheet: 'Who's there?' K. couldn't simply leave again now, and he looked unhappily at the handsome but occupied bed, then remembered the question and gave his name. This seemed to make a good impression. The man in the bed drew the blanket back from his face a little way, but in alarm, ready to disappear again if anything was wrong out there. But then, making up his mind, he turned the blanket right back and sat upright. He certainly wasn't Erlanger. He was a small gentleman, evidently in good health, whose features didn't quite fit with each other by virtue of the fact that the cheeks were childishly plump and the eyes childishly merry, but the high forehead, the sharp nose, the narrow mouth with lips that would hardly stay closed, and the almost receding chin were not childish at all, but indicated a capacity for deep thought. It was probably his self-satisfaction with that which had helped him to preserve a pronounced streak of healthy childishness. 'Do you know Friedrich?' he asked. K. said he did not. 'But he knows you,' said the gentleman, smiling. K. nodded; there were plenty of people who knew him, in fact it was one of the chief obstacles in his path. 'I'm his secretary,' said the gentleman, 'and my name is Bürgel.'* 'I'm sorry,' said K., reaching for the door-handle. 'I'm afraid I mixed your door up with another one. I was summoned to see Mr Secretary Erlanger.' 'What a pity!' said Bürgel. 'Not that you're summoned to see someone else, it's a pity you mixed the doors up. You see, once I'm woken I can never get to sleep again. Well, no need for that to upset you, it's my personal misfortune. Why can't the doors here be locked, do you think? There's certainly a reason for it. An old saying has it that the doors of secretaries are always open.

Still, it needn't be taken quite so literally.' And Bürgel looked at K. inquiringly and cheerfully, for despite his complaint he seemed to be well rested, and probably had never been as tired as K. was just now. 'Where are you going?' asked Bürgel. 'It's four in the morning. You'd have to wake up anyone you wanted to see now; not everyone's as used to being disturbed as I am, not everyone will take it so patiently, the secretaries are a highly strung lot. So stay here for a while. They begin to get up about five o'clock in this place, and then you'll be able to comply with your summons better. So please let go of that handle and sit down somewhere, not that there's much room, to be sure. You'd better sit on the edge of this bed. Are you surprised that I have neither a chair nor a table in here? Well, I had the choice of either a completely furnished room with a narrow hotel bed, or this big bed and nothing else but the washstand. I chose the big bed; after all, the bed is what matters most in a bedroom. Ah, this bed would be really excellent for a good sleeper, a man who could stretch out and sleep well. But it does even me good, always tired as I am without being able to sleep. I spend a large part of the day in it, I do all my correspondence here, and it's where I conduct my hearings with members of the public. It works very well. To be sure, the members of the public have nowhere to sit, but they can manage without, and anyway it's nicer for them to stand while the person conducting the hearing feels good than to sit comfortably while he keeps shouting at them. So I can offer only this place on the edge of the bed, but it's not an official place, it's just meant for nocturnal conversations. But you are so quiet, Mr Land Surveyor.' 'I'm very tired,' said K., who had sat down on the bed at once on being invited, abruptly and unceremoniously, leaning against the bedpost. 'Of course you are,' said Bürgel, laughing. 'Everyone here is tired. For instance, it was no small workload I dealt with both yesterday and today. It's out of the question for me to sleep now, but if that extremely improbable event should occur, if I were to fall asleep while you're here, then please keep perfectly still and don't open the door. Never fear, though, I certainly won't fall asleep, or if I do it will be at most only for a few minutes. The fact is that, probably because I am so used to the coming and going of members of the public, I always sleep most easily when I have company.' 'Do by all means go to sleep, Mr Secretary,' said K., pleased to hear this announcement. 'And then, if you will allow me, I will get a little sleep too.'

'No, no,' laughed Bürgel again. 'I'm afraid I can't fall asleep merely on invitation, the opportunity may come only in the course of conversation. Yes, a conversation is the most likely thing to send me to sleep. Our business is bad for the nerves, you see. I, for instance, am a communications secretary. You don't know what that is? Well, I am the main line of communication'—and so saying he rubbed his hands quickly with instinctive cheerfulness—'between Friedrich and the village, I deal with communications between his castle secretary and his village secretary, I am generally in the village but not all the time, I have to be ready to drive up to the castle at a moment's notice. You see that travelling-bag—ah, it's a restless life, it's not for everyone. On the other hand, it's a fact that I couldn't do without this kind of work now, any other work would seem to me dull. And what is land surveying like?' 'I'm not doing any of that; I'm not employed as a land surveyor here,' said K., whose thoughts were not really on the subject. In fact he was simply longing for Bürgel to go to sleep, although even that was out of a certain sense of what he owed to himself; in the depths of his mind he thought he knew that the moment when Bürgel might fall asleep was still incalculably far away. 'Well, that's amazing,' said Bürgel, throwing his head back in a lively manner and producing a notepad from under the blanket to write something down on it. 'You are a land surveyor, and you have no surveying work to do.' K. nodded mechanically. He had raised his left arm to the top of the bedpost and was resting his head on it. He had already tried various ways of making himself comfortable, but this was the most comfortable position of all. Now he could pay a little more attention to what Bürgel was saying. 'I am prepared', Bürgel went on, 'to pursue this question further. Matters here are certainly not in such a state that any professional skill ought to be left unused. And it must annoy you too. Don't you suffer from it?' 'I do indeed suffer from it,' said K. slowly, smiling to himself, for just now he did not suffer from it in the slightest. Moreover, Bürgel's offer made little impression on him. It sounded thoroughly amateurish. Knowing nothing of the circumstances of K.'s appointment, of the difficulties put in its way in the village and the castle, of the complications that had already arisen or looked like arising during K.'s stay here—knowing nothing about any of that, even without giving any sign that, as might have been expected of a secretary, he had some faint idea of it all, he was proposing to put the whole thing in order with the help of his little notepad, just like that. But then Bürgel said: 'You seem to have had several disappointments already,' thus showing a certain understanding of human nature again, and ever since K. entered this room he had told himself from time to time not to underestimate Bürgel. However, in his present condition it was difficult to judge anything properly except his own weariness. 'No, no,' said Bürgel, as if replying to some thought in K.'s mind and kindly sparing him the trouble of saying it out loud. 'You mustn't let disappointments deter you. A good deal here seems designed for deterrence, and when you're new to the place you feel it's impossible to get past the obstacles. I don't mean to try finding out how things really are, perhaps the appearance really corresponds to the reality, in my position I don't stand at the right distance from it to establish that, but note this: opportunities sometimes arise that have hardly anything to do with the situation as a whole, opportunities when a word, a glance, a sign of trust can achieve more than tedious, life-long efforts. Yes, that's the way of it. Of course these opportunities do agree with the situation as a whole in so far as they are never exploited. But why are they not exploited, that's what I always wonder.' K. didn't know. He did indeed realize that what Bürgel was talking about probably concerned him closely, but just now he had a great dislike for everything that concerned him closely. He moved his head a little way aside, as if he could thus leave the way clear for Bürgel's questions to pass him by and not touch him any more. 'It is,' Bürgel went on, stretching his arms and yawning, in confusing contrast to the gravity of his words, 'it is the secretaries' constant complaint that they are obliged to hold most hearings in the village by night. And why do they complain of it? Because it puts too much strain on them? Because they'd rather use the night for sleeping? No, they definitely don't complain of that. Of course there are both industrious and less industrious men among the secretaries, as everywhere, but none of them complains of being under excessive strain, certainly not in public. That is simply not our way. So far as that's concerned, we see no difference between ordinary time and time spent working. We are strangers to such distinctions. So what do the secretaries have against hearings conducted by night? Is it perhaps consideration for the members of the public involved? No, that's not it either. The secretaries are not at all considerate of those members of the public, although they are no more inconsiderate of the members of the public than they are of themselves, they are equally inconsiderate to both. And in fact this inconsiderate attitude, that is to say, the iron observance and performance of their duty, shows the greatest consideration that members of the public could wish for. Fundamentally—although a casual observer will not of course notice it—that is fully appreciated, and as in this case nocturnal hearings are particularly welcome to members of the public, there is no objection to nocturnal hearings in principle. So why don't the secretaries like them?' K. did not know the answer to that either; he knew so little about the subject that he couldn't even tell whether Bürgel was asking a question seriously or only rhetorically. If you'd let me lie down in your bed, he thought, I'll answer any questions you like at midday tomorrow, or even better in the evening. But Bürgel did not seem to be taking any notice of K., he was too interested in the question that he himself had just raised. 'As far as I know, and from my own experience, the reservations entertained by the secretaries about nocturnal hearings are more or less as follows. Night is less suitable for negotiation with members of the public because it is difficult or actually impossible to maintain the official character of negotiations at night. That is not because of outward details; of course the formalities can be as strictly observed by night as by day, just as one likes. So that's not it, but on the other hand official judgement suffers by night. One is instinctively inclined to judge things from a more private point of view then, the points advanced by members of the public seem to carry more weight than they should, consideration of the further situation of those members of the public, of their sufferings and sorrows, mingles with our assessment, where it does not belong. The requisite barrier between members of the public and officials, however flawlessly it may be present to outward appearance, is relaxed, and where usually only questions and answers are exchanged, which is just as it should be, a strange and entirely unsuitable exchange between the persons sometimes seems to occur. So at least the secretaries say, and they are people whose profession means that they have the gift of an extraordinarily sensitive feeling for such things. But even they—and this is often discussed in our circles—even they notice little of those unfortunate influences during nocturnal hearings; on the contrary, they make great efforts from the first to counter them, and in the end they consider that they have done particularly good work. However, if you read the records later, you are often amazed by the weaknesses so clearly exposed. And it is these errors, made to the only partly justified advantage of the members of the public, which cannot be dealt with summarily in the usual way, at least not according to our regulations. Of course they may be corrected by a supervisory office, but that will be useful only to the law and cannot affect the person concerned for the worse. Wouldn't you say that in such circumstances the complaints of the secretaries are highly justifiable?' K. had already spent some time half asleep, and now his slumbers were disturbed again. Why all this, he asked himself, why all this? From beneath his lowered eyelids, he observed Bürgel not as an official who was discussing difficult questions with him, but simply as something that kept him from sleeping, and he couldn't see any other point to him. Bürgel, however, given over entirely to his own train of thought, smiled as if he had just succeeded in leading K. slightly astray. However, he was ready to set him right again. 'Nor', he said, 'can one call those complaints entirely justified either, just like that. Nocturnal hearings are not exactly stipulated anywhere, so no one is breaking any regulation in trying to avoid them, but the circumstances, the excessive amount of work, the way in which the officials in the castle work, the difficulty of getting hold of them, the regulation saying that hearings of members of the public may be held only after the rest of an investigation has been entirely concluded, but must then be held at once, all this and more has made the nocturnal hearings an unavoidable necessity. However, if they have become a necessity—as I say—then that is also, or at least indirectly, as a result of the regulations, and finding fault with the nature of nocturnal hearings would then be almost—mind you, I am exaggerating slightly, so that as it is an exaggeration I may voice it—would then be almost to find fault with the regulations. On the other hand, it may be allowed that the secretaries seek to secure themselves as best they can, within the regulations, against the nocturnal hearings and their disadvantages, although those may be only apparent. And to a very great extent they do secure themselves; they admit only subjects of negotiation which allow as little as possible to be feared in that respect, they test themselves closely before the negotiations and, if the result of the testing demands it even at the last minute, they withdraw any agreement, they reinforce their authority by frequently summoning a member of the public ten times before really considering his case, they like to be represented by colleagues who are unqualified to deal with the case concerned and can thus handle it more easily; they at least hold the negotiations at the beginning or end of the night and avoid the middle hours—there are plenty of such measures. They do not let anyone get the better of them easily, those secretaries, they are almost as tough as they are sensitive.' K. was asleep. It was not real sleep; he could hear what Bürgel was saying perhaps better than during his early period of wakeful exhaustion, word after word came to his ear, but his troublesome consciousness was gone; he felt free, Bürgel no longer had a hold on him, he just sometimes made his way towards Bürgel, he was not yet deeply immersed in slumber but he had taken the plunge, and no one was going to rob him of that now. He felt as if he had won a great victory, as if a company had gathered to celebrate it, and he or someone else was raising a glass of champagne in honour of that victory. And so that everyone would know what it was about, the struggle and the victory were repeated all over again, or perhaps not repeated, perhaps they were only now taking place but had been celebrated earlier, and because, luckily, the outcome was certain there was constant celebration. K. was fighting a naked secretary who greatly resembled the statue of a Greek god, and who was getting the worst of it. It was very comical, and K. smiled slightly in his sleep to see the secretary's proud bearing upset again and again by K.'s advance, so that he had, for instance, to use his outstretched arm and clenched fist to cover his nakedness, but was always too slow about it. The combat did not last long; step after step, and they were long strides, K. pressed forward. Was it a combat at all? There was no serious obstacle, only a squeal from the secretary now and then. That Greek god squealed like a girl being tickled. And finally he was gone; K. was alone in a large space. He turned around in it, ready to fight, looking for his opponent, but there was no one there any more, the company had left. Only the champagne glass lay on the ground, broken, and K. trod it to pieces. But the broken glass stung, and he woke again with a start, feeling unwell like a small child who has been woken suddenly. All the same, at the sight of Bürgel's bared chest an idea came to him from his dream: 'Here's your Greek god! Get him out of bed!' 'However,' said Bürgel, raising his face thoughtfully to the ceiling as if seeking in his memory for examples but failing to find any, 'all the same, in spite of all the precautionary measures, there is an opportunity for members of the public to exploit this nocturnal weakness of the secretaries, always supposing that it *is* a weakness, for their own ends. To be sure it is a very rare opportunity, or more accurately I should say one that almost never comes. It consists in the arrival of the person concerned in the middle of the night, unannounced. You may be surprised that this happens so seldom, when it seems such an obvious thing to do. Well, you are not familiar with the way we go about things here. But you will have noticed the impenetrability of the official organization. However, that impenetrability in itself means that everyone who has any kind of request to make, or must be examined on some subject for other reasons, receives a summons at once, immediately, usually even before he has thought out his case, why, even before he knows about it. He will not be examined this time, usually he won't be examined yet, generally the case has not reached that point, but he has the summons, which means that he can't turn up announced and thus entirely by surprise. At most, he can come at the wrong time, when the date and hour of his summons will be pointed out to him, and then, if he comes back at the right time, as a rule he will be sent away, and there is no more difficulty; the summons in the member of the public's hand and the note in the files are weapons used by the secretaries, and if not always quite adequate they are still strong. That applies, however, only to the secretary responsible for the case; anyone would still be at liberty to take the other secretaries by surprise at night. But hardly anyone ever will; there's almost no point in it. First, anyone who did so would arouse the ire of the secretary responsible for the case. We secretaries may certainly not be jealous of each other where our work is concerned, each has only too great a workload to carry, we get more than enough of that, but in dealing with members of the public we cannot tolerate any interference with our responsibility. Many have lost a case because, when they thought they weren't getting anywhere with the secretary responsible, they tried to slip past the network in the wrong way. Such attempts are in fact bound to fail because a secretary who is not responsible for a case, even if he is taken by surprise at night and feels inclined to help, can hardly intervene in it because he is not responsible, any more than any random attorney can, indeed much less so, for even if he might otherwise do something or other, since he knows the secret ways of the law far better than all those legal gentlemen, he simply doesn't have any time for matters for which he is not responsible, he can't spare a minute for them. So who, with these prospects in view, would spend his nights on the trail of secretaries not responsible for his case? And the members of the public are fully occupied in trying to comply with the summonses from and signals given by those who are responsible for their cases, as well as pursuing their usual professions. I mean fully occupied of course as members of the public would understand it, which of course is far from being the same as fully occupied in the sense in which the secretaries would do so.' K. nodded with a smile. He thought he understood all about it, not because it troubled him but because he was now convinced that he would fall properly asleep in the next few minutes, and this time without any dream or other disturbance; between the secretaries responsible on one side and those not responsible on the other, and in view of the whole crowd of fully occupied members of the public, he would fall into a deep sleep and thus escape it all. By now he was so used to Bürgel's quiet, self-satisfied voice, as he obviously endeavoured in vain to fall asleep himself, that it was more likely to send him to sleep than disturb his slumbers. Clatter, mill-wheel, clatter, he thought, clatter on for me. 'So where,' said Bürgel, two fingers toying with his lower lip, his eyes wide, craning his neck, as if he were approaching a delightful viewing-point after an arduous walk, 'so where is that elusive opportunity I mentioned, the one that almost never comes? The secret lies in the way responsibility is regulated. For it is not possible, nor in a large and living organization can it be, for only a certain secretary to be responsible for every case. It is simply that one secretary has the main responsibility, but many others have responsibility, even if less responsibility, for certain parts of it. Who, however hard a worker, could accommodate all the papers relating to even the smallest incident on his desk? Even what I have said about the main responsibility is going too far. Is not the whole thing also contained in the smallest responsibility? Is not the ardour with which one approaches the case a crucial point? And is not that always the same, always present at full strength? There may be differences between the secretaries in everything, and there are countless such differences, but not in the matter of ardour, none of them will be able to hold back if he receives an invitation to take part in a case for which he has only the slightest responsibility. Outwardly, however, an ordered opportunity for negotiation must be created, and so a certain secretary comes to the fore where the members of the public are concerned, and it is to him that they must officially turn. However, he does not have to be the one who bears the greatest responsibility for the case; the organization and its particular needs at the time influence the decision here. Such is the state of affairs. And now, Mr Land Surveyor, judge what chance there is for a member of the public, through circumstances of some kind and despite the obstacles already described to you (which in general are perfectly adequate), to take a secretary with a certain responsibility for the case by surprise in the middle of the night after all. I suppose you haven't thought of such a thing yet? I'm happy to believe you. But it isn't necessary to think of it, because it almost never happens. What a strange little grain of matter, formed in a certain special way, how very small and clever such a member of the public must be if it's to slip through such a perfect sieve. You think it can't happen? You are right, it can't. But then—and who can guarantee everything?—one night it does happen. To be sure, I know of no one among my acquaintances to whom it has happened, but that doesn't prove much. By comparison with the numbers involved here, my own acquaintance is limited, and anyway it isn't certain that a secretary to whom such a thing has happened will admit it. It is always a very personal matter, and to some extent carries the stigma of official shame. However, my experience may prove that it is such a rare event, really known only by rumour and with nothing else to confirm it, that it would be going much too far to fear it. Even if it ever really happened you can—or so I should think—render it entirely harmless by proving, which is easily done, that there is no place for it in this world. Anyway, it is morbid to hide under the bedclothes for fear of such a thing, never venturing to look out. And even if that total improbability were suddenly to assume real form, is all lost? Far from it. The fact that all is lost is even more improbable than that most improbable of events. To be sure, if the member of the public is in the room, that is very bad. It inhibits you. How long will you be able to resist? you ask yourself. But you know there will be no resistance. You just have to picture the situation in the right way. There sits the member of the public, whom you have never seen before, whom you have always awaited, positively thirsting to see him, but whom you have always, and reasonably, considered inaccessible. His mere silent presence invites you to enter into his poor life, to move around there as if it were your own property, to feel sympathy for its vain demands. This invitation in the silence of the night is captivating.

You accept it, and now you have in fact stopped being an official. It is a situation in which it will soon become impossible to refuse a request. Strictly speaking you are desperate, but even more strictly speaking you are very happy. Desperate because the defence-lessness with which you sit there waiting for the member of the public's request, knowing that once it is made you must grant it, even if, at least so far as you can see, it positively wrecks the official organization—well, I suppose it is the worst thing that can happen to you in practice. One reason above all—and apart from everything else—is that it entails your forcibly claiming a higher rank for your-self at this moment, higher than any you can conceive of. Our posi-tions do not authorize us to grant requests such as those I am talking about, but what with the nocturnal proximity of the member of the public our official powers seem to grow, we pledge ourselves to do things outside our sphere of responsibility, indeed, we will even do them in practice. Like a robber in the forest, a member of the public surprising us by night forces us to make sacrifices of which we would never otherwise be capable—well, that's how it is if the member of the public is still there, encouraging us and forcing us to do so and spurring us on, and we set it all in train half unconsciously. But how will it be later, when that's all over, when the member of the public goes away, satisfied and free of care, and we are left alone, defenceless in the face of our abuse of office? It doesn't bear thinking of. Yet all the same we are happy. How suicidal happiness can be! We could make an effort to keep the true situation secret from the member of the public. The member of the public himself will hardly notice anything of his own accord. As he sees it, he went into a room which wasn't the one he wanted, probably quite by chance, tired out, disap-pointed, feeling dull and indifferent from weariness and disillusion-ment, he is sitting there knowing nothing and deep in thoughts, if he is thinking anything, of his mistake or his weariness. Couldn't we leave it at that? No, we can't. With the loquacity of the happy man, we must explain it all. Without sparing ourselves in the slightest, we must show at length what has happened and why, how extraordinar-ily rare and uniquely great the opportunity is, we must show how the member of the public who, with all the helplessness of which only a member of the public can be capable, has walked by chance into his opportunity, we must show him, Mr Land Surveyor, how the member of the public can now control everything if he wants to, and need do nothing but somehow or other make his request, there is a document for granting it already prepared, we say, ready to be handed to him—we must go into all that. It is a dark hour for an official. But when you have done that, Mr Land Surveyor, what's most necessary has been done, and you must possess your soul in patience and wait.'

K. heard no more. He was asleep, remote from everything that was going on. His head, which had first been laid on his left arm as it held the bedpost above, had slipped off in his sleep and now hung free, sinking gradually lower, for the prop of his arm above it was no longer enough and K. instinctively created a new one by bracing his right hand on the blanket, by chance taking hold of Bürgel's foot just under the bedclothes. Bürgel looked that way and let him hold the foot, though it was probably tiresome for him.

Then there were several heavy knocks on the side wall. K. woke with a start and looked at the wall. 'Isn't the land surveyor in there?' asked a voice. 'Yes,' said Bürgel, freeing his foot from K. and suddenly stretching with a wild and wilful movement like a little boy. 'Then tell him to hurry up and get himself in here,' said the voice, without any consideration for Bürgel or for the fact that he might still need K. 'That's Erlanger,' said Bürgel in a whisper. He did not seem at all surprised to know that Erlanger was in the next room. 'Go straight in to him; he's in a temper, so you'd better try to mollify him. He sleeps soundly, but our voices were too loud; when you're speaking of certain subjects you can't really control your voice. Go along, then, you don't seem able to wake up properly. Go on, what more do you want in here? No, no, you don't have to apologize for your drowsiness, why should you? Physical strength is enough only up to a certain point; who can help it if that very point is also very significant otherwise? No one can help it. That's the way the world corrects itself in its course and keeps its balance. It's an excellent, incredibly excellent arrangement, although dismal in other respects. Now do run along, I don't know why you're staring at me like that. If you hesitate any longer Erlanger will be down on me like a ton of bricks, and that's something I'd much rather avoid. Go on, who knows what you should expect over there, this place is full of opportunities. Well, of course there are opportunities too great, in a certain way, to be exploited; there are things that fail only of their own volition and for no other reason. Yes, amazing. Anyway, I hope I can get a little sleep now, though it's five in the morning already and the noise will soon begin. I do wish to goodness you'd go away at last!'

Dazed from being woken suddenly from deep sleep, still in dire need of more sleep, his body hurting all over as a result of his uncomfortable position on the bed, K. couldn't bring himself to stand up for some time. He clutched his forehead and looked down at his lap. Even Bürgel's repeated goodbyes couldn't get him moving, he was induced to move only by a sense of the total futility of lingering in this room any longer. The room seemed to him indescribably bleak. Whether it had become like that, or had always been like that, he couldn't say. He wouldn't even manage to get to sleep again here. That conviction was in fact the deciding factor. Smiling at it slightly, he rose, propping himself against anything he could find to support him, the bed, the wall, the door, and he went out without a word, as if he had taken leave of Bürgel long ago.

24

HE would probably have passed Erlanger's door with equal indifference if Erlanger hadn't been standing in the doorway, crooking his forefinger to beckon him in. Erlanger was already fully clothed, preparing to leave; he wore a black fur coat with a high-buttoned collar. A servant was just handing him his gloves, and still held a fur cap. 'You were supposed to be here long ago,' Erlanger said. K. was about to apologize, but by closing his eyes wearily Erlanger showed that he could do without that. 'It's about the following matter,' he said. 'There was once a girl called Frieda serving in the bar, I know only her name, I don't know the girl herself, I'm not concerned with her. This Frieda sometimes brought Klamm his beer. There seems to be another girl there now. The change is of no significance, of course, probably not for anyone and certainly not for Klamm. But the more important a man's work, and Klamm's is certainly the most important of all, the less strength he has left to defend himself against the outside world, and as a consequence any insignificant change in the most insignificant little things can be seriously disturbing to him. The smallest change on his desk, the removal of a dirty mark that has been there for ever, anything like that can upset a man, and so can the arrival of a new barmaid. Well, of course nothing of the kind bothers Klamm, there can be no question of that, even if it would bother anyone else in any line of work you like to mention. All the same, we are in duty bound to watch over Klamm's comfort by removing troublesome factors if they appear to us potentially upsetting, even if they do not, as is very probable, upset him at all. We remove these troublesome factors not for his sake, not for his work's sake, but for our own sake, for the sake of our conscience and peace of mind. So that girl Frieda must return to the bar at once; perhaps her return will itself be disturbing, then and only then will we send her away again, but for the time being, however, she must come back. I'm told that you are living with her, so kindly make sure she comes back immediately. Personal feelings must be left out of this, that's obvious, so I am not going to enter into any further discussion of it. I am already doing more than is really necessary if I say that, should you be of service in this small matter, it could possibly be useful to you in your further progress. And that is all I have to say to you.' He nodded to K. in farewell, put on the fur cap handed to him by his servant, and went down the corridor, walking fast but with a slight limp and followed by the servant. Sometimes the orders given here were very easy to carry out, but K. didn't like the ease of this one at all. That was not just because this order concerned Frieda, and indeed, while it was intended as an order, it sounded to K. like ridicule, but above all because it showed K. how useless all his own efforts were. Orders were given above his head, the unfavourable and the favourable alike, and ultimately even the favourable probably had a nub of something unfavourable in them, but anyway they all went above his head, and his status was far too low for him to intervene or actually silence them and get his own voice heard. If Erlanger waves you away, what will you do, and if he were not to wave you away, what could you say to him? K. was in fact clear in his own mind that his weariness had harmed him more today than anything unfavourable in the circumstances, but why could he, who had believed he could rely on his physical strength and would never have set out without that conviction, why could he not endure a few disturbed nights and one without any sleep at all, why was he so uncontrollably tired here, in this particular place, where no one was ever tired—or perhaps, more likely, people were always tired without its affecting their work, but instead seeming to be good for it? You could conclude from that fact that, in its own way, it was a weariness entirely different from K.'s. Here, it was probably weariness in the midst of enjoyable work, something that from outside looked like weariness but was really unshakeable calm, unshakeable peace. If you are a little tired at noon, that's part of the natural and happy course of the day. And for the gentlemen here, K. told himself, it's always noon.

Very much in keeping with that idea, signs of life were now heard all over the place, on both sides of the corridor, at five in the morning. At first the babble of voices in the rooms had something extremely cheerful about it. Sometimes it sounded like the happy shouting of children getting ready for an outing, or then again like chickens waking up in the henhouse, a joyful noise just right for the dawning day. Somewhere or other, one of the gentlemen was even imitating the crowing of a cockerel. The corridor itself was still empty, but the doors were beginning to move. They kept being opened just a little way and quickly closed again, there was a positive percussion of such opening and closing of doors in the corridor, and now and then, looking through the gaps where the walls didn't reach the ceiling, K. saw tousled morning heads appear, only to disappear next minute. In the distance, a small trolley laden with files was being slowly pushed along by a servant. A second servant walked beside him with a list in his hand, obviously comparing the numbers on the doors with numbers on the files. The trolley stopped outside most of the doors, and then usually the door was opened and the relevant files handed into the room, or sometimes just a note—in such cases a little conversation would go on between the room and the corridor, probably a gentleman telling the servant off. If the door stayed closed its files were carefully piled up just outside it. When that happened it seemed to K. as if the movement of the doors around him was no less, although the files had been distributed, but even increased. Perhaps the others were looking longingly at the files which were lying outside the door and, for some incomprehensible reason, hadn't been taken in yet; they couldn't understand how someone who had only to open his door to lay hands on his files didn't do so. Perhaps it was even possible that files which remained lying about would be distributed later to the other gentlemen, who were already looking out at frequent intervals to see whether the files were still outside the door, meaning that there was still hope for themselves. Furthermore, the files left lying there were usually in particularly large bundles, and K. assumed that they had been left where they were for now either out of a certain malicious desire to show off, or for motives of well-justified pride intended to encourage the colleagues of the gentleman in the room. He was confirmed in this assumption by the fact that sometimes—always when he didn't happen to be looking—after the stack of files had been on show long enough, it was suddenly and very quickly snapped up and taken into the room, and the door then remained closed as before. The doors all around calmed down at that point, either disappointed or pleased to see that such a provocative item had finally been removed, but then they slowly began moving again.

K. saw all this with interest as well as curiosity. He felt almost happy in the midst of this stir and bustle, looking this way and that, following the servants, though keeping a suitable distance behind, and indeed they had often turned to look at him with a stern glance, lowered heads, and pouting lips, as he observed their work of distribution. The longer it lasted the less smoothly did it go; either the list wasn't perfectly accurate, or the servants couldn't always tell one file from another very well, or the gentlemen made objections for other reasons, but at any rate, it turned out that many of the files already distributed had to be returned, and then the little trolley went back and negotiations about the return of the files took place through the crack where the door stood ajar. These negotiations themselves were full of problems, but it quite often happened that when something had to be returned, doors that had been in the liveliest movement earlier were now firmly shut, as if they didn't want to know anything about what was going on. Only then did the real problems begin. The gentleman who thought he had a claim to the files would wax extremely impatient, make a great deal of noise in his room, clapping his hands, stamping his feet, and repeatedly calling the number of a certain file out into the passage. Then the trolley was often left abandoned. One of the servants would be busy mollifying the impatient gentleman, while the other stood outside a closed door fighting for the return of the file. Both servants had a hard time of it. Attempts to placate the impatient gentleman often made him even more impatient, he wouldn't listen to the servant's empty words any longer, he didn't want consolation, he wanted files. One such gentleman poured a whole bowlful of water over the servant through the gap at the top of his door. But the other servant, obviously higher-ranking, had an even worse time. If the gentleman concerned would enter into negotiations at all, discussions of the facts ensued, in which the servant cited his list, while the gentleman cited his notes and the actual files that he was supposed to return, but was now clutching so firmly that hardly a corner of them was still visible to the servant's avid eyes. Then the servant had to go back to the trolley for more evidence. By now it had run on of its own accord down the slight slope of the corridor, or he had to go after the gentleman who was claiming the files and exchange the protests of the gentleman currently in possession of them for a new set of counter-protests. Such negotiations went on for a very long time, and sometimes it was agreed that the gentleman would give back a part of the files, or would be given a different file in compensation, since they had only been mixed up. But it sometimes happened that a gentleman had to give up all the files demanded at once, whether because the evidence produced by the servant had driven him into a corner, or because he was tired of the constant bargaining. Then he didn't hand them to the servant but instead, with a sudden decisive gesture, threw them a long way down the corridor, so that the string tying them together came off, sheets of paper flew around, and the servants had great trouble putting everything back in order. However, all this was relatively simpler than when the servant got no answer at all when he went to ask for the files back; then he stood outside the closed door, begging and pleading, citing his list, calling on the regulations, all in vain, for not a sound came from inside the room, and obviously the servant had no right to enter it without permission. Then even this model servant sometimes lost his self-control and went to his little trolley, sat down on the files, wiped the sweat from his brow, and did nothing at all for a while but dangle his feet helplessly in the air. All around him, great interest was shown in that, there was much whispering, scarcely a door remained still, and up along the tops of the walls faces, curiously enough almost entirely wrapped in scarves, followed all that was going on, but never stayed where they were for long. In the midst of all this turmoil K. noticed that Bürgel's door had remained closed the whole time, and the servants had passed down that part of the corridor already, but no files had been handed out to Bürgel. Perhaps he was still asleep, and what with all the racket that would have meant his sleep was sound and very healthy, but why had he not been given any files? Only a very few rooms had been passed over in that way, and they were probably empty. On the other hand, there was already a new and particularly restless guest in what had been Erlanger's room. Erlanger must have been positively driven out by him in the night, which would not have suited Erlanger's own cool and down-to-earth nature, but the fact that he had been obliged to wait for K. in the doorway of the room suggested that such was the case.

K. kept coming back from all these other observations to the servant; what he had been told about the servants in general—their laziness, the comfortable life they led, their arrogance—certainly didn't apply to this one. There must be exceptions among the servants too, or more probably there were different groups of servants, for here, as K. noticed, there were demarcations of which he had previously seen hardly any hint. In particular he admired the unyielding determination of this servant. The servant was not giving up in his battle with these obstinate little rooms—to K. it often seemed a battle with the rooms themselves, since he hardly saw anything of their occupants. He felt tired, to be sure—who wouldn't have felt tired?—but he would soon pull himself together, slip down from the trolley, and make for the door that must be conquered, walking very erect and clenching his jaws grimly. And it could happen that he was beaten back two or three times by very simple means, simply by the dreadful silence inside the room, and yet was not overcome. When he saw that open attack was no good he tried something different, for instance, so far as K. could make out, he tried cunning. He would appear to go away from the door, letting it exhaust its powers of silence, so to speak, and turn to other doors, but after a while he would come back, call in a loud and very audible voice to the other servant, and begin piling files outside the closed door as if he had changed his mind, and there was nothing to be rightfully taken away from the gentleman, instead he was to get more files. Then he went on, but kept his eye on the door, and if the gentleman inside, as usually happened, soon cautiously opened the door to take in the new files, the servant was there in a flash, wedged his foot in the doorway, and obliged the gentleman at least to negotiate with him face to face, which usually brought the argument to a conclusion that was at least partly satisfactory. And if that didn't work, or it didn't appear to him the best way to approach a certain door, he would try yet another trick. He moved on, for instance, to the gentleman claiming the files. Then he would push aside the other servant, who was still mechanically distributing files and was not much of a help to him, and begin persuading the gentleman himself, whispering in conspiratorial tones with his head well inside the room, probably making promises and giving assurances that next time files were distributed the other gentleman would meet with proper retribution, at least he pointed frequently at the door of the first gentleman's opponent, laughing as far as his weariness would allow. But then there were cases, one or two of them, where he simply gave up any attempt, although even here K. thought he was only appearing to give up, or at least giving up on reasonable grounds, for he went calmly on, putting up with the noise made by a gentleman who felt badly treated, and only the way he sometimes closed his eyes for quite a while showed that he suffered from the racket. But the gentleman would gradually calm down, and his protests were made less often, just as the uninterrupted crying of children gradually turns to isolated sobs. But even after he had fallen silent there was still an occasional screech from his room, or its door was swiftly opened and slammed again. At least it turned out that here the servant had probably done just the right thing. In the end there was only one gentleman left who would not calm down; he remained silent for a long time, but only to get his breath back, and then he started up again, making just as much fuss as before. It was not quite clear why he was shouting and complaining like that; perhaps it wasn't to do with the distribution of the files at all. By now the servant had finished his work, and there was only a single file, or really just a piece of paper torn from a notepad, left on the trolley; that was the other servant's fault. An idea went through K.'s head: why, he thought, that could very well be my file. The village mayor had called his a very minor case. And K., however random and ridiculous his assumption seemed even to himself, tried to approach the servant, who was looking thoughtfully at the sheet of paper. However, that wasn't easy, for the servant did not react well to the interest that K. was taking in him; even in the middle of his hardest work he had always found time to look round at K. with an angry or impatient and nervous jerk of his head. Only now that the files were distributed did he seem to have forgotten K. for the moment, and seemed indifferent, which his exhaustion made understandable. He wasn't taking much trouble with the sheet of paper either, perhaps he wasn't even reading it, just looking as if he was, and although he would probably have made any of the gentlemen in the rooms happy by giving them this sheet of paper, he decided not to. He was tired of distributing files. With his forefinger to his lips, he signed to his companion to keep quiet, and then—K. was nowhere near him yet—tore up the sheet of paper into small pieces and put it in his pocket. This was the first irregularity that K. had seen in all the office business here, although it was possible that he had misunderstood it. And even if it had been an irregularity, it could be forgiven, considering the circumstances; the servant could not work flawlessly all the time, a point must come when his accumulated annoyance and uneasiness must break out, and venting it simply by tearing up a small sheet of paper was innocent enough. The voice of the gentleman who wasn't to be mollified was still echoing down the corridor, and his colleagues, who in other respects didn't behave in a very friendly way to each other, seemed to be all of the same opinion about the noise he was making. It was coming to seem as if the gentleman had assumed the task of making enough noise for them all, and their shouts and nods of the head merely encouraged him to go on with it. But now it didn't bother the servant any more; he had finished his work, and taking hold of the trolley signed to the other servant to do the same, so they wheeled it away again just as they had come, only more contentedly, and so fast that the trolley jolted along in front of them. Only once did they stop suddenly and look back, when the shouting gentleman outside whose door K. was now wandering around—he would have liked to know what the gentleman really wanted—had obviously deciding that screaming was getting him nowhere. He seemed to have found an electric bell-push, and in his delight at being relieved in this way began ringing the bell continuously instead of screaming. Thereupon loud murmuring, which seemed to indicate approval, came from the other rooms. The gentleman appeared to be doing something they would all have liked to do for a long time, and had been obliged to leave undone only for some unknown reason. Was it perhaps the servants, was it perhaps Frieda that the gentleman hoped to summon by ringing? He would have to wait a long time. Frieda was probably busy wrapping Jeremias in wet towels, and even if he was better by now she wouldn't have the time to come, for then she would be lying in his arms. But the ringing of the bell did have an immediate effect. The landlord of the Castle Inn himself came hurrying up from a distance, clad in black and neatly buttoned up as usual, but the way he ran suggested that he was forgetting his dignity. His arms were half outstretched as if he had been called to the scene of some great disaster, and was prepared to seize the cause of it, clamp it to his chest, and so stifle it, and with every little irregularity in the ringing of the bell he seemed to jump in the air for a moment and then hurry even faster. And now his wife also appeared, a long way behind him. She too was running with her arms outstretched, but her steps were small and dainty, and K. thought she would arrive too late; the landlord would have dealt with everything before she got there. K. pressed close to the wall to give the landlord room to run by. But the landlord stopped right in front of him, as if K. himself were his destination, and next moment the landlady was there too, both of them heaping reproaches on him which in all the haste and surprise he didn't understand, particularly as the gentleman's bell joined in as well, and other bells began ringing too, not with any sense of emergency now but just for fun and in an excess of high spirits. Since K. was very anxious to discover exactly what he had done wrong, he was perfectly happy for the landlord to take his arm and frogmarch him away from all this noise, which was getting louder and louder, for behind them—K. didn't turn to look, because the landlord was talking to him, and the landlady on his other side was talking even more—behind them the doors now opened wide, the corridor was teeming with life, there seemed to be coming and going as if it were a narrow but busy alley, the doors ahead of them were obviously waiting impatiently for K. to come past, so that they could let the gentlemen inside those rooms out, and through all this the bells rang as the gentlemen pushed them again and again, as if to celebrate a victory. And now at last—they were in the quiet white yard again, where several sleighs were waiting—did K. gradually gather what it was all about. Neither the landlord nor the landlady understood how K. could have done anything of the kind. But what exactly *had* he done? K. asked again and again, although he didn't get the chance to ask for long, because his guilt was only too obvious to both of them, and they didn't believe for a moment that he was asking in good faith. Only bit by bit did K. find out what the matter was. He had no right to be in the corridor, in general he could enter only the bar, and that only as a favour which could be withdrawn. If he had been summoned to see a gentleman, he must of course go to the place to which he had been summoned, but must always remain aware—he did have his wits about him, they imagined, like anyone else?—that he was somewhere where he did not belong, to which he had been summoned only by a gentleman, and very unwillingly at that, merely because official business required and justified it. He therefore had to turn up quickly, go through his hearing, and then disappear, even more quickly if possible. Hadn't he felt how very wrong it was for him to be there in the corridor? And if he had, then how could he have gone wandering around there like an animal out at pasture? Hadn't he been summoned to a nocturnal hearing, and didn't he know why such hearings were held at night? Such hearings—and here K. did get a new explanation of the point of them—were held at night with the sole purpose of questioning members of the public the sight of whom would be entirely intolerable to the gentlemen by day, thus getting through the hearing quickly, by night and in artificial light, so that directly it was over the gentlemen could forget all that unpleasantness in slumber. K.'s conduct, however, had made a mockery of all these precautionary measures. Even ghosts disappear when morning comes, but K. had stayed there with his hands in his pockets, as if expecting that if he did not remove himself the entire corridor might remove itself instead, rooms and gentlemen and all. And he could be sure, they said, that just that would have happened if it had only been possible, for the gentlemen's feelings were extremely sensitive. None of them would drive K. away, or even say, which was obvious, that he ought to go away, none of them would do that, although they were probably trembling with agitation all the time K. was there and spoiling the morning for them, their best time of day. Instead of taking any proceedings to get rid of K. they preferred to suffer in silence, although no doubt hoping that K. would finally see what was so strikingly obvious, when he himself would suffer to the point where the pain of it was intolerable and matched the gentlemen's own suffering, for it was so very wrong to be standing here in the corridor in the morning, where everyone could see him. But such hopes had been in vain. The gentlemen didn't know, or in their kindness and condescension wouldn't acknowledge, that there might be insensitive, hard hearts which could not be softened even by proper respect. Doesn't even the night-flying moth, poor creature, seek out a quiet corner when day comes, flatten itself as if it would like to disappear, and suffer because it can't? But as for K., oh no, he stands where he is most conspicuous, and if he could prevent day from dawning like that then he would. Well, he can't prevent it, but he could, unfortunately, delay it and make it much worse. Hadn't he seen the files being distributed? It was something that no one was allowed to see except those most closely concerned. Something that neither the landlord nor the landlady could witness in their own house. Something of which they had heard tell only in hints, like those dropped today by the servant. Hadn't he seen the difficulties attendant on the distribution of the files, something in itself beyond understanding, since every one of the gentlemen was simply serving the good cause, never thought of his own advantage, and must work with all his powers to ensure that the distribution of the files, that important and fundamental part of the work, was done quickly, easily, and without any errors? And hadn't K. really had even a distant presentiment that the main point of all the difficulties consisted in the fact that the distribution of the files must take place with the doors almost closed, with no possibility of direct communication between the gentlemen, who could of course have agreed with one another in an instant, while communication through the servants was bound to drag on almost for hours, could never be done without complaints, which was a constant trial to both the gentlemen and the servants, and one which would probably have adverse consequences for the rest of the work done later. Why couldn't the gentlemen communicate with one another directly? Did K. still not understand? Such a thing had never before happened to the landlady, she said—and the landlord confirmed it for himself—even though they had been obliged to deal with all kinds of recalcitrant persons. Things that one usually dared not mention must be told to him openly, for otherwise he wouldn't understand the most essential point. Well, since it had to be said: it was on his account, only and exclusively on his account, that the gentlemen had not been able to come out of their rooms, since just after waking up in the morning they were too bashful, too vulnerable, to be exposed to the glance of strange eyes, they feel positively too exposed to show themselves, even if they happen to be fully clothed. It is difficult to say why they feel bashful, perhaps, constant workers as they are, they were just ashamed of having gone to sleep. But perhaps they are even more bashful when it comes to seeing strangers than they feel about being seen themselves, and they do not now want to be suddenly and immediately confronted, first thing in the morning, with the distressing sight of members of the public, large as life and twice as natural, a sight that, fortunately, they have managed to overcome with the help of the nocturnal hearings. They are just not equal to it. And what kind of a human being wouldn't respect that? Well, someone like K. Someone who would set himself above everything, above the law, above the most ordinary human consideration for others, and do it with dull indifference and lethargy, someone who doesn't mind making the distribution of the files all but impossible, who harms the reputation of their inn, and is the cause of something never known before: the gentlemen, driven to distraction, begin to defend themselves, and after summoning up what to ordinary people is almost unimaginable will-power, reach for their bells and ring for help in getting rid of K., since there is no other way of doing it. They, the gentlemen, calling for help! Wouldn't the landlord and landlady and all their staff have come long before if they had only dared to appear before the gentlemen in the morning without being summoned, even if it was only to bring help and then go away at once? Quivering with their indignation at K.'s conduct, inconsolable at being so powerless, they had waited here at the beginning of the corridor, and the ringing of the bell that they had never really expected had been such a release for them! Well, the worst was over! If only they could get a glimpse of the happiness of the gentlemen now that they were finally delivered from K.! It wasn't over yet for K. himself, of course, he would certainly have to answer for what he had done.

By now they had reached the bar; why the landlord, for all his anger, had brought K. here was not entirely clear, but perhaps he had realized that K.'s exhaustion made it impossible for him to leave the house at once. Without waiting to be asked to sit down, K. positively collapsed on to one of the casks. It was good to be there in the dark. Only one weak electric light above the beer-pulls was switched on. It was still dark outside too, and there seemed to be driving snow. He must be thankful to be here in the warm and take care not to be driven out. The landlord and landlady went on standing in front of him as if he still represented imminent danger, as if he were so totally unreliable that they couldn't entirely exclude the possibility of his suddenly setting out to try getting back into the corridor. They were tired themselves after the nocturnal alarms and rising early, especially the landlady, who was wearing a wide-skirted brown dress that rustled like silk, and was rather carelessly buttoned and done up—where had she found it in her haste?—and had now laid her head on her husband's shoulder, was dabbing her eyes with a delicate little handkerchief, now and then, like a child, casting angry glances at K. To mollify the couple, K. said that everything they had told him was entirely new to him, but that even though he had not been aware of it he would never have stayed so long in the corridor, where he really had no business and certainly no desire to upset anyone, except that he was so exhausted. He thanked them, he said, for putting an end to the painful scene. If he was to be called to account for it, he would welcome that, for only in that way could he prevent his conduct from being generally misunderstood. His weariness was solely to blame, nothing else. But that weariness arose from his not being used to the strain of the hearings. After all, he hadn't been here very long. Once he had some experience of it nothing of the kind could happen again. Perhaps he took the hearings too seriously, but surely that wasn't a bad thing in itself. He had been through two hearings in quick succession, one with Bürgel and the second with Erlanger, and the first in particular had worn him out, although the second hadn't taken long, Erlanger had simply wanted to ask him a favour, but both together had been more than he could stand at once, perhaps something of the kind might be too much for others too, even the landlord. He had staggered away from the second hearing in what was almost a state of intoxication—after all, he had seen and heard the two gentlemen for the first time, and had been expected to answer them. As far as he knew it had all turned out well, but then the misfortune had happened, although he could hardly be held to blame for it after what had gone before. Unfortunately only Erlanger and Bürgel had seen the condition he was in, and he was sure they would have spoken up for him and averted anything unfortunate, but Erlanger had had to leave directly after the hearing, obviously to go to the castle, and Bürgel, probably tired after the hearing himself—so how could K. have survived it unaffected?—had gone to sleep and even slept through the distribution of the files. If a similar opportunity had come K.'s way he would happily have taken it, thus avoiding all glimpses of anything forbidden, and that would have been all the easier in that he really had been in no state to see anything, so even the most sensitive of the gentlemen could have shown themselves in front of him without fear.

The mention of the two hearings, particularly the one with Erlanger, and the respect with which K. spoke of the two gentlemen, made the landlord more inclined to tolerate him. He seemed about to agree to K.'s request to let him put a plank on the casks and sleep there at least until daylight came, but the landlady was clearly against it, and kept tugging uselessly here and there at her dress, the disorder of which she seemed to have noticed only now, and shaking her head again and again. What was obviously a long-standing argument about the cleanliness of the house seemed about to break out again. To K., weary as he was, the conversation between husband and wife took on enormous importance. To be driven away from here seemed a misfortune greater than any he had yet known. It must not happen, even if the landlord and landlady were to unite against him. Slumped on the cask, he watched the two of them warily. Until the landlady, in her own unusual sensitivity, which K. had noticed long ago, suddenly stepped aside and cried out—she had probably just been talking to the landlord about something else—'See how he's looking at me! Send him away, do!' But K., seizing his opportunity, and now feeling sure, almost to the point of indifference, that he would be staying, said: 'I'm not looking at you, I'm only looking at your dress.' 'Why my dress?' asked the agitated landlady. K. just shrugged. 'Come along,' the landlady told the landlord. 'He's drunk, the lout. Leave him here to sleep it off.' And she told Pepi, who at her call emerged from the darkness looking tired and tousled, with a broom held listlessly in her hand, to throw K. a cushion or so.

25

WHEN K. woke up he thought at first that he had hardly slept at all; the room was just the same, warm and empty, all the walls in darkness, but with that one electric light above the beer-pulls, and night outside the windows. But when he stretched, the cushion fell to the floor, and the board and casks creaked, Pepi arrived at once, and now he discovered that it was evening and he had slept for over twelve hours. The landlady had asked after him several times during the day, and Gerstäcker, who had been sitting here over a beer in the dark when K. spoke to the landlady in the morning but hadn't liked to disturb him, had also looked in once to see how he was. Finally, it appeared that Frieda too had come in, and stood beside K. for a little while, but she hadn't really come on his account, only because she had several things to get ready here before returning to her old job that evening. 'I suppose she doesn't fancy you any more?' asked Pepi, as she brought coffee and cakes. However, she asked not in her old malicious way but sadly, as if now she had come to know the malice of the world for herself, and beside it any personal malice pales and loses its point; she spoke to K. like a companion in misfortune, and when he tasted the coffee and she thought she saw that it wasn't sweet enough for him, she went off and brought him the full sugar-bowl. It was true that her melancholy had not kept her from decking herself out today even more extravagantly, perhaps, than last time K. had seen her; she wore a profusion of bows and ribbons threaded through her hair, which she had carefully arranged with curling-tongs over her forehead and temples. Around her neck she wore a necklace hanging down into the low-cut neck of her blouse. When K., feeling glad to have had a long sleep and some good coffee, surreptitiously took hold of one of the bows and tried to undo it, Pepi said wearily: 'Leave me alone,' and sat down on a cask beside him. K. didn't have to ask why she was unhappy, for she began telling him at once, her gaze fixed on K.'s coffee-pot as if she needed something to distract her mind as she told him about it, as if even when she thought about her suffering it was more than she could do to give herself up to it entirely. First K. discovered that he himself was to blame for Pepi's unhappiness, but she didn't bear him a grudge for that, she said. And she nodded eagerly as she told her tale, to keep K. from contradicting anything. First he had taken Frieda away from the bar and thus made it possible for Pepi to rise to the position of barmaid. She, Pepi, could think of nothing else that might have induced Frieda to give up her post; she sat there in the bar like a spider in its web, casting her threads far and wide as only she could; it would have been impossible to remove her against her will, only love for someone of low status, a love that was unfit for her position, could drive her from it. And what about Pepi? Had she ever aspired to such a post for herself? She was a chambermaid, she had an insignificant job with few prospects, like every other girl she dreamed of a wonderful future, you can't forbid anyone to dream, but she didn't seriously expect to get very far, she had come to terms with what she had already attained. And then Frieda suddenly left the bar, so suddenly that the landlord didn't have a suitable replacement to hand, he looked around and his eye fell on Pepi, who had certainly done her own part here by putting herself forward. At that time she loved K. as she had never loved anyone before, she had been living for months in her tiny, dark room down below, and expected to spend years there, her whole life if the worst came to the worst, with no one paying her any attention, and then along came K. all of a sudden, a hero, a deliverer of maidens, and he had opened the way for her to rise. Not that he knew anything about her, he hadn't done it for her sake, but that didn't make her any less grateful. On the night when she was appointed barmaid—the appointment wasn't certain yet, but it was very probable—she spent hours talking to him, whispering her thanks into his ear. What he had done seemed even greater to her because the burden he had taken on his own shoulders was Frieda, there was something amazingly unselfish in the fact that to free Pepi from her predicament he was making Frieda his mistress, an unattractive thin girl not as young as she used to be, with short, sparse hair, a sly girl too, who always had secrets of some kind, just the thing you might expect from her appearance; although her face and body were undoubtedly a miserable sight, she must at least have had other secrets that no one could know about, perhaps to do with her alleged relationship with Klamm. At the time, Pepi even entertained ideas like this: was it possible that K. really loved Frieda, wasn't he deceiving himself, or was he perhaps deceiving no one but Frieda, and would the only result of all this be just Pepi's rise in the world? Would K. see his mistake then, or stop trying to hide it, and take notice of Pepi instead of Frieda? That wasn't such a wild idea of Pepi's, for as one girl against another she could hold her own against Frieda very well, no one would deny that, and it had been primarily Frieda's position as barmaid and the lustre with which Frieda had managed to endow it that had dazzled K. at the moment when he met her. And then Pepi had dreamed that when she had the position herself K. would come to plead with her, and she would have the choice of either listening to K. and losing the job, or turning him down and rising higher. She had worked it out that she would give up everything and lower herself to his level, and teach him the true love that he could never know with Frieda, the love that is independent of all the grand positions in the world. But then it all turned out differently. And what was to blame for that? K. first and foremost, and then of course Frieda's crafty, sly nature. K. first, said Pepi, because just what did he want, what strange kind of person was he? What was he after, what important matters occupied his mind to make him forget all that was closest to him, all that was best and most beautiful? Pepi was the victim in all this, everything was stupid, all was lost, and if there was a man with the strength of mind to set fire to the whole Castle Inn and burn it to the ground, leaving no trace, like a piece of paper in the stove, he would be the man of Pepi's dreams today. Well, so Pepi came to work in the bar, she went on, four days ago just before lunchtime. It's not easy work here, she said, in fact it's murder, but you could do a lot for yourself. Pepi never used to live in the moment, and although in her wildest dreams she wouldn't have thought of rising to occupy the post of barmaid herself, she'd kept her eyes open, she knew what the job was like, she hadn't been unprepared when she took it on. You can't take a post on unprepared, or you'd lose it in the first few hours. Particularly if you behaved the way the chambermaids here did. When you're a chambermaid you feel forgotten and forlorn, it's like working down the mine, or at least it is in the corridor where the secretaries stay, you don't see a soul for days on end except for a few members of the public flitting back and forth, never venturing to look up, no one but the two or three other chambermaids who feel just as bitter about their lot. You can't leave your room in the morning, the secretaries want to be on their own, the servants bring their food from the kitchen, the chambermaids don't usually have anything to do with that, and you can't show yourself in the corridor at mealtimes either. It's only while the gentlemen are working that the chambermaids are allowed to tidy up, not of course in the rooms that are occupied but in those that happen to be empty, and the housework has to be done very quietly so as not to disturb the gentlemen at their work. But how can anyone clean and tidy quietly if the gentlemen stay in their rooms day after day, and then there are the servants going around, dirty riffraff that they are, and when a room is finally free for the chambermaid to go in, it's in such a state that not even a deluge could wash it clean? It's true that the gentlemen who come here are very fine, but you have a hard time of it mastering your disgust so that you can clean up after them. The chambermaids don't have too much work, but what there is of it is tough going. And never a word of praise, only blame, particularly the frequent and vexatious accusation that files have been lost while you were clearing up. In fact nothing is ever lost, every tiny piece of paper is handed in to the landlord; well, files do get lost, yes, but it's not the maids' fault. And then commissions of inquiry come along and the maids have to leave their room and the commission of inquiry takes their beds apart; the maids don't have any possessions, their few things fit into a pannier you can carry on your back, but the commission of inquiry spends hours searching all the same. Of course it never finds anything; how would files get into the maids' rooms? What would the maids do with files? But once again the result is angry scolding and threats on the part of the disappointed commission of inquiry, conveyed only through the landlord. And never any peace—not by day or by night. Noise half the night, noise from first thing in the morning. If only the chambermaids at least didn't have to live there, but they must, because it's their business to bring small things ordered from the kitchen in between times, particularly at night. Again and again you hear that sudden banging of a fist on the chambermaids' door, the order is dictated, you run down to the kitchen, you shake the sleeping kitchen-boys awake, you leave the tray of whatever has been ordered outside the chambermaids' door, from which the gentlemen's servants fetch it—how dreary it all is. But that's not the worst. The worst is when there are no orders and in the middle of the night, when everyone ought to be asleep, and most people really do get to sleep in the end, you sometimes hear someone slinking around outside the chambermaids' door. Then the maids get out of bed—the beds are above each other, there's very little space anywhere there; the whole room where the maids sleep is really no more than a big cupboard with three compartments—they listen at the door, they kneel down, they clutch one another in fear. And you keep hearing that person slinking about outside the door. Everyone would be glad if he finally did come in, but nothing happens, no one comes in. You have to remind yourself that there isn't necessarily any danger, perhaps it's just someone pacing up and down, wondering whether to order something and unable to make up his mind. Well, perhaps that's all it is, but perhaps it's something quite different. The chambermaids don't really know the gentlemen at all, they've hardly set eyes on them. Anyway, the maids inside the room are half dead with fear, and when at last it's quiet again outside they lean against the wall without even enough strength to get back into bed. And that was the life waiting for Pepi; this very evening, she said, she was to move back to her old place in the maids' room. And why? Because of K. and Frieda. Back to the life she'd barely escaped, escaped with K.'s help, to be sure, but also by dint of her own diligent efforts. Because the maids on duty down there, even the most fastidious, do tend to neglect themselves. Who would they be prettifying themselves for? No one sees them, at most the kitchen staff, well, maybe a maid who's satisfied with that will prettify herself. But otherwise they are in their little room, or in the gentlemen's rooms, and again it would be silly and a waste of time to enter those rooms in neat, clean clothes. And you're always in artificial light and stuffy air—the heating is always on—and always dead tired. The best way to spend your one free afternoon a week is to find some quiet place near the kitchen where you can sleep undisturbed and without fear. So why make yourself pretty? You hardly bother even to dress. And then—then Pepi was suddenly moved to the bar where the very opposite was necessary if you wanted to hold your ground, where you were always before other people's eyes, those people including some very finicky and observant gentlemen, and where you must always look as fine and pleasant as possible. Well, that was a great change! And Pepi might boast that she left nothing undone. How things turned out later didn't worry Pepi. She knew she had the abilities necessary for the job, she was sure of it, she is still convinced of it now and no one can take that conviction away from her, even today, the day of her defeat. The only difficult bit was knowing how to prove herself at first, because she was a poor chambermaid without nice clothes and jewellery, and the gentlemen don't have the patience to hang about and see how you grow into the job, they want a proper barmaid at once, without any in-between period, or they'll go somewhere else. You might think their demands weren't very great if Frieda could satisfy them. But that wasn't so. Pepi had often thought about it, she said, had often been in Frieda's company, even shared a bed with her for a while. It wasn't easy to make Frieda out, and anyone who didn't study her very closely—and what gentleman is going to study a barmaid very closely?—would easily be led astray. No one knows better than Frieda herself how pathetic she looks; for instance, when you first see her let her hair down you clasp your hands in pity; a girl like that ought not really to be even a chambermaid; she knows it too, and she has cried her eyes out over it many a night, pressing close to Pepi and winding Pepi's hair around her own head. But when she was serving in the bar all her doubts were gone, she considered herself a beauty and knew how to make everyone think so too. She knows what people are like, that's her real art. And she is a quick liar, and deceptive, so that people don't have time to look at her more closely. Of course that won't work forever, people do have eyes, and after all their eyes would tell them the truth. But when Frieda realized there was a danger of that she had something else up her sleeve, most recently, for instance, her relationship with Klamm. Her relationship with Klamm! If you don't believe me, you can go to Klamm and ask him, said Pepi. How clever, how cunning. And if you daren't go to see Klamm on that kind of subject, maybe you wouldn't be let in to see him on far more important business, if Klamm is entirely inaccessible—though only to you and your like, because Frieda, for instance, can pop in and see him whenever she wants—well, if that's the case, you still can find out, you'd think you only had to wait. Klamm wouldn't allow such a false rumour to circulate for long, he really likes to know what's said about him in the bar and the guest-rooms, all that is very important to him, and if it's false he'll soon put it right. But he hasn't put it right, so people think there's nothing to put right and it is the truth. What you see is only Frieda taking the beer to Klamm's room and coming out again with the payment, but Frieda tells you what you haven't seen, and you have to believe her. Although in fact she doesn't tell you, she wouldn't reveal such mysteries, no, the secrets spread of their own

accord around her, and once they've spread she doesn't shrink from
speaking of them herself, but in a modest way, without claiming
anything, just referring to what's common knowledge. Not to everything, for instance not that Klamm drank less beer than before since
she was serving in the bar, not much less, but distinctly less, she
doesn't talk about that, and there could be various reasons; it could
be that a time came when Klamm didn't like beer so much, or that
Frieda made him forget about drinking beer. Anyway, surprising as
it may be, let's say Frieda was Klamm's mistress. But if someone is
good enough for Klamm, why wouldn't others admire her too? So
Frieda became a great beauty, just like that, the kind of girl that's
needed in the bar, almost too beautiful, too powerful, soon the bar
would hardly be enough for her. And sure enough, it seemed strange
to people that she was still in the bar; it's a great thing to be a barmaid, and from that point of view her connection with Klamm
seemed very credible, but if the barmaid is Klamm's mistress, why
did he leave her in the bar for so long? Why didn't he promote her to
better things? You can tell people a thousand times that there was
nothing contradictory about this, that Klamm had his reasons for
acting in such a way, or that some time, perhaps very soon, Frieda's
promotion would come. None of that had much effect; people get
certain ideas and in the long term they won't be persuaded otherwise, not by any arts. No one doubted that Frieda was Klamm's
lover, even those who obviously knew better were too tired to doubt
it. 'For heaven's sake, call yourself Klamm's lover then,' they
thought, 'but if you really are we'll notice by your rise in the world.'
However, no one noticed anything, and Frieda stayed in the bar as
before, and was secretly very glad to stay there. But she lost face with
other people, she couldn't help noticing that, of course, she does
notice things, usually even before they've happened. A really beautiful, attractive girl, once she's become used to working in the bar,
doesn't have to employ any arts; as long as she's beautiful she will be
a barmaid, unless something especially unfortunate happens. A girl
like Frieda, however, must always be anxious about her job; of course
she doesn't show it in any obvious way, she's more likely to complain
and curse the job. But in secret she keeps observing the atmosphere,
so she saw how people were getting indifferent to her; it wasn't worth
looking up when Frieda came in, even the servants didn't bother
about her any more, they understandably stuck to Olga and girls

like that. And she noticed the behaviour of the landlord, and saw that she was nowhere near so indispensable any more. She couldn't always be making up new stories about Klamm, there are limits to everything—so dear Frieda thought up something new. Who would have seen through it from the first? Well, Pepi had guessed, but unfortunately hadn't seen right through it. Frieda decides on a scandal; she, Klamm's lover, will throw herself at the first man who comes along, perhaps someone totally insignificant. That will attract attention, people will talk about that for a long time, and at last, at last they'll remember what it means to be Klamm's lover, what it means to cast aside that honour in the frenzy of a new love. The only difficult part was finding a suitable man with whom she could play this clever game. It couldn't be anyone Frieda knew already, not even one of the servants, he would probably have stared at her wide-eyed and gone away, and above all he wouldn't have taken it seriously. However much he might talk, it would have been impossible to spread the story that Frieda had been attacked by him, hadn't been able to defend herself, and in a crazy moment had fallen for him. And if it was to be someone very insignificant, it had to be someone of whom it could credibly be believed that in spite of his blunt, inelegant manners he longed only for Frieda, of all people, and had no greater desire than—for heaven's sake!—to marry her. But if it was to be a low, vulgar man, if possible even lower, much lower than a servant, it should be someone who wouldn't have every other girl mocking her, someone by whom another girl, capable of good judgement, might perhaps be attracted. But where would you find a man like that? Another girl might have sought him in vain for a lifetime, but Frieda's luck brings the land surveyor to her in the bar, perhaps on the very evening when the idea first comes into her mind. The land surveyor! Yes, what was K. thinking of? What strange ideas did he have in his head? Did he want to achieve something in particular? A good appointment, a distinction? Did he want something of that kind? Well, then he should have gone about it differently from the start. He is nothing, it is pitiful to see his position. He is a land surveyor, well, perhaps that is something, he has trained at something, but if there's nothing you can do with that training then it means nothing. And he was making claims without anything at all to support them, not making them straight out, but you noticed that he was making claims of some kind, and that was provocative. Does he know that even a chambermaid is losing face if she talks to him for any length of time? And with all these special claims, he falls into the most obvious trap on the very first evening. Isn't he ashamed of himself? What did he see in Frieda? He could admit it now. Could that thin, sallow creature really have appealed to him? Oh no, he didn't even look at her, she just told him that she was Klamm's lover, that was interesting news to him, and he was lost. But now she had to move out, now of course there was no job for her at the Castle Inn. Pepi saw her the morning before she moved out, the staff had gathered, everyone was curious to see the sight. And her power was still so great that they were sorry for her, all of them, even her enemies were sorry for her; so well did her calculations work out at first. It seemed unthinkable to everyone that she'd thrown herself away on a man like that, what a blow of fate, the little kitchen-maids, who of course admire any barmaid, were inconsolable. Even Pepi was moved, not even she could entirely arm herself against pity, although her attention was really elsewhere. She noticed how little sadness Frieda actually showed. After all, it was fundamentally a terrible misfortune that had befallen her, and she acted as if she were very unhappy, but that game wasn't enough to deceive Pepi. So what kept her going? The joy of her new love, perhaps? That idea could be dismissed. What was it, then? What gave her the strength to be as coolly friendly as always, even to Pepi, who was already regarded as her successor? At the time Pepi didn't have the leisure to think about it, she had too much to do with preparing to take up her new post. She ought really to be beginning work within a few hours, and she didn't have a smart hairstyle yet, or an elegant dress, or fine underwear, or a good pair of shoes. All those things had to be found within a few hours, and if she couldn't equip herself properly it would be better not to accept the post at all, for she'd be sure to lose it again in the first half-hour. Well, she partly succeeded in her aims. She had a special talent for hairdressing; once the landlady had even summoned her to do her, the landlady's, hair, the fact is that she has a very light hand, and can arrange her own wealth of hair just as she likes. There was help at hand over the dress too. Her colleagues were still friendly with her, for it was a kind of honour to them too if a girl from their group was promoted to barmaid, and Pepi could have gained them many advantages later once she had real power. One of the girls had had a length of expensive dress material, it was her great treasure, she had often got the others to admire it, probably dreamed of using it for herself in some very fine way one day, and now that Pepi needed it she gave it up, it was so kind of her. And the two other girls were happy to help her with the sewing, they couldn't have worked harder if they'd been making the dress for themselves. It was actually very cheerful and pleasant work. They all sat on their beds, one above the other, sewing and singing, and handed the finished pieces and the trimmings up and down to each other. When Pepi thinks of that, her heart is all the heavier to know that it was all in vain, and she would return to her friends the chambermaids empty-handed. What a misfortune, and brought about with such thoughtlessness, above all by K. How glad they had been about that dress at the time. It seemed the guarantee of success, and when room was found for yet another ribbon later the last doubts disappeared. And isn't the dress really lovely? It is creased and a little stained now, Pepi didn't have a spare dress, she'd had to wear this one day and night, but you can still see how beautiful it is, not even those dreadful sisters of Barnabas could come up with a better one. And then you can take it in or let it out again as you like, above and below, it may be only a dress but it's an advantage that it can be so easily altered, and that was really her own idea. Sewing isn't difficult for her, Pepi isn't boasting of that, and anything will suit a healthy young girl. It was much harder to get underwear and good boots, and here the trouble really began. Once again her friends helped as well as they could, but there wasn't much they could do. They came up with only coarse, mended underwear, and instead of ankle-boots with high heels she had to wear slippers that you would rather hide than show. People comforted Pepi by saying that Frieda wasn't very well dressed herself, and sometimes she went around looking such a sloven that the guests would rather be served by the lads from the cellar than the barmaid. Those were the facts of the matter, but Frieda could get away with it because she was in favour and highly regarded; if a lady happens to go out looking dirty and carelessly dressed for once, she is all the more enticing, but a beginner like Pepi? And anyway Frieda couldn't dress well, she had no taste at all; if someone has a sallow skin, she can't do much about that, but she doesn't have to wear a low-cut cream blouse against it, like Frieda, so that your eyes watered from looking at all that yellow. And even if that hadn't been so, she was too mean to dress well; she kept everything she earned, no one knew what for. She didn't need money in the job, she made use of lies and tricks instead, she set an example that Pepi couldn't and wouldn't follow, and so it was right for her, Pepi, to prettify herself so that she could make her mark at the very outset. If only she had had more funds to do it with she'd have defeated Frieda in spite of all her slyness and all K.'s folly. And it began so well. She had found out the few skills you had to master and the things you had to know in advance. As soon as she began work in the bar she was quite at home there. No one missed Frieda. It was only on the second day that some of the guests asked what had become of her. There were no mistakes, the landlord was satisfied, he had been so anxious on the first day that he was in and out of the bar all the time, later he came only now and then, and in the end, since the takings were right—in fact the bar was taking on average a little more money than in Frieda's time—he left everything to Pepi. She introduced innovations. Frieda had supervised everyone strictly, not out of industry but out of avarice, out of her desire to dominate and her fear of letting someone else have any of her rights, she supervised even the servants, at least in part, especially when someone was watching. Pepi, on the other hand, left that work entirely to the cellar lads, who were much better suited to it. That meant she had more time for the gentlemen's rooms, the guests were served quickly, and she could exchange a few words with someone, not like Frieda, who apparently kept herself entirely for Klamm, and considered every word or approach from someone else an insult to him. That was clever too, to be sure, for if she ever did let someone approach her it was an unheard-of favour. But Pepi hated such tricks, and you can't use them to start with in a job either. Pepi was friendly to everyone, and everyone was friendly to her in return. They were all obviously glad of the change; when those tired, overworked gentlemen can finally sit over their beer for a while, you can positively transform them with a word, a glance, a shrug of your shoulders. Everyone liked to run his hands through Pepi's curls, she probably had to tidy her hair ten times a day; no one could resist the allure of those curls and the bows in her hair, not even K., who usually noticed nothing much. So those exciting, hard-working but successful days flew by. If only they hadn't flown so fast, if only there had been more of them left! Four days are not enough, when you're working yourself to the bone, perhaps the fifth day would have done the trick, but four days were too few. Pepi had indeed won friends and patrons in those four days, if she could trust the glances of all eyes she had been positively swimming in a sea of goodwill as she walked around with the beer tankards. A clerk called Bratmeier is crazy about her, she says, he gave her this chain and locket with his picture in the locket, which was certainly very bold of him—this, that, and the other had happened, but it was still only four days. In four days, if Pepi had put her mind to it, Frieda could have been almost if not entirely forgotten, and she would have been forgotten too, perhaps even earlier, if she hadn't made sure to keep people talking about her by creating such a scandal. It had made her interesting to them again, they wanted to see her merely out of curiosity; what had become dreadfully dreary had fresh interest because of K., to whom they were otherwise entirely indifferent, they wouldn't have lost interest in Pepi because of that, not while she was standing here physically present to them, but the gentlemen are mostly elderly and set in their ways, it takes them some time to get used to a new barmaid, however much the change is for the better, but it will take a few days, even if it's against the gentlemen's real will it's going to take a few days, perhaps only five, but four are not enough, Pepi still seemed like the temporary barmaid in spite of everything. And then there was perhaps the greatest of misfortunes; in those four days Klamm, although he had been in the village for the first two of them, had not come down to the guestroom next door. If he had come, that would have been a crucial test for Pepi, and a test she didn't fear at all, indeed she was looking forward to it. She would not—to be sure, it is better not to put such things into words—she would not have become Klamm's lover, and would never have told lies elevating herself to such a position, but she would at least have been able to put the beer glass on the table just as nicely as Frieda, she would have said a nice 'Good-day', without any of Frieda's pushy manner, and she would have taken her leave prettily too, and if Klamm was looking for anything at all in a girl's eyes, well, he'd have found it in Pepi's to his full satisfaction. But why didn't he come? Was it pure chance? Pepi had thought so at the time. She was expecting him at any moment during those first two days, she waited for him to appear at night too. Now Klamm will arrive, she kept on thinking, pacing up and down for no reason other than the agitation of waiting and the wish to be the first to see him come in. This constant disappointment tired her out, and perhaps for that reason she didn't achieve as much as she could have done. When she had a little time she stole out into the corridor that the staff were strictly forbidden to enter, huddled in a niche there, and waited. If only Klamm would come now, she thought, if only I could take that gentleman out of his room myself and carry him down to the guest-room in my arms. I wouldn't collapse under the burden, however great it was. But he didn't come. It's so quiet in those corridors upstairs, Pepi said, you can't imagine how quiet if you haven't been there. It's so quiet that you can't stand it for long, the silence drives you away. But again and again, driven away ten times, Pepi climbed up there again ten times. There was no point in it. If Klamm wanted to come down he would come, and if he didn't want to come down Pepi wouldn't lure him out, even if she was half choked in the niche by the palpitations of her heart. There was no point in it, but if he didn't come there was no point in almost anything. And he didn't come. Today Pepi knows why Klamm didn't come. Frieda would have been much amused if she had seen Pepi in the niche up in that corridor, both hands to her heart. Klamm didn't come down because Frieda wouldn't let him. It wasn't her requests that had won the day, her requests carried no weight with Klamm. But that spider in her web has connections that nobody knows about. If Pepi says something to a guest she says it openly, they can hear her at the table next to the guest's too; Frieda has nothing to say, she just puts the beer down on the table and walks away, with only her silk petticoat rustling, it's the one thing she will pay good money for. And if she does say something for once, she doesn't say it openly, she whispers to the guest, bending down, so that they have to prick up their ears at the next table. Whatever she says is probably unimportant, but not always, she has connections, keeps some of them going through the others, and while most of them fail her—well, who would bother about Frieda in the long run?—now and then one will hold firm. So she began exploiting these connections, K. gave her the opportunity for that, instead of staying with her and keeping watch on her he hardly goes home at all, he wanders around, talks to this person and that, watches out for everything except for Frieda, and finally, giving her yet more freedom, he moves from the Bridge Inn to the empty schoolhouse. That's a fine start to a honeymoon! Well, Pepi is certainly the last woman to blame K. for not being able to stand life with Frieda—no one can stand life with Frieda. But why didn't he leave her entirely then, why did he keep going back to her, why did his wandering about give the impression that he was championing her? It looked as if only contact with Frieda had shown him how little he really meant, as if he wanted to make himself worthy of Frieda, as if he somehow wanted to work his way up and so, for the time being, held back from living with her so that later, in his own good time, he could make up for it. Meanwhile Frieda is not wasting time, she sits in the school to which she has probably been instrumental in bringing K., keeping watch on the Castle Inn and K. too. She has excellent messengers to hand, K.'s assistants, whom he leaves entirely to her—it is hard to understand that, even if you know K. you really can't understand it. She sends them to her old friends, reminds them of what has happened, complains that she is kept captive by a man like K., stirs up bad feeling against Pepi, announces that she'll be back any day now, asks for help, tells her friends not to say a word to Klamm, acts as if Klamm must be spared and so in no circumstances can he be allowed down into the bar. While she pretends to some that she is just being thoughtful for Klamm, she exploits her success with the landlord by pointing out that Klamm is not coming down there any more. How could he, when there's only a girl like Pepi serving in the bar? Of course the landlord isn't to blame, says Frieda, Pepi was just the best substitute he could find, only she's not good enough even for a few days. K. knows nothing about all this intriguing on Frieda's part; if he isn't out and about he's lying at her feet, suspecting nothing, while she counts the hours that still lie between her and her return to the bar. But the assistants don't just act as messengers, they also serve to make K. jealous, to keep him on the boil. Frieda has known the assistants since her childhood, they certainly have no secrets from each other, but for K.'s benefit they start making eyes at each other, and K. is in danger of assuming it's a great love. And K. does all he can to please Frieda, however contradictory it may be, he lets the assistants make him jealous but he allows the three of them to stay together while he goes off on long walks on his own. It's almost as if he were Frieda's third assistant. So on the grounds of what she's observed, Frieda decides on her master-stroke—she decides to come back, and it is high time too, it's remarkable how that cunning girl Frieda recognizes and exploits that fact, her power of observation and decision is Frieda's special skill. If Pepi had it, how different would her own life be. If Frieda had stayed at the school just one or two days longer, Pepi couldn't have been driven away, she would have been the established barmaid at last, liked and loved by one and all, she'd have earned enough money to complete her wardrobe and fit herself out brilliantly, another two or three days and no tricks could have kept Klamm away from the bar, oh yes, he comes in, he drinks, he feels comfortable, and if he notices Frieda's absence at all he is very happy about the change, another two or three days and Frieda, with her scandalous behaviour, with her connections, with the assistants, with everything else, would be utterly forgotten, she would never surface again. Then would she perhaps cling all the more firmly to K., and at last learn to love him truly, assuming that she is capable of such a thing? No, not that either. For it wouldn't take K. more than a day to tire of her, to realize how shamefully she is deceiving him in every way, with her supposed beauty, her supposed constancy, most of all with her supposed love for Klamm, only one day is all he'd need to chase her and those filthy assistants out of the house—you might think that not even K. would need longer. And then, between those two dangers, where the ground positively seems to be closing over Frieda, K. in his foolishness keeps the last way of escape open for her, a narrow one, and she takes it. Suddenly—hardly anyone expected it any more, it is unnatural—suddenly it is she chasing away K., who still loves her, still follows her, and with the help of pressure from friends and assistants she looks to the landlord like a saviour, more enticing than before because of her scandalous behaviour, evidently desired by the lowest and the highest alike, and she fell for the lowest only briefly, soon rejected him again as was only proper, and she is now out of his reach and everyone else's as in the old days, except that in the old days doubt, quite correctly, was cast on all that, but now her status seems to be confirmed. So she comes back, the landlord glances surreptitiously at Pepi and hesitates—is he to sacrifice her after she has proved her worth so well?—but soon he's been persuaded. There's too much in Frieda's favour, and above all she will bring Klamm back to the guest-room. And that's what this evening is all about. Pepi isn't going to wait until Frieda comes back and makes taking over the job again into a scene of triumph. She's already handed the cash register over to the landlady, she can go. Her bunk bed down in the maids' room is ready for her, she will go there, to be greeted by her friends in tears, will take the dress off her body and the ribbons out of her hair and stuff it all in a corner where it will be well hidden, and won't unnecessarily remind her of times that are better forgotten. Then she will pick up the big bucket and the broom, grit her teeth, and set to work. But for now she simply had to tell K. everything, so that he, who wouldn't have understood all this yet without any help, will just for once see clearly how badly he has treated Pepi and how unhappy he has made her. Although in fact he too has merely been misused.

Pepi had finished what she had to say. She mopped a few tears from her eyes and cheeks and then looked at K., nodding, as if to say it wasn't really her own misfortune that troubled her, she would bear it, and didn't need help or consolation from anyone, least of all K., in spite of her youth she knew life, and her unhappiness just confirmed what she knows, no, this was about K., she wanted to hold his own picture up to him, even after the collapse of all her own hopes she thought she ought to do that.

'What a wild imagination you have, Pepi,' said K. 'Why, it's not true that you have discovered all these things only now; they're nothing but dreams from the dark, cramped room you and the other chambermaids share. They may be in place there, but they look strange here in the open, in the bar. You couldn't have held your ground here with such notions, that's obvious. Even your dress and your hairstyle, on which you pride yourself so much, are just the fantastic outcome of that darkness and those beds in your room. I am sure they look very attractive there, but here everyone laughs at them, whether secretly or openly. And what else do you say? You say I have been misused and betrayed? No, dear Pepi, I haven't been misused and betrayed any more than you have. It is true that at present Frieda has left me, or as you put it has run off with one of the assistants, so you have hit upon some idea of the facts, and it is really very unlikely that she will be my wife now, but it is entirely untrue to say that I tired of her, or chased her away next day, or that she betrayed me as a woman might usually betray a man. You chambermaids are used to spying through keyholes, which means that when you really do see some small thing, it leads you to draw grand but erroneous conclusions about the whole picture. The result is that I, for instance, know much less than you claim to know. I cannot explain in nearly as much detail as you do why Frieda has left me. It seems to me that you have also touched on the most probable explanation, although you didn't make much of it: I neglected her. I am afraid that's true, I have indeed neglected her, but there were particular reasons for that which it is not right to mention here. I would be happy if she came back to me, but I would begin neglecting her again at once, and that's how it is. When she was with me, I was always out and about on those wanderings you ridicule; now that she's gone I have almost nothing to do, I am tired, I long to be even more entirely unoccupied. Have you no advice for me, Pepi?' 'Oh yes,' said Pepi, suddenly becoming lively and taking hold of K.'s shoulders. 'We've both been betrayed, let's stay together, come down to the other maids with me.' 'I can't talk to you sensibly while you complain of being betrayed,' said K. 'You keep saying you were betrayed because the idea touches you and flatters you. But the truth is that you are not suitable for this position. If even I, who in your opinion know nothing, see that unsuitability then it must be very obvious. You are a good girl, Pepi, but it isn't easy to see that. I, for instance, thought you cruel and arrogant at first, which you aren't, it is just this post that bewilders you because you're not suitable for it. I don't mean to say it is too elevated for you, it is nothing so very out of the ordinary, or perhaps, looking at it closely, its status is a little higher than your previous job, but on the whole there is no great difference, the two are very similar, in fact one might almost say that to be a chambermaid is better than working in the bar, for the chambermaids are always among the secretaries, while here, even if you may serve the secretaries' superiors in the guest-rooms, you must also meet very common folk, for instance me; it is right and proper that I can't go anywhere else in the inn, only be here in the bar, and is the possibility of meeting me such a great distinction? Well, it seems so to you, and perhaps you have your reasons. But that is just why you are unsuitable. Although this is a job like any other, to you it seems like heaven, and as a result you do everything with excessive enthusiasm, you deck yourself out as you think the angels are adorned—although they are really not at all like that—you tremble for your post, you feel persecuted the whole time, you try to win over everyone who, you think, might be able to support you, showing far too much friendliness, but that is a nuisance to them and puts them off, for they want peace when they come to the inn, not to add the barmaid's troubles to their own. It's possible that after Frieda left none of the distinguished guests really noticed, but today they do and they really long to have Frieda back, I suppose because she ran everything very differently. Whatever else she may be like, and however she valued her post, she was experienced at serving the guests, cool and controlled, as you say yourself, but you don't profit by her example. Did you ever notice the expression in her eyes? It was not the expression of a barmaid but almost of a landlady. She saw everything, every detail, and the way she looked at an individual was enough to subdue him. What did it matter that she may have been a little thin, not as young as she once was, that a girl can have thicker hair? Those are all small details compared to what she really did have, and anyone troubled by those flaws would just have shown that he lacked a sense of better things. No such accusation can be levelled against Klamm, and it is only a young, inexperienced girl's viewpoint that makes you believe Klamm couldn't have loved Frieda. Klamm seems to you—and correctly—out of reach, and so you think that Frieda couldn't have been close to Klamm either. You are wrong. I would trust Frieda's word alone for that, even if I didn't have incontrovertible evidence of it. Incredible as it seems to you, and little as you can reconcile it with your ideas of the world, and the life of the officials, of distinction and the effect of female beauty, it is true, as true as we're sitting here together and I take your hand between mine. No doubt that is how Klamm and Frieda sat side by side too, as if it were the most natural thing in the world, and he came down here of his own free will, indeed he hurried down, no one was lying in wait for him in the corridor and neglecting the rest of her work, Klamm had to come down of his own accord, and the deficiencies of Frieda's clothing that have horrified you so much didn't trouble him at all. You just don't want to believe her! And you don't know how you are exposing yourself, because it shows your inexperience. Even someone who knew nothing about her relationship with Klamm must notice that of its very nature it left its mark on someone above you and me and all the other people in the village, and that their conversations went beyond the usual sort of joking between guests and waitresses, which seems to be the whole aim of your life. But I am doing you an injustice. You know Frieda's advantages very well yourself, you notice her gift for observation, her power of decision, her influence over other people, only you interpret it all in the wrong way, you think that she uses all that selfishly for her own benefit and with bad intentions, or even as a weapon against you. No, Pepi, even if she did hold such arrows in her hand she couldn't shoot them such a short way. And selfish? One might rather say that by sacrificing what she had, and what she could expect, she gave us both, you and me, an opportunity to rise higher, but that we have disappointed her and have positively forced her to come back here. I don't know whether that is so, and I am not quite clear how I am to blame, but when I compare myself with you something of the kind does appear before me; it is as if we both tried too hard, too noisily, too childishly, and with too little experience to gain something that can easily and quietly be had with, for instance, Frieda's calm and Frieda's objectivity, but we tried to get it by weeping and scratching and tugging, just as a child tugs at the tablecloth but cannot get it, merely sweeps all the beautiful things off the table and puts them out of reach for ever—I don't know if that is the case, but I do know for certain that it is more likely than your version of events.' 'I see,' said Pepi. 'You're in love with Frieda because she ran away from you. It's not difficult to be in love with her when she's not around. But even if it's as you claim, and even if you are right about everything, including making me look ridiculous—what are you going to do now? Frieda has left you, neither my explanation nor yours gives you any hope of her coming back to you, and even if she did, you have to spend the time in between somewhere, it's cold weather and you have neither work nor a bed, so come to us, you'll like my friends, we'll make you comfortable, you can help us with our work, which really is too hard for girls on their own, we girls won't have to rely entirely on ourselves and feel afraid at night. Do come and join us! My girlfriends know Frieda too, we'll tell you stories of her until you're sick and tired of them. Do come! We have pictures of Frieda as well, we'll show you those. Frieda was even less striking then than now, you'll hardly recognize her, except from her eyes, which had a sly look even then. Well, will you come?' 'Is that allowed? Yesterday it was a great scandal when I was caught in your corridor.' 'That's because you were caught, but if you are with us you won't be caught. No one will know about you, only the three of us. Oh, what fun it will be! My life there already seems to me more bearable than it did a little while ago. Perhaps I'm not losing so very much by having to leave the job here after all. You know, even with the three of us we weren't bored, you have to sweeten the bitterness of life, it's made bitter for us in our youth so that our tongues don't get used to luxury, but we three stick together, we live as nice a life as possible, you'll specially like Henriette, and Emilie too, I've already told them about you, people listen to such tales and marvel, as if nothing could happen outside our room, it's warm if cramped in there and we keep close together, even though we have only each other to rely on we don't get tired of one another. On the contrary, when I think of my girlfriends I almost feel it's all right to be going back there. Why should I rise higher than them? That was what kept us together, all three of us having the future barred to us in the same way, and then I broke out and was separated from them, but the fact is I didn't forget them, and my next concern was how I could do something for them; my own position was still uncertain—though I didn't know just how uncertain—and already I was talking to the landlord about Henriette and Emilie. The landlord wasn't entirely inflexible in Henriette's case, but as for Emilie, who is much older than the two of us—she's about Frieda's age—he could give me no hope there. But just think, they don't want to leave, they know it's a wretched life they lead there, but they've adjusted to it, good souls, I believe their tears when I said goodbye were mostly grief because I had to leave the room we shared and go out into the cold—in our room everything outside it seems to us cold—and I'd have to go around in those great, strange rooms with those great, strange people for no purpose but to earn a living, though I'd done that before when we lived and worked together. They probably won't be surprised to see me coming back, and they'll cry a little and bemoan my fate just to oblige me. But then they'll see you, and realize that it was a good thing I left after all. It will make them happy to know that now we have a man to help and protect us, and they'll be positively delighted that it all has to be kept secret, and the secret will bind us even more closely together than before. Come and join us, oh do please come and join us! There's no obligation on you, you won't be bound to the room for ever as we are. When spring comes, if you find somewhere else to stay and you don't like it with us any more, you can go, only you'll still have to keep the secret, and not give us away, because that would be the end of us at the Castle Inn. And of course if you're with us you must be careful not to show yourself anywhere that we don't consider safe, and to follow our advice. That's all the obligation you have, and you will have to put up with it just as we do, but otherwise you're entirely free, the work we give you to do won't be too hard, don't be afraid of that. Well, will you come?' 'How long is it until spring?' asked K. 'Until spring?' Pepi repeated. 'Oh, winter here is long, a very long, monotonous winter. But we don't complain of that down there, we're safe there from the winter. Well, some time spring will come, and summer too, and they have their own time, but now, as we remember them, spring and summer seem as short as if they weren't much more than two days long, and even on those days snow sometimes falls in the middle of the finest weather.'

The door opened. Pepi jumped—in her thoughts she had moved too far from the bar—but it wasn't Frieda, it was the landlady. She seemed surprised to find K. still here. K. excused himself by saying that he had been waiting for her, and at the same time he thanked her for letting him spend the night here. The landlady didn't understand why K. had been waiting for her. K. said he had had the impression that the landlady wanted to speak to him, he asked her pardon if that had been a mistake, and anyway he must go now, he had been away from the school where he was janitor far too long, yesterday's summons had been to blame for everything, he still had too little experience in these things, he said, he certainly wouldn't make as much trouble for the landlady again as he had yesterday. And he bowed, ready to go. But the landlady stared at him with a look in her eyes as if she were dreaming. That look of hers kept K. there longer than he wanted. Then she smiled a little too, and only at K.'s expression of amazement did she wake up to some extent. It was as if she had been waiting for a response to her smile, but now, when none came, she woke up. 'You had the impudence to say something about my dress yesterday.' K. couldn't remember that. 'Don't you remember? You're not only impudent but cowardly too, then.' K. explained that it was due to his weariness yesterday; it was possible, he said, that he had talked about something or other, but he couldn't remember it now. What could he have been saying about the good landlady's dresses? That they were more beautiful than any dresses he had ever seen? Or at least, he had never seen a landlady go about her work in such dresses before. 'Never mind passing personal remarks,' said the landlady quickly. 'I don't want to hear another word from you about my dresses. My dresses are none of your business. I forbid you to mention them, and that's that.' K. bowed again and went to the door. 'What do you mean, anyway?' called the landlady after him. 'What do you mean, you never saw a landlady go about her work in such dresses before? Why say such pointless things? What could be more pointless? What do you mean by it?' K. turned back and asked the landlady not to upset herself. Of course his remark was pointless, he said. He really didn't know anything about dresses. In his situation, any clean dress that didn't need mending seemed to him very fine. He had just been surprised, he said, to see the landlady there in the corridor at night in such a beautiful evening dress among all those half-clothed men, that was all. 'Well,' said the landlady, 'at last you seem to remember what you said yesterday! And you compound your impertinence with yet more nonsense. It is true that you know nothing about dresses. So let me earnestly beg you, kindly desist from passing remarks on fine dresses and what they are like, or about unsuitable evening dresses, or anything of the kind. And anyway'—here a shudder seemed to pass through her—'you are not to pay any attention to my dresses, do you hear?' And when K. was about to turn away again, in silence, she asked: 'Where did you get your knowledge of dresses, then?' K. shrugged his shoulders to show that he didn't know. 'Well, you have none,' said the landlady, 'so don't make out that you do. Come over to the office and I'll show you something, and then I hope you will leave off your impudence for ever.' She went ahead through the door; Pepi ran to K. On the excuse that she wanted K. to pay what he owed, they quickly came to an agreement; it was very easy, since K. knew the yard with the gate leading into the side-street. There was a little gate beside the big one, and Pepi would be waiting on the other side of that in an hour's time and open it when he knocked three times.

The private office of the inn was opposite the bar, there was only the front hall to cross. The landlady was already standing in the lighted office, looking impatiently at K. But there was one distraction. Gerstäcker had been waiting in the hall and wanted to speak to K. It wasn't easy to shake him off. The landlady joined in too, pointing out to Gerstäcker that he was intruding. 'Where do I wait, then? Where do I wait?' Gerstäcker could be heard calling as the door was closed, and his words were mingled unappealingly with sighing and coughing.

The office was a small, overheated room. A lectern desk stood by one of the shorter walls, and an iron safe too, while a wardrobe and an ottoman stood by the longer walls. The wardrobe took up most of the space; not only did it extend along the whole of one long wall, but its depth made the room very cramped, and three sliding doors were necessary to open it completely. The landlady pointed to the

ottoman, indicating that K. should sit down on it, and she herself sat
on the swivelling chair by the lectern. 'Haven't you ever trained as a
tailor and dressmaker?' asked the landlady. 'No, never,' said K.
'What's your profession, then?' 'I'm a land surveyor.' 'What's that?'
K. told her, but the explanation made her yawn. 'You're not telling
the truth. Why don't you tell the truth?' 'You're not telling the truth
either.' 'I? There you go again with your impudence. And suppose I
wasn't telling it—do I have to justify myself to you? Anyway, in what
way am I not telling the truth?' 'You are not just a landlady, as you
make out.' 'Well, you're very sharp, I'm sure. What else am I, then?
Your impertinence is really too much!' 'I don't know what else you
are. I see only that you appear to be a landlady, but you wear dresses
that don't suit a landlady, and as far as I know no one here in the
village wears anything like them.' 'Ah, so now we're coming to it.
You can't deny it. Perhaps you aren't impudent at all, perhaps you're
just like a child who knows some silly joke and can't be brought to
keep it quiet. So out with it. What's so special about those dresses?'
'You'll be angry if I tell you.' 'No, I shall laugh, because it will be just
childish nonsense. So what are my dresses like?' 'Well, you did ask.
They are made of good fabric, expensive dress material, but they are
old-fashioned, over-trimmed, often too elaborately made, they are
wearing out, and they suit neither your years nor your figure nor
your position. I noticed them as soon as I first set eyes on you, about
a week ago in the front hall here.' 'So now we have it. They are old-
fashioned, over-trimmed, and what else was it? And how do you
think you know all that?' 'I can see it. One doesn't need any training
to know such a thing.' 'You can see it, just like that. You don't have
to go and ask anywhere, you know at once what fashion demands.
You're going to be invaluable to me, because I do have a weakness for
beautiful dresses. And what will you say when I tell you that this
wardrobe is full of them?' She pushed the sliding doors aside, and
dress upon dress was to be seen hanging close together the whole
breadth and depth of the wardrobe, most of them dark, grey, brown,
black dresses, all carefully hung up with their skirts spread. 'Those
are my dresses, all of them old-fashioned and over-trimmed in your
opinion. But these are only the dresses I don't have room for in my
bedroom. I have two more wardrobes full of them upstairs, two
wardrobes, each almost the size of this one. Are you amazed?' 'No,
I expected something of the kind. As I said, you're more than just a

landlady, you are aiming for something else.' 'I'm aiming only to dress well, and you are either a fool or a child or a very bad, dangerous man. So go away, hurry up, go away!' K. was out in the hall, and Gerstäcker was holding his sleeve again, as the landlady called after him: 'I'm having a new dress delivered tomorrow. Perhaps I'll let you go and fetch it.'

Gerstäcker, angrily waving his hand as if to silence the landlady from a distance, because she bothered him, asked K. to go with him. At first he wouldn't explain why, and he didn't take much notice of K.'s objection that he ought to go to the school now. Only when K. resisted being dragged off by him did Gerstäcker tell him not to worry, he would have everything he needed at his own place, he could give up the post of school janitor, and would he please now come? He'd been waiting for him all day, Gerstäcker told him, his mother didn't know where he was. Slowly yielding to his demands, K. asked how he planned to provide board and lodging for him. Gerstäcker just answered briefly, saying he needed K. to help with the horses, he himself had other business now, and he wished K. didn't have to be dragged along like this, making unnecessary difficulties for him. If K. wanted payment then he, Gerstäcker, would give him payment. But for all his tugging K. stopped dead now. He didn't know anything about horses, he said. That didn't matter, said Gerstäcker impatiently, and in his irate state of mind he actually clasped his hands pleadingly to persuade K. to go with him. 'I don't know why you want me to come with you,' K. said at last. It was all one to Gerstäcker what K. knew. 'Is it because you think that I can bring influence to bear on Erlanger for you?' 'That's right,' said Gerstäcker. 'Why else would I be interested in you?' K. laughed, took Gerstäcker's arm, and let the man lead him away through the darkness.

The living-room in Gerstäcker's house was only dimly lit by the fire on the hearth and a candle-end. By the light of the latter someone could be seen stooped in a niche under the sloping rafters that stuck out there, reading a book. It was Gerstäcker's mother. She gave K. her trembling hand and made him sit down beside her. She spoke with difficulty, it was hard to understand her, but what she said

EXPLANATORY NOTES

5 *Westwest's*: this name has provoked much inconclusive conjecture, usually associating 'west' with 'decline'.

6 *land surveyor*: Erich Heller maintains that the German word *Landvermesser* 'alludes to *Vermessenheit*, hubris' (*The Disinherited Mind* (Cambridge: Bowes & Bowes, 1951), 169), though nothing is made of this association in the text. E. T. Beck notes that the Hebrew word for 'land surveyor', *mashoah*, is almost identical with that for 'messiah', *mashiah* (*Kafka and the Yiddish Theater* (Madison, Wisc.: University of Wisconsin Press, 1971), 195); the possible implications of this are followed out in Ritchie Robertson, *Kafka: Judaism, Politics, and Literature* (Oxford: Clarendon Press, 1985), 228–35.

8 *to the land surveyor now?*: here a deleted passage in Kafka's manuscript has K. seizing his stick and terrifying the peasants.

9 *wife and child*: not otherwise mentioned.

14 *silk*: many figures associated with the castle have clothes that resemble silk: cf. Barnabas (p. 23), the Castle Inn landlady's 'dress that rustled like silk' (p. 249), and Pepi's dress of 'shiny grey fabric' secured with a 'silk ribbon' (p. 89). This person is mentioned later (p. 127), and is said to be ill from the air in the village (p. 129), but she plays no part in the action.

16 *Lasemann*: suggests Czech *lázeň*, 'bath'.

17 *Gerstäcker*: the name of a nineteenth-century author of adventure stories; in Richard Sheppard's view it 'inevitably calls to mind the German word for graveyard, "Gottsacker"' (*On Kafka's Castle: A Study* (London: Croom Helm, 1973), 105).

22 *That eternal land surveyor*: perhaps alluding to the expression 'der ewige Jude' (the Wandering Jew; literally, the eternal Jew).

23 *Barnabas*: though explained in Acts 4: 36 as 'son of consolation', this name more likely means 'son of the prophet'.

   I am a messenger: in the original, Barnabas inverts subject and object ('Barnabas am I called; a messenger am I') in a strange and solemn way. Kafka knew that in Hebrew *malakh* means 'messenger' and also 'angel'.

27 *Klamm*: suggests the Czech word *klam*, 'illusion'.

31 *didn't entice him*: at this point Kafka originally had a long and stormy conversation between K. and Olga, during which K., annoyed by Amalia's stare, seized her knitting and threw it on the table.

35 *Frieda*: a very common name, suggesting German *Friede*, 'peace'.

38 *whip*: Frieda uses the whip to drive away the bestial servants: not to provoke lust, but to tame it.

40 *song of some kind*: at this point in the manuscript Kafka deleted an over-explicit formulation of K.'s motives: 'K. was thinking more about Klamm than about her. The conquest of Frieda required him to change his plans, here he was getting a powerful instrument which might make it unnecessary for him to spend any time working in the village.'

rubbish: on the juxtaposition of love and filth, cf. Kafka's letter to Milena of 8–9 August 1920, in which he says that his sexual urge 'had something of the eternal Jew—senselessly being drawn along, senselessly wandering through a senselessly obscene world', yet that in sex 'there's something of the air breathed in Paradise before the Fall' (*Letters to Milena* (New York: Schocken, 1990), 148).

42 *fourth day*: that is, if one counts the evening of his arrival as the first day.

50 *those villains!*: the hostility shown by the villagers, here and later, to Barnabas and his family, is inconsistent with Barnabas's friendly reception earlier in the saloon bar (p. 23). Kafka must have changed his plans for the family, without amending his earlier text accordingly.

52 *eagle*: Klamm is associated with an eagle also in a cancelled passage where K. says that Klamm's sleigh has a golden eagle at the front, but is told by Pepi that it is an ordinary black sleigh like any other.

59 *Sordini*: possibly suggested by Italian *sordo*, 'deaf'.

70 *Gardena*: an unusual name, possibly suggesting 'guard' with a suffix common in Czech female names (e.g. Milena, Ruzena).

78 *on your own account*: the original phrase, 'auf eigene Faust', which recurs at p. 82 ('of your own accord'), may allude to Goethe's *Faust*, whose ambitious behaviour resembles K.'s (see Introduction).

89 *Pepi*: short for Josefine, an extremely common name in Catholic German-speaking countries.

98 *Momus*: the Greek god of laughter. That everyone promptly becomes serious is a little joke by Kafka.

104 *fire and brimstone*: cf. Genesis 19: 24: 'Then the Lord rained upon Sodom and upon Gomorrah brimstone and fire from the Lord out of heaven.'

117 *mere children*: this confirms that K. and Frieda form a kind of family, with the two assistants as children.

121 *to the south of France, to Spain*: these real places feel very incongruous with the geographical vagueness of the castle and village.

129 *Bitter Rue*: Jews are required to eat bitter herbs and unleavened bread at Passover (Numbers 9: 11). Combined with Hans's prophecy that in the distant future K. will 'triumph over everyone' (p. 133), this may suggest that Kafka, at least briefly, conceived K. as liberating the village in the manner of Moses.

144 *warmth of her presence*: Schwarzer's futile devotion to Gisa provides a parallel to K.'s obsession with the castle.

165 *Sortini*: possibly suggested by Latin *sors* (genitive *sortis*) and its derivative, French *sort*, 'fate'.

3 July: Kafka's birthday.

166 *Galater*: this is the German name for St Paul's Letter to the Galatians, in which Paul opposes the divisions between some Jewish and some non-Jewish Christians; Arnold Heidsieck suggests that such divisions are represented in the novel by the villagers' ostracization of the Barnabas family, and that part of K.'s mission is to unite the village (*The Intellectual Contexts of Kafka's Fiction* (Columbia, SC: Camden House, 1994), 160–72).

167 *Turks*: since the Ottoman empire formerly controlled large tracts of Eastern Europe, and besieged Vienna in 1683, 'Turks' have been proverbial for barbaric enemies.

190 *Bertuch*: the name of a publisher in Goethe's Weimar; perhaps suggesting German *Bahrtuch*, 'shroud'.

206 *the brunette*: an inconsistency—earlier, both sisters were said to be blonde (p. 31).

209 *Erlanger*: suggests German *erlangen*, 'to reach, attain'.

225 *Bürgel*: suggests German *Bürge*, 'guarantor'; cf. 'who can guarantee everything' (p. 234).